ALSO BY FERNANDO A. FLORES

Valleyesque: Stories

Tears of the Trufflepig

Death to the Bullshit Artists of South Texas

BROTHER BRONTË

Brother Brontë

A NOVEL

Fernando A. Flores

MCD FARRAR, STRAUS AND GIROUX NEW YORK

MCD

Farrar, Straus and Giroux

120 Broadway, New York 10271

Printed in the United States of America

First edition, 2025

Library of Congress Cataloging-in-Publication Data

Names: Flores, Fernando A., 1982– author.

Title: Brother Brontë : a novel / Fernando A. Flores.

Description: First edition. | New York : MCD / Farrar, Straus and
Giroux, 2025.

Identifiers: LCCN 2024034083 | ISBN 9780374604165 (hardcover)

Subjects: LCGFT: Dystopian fiction. | Novels.

Classification: LCC PS3606.L5886 B76 2025 | DDC 813/.6—dc23/
eng/20240724

LC record available at https://lccn.loc.gov/2024034083

Designed by Abby Kagan

Our books may be purchased in bulk for promotional, educational, or
business use. Please contact your local bookseller or the Macmillan Corporate
and Premium Sales Department at 1-800-221-7945, extension 5442, or by email
at MacmillanSpecialMarkets@macmillan.com.

www.mcdbooks.com • www.fsgbooks.com

Follow us on social media at @mcdbooks and @fsgbooks

10 9 8 7 6 5 4 3 2 1

for Taisia

Reason with him and then whip him!
was her instruction (age six) to her father
regarding brother Branwell.

—ANNE CARSON, "The Glass Essay"

La neta no hay futuro.

—CIUDAD NEZAHUALCÓYOTL MIERDAS PUNK

Book One

R AIN FELL HARD like slabs of ham as a squad car pulled into the nearly abandoned neighborhood surrounding Angélica Street. The car flashed its swampy red and blue lights over muck-covered potholes and downed serpentine power lines. Wet clusters of trash from rolling cyclones pushed through the air like the ghosts of trees. A revolving cast of squatters often occupied the unleased, half-burned houses on Angélica, most of which were patched with white tarps that now came undone in the wind, their ropes lashing like tentacles toward the gurgling wound of a sky.

The squad car surveyed the indecorous morning. Static and shallow breathing could be heard from its mounted trumpet speaker; the local law-enforcement emblem of a fig leaf in a passionate embrace with a diagonal bayonet rifle was decaled on the cruiser's every door. From the dented roof, it cast a pasty beam of light beyond the faded white picket fence of a corner home it'd made a stop at the previous evening. Beneath a drooping covered porch, by the front door, CHUPACABRAS BRRRN was freshly graffitied in brick red. The squad car idled like a displeased beast as the smog and clouds from the flash thunderstorm cleared, revealing distant colorless shells of vandalized downtown buildings, along with the three onyx smokestacks from the Big Tex Fish Cannery, which never stopped operating, regardless of the weather.

The clumps of rain slowed to a misty drizzle.

With a grumble from its engine, the squad car retracted its icy light and continued down the street, past the overpopulated Live Oak tenement building, where smoking barbecue grills could be seen by open windows on the fifth and eighth floors.

Neftalí was watching safely from behind the broken front-porch blinds of that graffitied corner home. Once the squad car was gone, she lit a cigarette and a jar candle to illuminate the living room. Muddy tracks had been mopped from the linoleum, shattered glass had been mostly picked up, and she could hear the neighbor's goat bleating a welcome to the morning sun as the clouds parted. Resigned to lying on the clean floor, she gazed achingly past the popcorn patterns on the nicotine-stained ceiling to some imaginary lunar terrain, and pleaded to the real moon for something, anything, to keep her from having to look for another place to live.

The day's electric hum, like an insect whispering in her ear, informed Neftalí that the power in the neighborhood was finally back on. She got up, found the pile of LPs the authorities had smashed, picked a random artless sleeve. Only the outer edge of the vinyl had snapped off when they'd stomped on this one.

She placed the gramophone stylus in the middle of side A, past the record's broken edge. As the introductory notes of the instrumentals swept in, the roof and living room walls of the house she'd lived in her entire life delicately peeled open, like a corpse flower—she saw a man walking toward her along the shore of a bright, expansive beach. His trouser legs were rolled up, and he carried a bucket half filled with seashells he'd been collecting. Neftalí wanted to wave but instead stood frozen by this vision: she knew somehow that this man was the famous composer playing on the gramophone, Juventino Rosas, though the record sleeve had no photographs, and she'd never seen his face. Sand gusted in pink and green whirls from a casket-brown ocean while a long-dead German orchestra performed the composer's music from the broken record.

A golden gull flew close to Juventino, then a bandmate of his—the percussionist?—slung a wadded ball of raw ground beef and hit the gull stone-hard on its belly.

The bird dropped to the ground, hurt and delirious—golden feathers and ground beef against fleshy hot sand.

"You shouldn't have done that," said Juventino. "That bird is a deity."

"What's a deity?"

"Un dios."

"What's a dios?"

"Un god."

"Oh."

The waltz ended; Neftalí's vision ceased.

She walked around the knocked-over, stripped bookshelves and the buckets catching rainwater from the leaky side of the house, through the kitchen, and out the back door. Flattened weeds had coagulated with mud on the trail to the canted toolshed, creating something like black ice that she balanced herself over. At the shed's slanted entrance she looked around, aware that her neighbors had witnessed the previous night's disruption: Neftalí, handcuffed, standing on Angélica

Street under a swelling sky, stomping, cursing aloud, as the authorities ransacked, confiscated, and shredded.

Once inside the misshapen toolshed, she left the door cracked open. An angled gray beam of sunlight revealed rusted garden shears, pickaxes, a shovel, musty walls, bricks, and the dried cobblestone well, which was covered with a flat board weighed down by a cinder block.

Neftalí set the cinder block aside, uncovered the well, and gazed deeply into its underground cataract oblivion, possibly to catch her reflection on the surface of the water, like she had when she was a girl. The well had been dry for years now; its sallow breath stung her eyes. The socket it had become smelled like a giant's discarded yellow toenail, a toenail mixed with rotting livers. She opened the shed door a little wider, stuck her face outside for fresh air and to watch again for the loathsome eyes of a nosy neighbor. Only the dripping aluminum roofs and trembling pecan tree branches seemed to be paying attention. Not a dove to be heard.

She leaned her body into the desiccated well, grabbed one of the moldy bricks in its throat, shook it loose with great effort, and placed it on the ledge. Neftalí breathed deeply and held that breath as she stretched her body inside again, being careful not to fall in, and from a secret compartment she pulled out a bundle wrapped tightly in cellophane.

It was past citrus-picking season; the eldest in Three Rivers, with nobody to provide rations for them, had been waiting out the rain to glean produce from the Pulga or to scavenge machine parts that could be sold to build new book shredders.

Neftalí was dumping accumulated rainwater from the living room buckets into her backyard when she heard the front-porch screen door slam shut. A tower of dishes in the kitchen sink rattled, and Neftalí listened closer for approaching footfalls. Three Rivers authorities rarely hit up a house on consecutive days, so she wasn't concerned about the cellophane bundle sitting on her bed.

She walked inside. The smell of chrysanthemums and jasmine flower sweat announced her old bandmate Proserpina even before she appeared, wearing her customary torn, long skirt and tattered, thrifted new-wave shirt. Proserpina tried not to react to the bookshelves that had been picked to the marrow throughout the house. Even the mahogany shelves built into the hallway between the kitchen and the living room had been smashed through, rendered useless.

"They took all my shit, 'mana," Neftalí said. "I don't even care, really, because I've read them all. But some of those books are all I got left of my mother. They said they're gonna raze this house by the week's end, and I can't even salvage my belongings. How'd you hear, who told you?"

"One of the twins. You know I can never tell the three of them apart, the little fucks. Cool graffiti out front, did you paint it yourself?" Proserpina asked, not waiting for an answer. "C'mon, let's go to the carnival and get drunk and talk about it. Or, what's the word your Spanish-speaking ass uses? *Peda?*"

"Hell no. My Spanish-speaking ass is not going to no carnival. Especially to get all *peda*. Is a carnival even in town right now?"

"Over on Conway and Three Mile Line, they got a wheel

of fortune going, hominy-in-a-cup, powdered cake, the donkey lady robot, and everything."

"God. I don't know if I'm in the mood for those artery-clogging things," Neftalí went on, picking up splinters from the broken shelves, almost tasting the hangover she'd brew for herself at the carnival. "There's real shit I've got to accomplish, and today's Bettina's birthday, remember? Are you still down to go with me to the fish cannery?"

Proserpina thought about it. "I guess I promised you I would, right? I'm only weird about it 'cause I haven't spoken Arabic in a while. I still get super self-conscious about it around my mother. Especially now. Plus, it'll depress me . . . to see her in there. And, you know . . . not being able to do shit about it. Did the chupacabras destroy, like, even your dictionary? And the big book of plays that was disgusting to look at, with the naturally red hair growing from the mold spot?"

"Every one of them."

"How awful. You'd just gotten that rare book you were birthday-gifting to Bettina, too, no?"

"Well, 'mana," Neftalí said in a lower voice as she finished stacking the empty buckets for future use. "Let me show you."

The cellophane bundle wheezed as it was gutted open by Neftalí using a butterfly knife. "For a while now, right before something terrible happens, I've been getting this mysterious feeling, 'mana," she said. "I don't know what it is. Got it right before they took away my permit to teach reading. Got it the morning the Bexar school library burned down. It takes me a while to process experiences after they happen. But by the end, every time, I carry a heavy need to visit my mother's grave. That's how I felt yesterday, right before the chupacabras showed up to shred my books. So hours before they got here, I hid these out back. In the well."

Two books lay on the bed by the now mangled cellophane: one with an embossed clothbound cover, to which Proserpina's eyes naturally gravitated first; and a smaller, aged paperback with nothing written on the mended cover.

"What do these words even mean?" Proserpina asked, pointing at the hardcover's title: *Understanding Urban and Agricultural Hydraulics*.

"Technical stuff nobody knows anymore. It's the one book Bettina's requested from me the last few times I've seen her, believe it or not. I do what I can, since they let them read books in there. Alexei managed to score it through his connections, after months and months of trying. He's out collecting bottle-tops by the cathedral. I promised I'd meet him before going to the fish cannery. Anyway, you down to go?"

Neftalí and Proserpina stepped through the looking-glass doorway of the old house into the real world of Three Rivers, Texas. Rainbow-less muck puddles riddled the fractured sidewalks and uneven pavement of Angélica Street.

They passed Rayman's smoky food cart across from the Live Oak tenement building, where most of the people in the neighborhood lived in cramped quarters. He had bratwursts already blasting on the grill, as a couple neighborhood kids watched him, grinning like clothesline crows as he worked the skewers and tongs. Rayman was going on about the old days, but the kids were too busy paying attention to the sizzling meat and vegetables to listen.

"You think this is the kind of city that would be attacked by aliens?" Neftalí asked. "I can see a bunch of interdimensional space aliens coming down on these crumbling houses, and even the kids and these dogs, to teach everyone a harsh lesson."

"That's hilarious, Nef. I wish aliens would attack and shut this shit down. But aliens probably know they can just chill. Why go through all that trouble? People in Three Rivers are too busy destroying everything themselves. Why would intelligent space aliens want to waste their energy doing something we're already doing for free?"

Four boys from the Live Oak tenement were huddled under its awning, sharing cured crickets out of a large chrome bowl and having a disagreement about the tabs from aluminum cans that they used as currency. One of them was mending the spokes on a chrome fixed-gear tricycle. They each wore a cap from a different defunct sports team. The aluminum tabs sat on the ground in a pile next to the bowl of crickets. None of the boys noticed the two young women witnessing their serious dispute.

"Yuck," Proserpina said. "I'm never gonna get this new generation of kids. All their mothers busting their asses at the fish cannery, just so their boys can eat these disgusting fucking bugs three times a day? The tenement boys especially, I hear, don't trust any food sold in stores. Hey, gentlemen."

The boys paused their arguing to look up at Proserpina. Using a stick of blue chalk from her bag, she wrote $2+2=5$ on the sidewalk. They ignored her and continued their discussion.

Proserpina reached into their pile of aluminum tabs, slid two over the number 2, then two more over the other number 2.

"What does that read?" she asked them. The boys blinked several times at the scrawled math problem. "It's easy," Proserpina continued. "Count how many tabs there are: one, two, three, four. Two plus two equals five, you little jerks. Don't ever forget that."

She managed to keep a straight face until turning the corner with Neftalí.

"Look at you," Neftalí said, trying not to melt into a puddle of laughter. "You love this shit. You love teasing these boys. Nobody's taught them simple math, or how to even read."

"Come on, it's just small-time morning fun. And you taught me that two-plus-two gag back in the day, Nef, don't act all Mother Superior on me."

Ticker tape, facsimile propaganda, and waterlogged cardboard protest signs littered the sidewalks and clogged the gutters of the part of the city the young women lived in, known as Old Freeway. Bags of trash piled up like coagulated desks on every street corner, as the search to replace the city's oversaturated landfill dragged on. Neftalí slipped a stick of clove gum into her mouth and rolled her eyes at the orange-peel sky.

The four boys in old sports caps glided by a little too fast and close on their souped-up tricycles, as if finally understanding that they'd been teased, and they weren't happy. Two of them smacked their lips suggestively, while motioning to their own crotches.

"Aw, look at these little muttonheads," Proserpina said,

"how effin' fucking cute they look, playing conquistadors and cowboys here," and then the boys turned the corner and their flight of the bumblebee pedaling faded.

"You know, you only encourage their bad behavior by treating them that way. They're little boys, 'mana. That's what they want: your attention. Try ignoring them next time and they'll leave us alone forever."

"Nah, I like harassing them. It makes me feel good inside. And it gives me the chance to call someone a muttonhead, which is a great thing to say."

Proserpina and Neftalí finished their conversation inside Doña Julieta's *depósito*, a tiny old depot with limited produce, premium and regular canned Big Tex verdillo fish, pan dulce, hard candy, dried grains and beans and noodles, pickled vegetables, passable cabbage heads, milk, soda, water, beer, cigarettes, spices, garlic, yellow onions, and housekeeping needs in narrow, crammed, easy-to-access shelves. The *depósito* was built of adobe, with a flat roof that goats often climbed onto, and the living quarters of the family who owned the place were attached to the rear. Its interior walls were painted bright green, with peeling patches that revealed an old coat of mellow red. The lighting was poor, but it was cool inside. A newscube anchor's tight-jawed enunciation could be heard faintly from behind the counter, announcing forthcoming sunny days.

Doña Julieta ran the store on her own, since her son had left Three Rivers to work on an Arctic oil derrick, and her husband, Sigifredo, had died from a pulmonary infection. Upon seeing the two customers entering, Doña Julieta sighed dreamily and lit up with excitement, even sprang up from her stool behind the register.

"Mi'jita," Doña Julieta said, and when Neftalí moved closer, the elderly woman held her face briefly with rough hands. She could feel Doña Julieta's two wedding bands cold against her right cheek. "You're so big now, Angélica, look at you now. Time sure flies. How are your mother and your father?"

"Good, good, señora. Les mandan muchos saludos, como siempre."

"I'm sure, I'm sure, mi chula. Please send them my best. And which of your sisters is this now? Soledad?"

Proserpina, not knowing much Spanish, gave Doña Julieta half a counterclockwise wave, like she was onstage, playing a part before a sold-out crowd only she could see.

"Qué bueno, qué buenas niñas mías. Y con qué les puedo alludar hoy?"

Neftalí grabbed a bottle of water and a small bag of almonds; Proserpina took a pack of Spirits, which, she managed to inform Doña Julieta, were for their father. Doña Julieta winked and rang up the Spirits as red beans. Proserpina paid for everything using her fake ration card.

As they walked away from Doña Julieta's *depósito*, a fire truck rushed past them, blaring its horn. The rhythm of the streets took them on as players in a hidden ballet. Neftalí and Proserpina crossed into the section of Three Rivers known as New Freeway: the bus routes for the 22 and the RRS were running; workers and street kids clustered at the stops every quarter mile; unhoused men dressed like federal employees panhandled, played the harmonica, and sometimes sang off-key tunes—almost none of them wore shoes.

Proserpina said, "That lady back there. Her enthusiasm and everything makes me so happy to see her. And it's badass she's the only one who lets us buy smokes with a ration card. But when I walk away, I get so sad. I can't believe she thinks you're your mother, and calls you by her name."

"It used to creep me out, for sure. Still does. Especially since she also thinks you're my aunt, and asks how my grandparents are doing every time. You know that I never really knew my grandparents, and the house my aunt drank herself to death in got turned into that empty bowling alley sitting on Valencia. But, I don't know, I appreciate her. It makes me feel good to tell her my long-dead relatives are doing well, and that they send her their love."

"What I wanna know is why she thinks I'm your sister," Proserpina said. "You and me don't look anything alike. We're both brown, but a different kind of brown. That lady's Mexican, she knows what her people look like. An older Syrian woman would definitely recognize me as one of her own but know right off you're not Syrian."

"That's just how Doña Julieta's memory works. It's not her fault she thinks it's 1988, fifty years ago."

Neftalí and Proserpina raced across the supposedly haunted pedestrian bridge, over the busy intersection of Fourth and La Cuchilla, then sat down to catch their breath at the far edge of the embankment. The onyx smokestacks from the fish cannery whirled in the distance, against scattered patches of purple smog. Yellow low-flying clouds often moved through the streets like packs of giant dogs, lapping up windows, leaving muck residue to harden on the pavement.

Proserpina pointed at a burning mass in front of the old tamale shack and said, "You see those gnarly fires happening constantly now. What do you think everyone's burning so much?"

"Probably garbage. What do people expect? The fires never get that big or grow out of control inside the city, anyway, and people gotta get rid of their shit somehow. Garbage is piling, stinking everything up, right when we'd figured out the rat problem, too."

They loitered where the pedestrian bridge met the embankment to look down upon gutted, abandoned tractors, and the mossy Brown Apollo statue on the grounds of the burned-down elementary school. Neftalí had memories of reading short-story anthologies by the statue's immense feet when she'd attended the school as a girl; at the same spot, Proserpina had first met the man who'd sold her the carbon papers and emulsion to forge ration cards. The Brown Apollo statue seemed to raise its arms in a flex as Neftalí and Proserpina wandered the charred foundations on the property.

With the skeletal remains of the gymnasium behind him, Brown Apollo watched as a thick ground-level cloud approached Neftalí and Proserpina from the direction of a discontinued bus stop. Laughter and the whirring of tires and gears were heard, as if the whale-sized, turmeric-colored mist had hidden wheels and levers operated by giddy, sadistic gnomes. There was another sound—like an empty can of soup trying to sing—and as Neftalí's eyes focused on the silhouettes emerging from the cream-thick haze, she made out the bad doom metal, all treble, playing out of a small, possibly broken speaker. Four souped-up tricycles rushed by them, grazing their arms and canvas bags.

Proserpina immediately recognized the riders as the four boys she'd teased before they stopped at Doña Julieta's. She chuckled to herself, and it took all her strength not to say the first thing that came to mind. They were inside the belly of this yellow mist, lost in an artificial desert dust storm, and hard-pressed to see anything beyond its organism—the oxygen thinned, making it somehow easier to inhale the industrial pollutants.

Doom metal continued chirping from the miserable little speaker, then a voice said, "Surprise, surprise, to see you sneaking into New Freeway, Neftalí. Maybe you recognize your neighbors here? They caught me up with what happened over at your house last night."

The voice fluttered out of Santo as he rode his fixed-gear bicycle like it was a miniature donkey with shuffling hummingbird legs. He wore a denim jacket with torn sleeves, old skinny jeans, and shoes with missing laces.

"Your old drummer, Proserpina, here, too? Very special. And where's big-money-machine Alexei?" Santo continued. "Bring in the old bass player, get a whole band reunion going. Surely he must be looking for old bubblegum wrappers to convert to dollar bills? Or maybe it's shit-stained toilet paper squares today?"

The tricycle boys were clearly amused by Santo's variety of humor. He sat taller on his bicycle than the boys did on their tricycles, and Neftalí quickly gathered that they made up a small gang. Dry axles begging for an oil reprieve could be heard creaking louder and louder from somewhere within the devouring mist, as if the gears were trying to fiendishly laugh, too.

Proserpina grabbed a stone by Brown Apollo's sandaled feet, tracked the speaker hanging from one of the tricycle boys' shoulders, and pitched it at a calculated moment. The speaker fell, hit concrete: the doom metal stopped, plastic and metallic guts spilled out unceremoniously.

Santo and his small gang were one of many units of boys sweeping Three Rivers, wreaking their brand of havoc on the population. Their antics came handsomely rewarded by Mayor Pablo Henry Crick. Ever since Crick's administration started deploying book shredders to average citizens, boys like these had had carte blanche to find and discard books that the Three Rivers authorities had missed.

A large boy emerged from the haggard fog, pedaling with the strain of Sisyphus, barely making it over the cliff—behind him, strapped onto a flat wagon with those pleading, thirsty axles, sat a mechanical beast with four wide, sharp, well-fed mouths, like a savage prince being promenaded through the jungle, waiting for fresh grapes for dessert.

Two of the tricycle boys stepped off their rides, approached Neftalí first, made as if they weren't afraid to put their hands on her.

"Don't make this hard, Neftalí. Just hand over your bag."

"What, you're gonna feed your machine my shit? What's in this bag is all I got left."

In three flashes, and perhaps blinded by the immeasurable depth within the lurking mist, the two boys effortlessly snatched Proserpina's bag, then slipped off Neftalí's like a choreographed magic trick.

Santo emptied both canvas bags at the feet of Brown Apollo, like an offering among thieves. Even within the diffused sunlight inside that abnormal, low-flying cloud, the two books that fell out of Neftalí's bag were clear as day. The boys' faces all wriggled into large smiles, as the largest boy unstrapped the four-mouthed oblong shredder from the bed of the squeaky wagon, balanced it on the uneven school grounds, then yanked on the cord to start it up.

After plenty of unsuccessful yanks, Santo ordered: "Clean the gasket."

"You're really gonna do this, Santo?"

"Neftalí, do I look like a politician? It's the law."

"Bullshit," Proserpina said.

"All right, all right, let's switch places, and you are me. And you find *me* here, carrying two books, when . . . when a literacy permit is required and strictly enforced. Now, seeing as how *you* know the person with said books, what's the nicest thing *you* could do, without having to call the bosses?"

"Listen to the way he talks," Neftalí exclaimed to the other boys, unable to contain her disgust at Santo's words. "We both learned how to read in a class together, once upon a time—"

"You don't need to invent lies," Santo cracked, as the large boy finally got the shredder's four mouths chewing, complete with thousands of micro-blades crunching, spinning, and shrieking to be fed through the miasma. "Now that you've considered my point of view, and given your lying nature, what would you do in my place?" he yelled.

Santo reached for the book on the ground that appeared

the most seductive to him—the hardcover. He traced the embossed title with his right middle finger: *Understanding Urban and Agricultural Hydraulics*, then slowly flipped through its pages, pretending to be interested in the knowledge it offered, to spite the young women.

Proserpina noticed Neftalí shaking, and felt that her friend was capable, at any moment, of making the rashest decision. In the blink of an eye, Proserpina imagined flying sparks involving crowbars, machetes, all sorts of vengeful madness, so upon returning to the present moment, she harbored an urge to keep the peace, and in the friendliest tone she exclaimed: "That book can be useful to somebody, even if you think it's trash. Why destroy it?"

Neftalí missed these words, looking up as Brown Apollo's torso and head seemed to descend on them with the passing of the yellow cloud, and for a sliced moment she indulged her innermost fantasies of why the two of them had even stopped to visit this monument; she imagined Brown Apollo approaching them with his cast iron muscles, and their conversation turning immediately to galloping horses: the difference between the wild horses on the pampas and the horses by the shores of bombed South Padre Island. Brown Apollo would give them tips about wearing seashells as masks; Proserpina and Neftalí would brainstorm questions for Brown Apollo, to take advantage of this rare close encounter with a god. But mostly they'd want to have a chill time with him, to have drinks and watch Italian movies about ancient Greece with the divine bulwark himself.

This was the delirium Neftalí found herself in as she watched Santo feed the nearly impossible-to-find hardcover copy of *Understanding Urban and Agricultural Hydraulics*, meant for Bettina on her birthday, to the buzzing, chomping, four-mouthed book shredder. It surprised most people, despite repeated firsthand accounts, that the machine's micro-blades pulverized the book entirely, dust blowing into the wind after the procedure like a wildflower bouquet's ashes. Brown Apollo seemed to turn his head away, perhaps in disgust, or perhaps reluctantly agreeing with the perspective of the young men and the book-banning laws.

Santo thumbed through the remaining dog-eared paperback. "*Ghosts . . . in the Zap . . . otec Spher . . . icals,*" he read aloud from its time-yellowed title page. "By Jazzmin. Mon . . . elle. Rivas. She's correct about one thing, boys. I was one of the last to attend this burned-down school. Learned how to read here. So take it from me. You're not missing much."

Dense boxcar fog floated over from the elevated pedestrian bridge, and with it appeared two women. They whispered contentiously to each other, then walked around Brown Apollo, stopping on opposite sides of his giant mildewed ankles. One of the women hunched low to the ground, inspecting the sputtering book shredder. She wore a dark purple cloth that covered her entire hair and torso, while her long-braided partner stood with immaculate posture, muffling her ears against the ornery machine.

Santo was mere moments from feeding the worn paperback to the wailing beast, when the braided woman grabbed a stone from the ground and gently lobbed it toward the machine's four clamoring mouths. The book shredder's micro-blades and manufactured innards crunched to a pained, smoky halt; it seemed to turn its mouths inside out, while spewing resin from every pore. A plume of swampy grease left the prostrate machine's body like a sin-soaked soul, forming a beast on three backs along with the yellow haze and natural fog copulating near Brown Apollo.

"That oughta do it," the braided woman said triumphantly.

"Lady," Santo said, coughing, batting the swirling smoke away, as the tricycle boys circled Brown Apollo clockwise, "now what am I supposed to tell the boss about this?"

"Don't *lady* me, I'm a tía," said the braided woman, pointing a violin bow like a switchblade at Santo.

"Sorry, ma'am. I mean, Miss Tía."

The covered woman used a ratchet set to dismantle the book shredder's metallic organs, while the braided woman, raising an eyebrow, said to Santo: "We understand the mayor gave anyone permission to use these shredding devices and take the new reading law into their own hands. Even young boys like you. Said it was for the good of the community to stop the spread of unholy ideas. Now, is Mayor Pablo Crick your boss?"

"These boys answer to me. And my superior, I guess, answers to Crick. But we don't know him in person," Santo said, now in a supplicating tone that echoed his schoolboy days.

"Well," the braided woman continued, using the violin bow to punctuate her syllables, while her diligent partner piled up oily bolts, gears, and screws from the disemboweled book shredder, "you tell your superior to tell Mayor Crick that the tías of Three Rivers killed this machine. And we'll keep killing many more. Got that?"

"Yes, lady," Santo said. "I mean, yes, ma'am. Or tía. Sure thing."

"Okay. Now hand this young woman back her book. It's nobody's business but her own. And every one of you *muchachitos*: get lost."

The patchy natural fog that had arrived with the tías passed like the freight of a ghost train. All that remained of the noxious yellow haze was a slight tail, as its elephantine mass floated sluggishly toward the labyrinthine skeleton of the burned school. Santo and the tricycle boys followed this tail, the large boy sheepishly pedaling away with the mangled shredder's pathetic, grease-stained shell.

The two tías departed in the opposite direction, whispering to each other in a scandalized yet composed manner that to an outsider could've appeared argumentative.

Neftalí stood in a near-catatonic state, clutching her book like a golden ticket in a sandstorm. Proserpina waved a hand before her friend's unblinking, dilated eyes, snatched away the recovered paperback, and stuck it in her bag. Neftalí returned to the moment with a gasp only after Proserpina snapped her fingers. Not knowing which course to take, they walked behind the two women—the tías, their temporary saviors—as the violin strapped to the tall one's back looked at them like an excited puppy, validating their decision.

A three-story building at a distance was graffitied with a globular city sprouting from a purple diving bell. Neftalí and Proserpina passed by the old boarded-up pawnshop, overwhelmed by the skillful design on the building before them. The young women crossed the street, trailing the tías around the building's corner, after an unmanned donkey cart filled to the brim with trash passed in front of them. Proserpina was the first to notice that the building's graffiti was an optical illusion, when it revealed the hidden, half-smiling face of Mayor Pablo Henry Crick, now looking down on them like an artificial second sun.

The braided tía stood with her admirable posture against a red door on the eastern wall of the graffitied building and set the sandalwood bow to the strings of her violin. After an improvised intro that flattened and stretched time like dough, a waltz began to unravel from the instrument's soundboard. A lush garden grew from the reluctant concrete in three-quarters time.

The tía with covered hair, as a helicopter flew overhead at a distance, sang: "'Stone to flesh, / then onward toward my kingdom. / And in the morning my true love comes, / for the morningtime's the only true love.'"

Sidewalks had turned to wild pastures: mulberry tree trunks sprouted, branches elongated, plump cherub leaves teased the rat-winged Three Rivers smog; thorny vines wrapped around the vandalized building, as well as all the houses, shops, and forsaken infrastructure clinging for dear life near the heart of the city.

When the tías had finished their sublime tune, the spell was seemingly broken—Neftalí and Proserpina clapped, as everything turned back into a pumpkin or a tired horse. None of the stray midday passersby had even noticed the spontaneous musical performance; kids could be heard playing soccer on rooftops, as their mothers hung washed clothing to dry along burning clotheslines, like on any other day.

The braided tía's eyes grew bright from the praise, like cinders or polished carnelian stones, and she said, "Ah gee, thanks," putting her stringed instrument away.

"Either of you two look up at the sky recently?" the tía with covered hair excitedly asked their two-person audience. "Smoke from the fish cannery's what's creating those abominable fogs . . . and that muck falling with the rain in recent years, that's from fish cannery smoke as well. Smoke pulp clumps together like a paste and clogs sewers. Hazardous. We don't want that."

The tías silently agreed on something with a look, invited Neftalí and Proserpina through the red door, motioned to follow them up the staircase and to keep quiet. The ground floor gave the impression that the building was abandoned; the tiles were layered with dust, and stalactite cobwebs clung to the window frames. Opaque green daylight filtered in through the windows, which had exterior grime as thick as oatmeal. Halfway up to the second floor, the stairs changed from filthy to painted, in a pattern of green apples and red strawberries.

All four of them walked through a dense beaded curtain into a large, dark, wood-tiled studio loft, with a ramp that zigzagged from the farthest top corner to its diagonal opposite near the floor. The upper edge of the wall facing the street was lined with closed horizontal casement windows, except for the cracked-open one farthest to the right. A fluorescent light was flicked on by a tía, and as Neftalí craned her neck to find where the complex ramp began, she recognized the contraption as a conveyor belt, not unlike the kind she'd used to sort good vegetables from rotten ones during her short career working night shifts at a supermarket. This particular belt ricocheted at thirty-five degrees from corner to corner, passed through a bulbous cavern floating in the middle of the room, then ended at waist level over a woven basket near an aluminum-foiled window.

The covered-hair tía walked to a kitchen nook, set a red pot of tea to boil. There was sliced rye bread on a chopping block, and a small ceramic cup of goats' milk on the counter by the toaster, waiting to be finished. She dipped the rye bread into the goats' milk and chewed mournfully as their two guests unraveled the wonders their eyes met.

"What," Proserpina uttered, "is all this?"

She bumped into a sturdy, barrel-sized woven sack that sprayed pale dust on her dark, faded clothes. A cluster of similar sacks with symbols she didn't recognize rested by a doorless closet. Along with Neftalí, Proserpina looked inside one that was torn open, taking in the impossibly distant smell of corn and wheat fields ground to powder.

From an empty room somewhere on that floor, the braided tía yelled, "Don't touch the assembly line, I'm turning it on," as the surrounding conveyor belt system jolted to life with only the faintest screeching, like gears in a clock tower suddenly gossiping. The braided tía reappeared, pointing toward the bulbous centerpiece, inviting the young women to take a closer look.

"See those things inside there, looking like giant insect legs? We're trying to get them moving, so the oven here can work."

"This"—Neftalí gestured toward the doghouse-like dome the conveyor belt passed through—"is an oven?"

"Oven older than your great-grandma. I guarantee. Once it's running, we'll have a way to feed our community. And forget those useless ration cards. This is what the mayor ought to be making, instead of shredding books. Ovens. Keep hungry people fed—"

"Let's be accurate," the other tía interrupted, chewing through a burnt crust of rye, "with our language, Celia. This is an industrial oven, yes, older than any of us. And those things you stubbornly call *insect legs* are actually called *hydraulics*. We need to get them pumping for the oven to heat up."

"Hydraulics," Neftalí echoed. The daze of the moment withered, images from her day flashed like polychromatic peacock feathers in her mind's eye, and she saw the hardcover book meant for Bettina shredded to dust again and again in the four mouths of the bestial book shredder, Santo laughing, the multi-faced Cerberus fog.

"Yes," the braided tía indignantly uttered. "Hydraulics. That's what I first said."

"No, you didn't. You called them *insect legs*. Didn't she say that?"

Both tías looked toward Neftalí and Proserpina to settle their argument.

The bleating of the red teapot stole the covered tía's attention, however. She grumbled her way to the kitchen nook, prepared a few cups of oolong tea, and brought them to her guests with no further discussion. As the braided tía climbed a ladder to the top of the ancient oven, Neftalí and Proserpina blew on and sipped at their steaming tea.

Whirls of browned yellow smoke snuck their thick, ghoulish hairs into the room from the cracked-open casement window in the far-right corner. The tía on the ladder flashed a light at the industrial oven's malfunctioning inner hydraulics and tapped them with a crowfoot wrench.

"Maybe we could take the entire thing apart. Get it going elsewhere," said the covered tía, dreamily looking toward the casement windows. "How charming, the honey color of this toxic fog. It takes me back to the smoke from when I was a girl, living near sugarcane fields. On a small island, with family. They'd burn sugarcane in a controlled fire every year or so. And all the animals that'd made the fields their home would run for dear life. Mostly rats. Vermin. We were never warned in advance, so the fire was a surprise each time. My father and mother armed themselves in a hurry. Us kids would arm ourselves, too. As a family, we battled every creature that tried to run into our house from the burning fields. We'd shoot them. Chase them. Club them. Then we gathered their carcasses afterward to bury them far from our property, downwind. Poor vermin. We laughed and celebrated every killing, us kids. My sisters and brother. My parents had many problems, and this was just another one. Not many laughs or celebrations from them."

The tea was consumed without solutions regarding the oven, then the braided tía stepped down from the ladder to help escort their guests back outside. Everyone said their goodbyes at the red door. As Proserpina and Neftalí walked away, the braided tía played a mournful waltz on her violin once again, but this time no garden sprouted.

Past the liquor store and the poultry and pork racks, the hellhounds of commotion were rustling between two police officers outside their squad car and a gathering crowd. Neftalí and Proserpina walked toward the locust sunlight reflecting from the vehicle's hood, looked around at people's intrigued, upset faces. A barrel of a policeman wearing fashionable shades waved a bayonet rifle to keep people away, and the other squinting policeman had his knee pressed onto the back of a young man wearing a denim jacket and skinny jeans, who pleaded, "What I do? What I do, huh? I didn't do anything, what I do, chupacabra? Somebody, please, get them off me, they're picking me up for nothing!"

Mouths agape, Proserpina and Neftalí recognized the young man: Santo. His fixed-gear bicycle, the crunched shredder, and the tricycle boys were all nowhere to be seen. Asphalt dust covered the right side of his face and he writhed under the officer pinning him down. Santo spit a pebble toward the sidewalk as his horrified eyes found two familiar faces in the crowd, and he yelled, "Nef. Pros. Tell them I'm one of them! Or, not exactly one of them, but not a bad one. You know what I mean. C'mon, Nef, we go way back to Mrs. Casas's kindergarten class! Tell them something, please, get them off me."

Proserpina smirked, threw him the finger. Neftalí couldn't decide whether to be ruthless or compassionate, so she did nothing.

Despite Santo's struggle to break free, the squinting policeman forced the cuffs onto him until his wrists went red and pale. As both officers shoved the kicking, jumping young man into the back of the squad car, Santo yelled even louder, in a hoarse voice, "No. No. Check her bag. The one with the big hair. She's got a book hidden in there, check her bag!"

Before anybody could say anything else, the squad car was speeding away up the hill.

An older man in trousers and suspenders spit as the crowd

dispersed, and said, "Serves that youngster right. Wearing his jeans like they're painted on him. Loitering up and down the hill all afternoon on that bike like he's out to start trouble. Maybe locked up, he'll learn the value of earning an honest day's living."

Neftalí was about to say something, no doubt with deep insight and meaning, when she spotted a figure walking toward them on the sidewalk curving from Figueroa Avenue.

It was either a heavy-metal D'Artagnan or a central Texan Kaspar Hauser, surviving on energy drinks and power chords alone; he wore old baggy jeans and a shirt two sizes too large for his slim frame, which displayed the emblem of the young women's long-broken-up underground punk band, Missus Batches. Neftalí watched Proserpina's expression change from annoyed, to perplexed, to delighted, when they both saw that the figure was their former number one fan, Po, a young rocker from their Old Freeway neighborhood, and one of the last people to remember they had once made up two-thirds of a three-piece band.

Po batted his hands around, pretending to cry, as if Neftalí and Proserpina were English pop stars landing at JFK, and the three of them fell into a group hug. Though neither of them had touched an instrument in years, the young women were amused.

Neftalí asked, "Po, did you see what just went down?"

"Nah. What happened? Someone get into a street fight? Chupacabras carting people off for no damn reason at all since the other night. Oh. I got to see some of what happened yesterday, too, Nef. Sorry we couldn't do anything to stop the shredding."

"Someone snitched on me in the neighborhood for sure, Po, but I know it wasn't you. You hear anybody cool looking for roommates or anything? I need to find another place to live."

Po laughed like it was the funniest joke he'd heard all day. "No," he said. "Everyone I know is still squatting. But I'll tell you if I do."

They moseyed down the sidewalks of the empty square block known as the Pantry, the seedy part of town, where older, infirm squatters sought refuge. Since it was plain day, with police aggressively patrolling, no one was around, and only the pickled stench of urine filtered through malfunctioning kidneys was left haunting the air—no poltergeists or ghosts. The three shielded their faces from the putrid stench and crossed the street in the direction of the cathedral.

"Hey, Po," Neftalí exclaimed, remembering that Po was once a reader—she pulled out her copy of *Ghosts in the Zapotec Sphericals* by Jazzmin Monelle Rivas. "Check it out! My lucky copy."

"No way," said Po, looking around nervously. He held the paperback and leafed through the aged pages, running over passages with his fingers. "I haven't seen one of these in forever. Pages smell so nice, like a clean, empty room. Seriously, Proserpina," Po said, "I know you don't like to read, but if you ever do, read this book."

"I will. But nah, I won't. My brain doesn't work like that."

"You know anybody that's read her new book, Po?" Neftalí asked.

"She has a new one? I thought she died a long time ago."

"She's still alive. But she's an older writer now. Obviously.

Doesn't have any family, because she never had kids and never married, and I heard the only person she talks to is her publisher, who is even older. She writes in English, you see. Still. Even after her deportation and not having lived here for decades. It's now the last book I own."

"Hold it close to you, like they say. I'm over here sometimes helping to scavenge for crickets to hustle a few bucks. Read it for those of us who don't have time, like you played music for those of us who don't have musical talent. Hey, but check it." Po pivoted, handing Neftalí the paperback. "Y'all are going to the cathedral? I don't think I can ride with you two all the way back there. Can't swing it . . . you know . . . emotionally. Still processing how the chupacabras shut down the protest the other day. And how they killed those worker-mothers. It's sad. Just not right."

The goodbyes were swift. Neftalí and Proserpina waved to Po as he disappeared down the vitreous curvature of the block, wearing quite possibly the last screen-printed shirt of their short-lived band.

Three squad cars were lined up along the curb on Chavez Boulevard. Inside the first car, a police officer sat watching a talking head spewing instructions from a monitor strapped to the dashboard; two other officers sporting shades stood by the open doors of the second squad car, having a loud conversation, bayonet rifles at their sides. The officer closest to Neftalí and Proserpina signaled for them to halt. He sized them up and, without asking questions, said, "All right," and motioned them to move it along. The third squad car was empty. On the opposite side of the street, an ambulance was standing by, flashing its lights.

The cul-de-sac in front of the cathedral had been sprayed clean with pressure hoses—drains were clogged with multicolored banners, discarded cups, and facsimiles reading CRICK OUT FOR OUR MOTHERS and DOWN WITH BIG TEX and FISH CANNERY MORE LIKE FISH CAN'T-ERY and, simply, VERDILLO = MURDER. City workers in brown polo shirts picked up the debris wearing thorn-proof gloves, and loaded bulging trash bags onto the bed of a lengthy, rickety electric wagon. The walnut and soapberry trees on the cul-de-sac were barren, and the mammoth cathedral appeared older than ever, with its deranged mixture of Roman, Gothic, and adobe architecture that for a time had made it a prime tourist attraction in this part of rural Texas. From the cathedral's rear, ascending to the sky, stood the tower and Epifanía—the five-ton unmaintained bell, which rang twice a week in the key of G before its hinges rusted.

Yellow barricades were carefully being removed from the road by workers, along with tall, bright orange road cones lining the cul-de-sac. A couple of officers dismantled and rolled up WARNING and CAUTION tape to use for future crime scenes.

A police officer raised his bayonet rifle like a shield toward Neftalí and Proserpina and yelled, "Loitering in this area is not tolerated at this moment."

Neftalí ignored him and noticed that a section of the sidewalk in front of the cathedral had been cordoned off; there were chalk outlines of bodies with bright green markings all over, along with stains she later realized were dried blood. Neftalí tried to remember how many escaped worker-mothers people said had been murdered by the military here the previous week. Twelve? Fourteen? Their asylum at the cathedral had been honored, even by the state, until the mayor had his people clandestinely haul the women out in a midnight raid— what occurred afterward had gone undocumented but was now common knowledge in Three Rivers, at least among those who cared to know.

Proserpina moved toward the scarecrow cathedral ahead of Neftalí. The first scheduled Mass since the killings occurred had ended a few hours earlier, and the tall, reinforced-steel cathedral doors were wide open. As the young women walked between soapberry trees in the cul-de-sac, then up the long concrete staircase, the votive candles burned beyond the throaty darkness of the cathedral doors, and on the far wall, a pale Christ was stuck on the cross.

Rusty echoes ricocheted inside the cathedral, while nesting pigeons croaked like bullfrogs up and down the steps and flying buttresses. Two officers kept crosshair eyes behind their shades, staring at the young women. A pair of disgruntled middle-aged nuns were escorting a grinning young man out toward the cathedral doors—Alexei. He wore skinny jeans, a beige T-shirt with a spray-painted backward CH, and a dark brown vest with shiny black shoes, the stylish kind he used to wear to their Missus Batches gigs. The two middle-aged nuns pushed him out, shut the cathedral doors as Alexei descended the steps.

Proserpina looked up at the dormant bell tower, half expecting it to wake up and ring at this rare little reunion of their permanently-on-hiatus experiment, Missus Batches.

They climbed down the remaining cathedral steps together, walked past the *paletero* and Katya the Elder selling pineapple juice in plastic pouches, ringing her high-pitched bell at potential customers.

Alexei said to his old bandmates, with his back to the police, "Let's get out of here, these goat suckers love giving me stink eye. They stopped and frisked me earlier, so I lay low at the cathedral until the nuns ran me out. I guess I was snoring loud."

It was springtime in Live Oak County and the remaining acres of rainforest were far away, being chopped up like a cold lobster on its back. Proserpina and Neftalí followed Alexei down the uneven brick road between Peony and Jones Streets, half a block from the cathedral. The streets and walls of the derelict buildings seemed chewed by the rats of time and stank like their own brand of rotting cheese. They stepped over empty tin cans, squashed cigarette butts, used condoms, half-burned Bibles, and placentas of partly digested food.

The brick walls turned into dark wood, the buildings slouched over them like scolding cypress trees, and Neftalí saw the haunted green eyes of an owl creeping from an air-conditioning unit up high. Proserpina had flashbacks to when she was a girl and lived in the big city with her parents and three brothers—before rumors spread that her extended family had made it out of Damascus, and they came to Three Rivers in search of them. Alexei carelessly hummed the bass line of an old battle hymn called "The Yankee Soldier and the Champlain Lass." They turned a corner in the alley, and the squalor disappeared—there were no steaming trash cans or threats of jacked rodents gnawing them to husks. Instead, an oceanic breeze swept down from the smoky quartz skies, and the alley up ahead hit a frowning dead end.

A small stereo blared Houston rap with no bass as a young woman with cropped yellow hair under a turquoise hoodie danced on her own. Her moves sank and swam with an improvised grace as the three approached her. A morose string quartet incongruously replaced the rap, filling the air like a hydrogen balloon.

Two boys sat with their backs to one of the walls, watching the dancer go. A boy with a black eye and a sports hat occasionally fiddled with the knob on the stereo. The dancer continued as the two boys clapped along off-beat.

"You know this kind of dancing," the dancer said to the boys. "They used to call this *disco dancing.* 'Disco' was short for 'discotheque.' Get it? It was a place where you would go and they would teach you all kinds of dances. Kinda like a library, but exclusively for dancing styles. And only dancing. Can you believe it? Discotheques were popular all over, even here in Three Rivers. My mom told me. Gonna see her today again, after a spell."

The boy on the right, with a pack-of-hyenas haircut, said, "Shit, I wanna go to a discotheque with you one day, Moira."

Moira said, "We can't. They don't have discotheques around anymore." She noticed Proserpina, Neftalí, Alexei, and stopped dancing.

Proserpina recognized the boy with the black eye and said, "Were you with Santo over by Brown Apollo earlier?"

The boy blushed, looked down and to the right, and said, "Nah, that's my brother, and some of the others."

"Who's your brother?"

"Santo."

"You better check up on him," Proserpina suggested. "'Cause a minute ago we saw the chupacabras picking him up."

"My brother can right his own bads," the boy with the black eye said.

"Excellently put," Neftalí interjected.

Alexei swung around the five of them, removed a false side from one of the alley's brick walls, and pulled out a blue canvas reenlistment bag stuffed to capacity. Alexei shoved the false side of the brick back in and hoisted the heavy blue bag over his shoulder with surprising ease.

"Bottle-tops," Alexei said. "We picked up a good amount. People just throw their plastic bottles anywhere, since the city removed all the trash cans from the sidewalks. The protest left a lot of shit out there for us. We're even helping clean up the city, if you think about it. The environment. Moira, Jaime, and Howie here have all helped."

"What happened to your eye?" Proserpina asked Howie.

"I was at the cathedral the other night when the protest was going down, after the killings. Something flew from the sky and bit me when the chupacabras shot their smoke cannons."

"Bit your eye?"

"That's what it felt like."

The boy with the pack-of-hyenas haircut, Jaime, gestured toward a carefully concealed Styrofoam cooler behind a brimming grease trap. Proserpina opened the cooler gently, like it might be booby-trapped. There was a frosty emerald-green forty for each of them inside. Everyone but Neftalí, who had recently quit drinking again, popped one, as Alexei recounted the story of Professor Pantano and the new kind of currency he was creating. Alexei described the coin machine assembled out of stolen tree house planks, boiler parts, gears, pumps, pipes, and a motherboard, which they would all finally get to see only if they agreed to cross to the roofed part of the city. He reached his coup de théâtre upon describing the coin machine's rattle and roar—Alexei lifted his arms like an enraged grizzly to demonstrate, and it was easy to envision thunder and lightning creating golden arches over his performance.

Every time Neftalí learned more about Professor Pantano and this crackpot plan of Alexei's, a heavy dread settled on her shoulders. She could see Alexei wearing a military uniform, haranguing like Ned Kelly while galloping on a mare, but there was no army behind him, only mesquite-brown, dry South Texas. *What about Proserpina and my people?* she'd asked herself before. *Where are* they *in this bullshit fantasy of his?* But Neftalí never got far on this train of thought before she lost her patience and interrupted her old bandmate Alexei. "Wait. Hold up, everybody. Time out for one minute. Hold your tiny horses. One immigrant at a time. Qué no panda el pinche cúnico. I'm sorry, I know you all are drinking and having a chill time, and that's cool and everything, I get it. I mean, I wish I had the mind where I could kick back and have a forty with y'all, but the last day, or two, or three or four, have been traumatic. Right? Cops killed those worker-mothers. You think they didn't stab them with those bayonet rifles? They destroyed my books. Both these things have to be fucking connected. Right?"

At first everybody was grateful for Neftalí's outburst. They held their forties out to give her props—she always said straight out what others collectively kept bottled up. Then, as the conversation took stark, somber, helpless turns, they became agitated, and resentful of Neftalí, until everybody was silent long enough to forget, trip out, and laugh about nothing all over again. The drinkers toasted, cheered, and poured some out for shredded books and the murdered worker-mothers, as Neftalí's chest heaved with an inner turmoil nobody seemed to understand.

She looked beyond the forties, her old bandmates, Moira, the two boys—the alley walls grew brighter, disappeared like a flimsy set, and were replaced by the blossoming shore of a wide beach. For the second time that day, Neftalí saw the composer Juventino Rosas picking up seashells along the coast of a bubble-wrap ocean. Each shell reminded Juventino of a past love, a different relative he'd left behind. He brought the shells up to his ear and heard his loved ones' secrets—beyond him was the casket-brown body of water, turning pink, then a deep ceramic blue.

Neftalí was rudely brought back to the present moment when her sweaty palms unmistakably cradled the weight of a book. "What—" she said, focusing on the book's binding, while Juventino and the beach mirage slipped away, as if into an empty forty.

She admired the hard cover and the colorless embossed cursive letters on the front. Neftalí traced the letters, which spelled out the book's title, using her fingers. Alexei couldn't help but smile as Proserpina, Moira, and the two boys—who were in on the surprise—looked on.

Neftalí carefully opened the book, trying to placate her undulating, rabbit-fanged emotions, and not to show the others that her eyes were tearing up, as she read the title page: *Brother Brontë* by Jazzmin Monelle Rivas, number 136 of 2,000. On the copyright page there was no year of first printing. Neftalí, with heavy fingers, turned a couple of pages, feeling the thick off-white paper. The dedication read "For Helena (Mina)."

Neftalí and Alexei slapped each other's hands in a failed embrace, acknowledged their mutual inability to give thanks for anything, then finally hugged it out. Though the shit-talking of the past was always hanging, they both cherished these moments when their connection as bass player and lead guitarist was rekindled. She showed the book to Proserpina, who said, "This is your girl, right? Your favorite writer? It looks beautiful. Makes me almost want to be a reader," to which Moira and the two boys emphatically agreed.

Alexei laughed like a sly pickpocket, and in his mind he, Proserpina, and Neftalí were Missus Batches, unloading equipment on the side of a rainy street in some black-and-white photograph he'd seen in a music magazine long ago.

Feeling he was on a roll, he said, "Proserpina, Jaime here doesn't have a mother at the fish cannery, so he's wondering about . . . requesting your services."

"Is that right?" Proserpina said. "It's gonna cost you up front. Seeing as how you two run with hoodlums like Santo. You don't have any cash? Like, at all? What do you got for me, then? And do you have a recent headshot on you, even?"

Jaime offered her a couple active bus passes as a trade. Proserpina accepted, against her worst instincts, and Jaime handed her a current headshot. She held the photo up to the light of the sun and trimmed it to a perfect square using tiny scissors. The type of ration cards Proserpina forged didn't require personal information. They could be used only for small purchases and would expire at random moments, but they were worth much more than what Proserpina often charged, if the purchaser played it right. She pulled out her manual card imprinter, inserted the photo face down in the slot, along with two lamination sheets and a barcode, then ran the handle across the little imprinting machine while applying the entirety of her weight. The ration card came out sealed to her satisfaction along the plastic edges.

Proserpina grinned approvingly as she inspected the card in the sunlight to make sure the glue had coalesced just right, handed it to Jaime. He and Howie peaced, wishing everyone a fine day. Proserpina bowed to them in a half-mocking gesture. Moira high-fived and hugged Jaime and Howie; Alexei offered them cigarettes from the pack he'd found. The boys plucked a single smoke each for the road.

Moira mentioned her plans to visit her mother at the fish cannery, so she tagged along as the remaining members of the group moved in that direction.

While they crossed the pedestrian bridge over I-35, filled with bumper-to-bumper traffic passing through Three Rivers twenty feet below, Alexei babbled, "We're gonna take over one street, one neighborhood, one city at a time, until they're forced to hand us *our* own part of the state, *our* own country. It's gonna start how everything starts—with a *tortilleria*, of course. We'll sell corn tortillas by the kilo, wrap them in special paper to keep them warm as long as possible. We'll abolish all kinds of pop soda, drink only águas frescas. Then the taco stands will take over. One per block. Burger joints are forever out. The butcher will be a very respected person, politically and within the community. Local farms will be places of worship, sanctuaries like the cathedral, but real ones, where we won't let people die. From these church farms we'll get our milk, our cheese, our vegetables, fruit, and butters. We'll do away with yellow government cheeses and carry only two kinds of white cheese, *asadero* and *panela*—"

"You're selling your people out, Alexei," Proserpina interrupted.

"Which people? Russian people? No way. How do you mean?"

"Well," she continued, scratching her head with both hands, "your given name is Alexander Fyodorovich Tolstoyevsky. If that's not the most Russian name on the goddamn planet, then I don't know what is. What are you doing, trying to start a new world hustling Mexican street food for, right under Mexican people's noses? What about borscht or piroshki? What about those little pelmeni, especially? What about the street food of *your* scattered people?"

"Geez. Okay. I'll consider it. But you ever try rolling hundreds of dumplings at five in the morning every day? It's hard to know how to bother with those."

THREE RIVERS WAS DIVIDED into three sections: Arroyo North, the well-off side of town, where the actual three rivers—Frio, Atascosa, and Nueces—flowed down from the Rockies and where the train station was first built in the 1850s, connecting the liver of Texas with the rest of the developing country; New Freeway, the east side, where 85 percent of the buildings once built for big-tech innovations had been abandoned; and finally, Old Freeway, named after the deserted highway system that ran through it, and known to most as *the bad side of town*—where the vapor mirage of the old city remembered the poetic scrolls of cosmic knowledge one minute, and forgot them the next, in an endless cycle.

Neftalí, Alexei, Moira, and Proserpina lived in the first community after crossing into Old Freeway, one that had suffered from rolling blackouts for most of their lives.

All three sections of the city converged in a vortex at its center, and slightly north of this center was where the Big Tex Fish Cannery lurched, stinking like a gangrened seaport thanks to its three onyx smokestacks, which perpetually released the grizzly rot of processed verdillo fish. It was against state law for any mother of a child to be unemployed, so with the scarcity of jobs, most grown women in Three Rivers ended up permanently barracked at Big Tex, which required its workers to also live there—working at the cannery was the only job guaranteed anywhere for Texan women, even those with zero experience or education.

As they approached the barbed, spiked perimeter fence, the miasma of verdillo fish presented a smothering welcome. Alexei dropped his canvas bag of bottle-tops onto the pavement and said he'd wait on the curb, since his mother had died in Dagestan before he'd immigrated to Texas. Alexei waved at Moira, Proserpina, and Neftalí as they walked toward the mechanical entrance gate, looked around, and sat on the ground by his bag of bottle-tops. He caught the sun staring down at him, so he stared right back. "The key," he said aloud, "is to simply return the sun's gaze. Everything else is merely formulaic."

Moments later a sports car pulled up next to Alexei. The driver was a woman in a red skirt and a yellow bikini top. The sports car was blaring an opera—the driver revved the engine, blew Alexei a kiss. Alexei caught the kiss and returned it as the sports car spun around and shrank like a rapidly deflating balloon, until it grew tiny and slipped into a crack in the pavement.

Three police squad cars soon followed. Alexei made eye contact with each one of the police officers driving, and when they were gone, he regretted doing so. He stood up, kicked dust, and watched it whirlwind and darken into a giant reptile, ready to breathe down hellfire on Three Rivers, Texas.

———

Proserpina grew anxious about the reality of walking into the fish cannery, which forced her to face her fear of bearing children; but mostly she was confronted with the fear of exposing herself to the great sacrifice her immigrant mother had made for her and her brothers after their father passed away. Proserpina's spirits sank into a vacuous trench. Her heartbeat churned, locomotively nostalgic and emotional—she braced herself to meet face-to-face her mother's pain and the pain of their entire family, which balanced itself like a white elephant on her back.

Neftalí, Proserpina, and Moira walked past abandoned skeletons of charred vehicles in the quarter-mile-long parking lot leading to the main building's entrance. The heretic smokestacks seemed to disappear as they neared the towering visitors' lobby. Two bulky male pylons were holding bayonet rifles and chewing bubble gum loudly by the revolving doors. The pylons eyed them up and down as the three walked into the phosphorescent vestibule.

The walls inside emitted a low meat-grinding hum, as if the vestibule would be compacted into a cube by robots at any moment. Behind a piece of thick glass halving the room, a crew of tall, blond women in brown jumpsuits were stressfully pacing and working. The blond women either organized stacks of manila folders, or stared into computer screens while typing furiously, or slammed rubber stamps down onto sheet after sheet taken from piles of documents.

Another pair of pylons stood at attention, holding bayonet rifles by a small window, and above them, painted on the entirety of the wall, was an elaborate scene commemorating the founding of Big Tex Fish Cannery. Furrows of moorland, sitting below the gaze of an ocean-blue sky, made up the mural's landscape. Destitute women in rags were thronged and scattered along this grassland, holding shiny verdillo fish in their hands—the women closer to the foreground were the only ones with anything like smiles, as they all greatly admired the painting's centerpiece: a larger-than-life Pablo Henry Crick, standing beside a gleaming white horse. Clutched in his hands, and pointed heavenward, was a diapered cherub cradling two haloed fish. A banner had been splashed across the ceiling at the very top of the mural, and the large Latin inscription, NON SIBI SED PATRIAE, had recently been retouched.

One of the blond women working behind the glass partition pressed a button, and from an overhead speaker her fuzzy, low-battery voice said, "You girls here to visit somebody? Got your ration identification cards ready?"

Proserpina made sure to grab her real ration identification card from the pocket she'd sewed inside her skirt; Moira found hers easily in her handbag. Neftalí seemed to walk into her bag like it was a two-story house; she climbed the stairs, found the main bedroom, dug through the closet until she found the right shoebox, retrieved the card, left the two-story house, and then the three young women placed their cards in the suction tube capsule, pressed the button, and they swooshed away. The capsule got sucked into the roof, and thirty seconds later it appeared next to the blond woman on the other side of the bulletproof glass. The woman cracked open the capsule, then scanned all three ration cards into the system.

"You girls are familiar with the dos and the don'ts, correct?" the blond woman said into the crooked microphone. "What you are allowed to do, and what you aren't? You got twenty minutes, starting as soon as you walk through those two doors. As a reminder, and for your own safety, your cards have been scanned, so there's never a moment when you're not being tracked. Make sure your passes remain visible."

They nodded silently in unison as the blond woman sent back three visitors' passes, along with their ration cards, which were promptly stashed.

Moira, Neftalí, and Proserpina clipped the visitors' passes on their right shoulders and all but ignored the armed male pylons as they walked through the long beige tunnel toward the fields of the Three Rivers Big Tex Fish Cannery.

Acres and acres of verdillo breeding pools were divided into plots, each the size of a parking space—as far as the eye could see there were worker-mothers wearing denim smocks, tending to the pools. Before each pool stood a worker-mother with a chronometer, in charge of timing the soil mixture and monitoring the growth of each batch of fish.

Some pools had no visible verdillo fish, but in others their stumpy little tails protruded from the soil like armies of silver prairie dogs. In the most advanced batches, thousands of fishtails slapped wildly like severed hands trying desperately to clap. Seven to ten worker-mothers operated each pool, turning the soil formula, pulling the muddy, slimy verdillo fish from the dark blue dirt, and piling them up in large yellow drum barrels, while other worker-mothers waited until the barrels filled up before moving them toward the canning stage of production. The worker-mothers were of varying ages: some were dedicated and energetic, with fit bodies from the demanding work; others were twisted and glum, broken by the enforced repetition.

"My mother's all the way in sector eighty-eight," said Moira. "What about y'all's?"

"Mine's actually in the downstairs back office," Proserpina said.

"Oh, fancy."

Neftalí said, "I'm here to say happy birthday to the other woman who raised me. Aside, you know, from my own mother."

The three parted ways, for the clock was ticking—two minutes had gone by as they adjusted to the grim regimented reality inside the fish cannery.

Moira cut through several empty pools, looked up at the watchtowers posted every hundred feet or so like vulture nests, where the male pylons with shaded eyes were hiding out. She winked at the armed pylon closest to her, certain he was looking down on her through his dark sunglasses as she ran past worker-mothers who sometimes smiled or asked rhetorically how she was doing.

Moira approached sector 88. A woman with an orange bandanna holding back her curly hair hollered, "My glorious daughter!" as she pulled out two bushels of verdillo fish from a fresh dark blue pool.

The pylons at the freight elevator scanned Proserpina's visitors' pass, and she was sent down two levels, toward the fish cannery's labeling center. Jobs here were reserved for worker-mothers with university degrees; additionally, once a year, any worker-mother who was "enrolled" at the fish cannery could take the Upwards Exam and potentially transfer to a less physically demanding job. If a worker-mother excelled at the exam, which was divided into five sections (Agriculture, Metallurgy, Engineering & Architectural Tendencies, Numerology, and Sanitation), she'd move on to another exam called the Entrance Exam, which tested a worker-mother's level of anarchic unrest, religious persuasion, and spiritual and moral attachment to her kin, and required her to write a three-page essay on her views and hopes for the future. Most worker-mothers who passed the Upwards Exam performed awkwardly or miserably on the Entrance Exam, and continued working the fields, performing the most grueling labor in the fish cannery.

Proserpina's mother was one of the few worker-mothers to have come into Big Tex without a college degree and still work her way up to the labeling center. After a second consecutive high score on the Entrance Exam, she was interviewed by the director of the fish cannery, the head supervisor, junior supervisors, and superintendents of Three Rivers' social education district, and was finally promoted to head proofreader—a new position, in which she oversaw each Big Tex label. Since the formula for the mass-produced fish was constantly changing, and grammatical precision was as important to the company as its famous logo (a fish wearing a raincoat in a rowboat, caught in a tempest at sea), the board of directors developed the position for a worker-mother to exclusively research and meticulously execute the correct spelling of every ingredient.

Proserpina walked into the labeling center trying not to

hyperventilate, wondering why she'd even agreed to a visit. Twenty desks sat evenly spaced in rows of five. The worker-mothers here wore brown jumpsuits, with blue bandannas holding their hair back. Each was assigned her own desk, but presently they were all huddled around a diminutive woman standing on the desk at the center of the large room. The small woman was holding up a sheet of parchment paper and appeared to be reading aloud from it. There were no pylons monitoring the room, but at least eight cameras were strapped to the ceiling, with blinking orange lights.

The worker-mother on the desk was Proserpina's mother. Each day was a different battle at the fish cannery, and Proserpina had been nervous about what kind of mood she might find her in. It was a relief to stand there silently among the other women, trying to make out the words her mother was reciting.

"Here she is, my daughter. To clear this mess up!" her mother yelled, interrupting her own reading.

Proserpina gave an awkward wave to the throng amidst what was clearly some dispute.

Her mother climbed down from the desk while gesturing at the parchment paper in her hands, then wrapped her arms around her daughter in a swift embrace. "Now," she continued, releasing her grip, "my daughter follows this ancient story very well. Better than anyone. Better than me, for she grew up with it. Even retelling it back to me. What a magical occasion that you are here, Proserpina, so you can help remind these women of the story 'The Barber and the Bearded Fish.'"

"'The Barber and the Bearded Fish'?" echoed Proserpina, dreading whatever this was and whatever might follow.

"My daughter, don't act at all surprised. You have known this story since you were a child—"

"The one about the bearded fish that jumps from the water and goes to the boardwalk every week to get a shave from the barber? Because the fish's beard can't stop growing, and even obstructs its vision when it swims?"

"Yes. That very story. And where did this bearded fish come from?"

"The salt water."

"But what body of salt water?"

"The sea."

"Which sea? There are so many, with particular characteristics, and individual names, in different corners of the planet."

"What sea, what sea?" Proserpina said, searching every vacant avenue in her brain for an exit. "I don't think it's ever mentioned in what sea. Right? Instead, they call it something epic like *the Just and Wayfaring Sea*—"

A scandalized-courthouse commotion broke out among the worker-mothers in the room.

Proserpina's mother waved the sheet of parchment paper triumphantly in the air, and, raising her voice over mild protestations, repeated, "The Just. And Wayfaring. Sea. Not the Red Sea. Not the Mediterranean. Baltic. Not even the Wine-Dark. But the classic Just and Wayfaring Sea."

"Jot it!" a voice in the crowd exclaimed, to end it all.

Proserpina's mother spread the large parchment paper on the center desk over murmuring, conceding voices, and with a micropigment ink pen amended the text as needed throughout. Then she opened a desk drawer with a false bottom, clipped the page to a larger bundle of pages, and shut the drawer while the worker-mothers shuffled back to their own desks and fell silent. Just as they each picked up a task and appeared busy, two male pylons with bayonet rifles entered the room. When they saw Proserpina, they scanned her visitors' pass again and she requested some time in the private visitors' room with her mother, which was granted. They had two minutes.

Proserpina and her mother sat on gray plastic chairs in a room with pink walls and a white tiled floor; a grandfather clock at the far end looked at them like they were in detention. One of the pylons shut the door and Proserpina whispered in Arabic, "Mama, what's going on, what was that all about?"

"It's okay, we can talk in a normal-volume voice, there's no bugs in here anymore. We took care of them, along with the cameras outside. These guards are brainless. They have no clue we are even speaking another language."

"Mama, are you all right? Why are you so thin, are you sick?"

"No, no, your mother is fine."

"What was that argument all about, asking me about a little kids' story like 'The Barber and the Bearded Fish'?"

"Proserpina, how are your brothers? My wonderful grown sons?"

"They're okay, I guess. Raf is still a supervisor at Sanitation. Benito is always working hard for his kids and to keep his wife out of the fish cannery. You know how that one goes. And I hardly ever see Ali. He's okay, too, though, just doesn't like to see anybody, ever, outside his job."

"That's good, that's good. They're all fine boys. Know

what they want in life. And you, Proserpina? How is my one daughter? Tell me about the style of music you are playing today."

"Not really playing any music right now, Mama. Our equipment got stolen, and finally we couldn't keep replacing it. Everything's too expensive. But it's been a while now, and we've sort of gotten over it. You know, the rock-and-roll dream. Trying to move along. I'm doing well enough, I guess, just—"

"You're all bones," her mother interrupted, running her hands along Proserpina's sides. "I can feel your ribs. Too skinny. What are they feeding you out there, Daughter? Are the ration cards not enough? Proserpina, tell me. I need to know. And I want you to be honest without fear of hurting my feelings. Was I a good mother to you and your brothers? Remember when your father would bring buckets of American ice cream, and we all sat on tree stumps and had it in cones for the first time? That was fun."

"It *was* fun, Mama—"

"Ah, your father. How we miss him. And you, my beautiful children. My dear girl, and my boys. How I miss us living together back then, as a family. Even the hard times, without electricity, when it was so hot and cold. A world away from Damascus, everything we've known. Proserpina, give me your hand. Before we run out of time. I have something for you. I've sewn a hidden pocket in my apron, like I taught you to always do. Please hide this halceamadon and take it with you. Tell your brothers you saw me and that I'm healthy and doing good. Are you still friends with that Neftalí? How is she? I like her, my favorite songs you did were always the ones you played with her. She's a good friend to you. Don't forget how hard she's had it, because her mother died when she was only a girl. She doesn't have a mother looking after her, like you."

A bar of Mahler rang from the grandfather clock across the pink room, which immediately summoned a pylon from behind the door. Proserpina stashed the halceamadon in her hidden pocket, hugged her mother, and in a trickle of a voice told her she loved her.

"I love you, too, beautiful daughter. Don't misbehave. Don't make the mistakes where you end up here, like your mother."

"I won't, Mama. Please take care. Don't get sick. You're going to retire and come live with me one day soon, Mama."

"I will, Daughter."

"You will, Mama."

"I will, my daughter. Goodbye."

"Bye, Mama."

Proserpina was guided past the busy worker-mothers at their desks; the pylon directed her back into the freight elevator. As soon as the elevator doors shut, Proserpina's chest heaved, and in that forty-four-second ride to the ground floor she sobbed—her first sob since the last time she'd visited her mother at the fish cannery.

Neftalí rapidly made her way to an interior corner of the fish cannery's perimeter fence, where she'd been told Bettina was on a monitored smoke break. Halfway into a drag, she spotted Neftalí and said, "I must be hallucinating—you remembered?

No way. I was just telling some of the other women last night after our shift that I don't have to see the people I love every day in order to feel them close to me. They were complaining about how none of their kids visit them anymore. But here you are. How are you doing, Neftalí?"

Neftalí stood a few feet from Bettina. Neither of them leaned in for any kind of physical contact; they kept their distance, since the traumas from Bettina's hard-drinking past were never far from either's mind. "Happy birthday, Bettina. I've been meaning to pay you a visit. I've been okay. Just thinking about the future. While trying to be very aware of the present moment."

"The constant battle to be ever-present. We heard of the protests at the cathedral. Glum atmosphere around here. As you can probably tell. But in here one hopes that people outside are finally getting it together. What's going on out there?"

"Chupacabras came into the house last night. They did away with the entirety of your and Mama's library. It was only a matter of time, I guess. Wish I could have brought them here to you one by one, since this is the only place where anyone in Three Rivers is allowed to have books now."

"That's cruddy. I don't like hearing it. Was going to ask if you'd by any chance tracked that book down for me."

"*Understanding Urban and Agricultural Hydraulics*? It's a long, sad story, actually. I couldn't find it," Neftalí lied.

"That's okay. It's not like I have much need for *Understanding Urban and Agricultural Hydraulics* in here. Hauling verdillo fish all day. Just thought one day it'd be nice to know about it. Maybe distract myself with the technical illustrations. But, like your mother always said, 'They'll never legalize the hustle.' Especially since our leaders already perfected their end of the hustle, when we can't even acquire technical books to learn new technical skills. I mean, here we are, all of us are called *worker-mothers*, first of all. Why do you think they even call us this? All these women and myself? They have us pretty much incarcerated. That's what the escape—and what happened at the cathedral—proved. Am I right?"

Two pylons passed them by; Bettina signaled that there was no need for her to answer.

"I do have this, though," Neftalí said, holding out the white hardcover edition of *Brother Brontë*. It felt good that the pylons here didn't care about books, as if Big Tex was tethered to a different set of laws than Three Rivers.

"Your favorite writer, right? I remember back when you were first discovering her. Check out the binding. Stitching. Immaculately constructed book. This is not easy. The mere craft of it as an object makes this book a work of art. You're giving me this?"

"I can't actually let you take this copy. Because it was given to me as a gift. I knew you'd admire its craftsmanship, so I wanted to show it to you. But here's something you can have instead."

Neftalí handed Bettina her treasured tattered paperback copy of *Ghosts in the Zapotec Sphericals* by Jazzmin Monelle Rivas. She'd saved it years ago from the Bexar elementary school library fire, shortly before Missus Batches's only mini tour; her sentimental attachment to the book went beyond the typeset story it contained.

"You're always asking for these intense, instructional, harrowingly demanding books," Neftalí said. "Thought you could maybe burn off creative energy with some fiction. You know, not having to constantly strain to decipher engineering terms, and consult the glossary over and over. That right there is one of my favorite novels, as a matter of fact. And I carry it around most days like an amulet. So . . . happy birthday, Bettina."

A pylon with glowing red eyes like a *nosferatu* appeared between them, because Neftalí's visiting minutes were up—Bettina needed to get back to holding the line of production. Between them there were never any goodbyes, so Neftalí waved her fingers and Bettina blew her a kiss.

"Thanks for the book. Remember that I miss you. Remember that your mother misses you."

Neftalí and Proserpina were escorted by three pylons through fields of verdillo fish, until they found Moira playing a card game with her mother on an upside-down maroon bucket by a reinforced-steel wall. The pylons waited for Moira and her mother to finish their hand before announcing that visitation time was up. Then they collected their three visitors' passes, scanned them, and the largest pylon signaled toward the exit. Moira, Neftalí, and Proserpina walked toward the visitors' foyer of the fish cannery and reentered its long beige hallway.

"How were your moms?" asked Neftalí.

"Honestly, I never really know. I always feel she's not being legit with me. But can't be great, right?" Proserpina said.

"Mine I think's okay," said Moira. "We just sat and played cards the entire time. But she did tell me about my identical twin sister, who I've never met. Apparently, she came here to visit her last week, out of the blue."

"Out of the blue, huh? What a thing to say, out of the blue. What blue? Anyway, wait, that's crazy about your sister. So you two look exactly alike?" asked Proserpina.

Moira shrugged.

"And how was Bettina, Nef?"

"She's fine, I guess. I don't know. I get the feeling she doesn't really mind it in here. They don't let anyone drink booze. At least she can read, and enjoys reading."

As they crossed the clinical vestibule, Neftalí paid especially careful attention to the details rendered within the commissioned mural looming above the two armed pylons: grassland unlike anything in Three Rivers; the look of reverence and gratitude of the ragged fish-clutching women toward the only man depicted, Pablo Henry Crick, as he presented a bright-eyed cherub cradling two fish while gazing in rapture at a vague spot in the sky; and the pale horse, a symbol of wisdom and sportsmanship and apocalypse, beside Crick, a barrier between himself and the devout women.

THIS PART BEGINS with loathsome midday sunrays squeezing between the thin clouds and smog to crunch down on Neftalí, Proserpina, and Moira, who were scattered throughout the quarter-mile-long parking lot outside Big Tex, looking for Alexei, yelling his name like they were in the middle of the *monte* and searching for their missing Labrador.

"Let's just leave him," Neftalí called out, exasperated.

All three met at the curb, where they'd last seen him. The sidewalk beneath them groaned like flushed old pipes; the sun brayed like a drunk man telling an unwelcome joke; the cracks on the quarter-mile-long parking lot turned into slithering worms.

Proserpina pulled out the paper her mother had hastily handed her in the pink visitation room from the secret pocket inside her skirt. The paper was intricately folded into a flat halceamadon. It took a minute and a half to carefully undo it without force, without tearing it. Neftalí tried to help while Moira watched. Together, Proserpina and Neftalí unfolded the parchment paper like a large map, flipped it over, and found that the entire poster-sized sheet was covered in tiny dots that could have been life-size portraits of fleas.

Neftalí pulled out a purple coin purse from her bag, found a magnifying lens, and when she looked through it, careful to avoid direct sunlight, the dots on the paper grew like fish swimming close to the glass in an aquarium. The unwrapped halceamadon was, upon examination, a narrative written in many columns in tiny typescript, as if it'd been dictated to an insect, starting in the upper-right corner with the title in bold, cursive script: *The Southerns: The Worker-Mother Tales.*

"What in the world is this?" Neftalí nudged Proserpina.

"I don't know. My mother just told me to take it."

"Well, what did she say it was?"

"I don't know if she did."

"What even happened when you were in there?"

"I don't know . . . Uh, uh, let's see. The worker-mothers in the labeling department. They were having an intense argument. And my mom was at the center of it all. They were arguing about an old story I first heard in Damascus, when I was a girl. My grandmother told it to me many times to get me to calm down. It was called 'The Barber and the Bearded Fish.'"

"What the hell," Neftalí said, reading through some of the sentences and passages. "Proserpina. This is a story. It's a lot of stories. Written very small. I think it's in English, but written backward, from right to left."

"Like in Arabic," said Proserpina.

Both of them scanned the paper from top to bottom, corner to corner.

Proserpina felt that something deep and personal that she'd never dealt with before was being exposed, spread open like a spatchcocked beast for anyone to see. She snatched the parchment paper and folded it back into a flat halceamadon, slipped it into her secret pocket as Alexei approached, carrying his bag of bottle-tops. Everyone was too lost in their own thoughts to ask him where he'd been.

On their way to the roofed part of the city they spotted a Chevron station. Proserpina had been scratching her head with every step. She looked at her fingernails and noticed there was blood underneath them. Then she turned to Neftalí and said, "I'm starving, Nef. We should've gotten a wurst from Rayman earlier. I kinda regret talking all that shit, now that I'm hungry. I'm thirsty, too, probably dehydrated, and I gotta pee bad."

Using their real ration cards, Proserpina, Moira, and Neftalí each picked up a bottle of water and an energy bar at the Chevron. They distracted the robot clerk and grabbed its key, then took turns using the exterior restroom.

Alexei had only teddys in his pocket, which government-run Chevron stations didn't accept, so he waited outside. It wasn't hard for Alexei, though, to picture a world in which his bottle-top currency would be widely accepted for the transaction of goods, even beyond Chevron stations.

When the three young women walked out of the Chevron after returning the restroom key to the robot clerk, Alexei said to Proserpina, "Remind me to get a ration card off ya later."

Proserpina held in her surprise—this was the first time Alexei had ever asked her for a ration card, since he usually went to one of his own boys. Rather than call it out as a sexist affront after all this time, Proserpina concluded that Alexei had tribes to be loyal to and tributes of his own to pay, which she concluded was sexist, too, but in a different way.

"All right, yes, Alexei, sure. I won't charge you for the first one, it'll be on me."

"Nah, here, let me give you teddys. Two teddys, how about that?"

"Please. Lemme just do this one on me, okay. And, no offense, but that's not real money you're offering right there."

"What? Teddys are real money."

Proserpina and Neftalí suppressed their laughter. "No, they aren't," they said in unison.

"Well, they're gonna be. I don't know why you two don't believe in the vision of the future that the professor and me have."

"That's because that professor is a creep," Neftalí said. "And kind of a pervert."

"Aw, you don't know how it is with these old guys, Neftalí. Sometimes it's hard for them to adjust. What with the professor being from the older generation and all. A guy like that's really gotta make an effort to treat women as actual people. Even for guys like me, during puberty it was hard not to notice the hot bod of a lady walking by. But look. You learn. Time passes. The generation of boys like the professor was never taught those things during their puberty, like us. It's what makes them old-fashioned—not being able to get their eyes off young ladies. You know?"

"That's the most ignorant thing I've ever heard you say, Alexei. Proserpina, let's go."

"Honestly," Proserpina whispered to Alexei, "I was trying really hard not to crack up during your little he-man speech, Alexei. You're like a long, skinny cigarette: sophistication: one hundred percent pure class."

"Did I say something offensive?"

"Men like this professor are the ones who have left this world the way it is," Neftalí said. "Didn't you say to me he had a hand in building those book shredders? I mean, we just visited the fish cannery, where the women in our lives are barracked and forced to work. And the fact that you associate with people like that professor is kind of a letdown. It feels old, too, that kind of letdown, like it derives from a story in our ancient mythology or collective subconscious or something."

"You know I don't mythologize anything, Neftalí," said Alexei. "But you two are right. I have to apologize. I shouldn't have to defend the professor's . . . how do you say? Sexism? Y'all don't have to come with me to the laboratory if you don't want. I just wanted you two to see the teddymaker in person, for yourselves. The machine the professor constructed, where I'm taking these bottle-tops, that y'all have been hearing me go on and on about—"

"Bullshit," Proserpina interrupted. "How does this teddy-maker work?"

"We'll simply feed the machine the bottle-tops and it'll make the teddys. Boom."

"But the machine is not a mammal. It doesn't eat plastic and shit out gold coins."

"No, no, of course the machine is not a mammal, it's a complex machine. I was there when he was first experimenting with building it. I got neighborhood kids to climb into the small chambers to tighten bolts or seal ventilation shafts. There's nothing else like this teddymaker. You two have to finally see it so you can understand how it's gonna change our lives. We don't get to play music, but we get to do this."

"So you've got neighborhood boys gathering bottle-tops for you?" Neftalí asked.

"Hell yeah. Me and Moira, here, together. As a team."

"They're all in this bag," Moira pointed out. "I hustled those boys you found me with to help us out."

Alexei shook the bag, and the bottle-tops rattled like a gymnasium of falling glass shards. Neftalí kept her disbelief at bay. She'd always been supportive of her friends' business endeavors, even when they bordered on crackpot. Neftalí no longer recognized what part of the city they were in; she wasn't sure if all the right turns they'd taken amounted to walking in circles, and she hadn't paid attention to any vacant shop signs. Cobblestone streets and alleyways were all vulture brown; hidden shadows fluttered like prehistoric bat feathers. The terrain made a slight descent and the sun hid behind the shell of a half-finished building.

"We're in the roofed part of the city, huh," Proserpina said, scratching the back of her neck. "Shay-deeeee."

Neftalí held herself in a hug as she walked along and said, "Remember when we'd get real creeped out just thinking of going anywhere far from our own neighborhood, even five years ago? Look at us now, way out here. I used to think the roofed part of the city was scary, with all the down-and-out folks we'd run into. But now that nobody's around, I find that it's even creepier."

A gush of the city's outer winds whorled through the roofed part of the city in black-hole moans, and echoed in such a way that all four no longer felt they were in the rusty-valve heart of Three Rivers, or even the liver, but somewhere deep in its long intestine.

"Check this out," said Moira, spreading her arms to indicate that everyone should stop walking and be silent. "Cukú," she called, like a mechanical bird, "cukú, cukú." The cooing of pigeons was heard from the pockets of inky darkness, like they were back at the cathedral, or at the foot of Suicide Bridge. "They're not pigeons," Moira continued, as if trying to scare everyone. "I think they'd fly or even flap their wings if they were. We don't know what they are. Nobody I know does."

"That's not really true," Alexei said. "We do know, kinda."

"He thinks they're birds that have inbred with the rats down here."

"Crossbred." Neftalí couldn't help but correct her. "However, that's probably not possible. Could be, I guess. I don't know. Listen to them scurrying with their tiny feet, and cooing. What are they doing? Pissing and shitting everywhere?"

"Is that what that burning-oranges smell is: their pee?"

Something like an empty coffin was heard hitting the ground—it thudded and boomed, which changed the rhythm of the scurrying and cooing and circulating dust.

"Anyway," Alexei said, moving along and bouncing the bag of bottle-tops, "rats don't coo like that in real life. Not in Three Rivers."

They reached a large steel door with a heavy, solid brass latch that Alexei lifted using the entire force of one arm. "Is this it?" Neftalí asked, fanning herself. It was humid deep in the guts of the roofed part of the city.

"This is it. Welcome to the professor's laboratory," Alexei said, stressing the *o* in "laboratory."

The door grated open, releasing orange daylight that

melted like cheddar along the brick tunnels of the roofed part of the city behind them. The room that housed the laboratory was high and wide, with a mosaic of transparent plastic parts as a ceiling, and sitting in the middle was an ancient, poorly conceived barn that had incongruous sections bulging with wooden compartments, pipes, and gears shiny with grease. It smelled like a mixture of sawdust and burnt oil. A harmonium played from the far end of the room, and Proserpina and Neftalí felt the presence of something sacred, profound, and even destructive.

Neftalí kept one hand to her chest, as if holding on to a handlebar on public transit. Moira skipped along and did her best rendition of a late-twentieth-century party call, announcing their arrival. The barn structure shook like a giant dog passing a stone and belched a thick exhaust that swirled upward through the ventilation shafts into the sky.

Alexei introduced this shack-like bride of Frankenstein, this madman architect's minimalist castle, this apocryphal Tower of Babel, as the teddymaker. Scraps of wood, metal, aluminum, clay, Sheetrock, and pipes, with a combination of electrical energy and densely leaded fuel, were the ingredients that kept the machine running, he informed them.

The teddy machine trembled on the concrete blocks that kept it propped a few feet off the ground. A chair was heard rolling down a corridor directly behind them—Neftalí and Proserpina turned as Moira and Alexei kept walking to the far end of the laboratory. Proserpina crept closer to the sound, scratching her head, but neither she nor Neftalí could see any chair in the corridor.

"What's up with you? You've been scratching your head a lot, 'mana, are you all *piojosa* or what?" Neftalí asked Proserpina.

A scraggly dog scuttled out from the corridor. It startled both of them. Then they tried getting the dog's attention, but the dog mistrusted them and strutted out the open door into the roofed part of the city.

Moira and Alexei stood by a long rectangular table stacked with small engines, large bolts, tubes, and gears that smelled like the gunky gallstones of greasy auto parts. To the left of the table was an older man of medium height, wearing a pristine white lab coat and a heavily stained denim apron over it. On both hands he wore tight rubber gloves that went all the way to his elbows. Patches of hair were missing from his head and thinning beard, as if they'd been singed off in a chemical accident.

Alexei said, "Neftalí, this is the world-famous Professor Pantano."

Professor Pantano tried removing one glove to shake her hand, but Neftalí intercepted him, and she shook it as it was. Proserpina introduced herself, since nobody else had done it for her, and told the professor, "We met your dog just now."

"My dog?" he exclaimed.

"Yeah, it ran away to hide. We must've lured it out by accident, then scared it or something."

"You mean you saw a canine just now in my laboratory?"

Nervously, Proserpina nodded, and Neftalí backed her up.

"I wasn't aware there was any such animal in here. I would've boiled it. No animals are allowed in my laboratory, much less a yummy canine," he said. Professor Pantano re-

moved his goggles to reveal light brown, quicksand eyes—
he held the hefty canvas bag of bottle-tops by the seams and
shook it like a giant baby's rattle.

"Big bag, Alexei. The equivalent of two regular bagfuls.
You've outdone yourself. You and your crew are real prodigies
of city life. When the streets catch fire, it's only so you can
shine, my boy. Did you help him using your prowess, Moira? I
had a feeling you did, my girl. You have the prodigy gift, too,
despite your lesser sex. Let's see now. I just oiled up Badebec
here. She's all ready to go."

"Badebec?" interrupted Neftalí.

"Yes," Professor Pantano said. "It's bad luck to build a machine of great sophistication such as this one and not name it.
Who am I to reject a commonly embraced superstition within
the scientific community? I present to you all: Badebec—"

"That's like . . . that's like," Neftalí said, snapping her fingers, scraping her memory barrel for the right image. "That's
like Pantagruel's mother . . . who died upon giving birth to
him."

"I think I remember that cat from back in the day. We
played with him, didn't we? He jammed in a glut-rock band,
they covered themselves with flour onstage," Alexei said, and
he looked over at Proserpina, who held a gaze of confusion as
she dazedly scratched through her bushy hair.

Professor Pantano lit up like a shorting electrical socket.
"What did you say? Alexei, this is your girlie, huh? Old
bandmate and friend, I see. Now, old bandmate and friend of
Alexei, Neftalí. May I ask you to repeat what you just said? I'm
an old man and I tend to mishear things."

"I pointed out that your machine's name is the same as

Pantagruel's mother's. In the old French stories of Gargantua and Pantagruel."

"Yes," the professor said. "Of course, young girlie. May I also ask . . . exactly how you happen to know this particular detail?"

Professor Pantano and Neftalí had both taken a step back, distancing themselves like duelists hitting their marks. Proserpina and Alexei were suspicious of what was unfolding, as Moira circled the girthy coin machine with a crowbar and wrench, making sure bolts were tight and panels intact. She wheeled a ladder to the far end, climbed it to reach the top of Badebec, and paid little attention to the concerns of the others.

Birds sprayed down from the flayed ceiling, where they'd been nesting by a ventilation shaft, and circled silently over the teddymaker.

Neftalí told the professor, "From reading books. How else?"

Alexei gritted his teeth at this. Professor Pantano clapped in astonishment, and hooted at Neftalí's courageous response. He took half a breath, then said, "Well. Alexei. Moira. Young girls. Let's make some future money with Badebec."

Moira wheeled the staircase ladder in their direction. Neftalí once again noticed Proserpina scratching her head, reached for one of her wrists, and said, "What's up, 'mana? You're making your scalp bleed, and that's bad. Be honest with me, for real. Are you all *piojosa*, or what?"

"You know my Spanish sucks, what's that word you keep using? My head's super itchy, that's all."

The hood of an old Buick was adjoined vertically to the

side of Badebec. Alexei propped the hood open then slid it into the coin machine. There was a red handle inside that Alexei pulled with one hand, as the professor situated himself on a platform at the other end, in front of an array of knobs and levers. The professor signaled to Alexei and pulled on four stiff levers, locking them into position. Steam hissed and the clunky equipment grumbled throughout Badebec like a giant beast having trouble digesting. A moment of crystalline stillness and silence hung in the laboratory like a snowflake; then Professor Pantano signaled with a thumbs-up. Alexei climbed the staircase ladder carrying the blue canvas reenlistment bag with the bottle-tops, and for kicks Moira went up with him.

As they did all this, the professor got ready. He massaged the pulley knobs gently with his fingers, as if they were tiny mice he was shoplifting for a revenge stew—then he yelled, "We have the power to ignore, my dear children. If we don't see the light, we can't ignore. We have the eighth tone at our disposal. If we can hear the eighth tone, then we cannot ignore it. The eighth tone should be everything, but we are stuck only with seven, leaving us with the bare minimum in tonality for our primitive ears."

Neftalí took hold of Proserpina by the wrist again. In an infinite moment that was a second and a half long, both of them inspected the drying blood on Proserpina's fingertips and nails, then locked eyes. Without saying a word, a horrified Proserpina turned her back to Neftalí, and Neftalí, as she'd been trained to do as a child, started sifting through the weeds and thickets of her hair in search of head lice.

Meanwhile, Professor Pantano waited for Alexei to reach the summit of Badebec, before pulling on the final levers, which controlled the main ignition starter for the fuel valve. He continued: "Remember the mountains we cannot see, children. For we are the forgers of the new currency: the new mountains. It will be a peaceful, complete takeover. This is how we will begin it together, children. You and I. This is how we end it together . . ."

Neftalí felt like a giant ape looking down upon the buildings and ruminations of a private civilization—she saw, in Proserpina's scalp, not one or two tiny, serious businessmen, but hundreds of determined businesspeople zipping up and down avenues, wrapped up in their own bureaucratic order.

"Oh no, 'mana . . ."

Alexei reached the top of the ladder with the canvas bag and untied it. He unsealed the lid at the crest of Badebec. Moira, standing beside him, posed as if they were preparing to make the greatest of human sacrifices. Without any signal, Alexei poured the first half of the bottle-tops into Badebec, and the professor pulled on the first, second, and third levers, and then twisted a knob at his feet using both hands. Moira grabbed the bag and poured the remainder of the bottle-tops into Badebec. Alexei sealed the lid, then he and Moira climbed down the stepladder as if descending the stairs of a great pyramid.

"'Mana . . . hermana mía," Neftalí said, shutting Proserpina's hair like a velvet curtain.

Badebec made a sound as if deep inside the machine there was a bowling alley pleading for dessert after a meal. Her planks shifted like the scales of a towering lizard that protected the machine from both aridness and excessive moisture. A locomotive was heard arriving from inside Badebec. The professor had pulled all the levers and, like everybody else, stood removed from the machine, and took off his elbow-length rubber gloves in a daze.

Proserpina detached herself from this calamity, looking petrified and confused. She searched for the shoulder of the road that had brought her here, and instead found the nearest wall, extended her arms toward it, then slid downward, her gaze fixed on nothing in particular upon the ground. A concerned Neftalí followed, then knelt down and took Proserpina's hand.

"I have to tell you something, Nef. Remember that kid Po? The Jazzmin Monelle fan we ran into this morning? I fucked him. That was my old band shirt he was wearing. I'm surprised you didn't recognize it. Don't judge me, okay. We did it without protection or anything. There's something unusual about Po, he can last a long time doing it. Like, a really long time. But look at me now, was it worth it? To get all lousy off that dirty kid?"

Neftalí, sensitive to Proserpina's feelings, and to this unexpected confession, said, "Well, I'm willing to believe that you could've gotten those *piojos* anywhere, 'mana. We can't just assume that, beyond being dirty, Po is lousy, too."

"We've been doing it constantly at the abandoned taco stand off Twenty-Five Mile Line, where he crashes by his sister's clothes and shoestring drive. I've spent a lot of nights in his cozy den. We shared a hay mattress, a pillow, with his cats and squirrels and possums and all his animals. They sleep around him like his babies, and he eats fruits and vegetables in their presence, too, using his unwashed hands. We did all this together while joking we were Adam and Eve."

"Oh."

Proserpina squeezed Neftalí's hand, knowing she'd understand. Steam hissed from Badebec's hidden and exposed valves. One of the pipes whistled loudly. The teddy machine came down from a great sob, or rowdy orgy. A motor was heard sputtering deep inside Badebec, even after the rest of the machine shuddered to a halt.

The coin machine went from spooky and menacing to weary, comical, and useless.

"Don't worry about it. It will grow back," Neftalí assured Proserpina. "It's just hair, right?"

"What do you mean, it will grow back?"

Moira wielded a pair of long pincers made of Anacortes steel, and Alexei, using a crowbar, pried open a tight, circular compartment on Badebec's side. Chilled steam grazed their shoulders, hinting at fancy parties and galas never to come. Wearing thick wool gloves, Professor Pantano reached into the circular compartment, unscrewed a large bolt while wincing against the gray, milky frost. Moira reached into the frost using the long pincers and pulled out a capsule the size and shape of a lunch pail. On both ends of the capsule were tiny holes similar to those on saltshaker lids.

Neftalí held Proserpina's hand—they suspended their conversation to watch as Professor Pantano cradled the capsule in his wool gloves. He extended it to both of them, said, "Feel this."

More out of their own curiosity than the professor's invitation, Neftalí and Proserpina felt the freezing-cold, sticky metal of the capsule. Proserpina ran one of her bloodstained fingers across it, and only then did Neftalí see the layer of sooty ice.

"We must be able to harden liquid metal in a matter of seconds, young ones," the professor said. "By the looks of it, we've accomplished this."

Professor Pantano wiped the frozen soot with a small towel, and Alexei opened the capsule by flicking a few switches at its base. Inside were about sixteen faces of the long-dead president Theodore Roosevelt, embossed in metal.

Proserpina shuffled toward a small garbage can near the wall and puked into it, as Neftalí rushed to stand by her. She suspected Proserpina was vomit-crying, and when she caught the all-too-familiar whiff of pinot noir, saltine crackers, powdered doughnuts, and avocados in the vomit, Neftalí said, "That's my girl, 'mana. Let it all out, baby. Just get rid of it. Let's start fresh."

Proserpina wiped her mouth with a handkerchief Neftalí offered. She looked up at Neftalí with bloodshot eyes. Half-dazed and horrified, Proserpina said, "Nef. Sister. You think they're gonna have to cut all my hair off? Is that what you're getting at? Don't you think the dog shampoo will do?"

Neftalí said, "'Mana. You're all *piojosa*," while stroking Proserpina's arms. "Of course they're gonna have to cut all the hair. It will probably be one of us who'll have to do it, sadly. So get ready."

"No."

"Buzz it, really, if we want to give it shape."

"No."

"But, yeah. You're all *piojosa*. If you want, I'll cut it myself when we get out of here."

Proserpina pushed herself against the wall, as if burrowing into it, or trying to disappear into the yellow wallpaper, not wanting to believe Neftalí's words.

Even before she registered what she was doing, Neftalí pulled Alexei aside as he balanced the teddys on both palms and talked to Professor Pantano.

"What are we doing here," she snapped at Alexei, as she let go of his arm and pushed away from him. He palmed the coins and made fists.

"What do you mean? *This* is happening. I got my money, look at it right here. Eight teddys, only for like a couple of days' work. So . . . what do you think? I mean, now that you've seen how the professor's invention works, how the coins are made, how we're slowly taking over—"

"You're saying you collected all those bottle-tops just to make those eight measly teddys?"

"Measly? Eight teddys is my cut, Neffy. The machine can only make eighteen teddys at a time, with two bagfuls. This is the way me and the professor split it, we're business partners and all. Plus, he built the machine and has to recoup a few costs, you know what I'm saying?"

"Let me take a look."

Neftalí held a teddy in her hand and tried to see herself in it. The coin was rather heavy. Otherworldly. Absurd in a manner that made her chuckle. Standing next to Badebec, holding her fruit, Neftalí felt she was in the presence of a rare, endangered animal, shackled to perform tricks for big business. She had an urgent desire to run, then something like a ghost or shadowy presence seemed to hold her in place by the shoulders.

"Let's just meet up later, Alexei. We can talk more about all this. Proserpina's all *piojosa* right now, so that has to be taken care of. Then I need to be alone for a while."

"Proserpina's all what?"

"*Piojosa*. Lousy. She's got an entire civilization of lice living in her head. Hopefully not anything else. She's not right in her mind at the moment, because we both just figured this out. I gotta see that she's okay, then go off and do my thing."

"Are you pissed at me? I know it's been forever since we've written a power ballad together—"

"It's not the power ballads, Alexei. It's that there's so much shit I gotta take care of, most importantly, finding a place to live. I need time and space away from all this bullshit to concentrate."

"All right, Nef. But I want you to keep that teddy. As a gift from your Missus Batches bass player."

They turned Badebec's corner to find that Professor Pantano had made Moira and Proserpina cups of hot cocoa and was sitting on the ground talking at them, hugging his knees. Neftalí took a good look at the professor. He had pale skin that was flaking in small and large chunks around his sideburns and ears; on the back of his neck, thick white pustules clustered in patches. His postcard teeth showed when he smiled, and his thin shadow slithered on the oil-stained ground like a varicose snake conducting fire. Neftalí's chest stampeded and she felt a deep pool of disgust. She took Proserpina's hand, then made eye contact with Moira and the professor and said, "We need to get going, unfortunately."

The professor shot straight up to his feet and exclaimed, "But we're just getting to know each other!"

"Sorry, but no. My friend here's got head lice. We have to cut her hair and get that special shampoo for dogs."

"This is absurd. The girl must already be vaccinated against parasites."

In a daze Proserpina clutched her own hair with one arm, as Neftalí pulled her toward the laboratory's exit. "Moira, you're coming with us—"

"This is ultimately rude, leaving my space here with such haste. Alexei, please . . ."

Alexei considered his options as Neftalí stopped near the doorway—he'd always thought Proserpina looked like an outer-space version of Neftalí, and as they stood there, Proserpina, with beads of sweat accumulating on her face and neck, looked more like this than ever. He turned to Professor Pantano and said, "We'll bring you more bottle-tops in a couple days, Professor. Bandmates' code, so . . . safety first."

They pushed the big steel door open, shut it behind them, and before they knew it, Alexei, Neftalí, and Proserpina were making their way back through the roofed part of the city, with Moira trailing behind.

"Bottle-tops," Neftalí said aloud, like it was a new way to curse.

"Shit yeah, Neffy," Alexei answered. "By the time you know it, we're gonna be loaded. We'll be riding in a limo, like we joked we would as a band, everywhere around town."

"But you can only produce eighteen coins a day?"

"Actually, twenty. Moira also gets a cut."

"Moira, you only get two?"

Moira nodded.

"That's fucked up, why doesn't she get as much as you?"

"Moira doesn't do any of the heavy lifting herself. She just gets the other boys to chip in their labor and help."

"Sounds fucked up to me. You and all these horny little boys, picking up bottle-tops to fill two big bags' worth and make only eight teddys?"

"Teddys aren't worth a damn thing, that's the worst part!" Proserpina blurted.

"But they're future money that's going to be worth something. This is our investment. Right, Moira? Tell them," Alexei pleaded. "Teddys are coming around. Teddys are happening. They might not be seen by folks as a legit currency worldwide, but that doesn't mean that they won't be. Moira knows this. And so does the professor. That's our investment together, and we're not the only ones."

"How many other people does the professor have doing this? While he stays in that temperature-controlled lab?"

"Just us. The professor—I don't know if you could tell, but he's kinda jumpy. Doesn't trust a lot of people. Likes to stay shut in at the laboratory most of the time and have his tacos delivered."

Neftalí was in a bind. Her mind felt carpeted with dead leaves that desperately needed raking. She remembered her tendency to be introverted during times of crisis—and the combination of the raid on her home, Proserpina's lice, and whatever Alexei was up to constituted a crisis. It'd happened when she was a girl during the Falfurrias barrio fires, when her mother had found her hiding in the corner of a closet, then wrapped her in a wet blanket and carried her out of the burning building; in her short-lived school days, during the Frankie J. Jimenez drug raid, when she'd panicked and climbed on the two-hundred-year-old oak tree and stayed there for three days to witness the military takeover; in the years after her mother died, which were mostly an emotional blur, more like a forgotten ball of yarn waiting to unravel in the back of a drawer.

She backed away from her old bandmates and Moira while clutching her heart like a talisman, and for the third time that day the curtains of reality were stripped away and Neftalí had a vision of the beach. A young man no older than herself had his trousers rolled up to his knees and was walking along the shore. His shins and feet were wet from the lapping waves, which turned his brown skin closer to copper. The young man whistled an indistinct melody as he drew a figure on the golden sand using a stick.

When Neftalí looked closer at the sperm whale drawn in the sand, she returned to her actual surroundings and saw Alexei's worried face as he held her by the shoulders, crouching down. "Nef," he said, "are you with me, Neftalí?"

She realized she was on the ground and shook his arms off, got onto her feet, wobbled, then found her balance.

"Geez, are you all right?" Alexei insisted.

"I just need some room, y'all. I need quiet. I need for time to go by as I sit still somewhere with nothing happening, and without worrying about dumb things like losing my books and losing my house. I think somebody is trying to talk to me, too. Somebody from beyond, like, time and space. What I mean is I keep having a vision. Of a man . . . a musician. A musician like we were, once upon a time, I guess. And he's somewhere on a beach, sometimes all alone. But I know he's far away. Far, far away . . . and somehow this musician needs me. Or maybe I need him."

Neftalí felt her eyes become hot with tears. She kissed Proserpina's hands, blew kisses toward Moira and Alexei, and they were left with no recourse but to let Neftalí drift away. Everyone waved in a grave manner as a hunched, pale Proserpina turned paler. Moira pulled her by the hand as they both walked toward their neighborhood in Old Freeway. Eventually, Alexei caught up with them.

NEFTALÍ PUNTED A CRUNCHED ALUMINUM CAN along the caliche road, and it flapped its wings like a bat toward the abysmal evening. It didn't cross her mind that she was taking the Old Nueces Trail, on which two hundred years ago strangers in this strange land had traveled westward. She muttered things she could've said to Alexei, like "Think of the last person who's ever gonna exist in this world, the very final person looking back on idiots like you and me and just laughing. Laughing at how stupid we are for making the choices we're constantly making."

The Acevedo neighborhood was on the failed side of the city's power grid, all adobe tenements with dusty roads, where some of the poorest people resided. It was an early-rising community. The streets were ghostly and still as Neftalí walked along them, thinking about her own mother, who was raised here in dire poverty. As she roamed the sinking streets, Neftalí remembered the problems with the stray, aggressive chickens Acevedo was known for, and her stomach growled. Her feet were also aching, so she slipped off her worn shoes.

A pod of adobe tenements before her was surrounded by mounds of dust. She stopped to rub her arches and soles while leaning against a lonely swaying palm tree. It didn't appear that anyone lived under those flat adobe roofs, and she was about to keep moving when the door to one of the tenements popped opened. An older woman, with great effort, threw out a bucket of dirty water that nearly reached Neftalí, and then she shot her a disgruntled look.

"Usted es del gobierno?" the woman asked Neftalí.

"No, señora, yo soy sola una persona."

The woman eyed Neftalí suspiciously as two windmill-eyed children emerged from the doorway behind her to take a look.

"You tell the government," the woman continued, gesticulating pointedly, "it's a disaster out here. We don't even have potable water. I'm bringing up these grandchildren of mine on nothing but grains and chickens, with their unfortunate mother doing time at the fish cannery, and her children not even receiving her earned rations. Where are those rations going, if not to her hungry, thirsty children? The only water they can drink out here is the water extracted from chicken feet. Now, how about that?"

Neftalí shuffled away without letting the woman continue airing her grievances, and considered again her caged hunger. She ignored the lamentable conditions the woman had described and snooped around for a chicken, trying not to think of the feet.

Three red hens clucked cautiously in an alley between two tenements. They paused to make eye contact with Neftalí. Neftalí hunched low, crept closer, and saw that the hens' feet were dark red, almost maroon, which was the clearest indication that these were completely edible street hens. As if reading her mind, the hens lifted their beaks and clucked toward an alley across the way, putting on thick airs. She stopped next to a mesquite tree and looked up at the peeling branches.

Brown feathers and yellow feet moved slowly within the golden and green foliage.

She remembered Proserpina's advice about the most efficient way to nab a chicken. Though Neftalí had chortled with laughter when she'd first heard Proserpina tell it, thinking it was another one of her crackpot theories about how shit worked, she now concluded, *Why not?*, and found the pressure point under her right ear. She pressed on it for a couple of minutes while massaging the muscles around her temples into a working rhythm.

Neftalí felt something profound, as if the Holy Spirit had entered one ear and gone out the other, or as if her ear had given birth to an entire Greek myth. Using her right thumb and index finger, she reached in and fished out a small ball of acetate earwax, like a clump of raw chocolate the size of a lead pistol pellet. She opened the palm of her left hand and rolled the earwax into a spherical marble, awed that her body could produce such a wonder all on its own. Then, reluctantly, she threw the ball of wax onto the ground before her and waited beneath the shade of a guayaba tree.

At first Neftalí was disappointed—the ball of earwax had gotten lost in the continuously blowing dust that teased and slithered over everything as if the arid atmosphere was a living, displeased thing. The sun released its purples and fiery yellows into the sky and crept behind distant hills and the three curling rivers.

She poked into her ear again to be sure all the wax had been retrieved, when a plump brown hen with maroon feet flew down from a mesquite tree branch and clucked.

Neftalí expressed inaudible shock as she stood stock-still,

afraid she'd frighten the hen. In a cartwheel flutter she grabbed the brown hen by its head, twisted its body clockwise, the head counterclockwise. Bones and tendons snapped and cracked between her fingers; she felt tiny bits of loose skin against her wrist, and grabbed a towel from her bag to wrap the hen and wipe up the hot blood. Neftalí inspected her outfit for stains and walked cautiously in a random direction.

Before it got completely dark, Neftalí found a clearing near the Segovia Woods and managed to start a fire with an old matchbook, logs, and twigs. She plucked the hen merrily by the campfire, repeatedly singing the same verse she'd learned earlier from the two tías: "Stone to flesh, / then onward toward my kingdom. / And in the morning my true love comes, / for the morningtime's the only true love."

She lopped the chicken's head off using the edge of the sharpest stone she could find, while the water in her portable cauldron, rigged on a spit over the fire, came to a boil. Neftalí gutted the chicken and buried the innards and blood to dissuade scavengers, then dropped the chicken into the boiling cauldron. There was a mossy boulder about twenty feet away that she rolled toward the campfire.

Neftalí sat on the boulder, staring into the crackling flames. She recognized the fire as another living being, accepted the possibility that it was an extraterrestrial, here to be a troublesome companion to cold humankind. After the chicken had boiled awhile, she poked into the bones to encourage their separation from the flesh. Then she took the cauldron off the spit while wearing her woolen gloves. Crickets and distant bullfrogs made Neftalí wonder if she was near a small body of water.

She lost her train of thought to mad hunger, made herself as small as possible on the ground as chicken juices dripped from her mouth, down her chest, and onto her thighs. Neftalí felt herself losing control and tore the bones and flesh off the chicken with her bare hands. She chewed loudly with her mouth closed. The chicken grease formed a glowing rim around Neftalí's face that winked at the battery-shaped moon.

Floppy chicken skin clung to her hair, meat chunks dug into her fingernails, and she threw the mangled carcass down, looking at her hands as if she were a feral creature finally understanding a simple math equation. Her body trembled. She thought of the chicken as another living creature simply trying to survive in this tough city. Though stupid, it was a sentient being—as a person with a conscience, Neftalí felt ashamed.

Neftalí wept, and out of the same feral instinct she'd had to eat the chicken, she took off all her clothes and folded them and set them by the fire. Neftalí grabbed the chicken carcass as she wept, and rubbed it clinically all over her body, including her neck and face and thick black hair. She buried the remains and bolted into the long-haired night. Neftalí sensed the wild creatures of the landscape sniffing her out.

The brush was soft and dry then damp and cold. She almost turned back to her fire but was startled when the terrain a few feet ahead suddenly mirrored the audience of stars in the sky. A stream of water. Neftalí couldn't believe it, but at the same time she could, as the placid, crystalline stream seemed to say, "Yes, dear, you found me. Go on, get in, use what I have left to offer, while I continue searching for my people. Rejoice and forget the world out there. Cleanse your spirit and your being."

Neftalí obeyed, and dipped one foot into the water, then the other, then silently dunked her entire body while holding her nose. She came back up and the soapy moonlight lathered her. Neftalí scooped water with her hands and scrubbed under her arms with all its silver and gold. She submerged herself in the water once again, and it was then that Neftalí heard something moving within the undulations, like a song was being carried from a wooden flute buried in a sunken box.

When Neftalí came back up for air she listened past the murmurs of the stream and the chatter of the nighttime woods. Her ears searched as she waded around a short bend in the stream, never straying far from the embankment. The sound became unmistakable: it was the rhythmic, ancient, yet Gothic sound of a wooden *duduk*.

She kept low and silent, with only her head sticking up above the surface of the water. To her surprise, she saw that the instrument's player was close, sitting among a cluster of smooth boulders about ten feet away from the river. She could hardly make out this person in the smeared darkness.

The song from the *duduk* was devastating to Neftalí. Its melody brought back the tragedies and irregularities of the past few days: losing her family library to the chupacabras; the killings of the escaped worker-mothers; her recurring, all-too-real vision of the Mexican composer Juventino Rosas. The sound of the stream became a Greek chorus, its volume and size crescendoed into a powerful, stampeding river as it grew animated, narrating the story of Neftalí's present moment.

The *duduk* player stopped playing mid-song, straightened their arched back at something moving in the water.

Before anything else transpired, Neftalí vanished back into the stream on all fours and tried to find the shore where she'd originally entered, feeling her troubles briefly lifted by the music of the mysterious player.

She got out of the water and wrung out her hair under the terror of the cosmos while once again walking through the dream-piercing silence that can exist only in a patch of woods.

The campfire she'd started had turned to shy embers, and her clothes were folded right where she'd left them. As she slipped them back on, she noticed that a large doe in the brush had been staring—perhaps had even followed her from the stream. Thinking the doe was simply being a protective mother, she kept moving, collected her belongings, and as she walked away, Neftalí turned to the doe and said: "You're gorgeous, baby."

Coyotes and street dogs mourned the distance of the stars from every corner of Three Rivers as Neftalí arrived at the bolted gates of D'Hanis Cemetery. The statue of a steel anchor embraced by a marbled angel like they were drowned lovers greeted her; the cemetery's sinking limestone perimeter wall was more or less six feet high. A phosphorescent moss had accumulated along the limestone, so that instead of silver the walls appeared dark and grimy, as if the entire cemetery had been at the bottom of the sea for many centuries before finally emerging here.

Neftalí didn't allow herself to feel anything at this familiar sight, even as the memories came pouring out. She walked counterclockwise around the perimeter until she found the cracked opening within the limestone, pulled at the loose, heavy boulders, and set them aside to enter.

Once inside, Neftalí imagined an asteroid field as she read the gunky names, dates, and epitaphs on the headstones—some protruded from the ground with an ecclesiastical, Gothic flair, like ancient thrones or jukeboxes; others resembled vanity tables or walk-in closets. The majority of the headstones were chipped, faded, and centuries old. Neftalí scratched the roof of her mouth with her tongue. She came across the display of the cemetery map, spotted her location, walked past the broken-molar gravestones toward the rear center of the cemetery.

The mass rustling of leaves and distant howling from the ashes of placated hill fires rushed through the graveyard. An inky, hazy sky looked down like our third-person narrator, and cynically, out of some mysterious revenge, Neftalí shook her fist at the vague stars as she approached her mother's plot: ANGÉLICA BARRIENTOS.

She traced with one finger the large lettering of the name, which was the only thing inscribed on the headstone. There were drying bouquets of roses and clumped dead leaves that Neftalí cleared away after dusting the plot, and she forgot what she had to do or say, now that she was here. Neftalí knelt and shut her eyes and cleared her mind of any amusement or anxiety or pious thought. Upon opening them, she scooped dirt from directly behind the headstone. Neftalí pulled a spider-webbed half bottle of Old Southern Veil bourbon from a buried tin box. She uncorked the bottle, poured some out for the moonlight first, then some more for her dead mother.

Neftalí took a long pull for herself and sat beside the grave.

A great disappointment, one she'd never quite gotten used to, and that even reading books had left Neftalí powerless against, was the way language changed for the departed. It had taken various visits to her mother at the cemetery for Neftalí to realize the dead have their own logic that no longer lines up with human reality. The times Neftalí had tried to follow advice from the dead—like filling a barrel with old phones to get rich, or lighting the tips, but only the tips, of all the palm trees on fire to avoid the flu in the winter—she'd suffered only heavy, lamentable consequences.

Neftalí inspected the damp grass in front of the headstone while taking pulls from the bottle of bourbon. Finally, she stood up and poured a good pour onto the earth's sweet spot. The bowels of the ground below shifted, the surface gurgled, as if water or oil was about to spray out. Angélica Barrientos clawed herself out of the bare earth, stretched her neck, and said, "*Mira*. Look who remembered her mother," dusting off her floor-length hair and the orange dress she'd been buried in.

Neftalí offered Angélica the bottle of booze. Politely, but with slight airs, Angélica said, "No," then changed her mind, snatched the bottle, and took a big gulp. She laughed like a parliament of owls flapping their wings, looked up at her quiet neighbors in the cemetery, and said, "Where is everybody? I bet they're all surprised, actually. That's why they've hidden. They're surprised to see me out here like this, with a visitor. That's right, everyone, my own *daughter*, who I birthed, came to visit me. What, do you think it's only dead kings that can come back to haunt from the grave? Get real. Did you come here to tell me something, mi'ja? Did I leave the oven burning again?"

"You didn't leave anything burning, Mama. I'm gonna have to find a new place to live soon. That's all. They're forcing me to leave the family house. We had a good run there, I suppose. The city named the street after you, and now we have to move. *Gacho.* Remember I told you none of the new kids believe me, because they didn't add the accent in your name on the sign? Shit. But now it doesn't matter, because the newer kids don't even know how to read, so . . ."

Somewhere near the cemetery there was the buzzing of a chain saw; echoing voices crawled on four legs and scratched themselves; feathers ruffled behind blotter-colored headstones; an uneven mist touched down, which gave the twilight a grainy, unexposed celluloid look as Neftalí and Angélica passed the bottle back and forth, laughing and crying.

How does silence prevail under the gasping harrow of Three Rivers? What is the sound of cypress tree branches reaching for the distant weeping willows over the years, the sound of an insect's glory, of a rainbow bouncing from one cauldron of boiling bones into another? Out of one of these mysterious kernels of silence emerged the void that Proserpina waded through, after Moira ran the loud, buzzing clippers over her cranium and she was forced to stare hard at her hairless self reflected in the looking glass, sitting in the backyard of her family's trailer.

Proserpina roamed the wooded reality within the looking glass wearing a red cloak. Meaty roots from birch and redwood trees kicked up from the mud, trying to trip her. There was a wooden desk on an oak tree above, and Proserpina saw her mother propped on a floating high chair. She was wearing her worker-mother uniform, with her hair tied back, while she intricately folded a large sheet of paper with tiny scribbles into a mysterious, multi-surface halceamadon.

Bare-headed, covered from head to toe with strands of her own hair, Proserpina approached her: "Mama," she said. "Look at the shape of my head, Mama. It's just like your own."

"Yes," her mother replied, holding up her immaculate paper creation. "This is the natural way the story told inside our minds is written. Through our family hair. Before today,

I was the only person to ever cut that hair of yours, my daughter. No other person. Like my mother cut mine, as a girl."

Proserpina rudely emerged from the brown woods of her own eyes: within the looking glass, reflected in the backyard all around her, were old filing cabinets; a manual lawn mower with tall grass growing around it and a graceful vine weaving through its rusted blades; defaced PABLO HENRY CRICK campaign signs from previous election cycles; the old Cadillac that'd once been a good chicken coop and was now an occasional nest for unfriendly possums; the empty, bulging natural gas tank named Ollie and its sidekick, the smaller empty natural gas tank named Squirrel; the occasional dandelion sprouts; the rampantly reproducing neighborhood cats—all this, along with bits of her hair blowing away, as Moira collected clumps of it in a paper bag. One Proserpina walked out of the center of the looking glass as another walked in, swapping realms. She came to.

Moira held up the paper bag of Proserpina's thick hair and said, "So are you sure it's cool for me to keep all of it?"

"Take it," Proserpina barely managed to utter.

"Thanks. I'll see how many bouncy balls I can make. You can have a few."

A tabby cat that Proserpina had named Bog crawled out from under the junked Cadillac and elegantly moved toward the mirror. Bog studiously licked the part of the glass where Proserpina's left toes were reflected. Proserpina wiggled her toes, calling her over, but Bog preferred the reflection to the real thing. Proserpina stood from the upturned green bucket she was sitting on and gently grabbed Bog. The long mirror was actually a vertical rear bus window, coated with nickel on one side. Within the reflection, a buzz-cut Proserpina disappeared into the labyrinthine backyard carrying Bog.

She climbed the concrete steps to the beige trailer, walked through the kitchen. Proserpina passed her brothers' empty bedrooms and walked into the restroom, where she set Bog on the sink as she ran a bath from the garden hose into the tub and heated the kettle on the hot plate by the door. She heated three kettles' worth of water and poured them into the cold bath, along with the second-to-last herb bundle she'd been hoarding, then shut the garden hose.

Proserpina dipped into the bath without making the slightest sound and sank like a stone to the bottom, trying to make herself into the smallest-possible ball as her dead hair floated to the surface, mingling with the iridescent, bubble-free concoction.

Bog balanced herself on the edge of the porcelain tub, looking back and forth between Proserpina at the bottom and her own reflection on the surface.

Proserpina heard a wind-tunnel sound that can come only from inside a seashell—only it wasn't a seashell she heard but a voice. A woman's voice. And the woman was welcoming nature: calling a flock of sheep, saying goodbye to the mist, hello to the morning dew, then hello to the sun to burn away the dew. It was a song full of yearning, echoing so Proserpina could hear it at this moment at the bottom of her family's American bathtub.

When she surfaced and got out, Proserpina was grateful for the last clean towel. She caught her reflection, this time in the small bathroom mirror, turned to the left, then to the right, and with her nails scratched her buzzed head and made sure nothing was crawling on her scalp.

Proserpina put on an oversize metal shirt, poured herself drinking water after churning it from the sink, and lit Atascosa sage. She piled her clothes in the corner of her room, then she meditated and prayed in Arabic for the first time in many years.

About an hour later, she grabbed a thick orange rubber band to tie her hair back into a bun, and hadn't even reached back before remembering, with no small shock, that it was all gone.

She opened the west-facing blinds and the sun shot through from beyond the tall, clustered palm trees. Proserpina imagined living inside a giant fruit, making her home there, and if she ever got hungry, she could simply take a bite from the wall; the community would be in a giant tree, and she could picture the wicked young children below shaking the tree, trying to make everyone's home fall to the ground to devour.

The family trailer had lacked electricity ever since she was a girl, so the icebox was attached with jumper cables to a bulky car battery. The only thing inside the dark icebox was a transparent jug with a dark red liquid labeled BEET-BEAT. She grabbed a porcelain cup from the cupboard and poured herself a good helping. The drink glowed a hibiscus red with the white evening light piercing the open blinds. She tilted the weight of the juice into her mouth eagerly, then gratefully.

Proserpina inserted a barrio oldies mixtape into a flat, rechargeable Texaphone cassette player and sat on a stool by the kitchen counter in the middle of what had once been a living room. She heard distant thunder, or cannon fire, or maybe just the cassette's worn magnetic tape, as she lay on the linoleum floor of the trailer with her eyes closed.

Bog moved between dirty teacups and moldy bread on the small table, jumped off, and surveyed the scene like a strict schoolteacher forced into retirement. Bog lay down on the ground next to Proserpina with her head erect and attentive, as if she was taking notes for a poem to be written at a later date.

The sun no longer shined through the blinds the next morning when Proserpina awoke to footsteps and the screen door and the sound of chuckling little boys. When she saw it was Huicho, Luismi, and Cua—her ten-year-old identical triplet neighbors—Proserpina shifted seamlessly from feeling annoyed to somehow entertained, like she was about to witness a folksy performance or show. "What are y'all kids laughing at?" she asked them.

"Your hair."

"Where did it run to?"

"Did you get the *roña*?"

The three boys laughed, and Proserpina got up, nudged one of them, who passed it on to the rest. She realized that hair being gone—hair that had been her mother's and her grandmother's and her mother's before that—could be comical to outsiders.

"I don't know what that Spanish word means, but nah, you little freaks. I got lice. Probably from one of y'all, since you come bother me with your stinky heads so often."

Huicho, Luismi, and Cua laughed hysterically, slapping their hands together and raucously stomping their feet—a sight that brought joy to Proserpina, but also turned her into something superior to them, and she said, "You boys laugh, yeah. Hysterical, *ha-ha*. It's nothing to laugh at once you got them, I'll tell you that."

"All three of us had *piojos*, Pros."

"It was *gacho*. But they gave us the pills."

"Did your head bleed, too?"

"No," she lied. "It didn't get that bad. Moira had buzzers and she cut it before it got to heavy bleeding."

"We saw her."

"She said you went to the fish cannery together."

"Did you see our mom?"

"You know, I'm sorry to say that I didn't," Proserpina said, and immediately felt terrible when their faces dropped.

"We thought so."

"Thought we'd ask."

". . ."

"Okay, well, boys, is that what you came here for? To laugh at my almost-shaved head? Well, here it is, laugh it up."

"No, not only to laugh."

"Mostly to look at it."

". . ."

"All right, take a good look, get your laughs out of your system before I lose my temper and we never see each other again."

Huicho, Luismi, and Cua hesitated, thinking it was a trap, but then couldn't help themselves and laughed boisterously, slapping their knees and heads, jumping, pointing, and rolling around on the linoleum. Proserpina had to let out a chuckle, grabbed the skillet hanging from a grappling hook in the middle of the kitchen, and faced her reflection on the chrome surface.

"Your head looks sooo small."

"It was your big hair that made the head look big."

"Made you way bigger."

"Look, boys," Proserpina said, "I'm not kidding around. I need some space, need some room to sprawl out here on my own. I've been away from the neighborhood. How is it out there? Any big news?"

"Just the usual."

"You know."

"The usual."

"People angry and mean all the time."

"Don Rogelio always trying to get us to catch him a pig for his sausages."

"We pretend to be them, too, the animals."

"How do you mean?" asked Proserpina.

"We get on the ground," Luismi said, and the three of them got on all fours and quietly started sniffing and rooting and doing their best imitations of swine. Outside, migrating birds flew to the Tropic of Cancer from downed neighborhood trees as the smoke of the wildfires beyond Three Rivers got sucked straight through the razor-thin ozone.

"You boys crack me the fuck up," she said. "I'm so glad your mother is put away so I can have you all to myself." The boys remembered their earlier disappointment at hearing how Proserpina hadn't seen their mother at the fish cannery. She felt slightly bad again for making a joke out of it, even if it was her style and something these neighborhood boys were used to.

"What now, little toads," she asked them.

"Pros, we actually came here for something," said Huicho, and his brothers nodded.

"We found a big animal we want you to see," said Luismi.

"What do you mean, animal?"

"We don't know what kind it is, to um . . . imitate."

"How big is it?" she asked.

"Like," Cua said, "from here to there," pointing at the farthest wall.

"Guys, that's impossible. Where is it? Show me this animal."

Proserpina rigged the trailer door shut and noted the way she postured among the neighborhood youth when separated from Neftalí. She took on Neftalí's warmth, whereas Proserpina typically thought kids could benefit from brashness, ridicule, and tough love. She slipped on her sandals and moved through the neighborhood alleyways behind the triplets. A red dune buggy raced through and all of them squeezed along the edge to watch the large older man behind the wheel rush by, his blue scarf blowing out the open window.

They passed old satellites the size of dump trucks that'd faded, rusted, and chipped from decades of uselessness; passed broken refrigerators, burnt mattresses, and motor vehicles that'd become part of the landscape, with ferns and oak trees growing through them against the hazy skyline of the city.

Thick aluminum smoke appeared fifty feet from the alley, where a crew of older men stirred molten liquid in a steel barrel beneath a blue tarp. They poured the contents of the steel barrel slowly into arranged molds. One of the men, wearing dirty goggles, grinned a shattered-gymnasium-window grin, while other men in overalls paused their tasks to turn their attention to the young woman with no hair.

"Where are you taking me?"

"To the barn."

"You'll see."

"The one by the *naranjos*."

"I don't want to deal with that crazy old murderer who owns the barn," Proserpina said.

"The colonel is gone," Huicho replied.

"Where did he go?"

"Nobody know," said Cua.

"But—but," Luismi said, "the colonel's wagon and car are still put."

"Maybe he's dead inside his house," Proserpina joked.

They approached a long, unpaved driveway within the expanse of land known as *el monte*—knee-length grass that this time of year turned mosquito copper as the ants sang folk songs from the caked, dry soil below.

P H CRICK SQUEEZUS GRAPFRUTS 2 LAST DROP was spray-painted in a cosmic orange across the side of an abandoned barn that seemed to slobber and bounce around like a giant old basset hound.

"The barn door is wide open," Luismi whispered.

"They tag the grossest fucking shit," Proserpina muttered, and Cua respectfully signaled for her to keep quiet.

She winced but had to admire the calculated efficiency of these boys: how Luismi carefully held the swaying barn door as Huicho scoped inside. It was dark in the barn. Bundles of hay were stacked in disarray to the right and the left, with a cleared path down the middle. Proserpina didn't feel it was safe, and she wondered if she had brought her switchblade, or lighter, in case she needed to burn it all down. Her heartbeat became hoofbeats, galloping to a desert she'd never see.

The path among the haystacks made a hard turn to a clearing in the barn. Lying in the middle of the clearing, nestled by bent planks, was an indistinguishable mass of pink, seared flesh. A rectangular window in the barn's roof allowed in a white strip of daylight.

At first, Proserpina suspected this thing was a giant, breathing pile of old lard, but then she made out its black claws, its calluses—the wrinkled, beastly stuffed animal's face.

"What do you fellas know about this?" Proserpina asked in a loud whisper.

"We can talk in normal voices in barn," Huicho informed her.

"Señorita Pros," Luismi said, "which name of the cats is this?"

In a gesture that would become a habit, Proserpina ran one of her hands across her buzzed head like it was a crystal ball that held all the answers. She moved carefully around the creature and noticed its sporadic wheeze, its undulating belly.

"Have y'all told Neftalí about this? She knows more about animals than me."

The three boys shook their heads. Proserpina signaled them back out of the barn, and Luismi latched the door behind them. "One of you go find Neftalí," Proserpina ordered, forgetting that what one of these boys did, they all did. She walked toward the main house as the triplets headed back in the direction they'd all arrived from.

The two-story house was a faded jungle green, with decks around the perimeter of both stories, and three gables. Its roof was patched with blue tarps in several spots. Proserpina registered a low buzzing coming from the chestnut tree past the house's long shadow. Below the chestnut sat a white bucket with flies hovering in a vicious frenzy. When she looked into the bucket, prepared to see a severed human head or similar atrocity, Proserpina saw a pile of fast-food chicken wing bones. She headed back to the barn in disgust, then a distant birdcall made her change direction.

All of Huerta's horses were missing from the stable, but his wagon was intact; she tried to remember whether or not the old colonel had a dog. Or had the dog died? She couldn't recall the rumors, only Huerta's temperament, and, risking getting shot by him as a trespasser, she tried the broken buzzer, then knocked twice on the screen door. When nobody answered, she found the door already cracked open, and walked inside.

Proserpina left the screen and main doors unshut behind her. The morning sun was sneaking its flanks through the dusty, shaded windows. Family photographs that'd once been hanging were now on the floor, resting along the edges of the walls. It was cool in there, since the windows were partly open and air circulated liberally.

As she moved from room to room, this place of cursed neighborhood lore was more like an abandoned hospital vessel. Proserpina felt the weight of the immigrant German family who'd inexplicably died in the house over a hundred years ago, long before Huerta and his family moved in. She picked up a framed photograph by the staircase, unraveled the cobweb around it: a trio of smiling young girls wearing long dresses on the dock of some lakeshore—Huerta's daughters. Proserpina remembered their gruesome deaths, felt their fatal wounds around her own reproductive organs, and quickly put the photograph back down, fearing that her presence might set a curse in motion.

The tinted windowpanes along the creaking stairwell filtered oblong light patterns onto the flowered wallpaper. Proserpina at last thought to say something, maybe to give warning: "Hello," she shouted. "Are you here, old man? The door to your barn was open. There's some big creature dying in there. And your horses are gone. What's up with the chicken bones in the bucket, too, that's freaking gross."

When she heard no response, she added: "I'm gonna come up. You better not shoot me, or I'll be real mad."

She climbed the stairs, nervously walked down the empty argyle darkness of the second-story landing, which led to an ample main room. Beige sheets covered most of the windows and diffused the daylight. The walls were bare, while a clicking ceiling fan had been left on the lowest setting. There were no signs that anybody had occupied this space for some time. Proserpina did her version of a howling coyote, pulled down one of the sheets covering a tall window, and let a wall of sunlight tumble in. The doors it revealed were all locked.

Proserpina descended the stairs to look for drinking water and walked into the dining room by the kitchen. On a velvet-cushioned mahogany chair sat a pale bald man with drooping ears and wearing a ranking military uniform from an old war. A pair of binoculars sat next to him on the table, along with a candleholder standing over a pool of yellow coagulated wax at its base. The man's cheeks bulged like puffed corn. To Proserpina, he looked like a sleeping, mustached infant doll.

She clapped in front of his face and yelled, "Huerta. Old man. You killed your family, you fool. You're a murderer, wake up."

When he didn't respond after a few seconds, she pushed him aside, suspecting this was some perverted joke Huerta was playing to feel her up. But then when she focused under the gray light sneaking through the outside foliage, she saw that his eyes were rolled back and only the whites showed— but they were a yellowish-purple color. She crept closer and carefully placed the back of one wrist over his mouth to check for breath.

Proserpina groaned upon noticing a folded note on the kitchen table. She spread open the parchment paper:

To whoever finds this note, I bequeath my property and estate unto you. Rid this place and belongings of my shamed family name. Present this note to the magistrate and cleric's office. Have them transfer all of it over to your name. Life has given me enough, and I have taken enough.

Dutifully,
Colonel J. Eusebio Huerta III

Proserpina walked to the closest window and held the paper up to the daylight and carefully reread every word. The paper had the official state of Texas watermark, along with the javelina hologram stamp from her district's notary public.

She circled the long dining room table, hoping for another note or instructions on what to do with the dead body. Crusted dishes and stained cups were piled around the kitchen sink. Pestilential pots and pans lurched on the stove like junkie gargoyles. She searched the rest of the house, found the place otherwise empty. While admiring the handcrafted chairs and rustic furniture by the door, she caught her buzzed head reflected in the glass face of an antique cuckoo clock. Proserpina walked out of the house to get some air and, feeling dizzy, rested on the steps of the back porch.

Scores of doves and mockingbirds circled the house at various radial distances. She paid close attention to their cooing, warbling, seemingly eternal shattering that hit a variety of sharp notes and distilled fear through Proserpina's veins. She read the death letter one more time, ran a hand across her buzzed head, then walked back toward the barn where they'd left the creature.

A three-headed squeaky wheelbarrow slowly pushed through from the alley. Two of the triplets—Proserpina couldn't tell which—each held a wheelbarrow handle as the third triplet guided it and maintained its balance along the bumpy back roads. A pile of dark hair with two pale brown feet was sticking out from the barrow.

Huicho, Luismi, and Cua eased the wheelbarrow to a halt, gathered in a circle around it.

The pile of hair in the wheelbarrow was unresponsive to the commotion, so Proserpina gave the metal rim a couple of nudges.

"Where'd you find her?"

Huicho said, "Outside her house."

"How'd you get her into the barrow?"

"She was sleeping there already," said Luismi.

An image of choking on vomit flashed in Proserpina's mind, she panicked and tossed Neftalí's hair aside and said, "Ey, Neftalí. We're being deported. Wake up," and slapped her cheeks lightly.

Neftalí lifted her head and squinted, sluggishly opened her eyes, as if she'd peeked out of a deep burrow to discover bright mayonnaise sunlight. She had eye-crusties attached to her lashes like tiny cacti. Her head felt like it was a tiny head trying to break out of a larger, more oppressive head, and her stomach held smoldering cinders.

She had been passed out on her handbag, which she now grabbed, and she walked toward the edge of the orchard behind the barn, saying, "I need a minute, y'all, jus' give me a minute," barely able to keep her balance.

Neftalí returned moments later looking far from well after her brief retching, and said, "You know what I crave most, my babies? One of those gooey, fun treats that hip European lady one time made for us: *Schnecken*. Remember those? That moment in time when we could have them was like magic. If I could go back, it would be only for *Schnecken*. Those little buns are the best."

Proserpina walked away, not wanting to show emotion in front of the triplets, and sat on the uneven ground halfway back toward the house. Neftalí asked herself if she'd been rude, then finally took in the fact that all of Proserpina's nimbus cloud hair was missing. She walked to Proserpina and sat on the ground next to her.

It seemed like the perfect occasion to resurrect an old band joke of theirs, so Neftalí said: "All of this land will be yours one day, mi'ja," which made Proserpina laugh.

"Hey, that may be no joke," she said, and handed Neftalí Colonel Huerta's suicide note.

Neftalí held it up to the soggy light.

"He offed himself? And had his suicide note javelina-notarized? Baller. Wait, hold up. I need some water or something 'cause I'm super dehydrated. Your head looks great, I must say, my little beast."

"Do I look like a stupid outer-space alien because of my large eyes, even more? Alexei always says I look from another galaxy—"

"You look fabulous, dear. You have the right face and build for a shaved head. I'd look pretty gnarly. So Huerta offed himself? Is his wormy body in there, stinking the house up? Let's go see. How did he do it? Is it a mess? I don't wanna go if it's a mess, I can't handle that right now, all *crudota* and shit. I'd probably puke on it."

Proserpina looked over at the brothers. The three were huddled on top of the wheelbarrow, leafing through an open book.

"Wait a damn minute," Neftalí said, feeling a sensation, once again, of puncturing from one reality into another. "Where is this place? Are we on psycho Huerta's property? And he's dead now? Did we party here last night when we found out or something? 'Cause I don't remember."

"The twins wheeled you over just now, in that barrow."

"Why do you always say *twins*? These guys are triplets."

"No, they're obviously twins. Luismi, Huicho, and Cua."

"Uh," Neftalí said, not wanting to break it to her. "That's three of them. So they have to be triplets. One-two-three."

"You can be twins and be triplets, too. It's not about math. Yeah, 'cause they all look the same. If they all looked different, then they couldn't be twins."

Growing increasingly concerned about other matters, Neftalí said, "I suppose."

She got up, looked toward the boys, and took Proserpina by the hand. As they got closer to the triplets, Neftalí saw they were reading her white hardcover book, and said, "Oh, shit, my new novel."

"You dropped it back there," said Luismi.

"God," Neftalí blurted, not thinking about what she was saying, "why do there have to be three of y'all's names to remember? Proserpina's right, you're indistinguishable." She pulled a water thermos from her bag and a bottle of aspirin, offered pills to everybody around, but they declined. Neftalí popped two aspirin, chugged from the thermos. "Y'all are getting your grubby little fingers all over my book. It was a precious gift to me. What use d'y'all have with a book, can y'all even read? You're gonna get us all pinched, reading in the open like that."

The triplets handed it back.

Neftalí wandered toward the back road that had brought her there, and yelled, "All right, enough fucking around. I'll see all of y'all later. I'm going home to make some eggs, if I can find them."

"Señora Matilda's goose has eggs, and she let us have some on credit today."

"For real?"

Each of the three boys nodded in his own style.

"Thanks for the tip. She owes me after I helped save some of her hens from those bloodthirsty red foxes last summer."

As Neftalí strayed, Proserpina climbed onto the wheelbarrow to test how sturdy it was, and Luismi called out: "Wait! We have something to show you."

Proserpina jumped down from the barrow, shrugged at Neftalí's puzzled look, and Huicho signaled for them to follow. The group of them moved toward the barn, unlatched the door, and walked along the narrow path between the haystacks.

There must have been a moment when Neftalí lost control of her mental faculties or blacked out—she'd been clutching the white hardcover book to her heaving chest as she surveyed the slab of pink, seared flesh before her. Neftalí's jaw shook as if a spirit had taken possession of her body and was trying to use her mouth to relate a message—but she couldn't utter a word. She circled the creature as Luismi said, "Do you know what name of the cats this is, Neftalí?"

"A guinea pig?" Cua wondered.

"A lion," Proserpina suggested, with cautious authority.

Neftalí was on her knees before the head of the creature. The black and brown blotches around its body were deep wounds in various healing stages—here was the sight of a rainbow that'd dipped its body into an overflowing pot, and all seven colors had hardened into a mass of flesh.

Neftalí reached out to touch it, and everybody else became visibly concerned. But nothing happened as her hand grazed the placid creature's face. The golden glow of haystacks transported the moment onto a stage, where Neftalí drew her hand back, looked down to stage right, and said to the audience: "It's maybe a tiger. A female tiger. Tigress, they were often called. Look at her over here. She doesn't have a tail. Somebody must've chopped it off."

Huicho, Luismi, and Cua asked what cutting off a tigress's tail was for. Proserpina added up the terror of this equation, and found Huerta could have had a hand in this, too.

"What do we do about it?" she asked Neftalí.

Neftalí's hangover took a brief clairvoyant turn; she felt light refracting through her thrashed body. The hardcover book was in her hands. She had a flashback to when the military had invaded the public school while she hid in that ancient oak tree as a girl, then ricocheted to thinking about her mother buried in that baroque cemetery, singing duets by herself for all eternity.

"Leave me alone here with the tiger, and get out."

Proserpina looked at the haystacks in the barn, then at the triplets, unsure whom Neftalí was referring to. "What?" she asked.

Neftalí raised her voice: "Leave. Close the door behind you and lock us in here. Do it, please."

Confused, and with great reluctance that bordered on offense, Luismi, Huicho, Cua, and Proserpina did as they were told.

Outside the barn, Proserpina shrugged at the triplets and went to find a place to pee. She walked rapidly past the orchards and came across the caliche path by a canal that led her to a reservoir she'd forgotten existed. The triplets hadn't followed her, and Proserpina did her business as she heard a metallic clamoring from the reservoir. When she had finished, she spotted about ten feet away from her, near the embankment, a sealed bottle labeled xxx. Proserpina kicked the bottle hard. It hit a cinder block on the side of a ridge, shattered, and fell into the shallow canal.

"Uh-oh," she mumbled. "I hope that bottle gets people fucked up. And doesn't poison everyone."

Proserpina stood carefully on the steep embankment's edge, admiring the viscous, sparkling stream about thirty feet below. She wondered where the canal started and where it might end. There were canals she knew of that traveled in complete circles around Three Rivers and were breeding pools for mosquitoes. Like a phantom scythe mowing down grass, a loud, insistent *hwenk-hwenk-hwenk, hwenk-hwenk-hwenk* rushed from behind her. Proserpina jumped out of the way, startled, and lost her footing, tumbling down the embankment.

She had just enough time before sliding into the canal to see the flash of a determined mother javelina scuttling out of the bushes with her cocky offspring. *Hwenk-hwenk-hwenk, hwenk-hwenk-hwenk*, the javelinas continued through the brambles.

As Proserpina got sucked into the pit of water, crying out in curdling horror, a baby javelina stayed behind to snort, whiff, and take a brief leak before joining the others. *Hwenk-hwenk-hwenk, hwenk-hwenk-hwenk*.

A cathedral of silence passed through the creature and Neftalí after the barn doors were shut. Neftalí sobbed before the prostrate tiger with a gyrating, pathetic intensity she hadn't felt since she was a girl, when her mother died. The light in the barn dimmed. She wiped away her tears, peed in the far corner behind a row of haystacks, then sat by the head of the tiger once again.

Neftalí breathed deeply, opened the book *Brother Brontë* by Jazzmin Monelle Rivas, thumbed past the epigraphs.

"'*Brother Brontë*,'" she read aloud. "'Chapter one. Pulling at her patterned stockings in the empty ambergris gallery, Prejudice struck a pose and made a face she once considered to be very nineteenth-century. It was a pose she'd associated with the boy poet A. Rimbaud, and one she saw again presently, standing before a painting by the seventeenth-century painter Claude Vignon, of David with the groaning, severed head of Goliath . . .'"

Book Two
~~~~~

Pulling at her patterned stockings in the empty ambergris gallery, Prejudice struck a pose and made a face she once considered to be very nineteenth-century. It was a pose she'd associated with the boy poet A. Rimbaud, and one she saw again presently, standing before a painting by the seventeenth-century painter Claude Vignon, of David with the groaning, severed head of Goliath. In the painting, David sits with his back to a wall inside a dark cell, where a beam of light shines from an open window upon his face and Goliath's supplicating head, blood dripping from the laceration. Young David's gaze, his eyes, nurture a calm, divine damnation, like he just got out of the juvenile rehab hospital, clean for the first time in months, which to a young man like David could feel like years. His eyes are neither triumphant nor afraid of what's to come. A century and a half later, Arthur Rimbaud would own that same stare in those two surviving photographs taken of him as a boy, and now Prejudice, standing before the Vignon painting in the academy's gallery the morning of her graduation, imitated that haunted expression herself.

So begins the novel *Brother Brontë* by Jazzmin Monelle Rivas, written in a contrived style she later confessed felt like it never belonged to her: unlike in Rivas's other work, the narrative doesn't take place on more than one psychic plane, and doesn't include a subplot involving creation or the planet's environmental collapse. The plot, at first glance, appears conventional—bucolic, even—and has only one setting: Our Brother Branwell Academy for Girls. It is Monelle's third published novel—her first since she was deported and had her first two published books blacklisted by the education department of the government, which, among other things, presided over the entirety of manuscripts published by native presses, and discarded works it felt went against the interests of the country. Libraries were systematically defunded and subsequently looted and vandalized.

But before all this, when she was twenty-one years old, Jazzmin Monelle wrote the novella *I Was a Teenage Brain Parasite*. She wrote it after a bad bout of dengue fever that the doctor on call had felt, but never said, she would fail to overcome. Jazzmin had still been living with her mother, almost three years after prep school, off Polk Street in the immigrant neighborhood of a Midwestern city. Jazzmin's mother, Silvia Cruz, was a custodian at the state library, and it was there that Jazzmin had spent most of her days after school—reading, getting lost in the treasures of old books, imagining her life as if it existed inside a test tube or a terrarium, with clouds becoming pages, browning like the insides of a sliced apple.

After the defunding of the government scholarship program for the financially disadvantaged, it became clear to Jazzmin Monelle that with her mother's salary and the rising cost of living, she'd never be able to pursue a university degree.

Other than her voracious reading habit and growing interest in visual art, Jazzmin hardly enjoyed her schooling—even as a little girl, hauling a paperback to the market with her mother, or to church, she rarely felt the act of learning was exclusive to an institution. School was a great introduction to ideas and facts, but she believed her everyday life around the city held a deeper, hidden language, one she couldn't quite pinpoint the origin of until she discovered fiction.

Waiting tables at Marf's was her first job, in her senior year of high school, and Jazzmin kept it until she turned twenty and got hired at Leroi's Diner, a landmark pancake house a stone's throw from the train station and Wright's Ball Field. Jazzmin Monelle picked up the habit of writing down on her guest checks tiny phrases she'd overheard, so when she got caught in the steaming wind tunnel of dengue fever, these phrases slithered into and out of her like phantom serpents, and deep inside herself she saw a tiny worker who was a simple dot—one tiny dot among many identical dots, all foaming in a growing cesspool that existed only in a petri dish. And inside this petri dish thrived an entire society, making itself known through her perilous disease.

When Jazzmin Monelle awakened after her fever broke, she was naked, and a male doctor was lying down fully clothed next to her on the bed. *My mother*, Jazzmin Monelle thought, her hair wet and rubbery. She got up and noticed the doctor was fast asleep, snoring. Jazzmin went to the bathroom in the chamber pot, chugged water from the pitcher on the bureau, and pulled a notepad and pencil from her bag.

At the top of the first blank page, she wrote the words that had echoed repeatedly from the jungle of her fever dream, and for a few minutes Jazzmin Monelle Rivas admired them as if they were caryatids: *I Was a Teenage Brain Parasite*. She was still completely unclothed, and writing on the bed, when the doctor came to. In that moment her mother arrived from work to witness this scene.

Within a few days of her convalescence, Jazzmin Monelle had completed a thirty-four-thousand-word novella, writing in her every waking moment. Its opening lines were also the first string of words she was able to tie together, like sausages from the inner workings of her then-fevered mind: "It's true, I was a teenage brain parasite. That much is true, yes, I'll admit. But what they'd never tell you is the golden next. That I'm responsible for the wolf's appetite, and for harebrained economics emboweling you, sculpting your insides throughout life. Here we go, hand in hand . . ."

Jazzmin Monelle went back five days later to waiting tables at Leroi's. The managers noted how spaced-out Jazzmin had been since her return, screwing up orders more than once per shift, losing her balance, spilling drinks. One day, while taking an extended break in the middle of working a double, she walked six blocks to the library and checked out a book on the publishing industry and how it worked. Jazzmin Monelle was given a verbal warning and write-up for clocking back in twenty minutes late. The diner by then was slammed with a choir singing a gospel rendition of a rock hit, while the spent staff at Leroi's resurrected the dead to run their orders.

That week Jazzmin Monelle also checked out a typewriter from the public library, and with her yellow notebook by her side began transcribing the manuscript for *I Was a Teenage Brain Parasite*. It took her thirty-five and a half hours to get the entire thing down in 158 double-spaced pages. Sixty pages into it, she realized she'd have to do this several times if she wanted to send the manuscript to several publishers.

In three weeks' time she rapidly typed two more relatively clean manuscripts varying in length, and checked out a copy of *The Writer's Almanac*. She quickly picked up the technical jargon of the publishing industry, and chose her two favorites from the list of operating presses in New York City: Pilgrimage Publishers and Duet Books. Five days after mailing off her first round of manuscripts, Jazzmin Monelle was handed her last meager check and fired from Leroi's Diner by Leroi's son himself, who had a soft spot for her and hated to do it.

Later, as she recounted the bad news to her mother at the kitchen table, Silvia kicked off her shoes, lifted the hem of her work pants, and casually showed Jazzmin her feet. They were knotted in a way that, to Jazzmin, made her feet look like python heads in the process of swallowing mice. She got onto the floor to look closer under the light in their measly apartment, while her mother confessed that the pain had been unbearable in recent days.

Jazzmin put water on to boil, rinsed a tin pail in the bathtub. Silvia soaked her feet in Epsom salts as she watched her favorite evening shows and drank herbal tea, with Jazzmin reading a book by her side. Three rapid knocks came from the door as Jazzmin turned to page 347 of her paperback. It was their neighbor—a man in his early thirties whom her mother referred to as *the immigrant*, though by all means, Jazzmin reminded her, Silvia herself was an immigrant.

The grinning neighbor held two small jars devoid of labels, containing a dark yellow paste. He handed one to Jazzmin, one to Silvia. Jazzmin held hers up like a bag with a goldfish inside. The neighbor gestured to untwist the lid, and Silvia opened hers while soaking her knotted feet. The freshness seals popped on both jars, which excited the neighbor.

"Ah," he said, "what think you?"

"What do you think," Jazzmin politely corrected him—a gesture he'd encouraged in the past, and almost automatically he repeated, "What *do you* think?"

"Mustard," Silvia said, unable to contain her displeasure.

"This is quite an intense smell you got here, sir," Jazzmin told the man.

"It's my family recipe. See?" he said, and pointed to the hallway. There was a red dolly parked by stacks of cardboard boxes. Jazzmin could see that the open topmost box was full of similar unlabeled jars.

"Oh!" exclaimed Jazzmin. "You sold out your family's mustard recipe so you could mass-produce it and sell it here in this country?"

"Very much, very much," he replied, unable to contain his excitement. "Always my family dream for me. They say, 'Filomeno, go to America and make the family name rich. Use all the recipes,' they say. 'Soup recipe, bread recipe.' Easiest to make for me was this, Tía's Dijon."

"Just so you know," Jazzmin said, "in America, you can't make food yourself at home and then sell it. Me and Momma tried that with chicharrones and churros and got fines that we only recently finished paying off."

He produced folders, then paperwork, from a briefcase

and said, "I have every permit. Industrial kitchen permit, permit of sales . . ."

Jazzmin shuffled through the official papers and handed them to Silvia, who also leafed through them in disbelief.

". . . registered ingredients, and the name: Spice Orchard Sauce . . ."

The neighbor recounted how he needed to print labels, and confided that his less-than-perfect English wouldn't suffice for a product marketed to Americans. He showed them the large-scale prototype of the logo: a single tree growing from a mustard seed in the ground. Hiring a writer to collaborate with him on the label had proved to be the hardest part.

"Well, what do you know," he said, one of the phrases he'd perfected in English. Then in his own language he continued: "They say America's writers make starving wages. But they're still too proud for honest job like *this*?"

Jazzmin Monelle, taking a leap from the precipice of her impecunious state, told Filomeno she could draft something up for him—if he felt that was a good idea. And if he approved of it, maybe they could discuss a contract and money. Filomeno thought about it, then shared a convoluted story of how his family came upon the sauce's ingredients, and what ultimately made the mustard special. Jazzmin jotted down bits of all this information, along with the ingredients, as Filomeno went through them one by one.

The following day, Jazzmin presented him with this sentence: "From our garden to your kitchen table." Filomeno hired a typographer and had an attorney draw up a fair contract. As Jazzmin and her mother read through the contract's points, Filomeno pontificated in a mixture of English and his native language: "You see, I notice from the first the American diet is absent of much taste and condiment, outside of catsup and sandwich food. The popular condiment here is for on the go, on the run, from one taxi to another with briefcase. This sauce will be reserved for days at home. Days with being among family. Days even among strangers, who become family."

He bought an ad in every major newspaper using the last of his inheritance, and within a week rented a larger, industrial kitchen, hired workers, and a whole new shipment of jars and labels was filled, assembled, and distributed all over the Midwest. Jazzmin and her mother opted to buy equity with a portion of their contract money, and as the company boomed, Silvia was able to quit her job and afford physical therapy for her legs twice a week, which significantly alleviated her gout. Jazzmin never had to wait tables again. Though the money they made as mother and daughter wasn't a fortune, it was able to cover their rent, bills, and food. Jazzmin ticked up her voracious reading to two, sometimes three books a week, and for a while became invested in tracing the scarce subject of motherhood and babies throughout literary history.

This is how, a short time later, she came upon writing her novella-length story "The Nineteenth Mary." Approximately fourteen thousand words, it tells the story of a young woman who is the lone survivor of her native village's pillaging. The setting is a desert landscape, and the story's wildest adjectives are reserved for the heat. The young protagonist's age is never disclosed, but we are given contextual clues that she is no longer a child. At the story's opening she's riding a mule in a state of shock, when suddenly her beast of burden collapses and dies from exhaustion. Far from the plundering fires, and carrying the trauma of her loved ones' murdered, mutilated, burned bodies, she runs to the nearby shelter of a cave. Once inside, she decides life can't be worth living, and is determined to find a comfortable spot to die. She finds an ideal clearing after a period of groping in the dark and lies down, her face cold and filthy with tears. The young woman falls asleep and has dreams of worms slithering over wet soil in a manner that is not grotesque but nourishing. The worms slither into her skin, her pores sprout hairy roots like a potato, tangling with stems of grass and sun-facing flowers—from the cave's oceanic darkness, the young woman feels warm hands stroking her arms, her wrists, then the inside of her right palm, as if reading her fate. Not knowing if this is a dream or a hallucination, if this is what it feels like to become a vegetable, she finds herself walking, being guided by this hand toward an orange light, as if emerging from a dark lagoon. Under the quarter moon (which feels much too bright to the young woman), she sees that her guide is an older woman wearing a hooded tunic woven out of a coarse fabric, and this is the last thing she remembers before waking up moments before dawn, slumped over a beast of burden within the walls of a small agrarian community of adobe houses, and being helped down from the beast by three similarly robed older women. When the young woman wakes up days later on a simple bed with all her clothes off, she finds that the scratches and wounds from her escape have completely healed. Hanging from the wall, and the only decorative thing in the sand-brown room, is a hooded tunic. She slips it on and doesn't mind the way the spidery fabric crawls along her skin. It is a bright blue day, and she walks out to find other doorless rooms built of adobe clay. The young woman can hear a quiet, polyphonic chant and running water coming from a profound well nearby. She spots a green shadow reflected in a makeshift pond in the small garden. The young woman explores the grounds and the different quarters of the agrarian community. After encountering several residents, she finds it odd that they are all older women thus far. The young woman is guided to a cottage at the center by the woman who found her in the cave, and here she meets all the members of the community: eighteen women. All of them have the same name—which is also the name the young woman will be called inside the community, and that name is Mary. We discover the women are all survivors of tyranny carried out by violent, fanatical, ignorant men. The women are rightly distrustful of the outside world, and only a few have clearance to leave the confines of the community's walls. The young woman discovers that during the daily prayer sessions, the eighteen Marys are in contact with a higher, extraterrestrial being that manifests in a dilating purple cloud within the prayer room. Weeks go by, and the young woman—the Nineteenth Mary—gets accustomed to her life in the community, while outside the winds shift constantly, and the older women become aware of a storm rapidly approaching. One evening, all nineteen women start a prolonged communal vigil under what the author calls a "blood jackal moon"—the young woman, for the final prayer of the night, is placed lying face up on a rug, while the other Marys form a circle around her, praying in an enhanced silence. The young woman awakes the following day feeling sick. Within a few weeks, she is encouraged to work in the garden only lightly, and to be in touch with the few living things around the compound as much as possible.

Though the reader gets plenty of thickly laid foreshadowing, the climax arrives as a surprise. The community of Marys is discovered by an outsider. The outsider is a man, and one of the Marys spots him as she's having her twilight bath. Naked and dripping with water, this Mary tackles and restrains the male intruder. He is tied up with the help of another Mary, and in short time the nineteen Marys hold council about what to do with their captive. A tense moral dilemma unfolds amongst the women, who fear the man will reveal their hidden community to others. They finally agree not to make any hasty decisions, and await the dawn.

In the middle of the night, however, the young woman, the Nineteenth Mary, already carrying a huge mound in her stomach, full of compassion that possesses her like a ghost, cuts the male prisoner loose and sets him free. The man runs into the cold desert night, and come dawn the young woman is severely reprimanded by the eighteen elder Marys.

They begin what they call *preparations*. The Marys burn bushels of dried herbs from their garden, bury a chest filled with crystals and a jar of their collected nail clippings (over five years' worth), and form a meditative circle around the pregnant Nineteenth Mary. Moments later, amidst a distant rumble that is more like a stampede, Joseph, the young shepherd they've commissioned, arrives pulling a singular spry mule. He'd been told only to deliver a package, so the acne-scarred shepherd is surprised to discover that the package is actually a pregnant young woman close to his age.

The eighteen Marys say their hasty goodbyes to the nineteenth, with various levels of affection. The Nineteenth Mary climbs onto the mule, and the shepherd escorts her to the mouth of the desert, thinking of all the different ways he could be in trouble if discovered—and this is where the readers get the author's confirmation of what they might already have suspected.

The following evening, when they are a couple hours away from their destination, the Nineteenth Mary informs the clueless shepherd that she's beginning to feel intense pains. A peaceful manger appears before them, and the mule decides on its own to strut inside, where our Mary gives birth surrounded by cows, horses, sheep, hens, as another mule makes lovey-dovey eyes at Joseph's mule, and Jazzmin Monelle Rivas's novella-length story "The Nineteenth Mary" concludes.

"The Nineteenth Mary" was submitted to *The Sunday Literary Supplement*, and was cold-read by two overworked, undercaffeinated interns, who tossed it to the slush pile, where it sat for months. One morning, after a night of binge drinking, the senior editor Heidi Monrow knocked over a pile of submissions, and as she collected them she read aloud a random title she saw: "The Nineteenth Mary."

She gathered the papers in a shoddy yet meticulous fashion, walked into her office, closed the door, and passed out on the couch. Three and a half hours later, after she used the restroom, washed up, and brushed her teeth, all while remembering her long-dead grandmother Mary Vazquez, Heidi Monrow buzzed one of the nervous interns and asked them to find the submission titled "The Nineteenth Mary."

Heidi read the entire story with great interest in one go,

shifting from chair to chair around her office while getting hydrated and chugging a pot and a half of French roast. The story was riddled with grammatical errors that she underlined in green ink with lightning bolts for effect, but there was something about it that didn't allow her to toss the pages aside. She looked through the paperwork of the submission, even had her assistant track down the mailing envelope, but no author bio was found attached to the story. Heidi Monrow edited "The Nineteenth Mary," had two interns each type up a copy, and the following morning, finally un-hungover, she read the story anew. A copy of the edited pages, along with a standard contract, were sent to the postmarked return address, and Jazzmin Monelle Rivas received it five business days later. She promptly, excitedly returned the contract with her signature, fearing she'd die at any moment, now that her wish of being published was coming true.

Upon receipt of the contract, Heidi Monrow sent the story to be proofed, filed the contract, and poured herself an old-fashioned, light on the sugar, from her office minibar.

After this small win, Jazzmin Monelle felt the fire still burning when she received a letter from Woodbird Books, which she opened with haste. Her heart pickled in a jar as she scanned the letter, reading through the parts informing her that her first novel was rejected. By then, *I Was a Teenage Brain Parasite* had been rejected by seventeen publishers, big and small.

The week her story appeared in *The Sunday Literary Supplement*, five journalists covering Washington, DC, were arrested at the culmination of a national scandal that had been unfolding for months as the American public became more restless and divided.

Jazzmin Monelle's novella-length story was overlooked in elite literary circles, but that week Heidi Monrow got an offer to lead her own imprint at Morik Books, which she accepted on the spot. The position paid relatively the same salary, but she was given a generous acquisition budget and an award-winning creative team. One of the first things Heidi did was write a personal letter welcoming novel submissions to a short list of writers she'd published throughout the years— particularly writers she felt she'd discovered.

One of these letters was mailed to Jazzmin Monelle Rivas in the Midwest, perhaps despite Heidi Monrow's better judgment. Fourteen days later, Heidi Monrow received a package with two bound manuscripts and a letter explaining how one draft was Jazzmin's first novel, and the other was her most recent unpublished novella, titled *Ghosts in the Zapotec Sphericals*.

Heidi Monrow read both manuscripts with extreme editorial prejudice and curiosity, before passing them on to the rest of her creative team for their thoughts. After intense discussion and debates, in which everyone offered harsh, unretractable criticism, they unanimously moved from "to hell with this writer" to agreeing that Jazzmin Monelle deserved a two-book deal. The contract was delivered the next day, along with an invitation to visit Morik's editorial offices upon the book's publication. An agent who'd been keeping up with Jazzmin's career contacted her and signed her not long after.

Jazzmin's mother had in the meantime been doing record-keeping for Spice Orchard Sauce, which, in less than a year, was distributed nationwide. Silvia continued getting the best physical therapy for her legs, and wore the most comfortable footwear available. Jazzmin Monelle worked up the courage one evening to share the careful plans for her writing career that she'd been secretly arranging, and was surprised when Silvia voiced her complete, enthusiastic support. Jazzmin could finally see something like independence from her mother as attainable, after years of worry, self-doubt, and guilt as her only daughter. In what they both felt to be no time at all, Jazzmin packed her one suitcase, bought a slipcase for her typewriter, took a long train ride to New Orleans, and boarded the ship the *Mandarina*.

Politics had shifted drastically in the country, and the founding principles attached to the Constitution were being corruptly rewritten. As a successful immigrant business, Spice Orchards Sauce, its owner, Filomeno, and employees, including Jazzmin Monelle and her mother, became open targets for hatred.

On their way to deliveries early one morning, three Spice Orchard Sauce trucks were run off the road by armed young men; one driver fled, another tried to negotiate and was seen as sympathetic by the youths, the third was beaten and taken to the hospital, and all three trucks were hijacked; the sauce shipments were discovered in the river three days later.

Filomeno received bomb threats, and regularly looked over his shoulder, even when alone in a room. Silvia decided to retire from the company after watching a woman her age, walking twenty or so feet away from her, get her satchel stolen in a systematic operation by youngsters who looked like children to her, and Silvia thought, *Dios Santo, could this be our marked hour?*

It felt like a cloud of resin had been vacuumed clean from inside Jazzmin Monelle's chest once the *Mandarina* departed from the Port of New Orleans. She settled in room 127 for her twelve-day voyage, on the lower deck of the ship, where she'd been guaranteed there'd be a desk.

There was. One about the size of her luggage, which suited her typewriter and allowed space for some books. Jazzmin was twenty-four by then, and felt really good being away from the city and her mother for the first time. She'd turned in her proofs for *I Was a Teenage Brain Parasite*, and was proud—also, she felt like a writer, an actual living writer.

It was Jazzmin's first time on a boat. She had a scroll-down curtain over the small oval porthole, and a postcard reproduction of a landscape by an uncredited painter was mounted on the wall. It was a painting that, years later, she would see in person at a Venetian museum, and she discovered its title there: *Windmill and Pond by the Home of a Wicked Lady, Before 1985*, by Denys Delourdes-Price.

She kept the curtain scrolled up to let in the moonlight and sunshine reflected off the sea; drank her coffee, or water, or bourbon; and wrote. Mostly, she typed nonsense: Jazzmin Monelle had taught herself the art of letting go beyond a narrative and characters, even beyond cohesive language, before conjuring a discernible idea for a story. She switched the meanings of Spanish and English words for fun. When she wasn't promenading on the *Mandarina*, Jazzmin Monelle was working away. At the ship's souvenir shop, she bought a curtain of shells to veil the threshold to her room, and during the late-morning hours she wrote for a few hours with the door open, shells dangling.

In the middle of writing an intense scene, a young boy stuck his head in amidst the loud typing and asked, "What happens here?"

Jazzmin Monelle halted her typing, looked the boy in the eye, and said, "Life and death and the womb of the universe happen here, young man."

She offered a peanut butter energy bar to the boy as his head continued floating in the curtain of floating shells. He took it and ran away. She walked out of her room and for the first time took real notice of the other faces. She'd been so entwined in her own inner pursuits that she'd forgotten to catch up on her immediate, surrounding reality aboard the ship. It was curious that most of the people in the rooms neighboring hers were young-to-middle-aged women. Some of them were two-to-a-room and had small children. The women were polite and timid in their brief exchanges with Jazzmin Monelle, and absent of many formalities, she assumed a passive kinship with them.

It didn't come as a complete surprise to Jazzmin Monelle when she discovered the women at her end of the ship were refugees escaping domestic abuse and the new laws back home. Though all the women were citizens, they'd been forced to leave the country. Rather than face jail time and crippling financial repercussions, they'd been given the option to renounce their citizenships, while their abusers ran free without so much as sullying their social standing. An organization was funding the relocation of the women, and certain countries in South America had opened their borders to them. When Jazzmin learned all this, she felt outraged at being the only person who wasn't a refugee in her quarter of the boat.

One of the women, in a room adjacent to hers, had a phonograph, and played only one record of classical compositions that Jazzmin Monelle had never heard. The musicians played waltzes that featured the violin. Jazzmin imagined this music emerging from the center of the earth a billion years ago like magma to give shape to the shapeless.

When the record wasn't playing, or when she promenaded along the deck, Jazzmin found herself humming what she considered to be the centerpiece of the album, a tune she later came to know as "Sobre las olas." She recognized its motif from a modern song played on one of her mother's beloved country music stations, and, with repetition, she responded deeply to it.

Jazzmin Monelle was humming it at the ship's main bar while sipping espresso one afternoon. As the frenetic jazz band onstage announced a break, Jazzmin made eye contact with a woman a few barstools away, in conversation with a sweaty, red-faced man. The woman wore a corduroy suit that matched her inebriated partner's outfit. The sweaty man stepped aside to talk to the band.

The woman smiled at Jazzmin Monelle, and Jazzmin succeeded in not smiling back, then said, "What?" but in a comedic manner.

The woman then accidentally spilled her mimosa on the bar. Jazzmin Monelle felt responsible, spotted the bussing towel, and wiped up the spot, as the bartender was helping other drinkers and hardly noticed.

Introductions: the woman was Mina Johnson, and she ordered herself another mimosa on Jazzmin Monelle's tab. The two of them talked as if they'd been coworkers at the same small-town supermarket years ago.

Mina gestured to her husband, Daryl Johnson, who was a manager of independent musical acts, including the musicians currently breaking their equipment down.

Jazzmin Monelle said she was an author. After ordering yet another mimosa, while Jazzmin Monelle ordered some tonic water, Mina said, "I am something of a diarist myself."

"How do you mean?" said Jazzmin, sipping her tonic water.

"Well," she said, "there's a diary I've been keeping. Since I was a teenage girl. I've accustomed myself to taking a few moments every day to jot down my account of what happened. And I'll continue to keep it for the rest of my days."

She looked away toward her husband, Daryl, as he walked back from speaking to the musicians. Mina introduced them, mentioned how clumsy she'd been to spill her own mimosa, and how courteous Jazzmin had been in sopping up the mess and buying her another one. Daryl thanked Jazzmin Monelle for her kindness and, along with Mina, wished her a good night and a pleasant remainder of the voyage.

Jazzmin Monelle noticed Mina glancing her way as she ordered herself a ginger beer. Back on the ship's deck, Jazzmin admired the clothing of other passengers, which seemed from another century, not unlike the waltz recordings still stuck in her head. By the edge of the deck, facing the spot where the cellophane sun would later set, were three women, all breast-feeding their babies. To Jazzmin Monelle's eyes, the women were identical.

"Buenas tardes," one of the breastfeeding women said, squinting at Jazzmin through the sunrays bouncing off the sea. Using the language of her grandparents and her mother, Jazzmin responded in kind.

She excused herself from the women and their babies with a half nod, and walked toward the bridge of the ship. Through the window that allowed passengers to look inside the wheel-house, she saw the large wheel, and steering it was a man wearing a three-piece suit. He wasn't looking forward, toward the ocean, but back over his shoulder at a small television screen.

The captain huddled with two other men beside him, who also gazed down at the television. They were immersed in a kind of courtroom drama being broadcast. The editing appeared unconventional to Jazzmin, and as she continued watching she discovered it wasn't a movie or show. Upon re-membering the ongoing New Way Forward Senate hearings back home, her heart accelerated, and her hands began to sweat.

The men in the wheelhouse watching the men on the screen—to Jazzmin Monelle, the men seemed to be watching themselves, as if the Senate hearings were a recording of a former school play they'd all been actors in.

Jazzmin's heartbeats multiplied exponentially. She man-aged to calm herself while having flashbacks to the time when she had been feverish and drafted her first novel; as if holding a mirror to her face, she remembered her mother and her ancestors and considered all the sadness that had to have happened to bring her to this precipice of time.

She got back to her room and burst with sentences before her typewriter. Jazzmin ripped through eleven single-spaced pages. Across the hall the sound of a cuckoo clock struck an indiscernible hour. There was a commotion outside, and from her window she saw a flock of seagulls fighting over a string of raw sausage. The *Mandarina* was ashore.

She packed up her things and readied herself with haste, while on the ship's deck people bottlenecked toward the boarding area and down the gangplank to the dock. Jazzmin heard the faint melody of a harmonium and people cheering, gulls screeching, and marital vows being exchanged.

Years later, she'd look back on her first encounter with this great city and its lights—bright greens and blues, but mostly the hunched orange shadows from the gas lamps. She'd remember the cobblestone fabric of the streets, sounds from accordions, the *clickety-clackety* of people's shoes, colorful buildings shimmering like giant, wise boulders. Most storefronts had the names of their business painted onto the buildings themselves, using flamboyant mural styles that Jazzmin had never encountered.

She inhaled the aroma of grilled zucchini, and wandered into a café with its door propped open. Jazzmin sat at the bar, and the bartender, thinking he recognized her, said, "Se acuerda de mi?" and poured her a shot of steaming turmeric-gold liquid, while dancing his eyebrows up and down suggestively. When they made eye contact, and the bartender saw he was mistaken, he felt embarrassed. Then, upon hearing

Jazzmin's imperfect Spanish, he grew relieved, and in his best English told her this first shot was on the house.

Jazzmin Monelle sipped on the hot, spicy beverage.

The bartender asked if her boat had just docked and, if so, where it had come from.

She responded using Spanish that wobbled like a drunk on stilts, as the bartender put on a record of a female lounge singer. Jazzmin leaned in, noticed the man wasn't actually putting on a record but lowering the volume of the music already playing, as a woman stood on an otherwise-empty stage by the entrance and sang. There was nobody else present except Jazzmin, the bartender, and this singer, going for the prize, as if in front of multitudes with a full backing band.

A glowing sensation from the drink was making its way through Jazzmin Monelle's insides like white light. The singer finished her tune, laughed, clapped once, and said, "The acoustics are incredible in here" in Spanish. Jazzmin Monelle paid attention to the poster beside her barstool advertising a performance on the twenty-eighth.

She rented a room thanks to a tip from the bartender, whose sister had a couple of vacancies not far from where they stood. Jazzmin Monelle unpacked her bags and set her typewriter on the nice, small kitchen table of one of those available rooms, occasionally taking hits of the concoction the bartender had insisted she take to boost her immune system after the long voyage.

It took almost a week, but one morning, without a vision for what she was doing, Jazzmin Monelle wrote a page and a half of a new story, took a nap, and in the evening awoke to firecrackers or distant gunshots. She looked out her third-story window into the alley below, and found a young, shirtless man playing percussion on an upturned bucket while facing the touristy sidewalk. She sat back down at her typewriter with the window open, wrote a full four pages, without thinking, to the accompaniment of the young man's beats, showered, and dressed to take a stroll around town.

Down in the streets there were streamers and paper lanterns hanging from power lines. Pumpkin-shaped taxis zoomed by, as multi-tongued pedestrians walked around and crossed the streets at will. An upright harmonium was positioned on the sidewalk, and a woman wearing a glowing violet dress played a somewhat familiar mazurka. Jazzmin Monelle wondered if this was her lot in life, to constantly hear music she could only half place, in a manner that would eventually drive her mad.

A blind woman around her age held a small stack of flyers and handed one to Jazzmin Monelle. It was a ticket for a cabaret show. As she walked along the sidewalk, the young woman held on to Jazzmin's arm, and seemed to be guiding her through the chaos. A man on a curb milked two goats as clients waited with their coins for their eight-ounce servings; by an intersection, young children played hopscotch over a labyrinthine diagram, which looped back to the beginning endlessly; flowerpots hung from apartment windows up above, and invisible stereos played their unique stations or maddening drones.

The sounds of the sea echoed all around, and Jazzmin Monelle paused to absorb this city that had once been so distant—that had existed for her only in books. The young blind woman let go of her arm and continued across a busy intersection, through the breaks in the high-strung traffic. Jazzmin Monelle watched her safely disappear, then looked up: she was standing under the sign of Café Teatro Sandoz, the venue advertised in the flyer in her hand.

She walked inside and was greeted by an empty vestibule.

Jazzmin looked for a box office or an usher, then made her way into the theater, amidst applause. A small crowd was giving a hearty standing ovation to performers, who were bowing and waving, blowing kisses at their generous audience from a small stage. Jazzmin Monelle shifted her shoulder bag and clapped along with everybody, admiring the robes and costumes of the actors. One of them was dressed as a minotaur, with an impressively crafted horned mask resting by the sweaty performer's side. As the audience began shuffling out, Jazzmin Monelle stayed to watch the actors congratulate one another with big smiles, and vanish behind the dark blue curtain.

In the vestibule on the other side of the theater stood a bar and lounge, where a piano player played a catchy ragtime number. A woman Jazzmin half recognized stood at the bar, holding a martini glass with two fingers, as if she was about to pin a thumbtack on a map—Jazzmin wondered if she had served this elegant woman before, maybe when she worked at Leroi's Diner back home.

"We must have similar tastes," the woman said to Jazzmin. "Could two encounters like this be called fate? Or is it just a plain old coincidence?"

Jazzmin thought this was clever, and placed her as the woman whose drink she had watched spill aboard the *Mandarina*. She ordered a ginger beer like she had then, and when the woman told the bartender to put it on her tab, Jazzmin recalled her name and said, "Mina."

"Aha," Mina said. And clinked her glass with Jazzmin Monelle's. "You didn't forget. Short for Wilhelmina. It's an uncommon name, I'm aware. I never expect people to remember it the first couple times they hear it, honestly. I'm impressed. And you're the writer?"

They found a table in the lounge near the piano player, who immediately went on break after they sat down, which seemed to distress Mina. But once the level of noise from the bar and lounge rose, she felt at ease again.

Unprompted, Mina revealed to Jazzmin Monelle intimate details of her life's burdens. Her father had been a wealthy paint manufacturer who divorced her mother when she was a girl. Mina had never felt she was the rebellious daughter, because unlike her sister McKenza, she'd finished college, and unlike her sister Carmen, she'd never switched political parties just to marry a corrupt lobbyist back home.

Mina ordered another martini and demanded that Jazzmin Monelle tell her everything about her life, too. Jazzmin hesitated, then did her best to condense her life experience for a complete stranger. How her parents had crossed the southern border as a newlywed couple; how her father had died from a treatable but complex pulmonary infection; how she'd had a fever and discovered the purpose of her life was reading and writing fiction and publishing books.

Mina's needlepoint gaze drifted. Jazzmin stopped talking, fearing she'd bored her, then Mina stood up, waved one arm toward her husband, Daryl, who approached them and said, "Making sure you're okay over here."

Daryl extended his hand to Jazzmin. "Ah, good to see you again, here on dry land, where it's more pleasant. Away from the terror of the Atlantic. I'm joining the band for some drinks, you two interested in coming along?"

Mina downed the rest of her beverage, and the three of them walked out of Café Teatro Sandoz. The gaslights haloed the sidewalks, and as they walked through the port city under the blue twilight, it seemed to Jazzmin Monelle that this was the hour that suited this place, and she imagined the scene painted on a large canvas as she walked below the paper lanterns. A young man played music from a calendolia, accompanied by a young girl on a fandolin, and both of them were painted on the canvas in her mind, too.

The trio took a sharp turn into an alley, where the world went pitch black, and Jazzmin Monelle became aware of the smoky quartz moon. The alley was in its natural state: filthy, with dumped trash and abandoned, moldy furniture. They reached an intersection where many buildings met, and a choice had to be made about how to proceed. Daryl pulled Mina's shoulder, and she reached for Jazzmin's wrist, and they continued walking.

The alley got narrower, and Jazzmin Monelle felt the image of a snake slithering through a crevice between the concrete and the red earth. About fifty feet ahead there was a dim yellow bulb softly illuminating the vandalized and much-faded painting of a tall angel with its left eye open and the other eye closed. Daryl ran one hand along the wall until he felt a cylindrical impression and pressed it hard. A muted buzz rang from the other side of the wall. The putrid layers of all the filthy alleys in the world crept closer and closer around them.

A thumping was heard from the wall behind the angel—Daryl, Mina, and Jazzmin Monelle stepped back, and the winking angel turned out to be a back door. A silhouetted figure wearing a top hat and a purple-and-black suit pushed it open from the inside. The figure motioned them in like a bouncer, then recognized Daryl, and they shared a mutual *gotcha* laugh.

Jazzmin Monelle took one last look at the alley, which became the bottom of the ocean holding the wreck of an ancient ship, then shut the door. The group made its way between stacked boxes labeled as various liquors or sardines, beneath the clatter and drone of ventilation shafts and bundles of wool and buckets of silverware and dill pickles, then crossed a small bridge between two buildings, walked through a wide door, and entered a large ballroom with high ceilings, filled with people enraptured in wild celebration.

Mina hollered, hugged their top-hatted escort. Jazzmin Monelle admired the tall velvet curtains adorning the walls, the large band onstage playing a boozy jazz number, stringed and horned instruments stumbling through the wafts of smoke; a candelabra looked down on everyone with its thousand diamond eyes. Hanging even higher was a hard-to-spot person inside a cage, who threw confetti, feathers, and ticker tape from a tiger-striped pillowcase onto the dancing crowd below. A light palpitated from dim to pitch black, as red and dark blue beams bounced from mirrored Roman sculptures.

A woman sitting at a cluster of tables jumped up and screamed, "Daryl" over the band, and she hugged and kissed him—passionately, the way a lover does, with tongue and groping and sweaty hair. Jazzmin Monelle, of course, noticed this, and when she turned toward Mina, Mina smiled and tapped her on the shoulder as a signal to leave them alone. Jazzmin followed Mina, who ordered two sparkling drinks for each of them at the bar, and after they'd toasted and taken a first sip, a sailor emerged from the dance floor. In a buttered-up drawl, he asked Mina for a dance.

Mina accepted.

As she leaned against the bar, Jazzmin Monelle admired their dance to a solo fiddle number. Mina was an exceptional dancer—it was obvious to anyone paying attention. The sailor didn't have much to do as a result, and behaved mostly as a prop so Mina could burn a hole through admiring minds— her red shoes and long dress came alive, and one could easily see how we attach magical properties to things like shoes instead of giving credit to the skilled dancer wearing them.

As the song reached its coda, the lights in the venue came on. A tall-haired woman with an amplified voice walked in with two punky young men, and they started passing around clipboards. The woman announced they were members of the Terésa de Mier Liberation Army—and that everyone in attendance, if they were to continue throwing their elitist parties and enjoying the many cultural riches this city had to offer, also had to remember there was a civil war potentially about to break out. She demanded everyone sign one of the forms going around, print their name, and also state their nationality if they were foreigners.

The members of the band and the bartenders, along with the scores of partiers at the venue, signed their names. Everyone had adjusted to the unflattering fluorescent ceiling lights and was starting to crash from their highs. The person in the cage had long since stopped throwing down anything, and after the members of the band had all finished signing, the tuba player yelled at the person in the cage to give their information, and they yelled it back, and the clarinet player was given permission to sign on the caged person's behalf.

The embers of the festivities had managed to come to life again by the time the clipboard reached Mina and Jazzmin Monelle. After signing her name and peeking at Mina's information, Jazzmin learned that Mina was originally from a country she knew next to nothing about. The Terésa de Mier Liberation Army thanked everyone, made the revelers sing along to their short anthem, saluted, then exited the building. The lights were dimmed again, and the band broke into a 5/5 number to dig everyone out of their buzzkilled trench. People clapped and toasted the Rentists (*los rentístas*), which was the nickname given to the Terésa de Mier Liberation Army and its allies.

"Rentístas hasta el mas allá," a woman yelled—one of the Rentists' slogans: "Rentists until the great beyond" was the way Jazzmin Monelle translated it in her mind, since it was her first time hearing it. She looked over to Mina, who was tearing through a cigarette.

"What a night already, huh?"

Mina set her glass on the speakeasy bar counter, took Jazzmin's hand. "Let's get some fresh air," she said, batting away cigar smoke.

Outside, bottle rockets had been cast into the sky—gaslights illuminated the streets and sidewalks between the patches of white-stallion fog. Mina let go of Jazzmin's hand and both looked up as the millions of golden fireworks sparks turned green, then red, then blue, and disappeared completely. "What's the occasion?" Jazzmin asked.

"I don't know," Mina admitted, putting out her cigarette. "Felt we were around so many stuffy people in there, thought we could take a walk and get away from the loud music."

"No, I mean for the fireworks going off, and the party. Is today a holiday here?"

Over the polite laughter of passersby, Mina said, "Fireworks are illegal here, and they have been for years. The Rentists are fighting the revolution without weapons. Did you know that? It's the first revolution of its kind, that's why it really feels like things are happening, that things are finally *real*. So some Rentists started stealing ammunition from the fascists and converting it to fireworks. To get rid of the gunpowder safely. At first they were cheap-looking fireworks, but, as you can see, now they get pretty creative."

Mina offered her newly lit cigarette to Jazzmin and they shared it, until a young boy going around selling portioned dried noodles made a cautious smoking gesture toward them.

"Oh, right. Women can't be seen smoking in public here. I don't usually smoke, so I haven't given it much thought—"

"Nobody really enforces it," said Mina. She stubbed the cigarette out against a water hydrant and left it there.

The women purchased a couple of fruit cups from a street vendor, and as they walked among the throngs of people, it was easy to forget the worrisome rusted gears currently turning the larger world. A group of formally dressed youngsters lit sparklers, and Jazzmin Monelle wondered if sparklers were considered fireworks as well; then her attention wandered to an older woman standing on an apple box reciting words through a ripped-up-carton megaphone and reading from a book that didn't appear to be a religious text.

A clique of teenage girls in school uniforms and berets were openly smoking cigarettes, sitting at a table outside Casa Gallardine. They all wore stockings with various patterns strategically cut into the fabric, some subtle, some not so subtle. One of the girls extended her pack to Mina and Jazzmin. Mina took one cigarette, which she and Jazzmin agreed to share, and for the next eleven minutes they did, as Mina explained to Jazzmin the significance of the patterns in the stockings. Since teenage girls were forced to wear them, they'd created their own language of protest through the patterns, which disturbed parents and most other adults. Many schools and public places now had rules against patterned stockings.

When they reached Café Teatro Sandoz, Mina asked the young man working in the box office if there was a late-night one-act, and if it was okay to go in. He pointed at the hand-painted poster advertising the play *Great Headwounds in Underground Art Movements*, by a playwright Jazzmin Monelle had never heard of, Salamandra Cortina.

A small audience was gathered close to the stage, with many empty chairs behind them, and a clearly passed-out man on the floor in the back corner. Two chairs were placed about ten feet from each other on the stage, and between them was the prop of a nonsensical flow chart. The performers stood beside the chart, and in the humble program Jazzmin read that the characters were the Transcendentalist Poet and Suzanne.

The box office attendant had warned them that the play was approaching its climax, and as they found their seats the

Transcendentalist Poet said, "Have you read the headlines these hedgehogs are publishing? With the way things are going, I'd rather be amongst the foxes than the hedgehogs . . . if I may be completely honest."

Suzanne looked away from the Transcendentalist Poet and said to her, "I knew you'd say that. You're such a freak, for God's sake."

"But I'm serious," said the Transcendentalist Poet. "It has to do with their habits as a collective. Hedgehogs are snakes. The foxes are less likely to rat you out than the hedgehogs."

"Snakes? Rat you out?" exclaimed Suzanne. "You've been overusing those terms lately. 'Don't mess with this person, he seems like he'll rat you out,' you warn me. 'Oh, so-and-so is a snake.' Rat me out to who, exactly? Why are you so obsessed with this 'ratting out'?"

"Must you always interrupt me in the middle of an epiphany, Suzanne? You know darn well to who. Have you forgotten that there are novelists around every corner, stalking me for the precise moment they can put their manuscript in my hands? I'm just one person with a printing press. Not an army. Wait. Why are you saying this? Are you cornering me to reveal the name of my sources out loud? Is that it? Have you crossed over to the feds now? Are you wearing a wire on me?"

The Transcendentalist Poet tore open Suzanne's blouse, snapping a few buttons, to reveal beige underwear laced with a bronze wire and a battery pack taped to her back—the few folks in the theater leaned in, even Jazzmin and Mina, who were mesmerized by the performances.

"So it's been you," the Transcendentalist Poet said, "all along, Suzanne. Is this why my little grasshoppers froze like chess pieces after playing 'Old Wicked Annie from the Pampas'? Is this why the snooze machine, and the morning crows, no longer delay? Is this why my time zones ignore my English, Suzanne? Answer me!"

The play concluded in tragedy; the audience clapped politely for the performers. Jazzmin stood up to join them, along with Mina.

At the bar, alley cats and players from the performance were elevated with drinks and cigarettes. A third done with her cocktail, and perhaps inspired by the play, Mina said, "Did I mention that Daryl is my biological brother? My twin brother, actually."

She explained that the woman Daryl had kissed at the party was his real wife, Pauline, whom he'd had a scandalous relationship with since they were teenagers. To gain passage from overseas, Mina had had to pretend to be her brother's wife, and had even commissioned forged papers. Their parents disapproved of Daryl's marriage and had done everything in their power to stop him and Pauline from reuniting over the years.

Jazzmin had many questions. The way Mina told the story left significant gaps in the narrative, but the bottom line was understood: Mina was single and seen by her right-wing aristocratic family as problematic and rebellious. They somewhat blamed her for Daryl and Pauline's elopement, to which Mina had replied with raspberries and pride.

Jazzmin and Mina raised their drinks, and absorbed the alcohol with the complimentary peanuts and bread. The phonograph at the bar played a new style of music people called *jalénco*. Jazzmin noticed a gray-haired woman sitting in the rear corner with a glass of absinthe by her side. She was playing an accompaniment to the prerecorded music on a violin.

"That woman," Mina said, pointing. "Do you know who she is?"

Jazzmin replied in the negative.

When the song ended, Mina said, "Let's introduce ourselves."

But Jazzmin remained seated and resisted; for, of course, she could see who the woman was: Mata Rivereña, author of the novel *Piano Lifeboats*, released only six years prior, and which she had written in Romanian and translated herself into Spanish and English. The book had made a profound impression on Jazzmin Monelle during a time of great hardship. There was no way she could simply get up, just like that, and allow herself to be introduced to Rivereña in some dive bar. But before she knew it, that's what was happening, and she was clasping the hand of the master herself.

When Mata Rivereña shook Mina's hand, the lauded author said, "Your hands have the texture of sand dunes . . . let me feel them again. Yes. They are hands I've encountered only a few times before. You have what I refer to as *Helen's hands*. Is your name Helen, by chance?"

Mina retracted her hand during this exchange and turned bashful. "No," she responded. "I'm afraid it isn't."

The intro to a thirteenth-century Scottish song blared from the speakers. Mata Rivereña smiled at Jazzmin Monelle, excused herself, put the violin to her shoulder, and played along. She winked at Mina right before closing her eyes and submerging herself in the tune. Mina and Jazzmin expressed their gratitude by nodding and slightly bowing as they stepped back to their table.

A horn blared from the street, and an automobile screeched to a halt. People were heard running, a man screamed sexist slurs, then gunshots blasted. The drinkers and the bartender crouched as Mina pulled Jazzmin under a table.

The bar went dark, killing the music, as the hollering outside grew louder and more shots were fired—the only other thing that could be heard was Mata Rivereña's freestyle violin.

The bartender moved in a crabwalk over to Mata and implored her to stop playing. People on the ground took sips of their beverages and waited out the ensuing silence—a gloomy silence. Sobbing trickled in from the street, another man screamed in sorrow, then an automobile peeled away.

Jazzmin and Mina emerged from under the table and walked outside with the other patrons as the bar's electricity came back on. A group of people were huddled across the street—Jazzmin saw a pool of blood on the ground, which she at first mistook for a spilled drink.

An older man, in tears, said to nobody in particular: "They are just schoolgirls . . . only smoking cigarettes. Who were they bothering? Nobody."

On the sidewalk were two shot teenage girls wearing berets and school uniforms, with their stockings cut in patterns of their own design—one of them was unconscious, while the other squeezed the hand of a young, ragged boy holding her in his arms as she bled profusely.

An older woman got onto her knees next to the shot teenage girls and yelled for someone to do something, for an ambulance to be summoned, a doctor to be found, somebody, for God's sake, needed to do something, the girls required urgent medical attention.

Jazzmin and Mina felt shocked and useless, then, along with the throng of witnesses, rapidly shifted from a partying mode to one of doom.

The unconscious girl was still wearing her beret; she'd been shot in the abdomen; the other girl's braids were coming undone while her right shoulder bled the darkest blood Jazzmin had ever seen, even in movies. In a few moments, all those present felt something vanishing from deep inside them, like the fabric of time unspooled—the last gasp of breath from the bleeding girl. Everyone felt her ghost holding their hand, as the sobbing older woman embraced the girl's body and she died.

Mina walked away, realizing she still had her mixed drink in hand. The dead braided girl had been the one who, earlier in the night, had offered her a cigarette, and Jazzmin recognized that the boy holding her was the boy who had warned them against public smoking.

A middle-aged woman arrived on the scene, announced herself as a medical doctor, and confirmed what nobody could bring themselves to admit.

By then Mina and Jazzmin were quite removed from the group. Mina poured out the drink in her hand, thought twice about shattering the glass, before carefully placing it by a winged-hog altar near the storm drainage.

Jazzmin kept an ear out for ambulances that never came.

As Mina walked about five feet ahead of her under the

gaslights, Jazzmin thought to ask, "That girl. They shot her dead? For smoking cigarettes openly in the street?"

Mina didn't face her when she mumbled a response.

They walked the empty streets and passed a couple of trolleys carrying early-shift workers and late-night clubbers; a white carriage with a man smacking his lips at his horse; people sleeping in every crevice of the city, sometimes with leashed pet cats and dogs.

Mina and Jazzmin continued along a path near the jetties where the waves were breaking. To avoid the dark boardwalk, they took an illuminated trail toward the twin lighthouses—the one nearest to them was the only one with a working light, and to Jazzmin Monelle that solved the mystery of the occasional flapping skylight. Mina unlocked the door to the second lighthouse, Jazzmin followed her up the winding stairs. As she trailed Mina in quiet obeisance she looked down at her own hands and remembered that the Greek Sirens had been depicted as appendages of a larger beast.

Variations of this Greek myth flashed before Jazzmin Monelle the following morning, lying on a queen-size mattress in a large room at the top of the lighthouse, with Mina holding her hand. She got up before Mina and in the little lavatory downstairs she saw the parts of her face crusted over from crying in the dark, and washed up in the low-flow sink. Back in the room upstairs, she sat on the only chair by the screenless window and placed the notebook she always carried on the concrete sill. She watched the sun stretch its arms along the expansive beach, and asked herself if it was supposed to look that way, like an oil spill instead of a sea. Mina lay on the bed, still wearing her dress from the night before, and Jazzmin saw how long and auburn Mina's hair was in the morning light.

From a distance, she spotted a group of young men gathering to do stretches by the shore. A small family was pushing a baby stroller toward a large mound of trash that Jazzmin Monelle found disturbing, then as she gave it a closer look she saw it was the beached gray whale people had been gossiping about the previous day. She gazed at the decaying plastic flesh and felt again the yearning to sob. Farther up the shore, she saw a fisherman pushing a boat into the low tide with the help of two small girls. A young man arrived kicking a soccer ball, and joined the stretching group, passed the ball to another young man, who then kicked it vertically and tapped it several times with his forehead.

When Jazzmin looked back toward the bed, it was empty, and before she knew it, she was at work on a new short story. Some time passed, then she became aware of a sunflower-yellow robe moving about the room. Mina had bathed, and Jazzmin admired her dark feet, legs, and exposed arms for the first time. In the moments that followed, something like a word came to life—the word "imperishable" sprouted from the earth, then flowered its children to gaze at the moon for twenty-eight glorious days, to push it along, to wade in its melted mirror across alleyways and tilted horizons.

Jazzmin Monelle's notebook pages fluttered in the cool Atlantic breeze, and outside, the kicking of the ball and hollering could be heard as the shirtless, copper-skinned teenage boys played a soccer match, while up in the second lighthouse,

Jazzmin Monelle made passionate love to a woman for the first time in her life.

Ripe, earthy pears and tiger-striped bananas in a bowl, sitting on a wooden table before an oval window facing the ocean. The lighthouse door bolted from the inside. Nothing could climb up or down those steps sneakily enough to avoid being heard from the top. The wandering sun shone through the window onto the bed, casting its rays like buttered treasure coins.

Jazzmin Monelle paced in the small confines of the lighthouse, eating her meal, swaying as if to a distant tarantella. She stopped several times in front of a four-by-six glossy photo of a painting tacked to the wall. The image had initially creeped her out, but after circling it a few times she felt a fellowship with it. The painting depicted the abnormally large, groaning, severed head of a bearded middle-aged man; by his side was a young, androgynous teenager—a child, possibly—holding the sword that had presumably done the severing. Jazzmin finally asked Mina about the image, as she sat at the small table breakfasting and doing the previous day's crossword puzzle.

Mina told her she'd torn it from a magazine featuring an art gallery's permanent collection—but she'd remembered the painting as a staple of her own girlhood, during the time when she was attending boarding school, when she'd yearned to be the young David the way some kids yearn to be rock stars.

Jazzmin Monelle pressed her for more details, and finally Mina recounted the story of how she'd attended Vesper

Hymns Academy, an all-girls boarding school that years ago burned to the ground (upon mentioning this detail, Mina laughed). The image of the severed head was the only work of art that had hung in the entire school and survived the fire. Mina elaborated that the painting was a depiction of the biblical story of David and Goliath. The gaze of the child who was cradling the severed head had been a thing of great romance and beauty to her classmates back then. By her senior year, Mina and a friend were downright convinced that David was not a young man, but a young woman. They circulated the rumor that this young woman had been robbed of her legacy way back in biblical times, and still today, given that it was she who had slain Goliath.

Together the women finished their breakfast and got dressed, for they'd agreed to go to Jazzmin's place to pick up some things, then wander around the town. On the way, Mina rolled her eyes and complained about the leftist paper's word choice in its headlines, which she felt had been downplaying current atrocities with innocuous, even cynical language.

They stopped at a *vinoteca* for a glass of rosé, and behind the bar was a digital television airing a live news broadcast. It took Jazzmin about twenty-six seconds of viewing, sitting on a stool, to realize it was footage from something happening in her home country. An off-screen reporter held a microphone in front of a determined woman with a green bandanna holding her hair back and a black mourning bandanna tied around her right arm; cradled on her left arm was a breast-feeding child. The chyron on the screen read: ANGÉLICA BAR-RIENTOS, REBEL LEADER IN THREE RIVERS, TEXAS. The volume was muted, and no captions ran across the screen, as a montage of burning buildings and armed troops played on a smaller screen within.

"That city is in Texas, huh? Is that close to where you live?" Mina asked, downing her chilled sparkling rosé.

"Not really," Jazzmin replied, her eyes glued on the woman from Three Rivers. "I live in the Midwest. But I'd like to live there one day." The camera often tried to unframe the baby and exposed breast, but the woman seemed to insist on them being seen. "To see what it's all about. This is down in Texas. A bunch of tech companies and big money were moving into this desert town," Jazzmin explained, "supposedly to give rural people opportunities after the oil bust, but it was always obviously for cheap labor. Look at all the buildings! They managed to turn this small town of Three Rivers into a big city pretty quickly, but then all the investors pulled everything out at the last minute after they found a way to get even cheaper labor in another state. Nobody living in Three Rivers even wanted the outsiders anyway, except the politicians. Now look at all the chaos they've created for the poor people who live there. And they're blaming it on this activist, Angélica, who has been organizing against the tech companies all along."

Jazzmin Monelle signaled the barkeep to raise the volume, but the barkeep misunderstood and instead changed the channel to a frenetic game show. By the time he'd figured out what Jazzmin meant and turned it back, the news coverage had moved on.

The following day was to be the last Jazzmin could legally stay in the country with her temporary visa. She had already purchased a nonrefundable plane ticket. While packing her typewriter and suitcase and arranging her pages, she lamented how long into her getaway it had taken to connect with Mina.

They shared a parting meal, a parting drink, a passionate parting kiss. Jazzmin Monelle was in a daze during that final stroll through the airport with Mina. In the years ahead she'd look back on this stroll and her throat would clench with regret at not having found the words to express what she knew in hindsight to be deep love.

As her ticket was scanned and passport stamped, she was passively interrogated by the green-suited officers. Jazzmin Monelle, instead of answering, felt the urge to ask the officers if they were doing well—they all seemed irritated, sweaty, dehydrated, and on edge.

Rumors of widespread protests were circulating among the passengers on the flight back home, and a few hours before touching down, the pilot began giving regular updates on the concerning situation, which for the moment appeared to be frenzied but safe. He urged passengers to be cautious as they deboarded, and to have a nice day. It was impossible to miss the hundreds of protesters with their signs, surgical masks, and painted faces. They sat on the floor in nonviolent clusters throughout the airport, and nothing appeared to have gotten out of hand.

A sinister detail that took several days for Jazzmin to register was that the police were wielding bayonet rifles— something she, until then, had seen only in history book illustrations and period films. SWAT trucks were parked beyond the glass airport dome, past the loading-and-unloading area in front of the airport, along with some armored tank-like vehicles she couldn't identify.

On the cab ride home, society seemed to be functioning—green meant go, shops flashed OPEN signs, gravity clasped to everyone's skin. Jazzmin had a sudden change of heart and told the driver to drop her off in front of the Crown Royale Hotel. She dragged her bags into the lobby, and luckily the hotel had a room immediately available. Jazzmin set her bags by the door and collapsed onto the bed, as ambulances and fire trucks blared their sirens below along Windsor Avenue.

A sense of relief washed over her. She was grateful to claim this time before going home. Jazzmin felt distant from whatever horrors had developed in her city, state, and country, and now that she was in the middle of it again, she felt the palpitations of people's terror.

Jazzmin longed for Mina. She stared out the window at a neighboring building that seemed more like a phantom ocean liner moored in a foggy harbor and wondered if she should board it, as hot tears fell down her cheeks. The ocean liner departed without her, and she felt stranded and lonelier than ever, caught between timelines that were not her own. Jazzmin Monelle feared this was the point she'd always come back to during future depressions, the point when she went from being someone's lover to a mere memory; the point when she went from being someone's daughter to lost in a kernel of space expanding into a past, present, and future.

Early the following day, Jazzmin discovered that the apartment building where she'd spent her formative years had been entirely vandalized. It was surreal to walk through the structure and feel as if nobody had lived there for decades. Both flights of stairs were graffitied and charred and stank of urine, with clothes and broken appliances scattered over the widespread shattered glass. She tried not to panic upon seeing what had become of the apartment she'd shared with her mother. Everything was gone—either moved out or looted. Jazzmin Monelle had been on her trip for mere weeks and couldn't imagine what had occurred. She was frantically dialing numbers to patch her through to the nearest hospitals when she heard a loud voice echo in the hallway of her floor.

Desperate for answers, she rushed out in search of the voice, and found her neighbor, the creator of Spice Orchard Sauce, Filomeno—a man who, in many ways, she'd grown to feel was a sort of benefactor, straight out of a Victorian novel. He was disheveled, with his graying mustache going every which way, shirt untucked under his blazer. He looked like he'd barely survived running across a collapsing bridge.

Jazzmin Monelle felt he required medical attention. He seemed lost, as lost, probably, as she was. "Filomeno," Jazzmin said. "Where is everybody? Where's my mother?"

Filomeno, mournfully looking toward the windows as if expecting the arrival of something from the skies, said, "They took them to Bethesda."

"Who took who to Bethesda, Filomeno?"

"The rats."

"Who are the rats?"

"You can see," he whispered. "Anti-immigrant rats. They get upset when you call them that, don't let them hear you."

"Bethesda the hospital or the jail?"

"Both."

"Why? Where did they take my mother?"

Filomeno leaned against a graffitied wall with peeling, blackened wallpaper as he began to weep. Jazzmin Monelle called a cab, and when she invited him to leave the building with her, Filomeno waved her away. He wanted to be left alone in his destroyed home.

When she'd made it down to the second story, she ran into blue-eyed, hooded teenagers pouring oil over the staircase, and watched as they lit the oil on fire. The kids saw Jazzmin Monelle and howled at her—she feared the building would burn down and Filomeno would be trapped. Jazzmin climbed back up the stairs, but her old neighbor was gone. She yelled his name—"Filomeno! Filomeno!"—up and down the wet hallways and into the ransacked rooms, but she couldn't find him. Jazzmin made it out the emergency exit to the ground floor, and only after she found the cab and hopped in did she begin to catch her breath.

She rode to the Bethesda jail first, and when its records didn't yield signs of her mother, she rode over to the hospital, whose records did. The hospital was over capacity, with people lying on stretchers and attached to respirators along the hallways. Jazzmin Monelle felt she was walking through a hospital near a war zone.

She was given an N95 mask, and was guided by a nurse into a room with curtains separating it into eight partitions. In the partition by the window lay Silvia, her mother. She was unconscious, attached to a respirator, and along her hands and arms Jazzmin saw bulging dark veins under taut and yellowing brown skin, glazed under the pallid light of an indifferent, cloudy sky. A nurse brought her a short stool, and Jazzmin sat by her mother, holding her hand. She wept quietly, trying to not disturb the other patients, focused on the beeping machines, the low voices from the fluorescent-lit hallway. As she sobbed and looked out the window at the overpass billboards, Jazzmin was grateful it was her mother who'd been given this view.

Days after she'd disembarked from the *Mandarina*, Jazzmin learned, a team of the newly formed Immigration Federal Unit had raided her apartment building, in one of many calculated sweeps across the city. The officers had sounded the building fire alarm, caught everyone off guard in the middle of the night. Jazzmin's mother, as she rushed into the hallway, was asked to present her papers at gunpoint, like everyone else. She did so as officers forced others against the wall or onto the ground, arresting them before crying children and protesting elders. There was even a barking dog somewhere, and squawking caged birds from Doña Sarita's apartment. The officers had scanned Silvia's papers and instructed her to evacuate the building and stay out of their way, or risk danger.

Silvia had carefully climbed down the stairs, since she found the elevator was off-limits. When she got to the curb, Silvia had slipped on a puddle of foam the officers were spraying into the eyes of dissenters and anyone who resisted. Her left ankle twisted, and it took an ambulance three hours to arrive. At first, she'd showed the normal signs of convalescence for a person her age, but then doctors had found inflammation in her bones that had spread throughout her body.

Lamentably (their word) there was nothing that could be done—it was a rare inflammation that, regardless of her sprain, and probably due to years of working on her feet with only passable footwear, had been rigidly manifesting throughout her body.

Silvia Morelia Cruz was laid to rest on Palm Sunday, and, aside from Jazzmin Monelle, only a few former coworkers from her days at the state library attended the ceremony. It rained after the funeral, and Jazzmin took the bus to get a couple of powdered doughnuts and a cup of flavored coffee at the same bakery where her mother had treated her as a girl on special occasions, when they crossed over to the part of town where the rents were high.

For weeks on end, as the state of the world deteriorated every which way, Jazzmin Monelle spent her savings on corn liquor and her evenings drinking it, listening to AM talk radio, often undressed, in a cheap apartment she rented. She got plastered only rarely, keeping the blues steady, easing toward darker shades. There were a couple of neighborhood taverns with jukeboxes she enjoyed when she did leave the house, and she had love affairs that never lasted, with sober bartenders and drunk locals alike.

There came a time when the invading fog of the exterior world caught up with the fog emerging from her subconscious— there were sunshine and coffee grounds and empty bottles of mezcal and red wine, ashes and books, and a knock on the apartment door, which Jazzmin answered on something like a morning. Through the protective latches and bars, a man in a fucking hat demanded, "Is your name Jazzmin Monelle Rivas?"

Barely looking at the shape of this man, Jazzmin Monelle said, "I didn't burn that goddamn building down."

The man in the fucking hat, thinking he had misheard, said, "Excuse me, ma'am?"

Jazzmin Monelle yelled: "I. Did not. Burrrrrrrrrn. That idiotic building. Down. For the last time. It was somebody who looked like me. Either present me with your papers and identification now, or I'm closing the door. So get the fuck out of my face."

The man in the fucking hat, eager to settle the confusion, held up a hardcover book: *I Was a Teenage Brain Parasite* by Jazzmin Monelle Rivas, the title in red Gothic lettering. The man in the fucking hat noticed the person behind the door looking suspiciously at the cover, and said: "Is your name the same name as the person who wrote this?"

Jazzmin Monelle shut the door to her apartment softly.

After a minute or so the man in the fucking hat gave up—he had a couple more leads and addresses to check out. As he was halfway toward the staircase, Jazzmin Monelle opened the door to her apartment all the way and appeared in jeans and an oversize gray sweater. Though she was ambivalent about the man's authority, he had been carrying the first copy she'd ever seen of a book she'd written, and for this alone she presented him with her identification.

The man in the fucking hat was a low-key private investigator—"Just a retired journalist with a permit," he told her.

He'd been hired by the New York publishing company to track down Jazzmin Monelle, whose address no longer matched the publisher's records and whom nobody at the company could get hold of. Heidi Monrow's headquarters had moved office buildings twice in eight months and all her assistants had turned over as many times. Though most of Morik Books' front list had been trimmed or considerably delayed, a famous pop sensation had stated in various interviews how excited she was to read *I Was a Teenage Brain Parasite*, based on the title alone, and preordering demand started unexpectedly to build. It was a shocker that nobody at the publishing house or at its parent company could've seen coming.

Jazzmin Monelle agreed to take an early flight the following day to the legendary publishing district of New York City. She gathered a few things in her bag, locked her apartment, and it was still morning as she took the AirTrain service with the man in the fucking hat. Once in the city, she followed him to the seventh floor of the Beaumont Building, and after making it through a maze of hallways they reached the front desk, where there was a bow-tied young man waiting to escort Jazzmin Monelle to the main office.

Heidi Monrow and the six other publishing people working at Morik Books were already sharing a bottle of bubbly champagne when they greeted her. Jazzmin was handed a glass with a generous pour, Heidi slurred her words through a toast, and the man in the fucking hat joined them as he waited for a check from the parent company to be cut.

Considering the systematic defunding of libraries and public literacy programs, the fact that bookstores were not doing so well, and that society's economic problems left people with little money and free time for buying books, *I Was a Teenage Brain Parasite* did remarkably well in certain demographics.

Weeks after she'd earned out her advance and received her first royalty statement, Jazzmin Monelle pulled a maduro cigar box out from a drawer by her typewriter desk. She'd kept it buried in the back, behind unlabeled files and old monographs she'd collected for light research like *The Brontë Family's Landscapes* and *Do You Know the Difference Between a Bog and a Fen?* The cigar box contained various postcards of paintings and landscapes. One of the postcards was of the painting *David with the Head of Goliath* by Claude Vignon. They were all unmailed and addressed to the same person: Mina Johnson.

Jazzmin Monelle considered the deportations and revocations of people's passports occurring all over the country as she sifted through the postcards. She wondered what her mother would have opined about the current political climate, what witticisms she'd have cracked about these bleak, hostile surroundings. With displaced determination, Jazzmin Monelle booked a one-way flight to the city that held the one she loved.

At the airport she took a taxi that dropped her off close to Camiseta Beach. It was morning and she could feel the shore's grand theater under her jet lag, smelled frying butter and dark-roast coffee crashing along with drowned-out music and distant waves.

The twin lighthouses appeared beyond the taxi's unadorned rearview mirror, tilted in different directions, as if their opposite ends were sinking into the rocks. When she'd paid her fare and gotten out, a beam of light revealed that the door to the second lighthouse was cracked open. She banged on it with an open palm and yelled, "Aló."

"Aló," a voice from the top of the lighthouse yelled back; crawling sounds of aluminum shook the structure as Jazzmin Monelle climbed the stairs and the person up top climbed down. Daryl appeared with a face full of tears, carrying a lantern, looking more the color of fire than human. He recognized Jazzmin after a confusing initial exchange. Daryl shook her hand, embraced her, then fell apart with watery tears until she managed to get him to keep climbing. She offered him water from her bag.

"I thought you were Helena," he said.

"What do you mean, Daryl? Where is Mina?"

"My name is not Daryl. It's Daniel. Sorry. But when we met there were certain precautions that had to be taken."

After many pauses filled with anguish and regret, Daniel managed to get across the story leading up to Helena's (Mina's actual name) death. Jazzmin Monelle learned that Daniel and Helena had had connections in their country to forge papers for him and his twin sister to evade authorities. Helena's alleged crime started with not having respect for any of her suitors, and one of the most prominent reported her to the authorities when he discovered her sexual inclinations through a private eye. In a pact with Daniel, Helena changed her name for the sake of the fake papers. Since he'd done his studies in America, Daniel had passed as her American husband, and Helena hid out in the lighthouse—a property inherited from a distant relative, who'd initially been stationed here, before the more advanced, neighboring lighthouse rendered his occupation obsolete.

Eventually Daniel managed to calm down enough for him and Jazzmin to take a stroll. They sat at the sidewalk table of a bistro called Pavaronerón to have a few drinks, and ordered light confections. Daniel revealed that Helena had walked out into the sea. The authorities believed she was caught by the riptide, because they found her on a northern beach, twenty-five kilometers away. He hypothesized it'd been a tragic accident: Daniel refused to believe Helena's death was by her own hand.

At the brink of the waitstaff's shift change, Daniel and Jazzmin closed out their tab and strolled back toward the lighthouse, where he handed her its heavy dungeon-master keys. "Due to your proximity to my sister . . ." was all he could say, however awkwardly. Daniel lived two hours away, and he'd been taking weekly trips to sit in Helena's room at the lighthouse. He got a kick out of the fact that Jazzmin had brought along her portable typewriter, and he typed his contact information on a blank page without her permission. Then he walked downstairs in a sober manner and eventually yelled, "Goodbye."

On Jazzmin's first night alone in the lighthouse, she made herself chamomile tea and listened to the waves crash in absolute darkness. She was afraid she would fall apart if she lay on the mattress, so in the morning she awoke with neck and back pain from sleeping with her head on the concrete sill.

The small postcard photo—of the young, beautiful David with the head of Goliath in its natural state by his side—was still tacked on the wall, with curled corners. Jazzmin's crying arrived like a slow train—one barely seen and heard at a distance, then wildly inescapable. She dropped onto the mattress, clutching and wrestling with it as if it was the ghost of Helena herself that she writhed with.

It was difficult, but Jazzmin Monelle worked hard to not fall into the same destructive patterns she'd cultivated after her mother passed away. She bought running shoes and did her best to jog on the beach each day at dawn, where she noticed that bones large and small were scattered, but none of them were ever human, and she ran through a group of young men playing soccer, and the people who made their lives up and down the shore.

One morning upon waking, Jazzmin Monelle decided not to jog, and instead bought coffee, oyster mushrooms, yogurt, nuts, and bread, and brought it all back to the lighthouse. She'd set her typewriter on the table by the oval window, with the bowl of fruit and a jug of water within reach. She went through her nonsensical notes as well as a jumble of character sketches and story lines for her new idea. The shoddy illustration of the setting of this novel, "Our Brother Branwell Academy for Girls," took up an entire two-page spread.

She had jotted micro-plots and monologue snippets for her main characters. The protagonists are teenage twins named Pride and Prejudice, and they attend an academy named after Branwell Brontë, the renowned writer of such exemplary novels for women as *Jane Eyre*, *Wuthering Heights*, and *The Tenant of Wildfell Hall*, among others. The older woman who is the director of the academy is known as the Director, or Madame

Director, and from the beginning it becomes clear she has a peculiar mole on her left cheek that later becomes a spider growing beneath her skin in a rather painful manner. As the narrative progresses, her pain contrasts with the increasing horror and rage of not only Pride and Prejudice but all the other girls attending the academy, when they discover the truth about the authorship of these beloved novels.

These were the only details Jazzmin Monelle Rivas was more or less sure of as she sat there in the lighthouse before her typewriter and a blank page. She turned on a little radio and set it far enough away that it would echo throughout the lighthouse and she could still ignore it. Though she knew she'd dedicate the work to Helena, she had to save setting the dedication to paper until the end.

At the top middle of a blank page she typed the title: *Brother Brontë*, and manually added the diaeresis using a black-ink pen.

Then, as if tearing apart a fox with her bare hands, she began to type what would become the unedited beginning of her novel, with the words "Pulling at her patterned stockings in the empty ambergris gallery, Prejudice struck a pose and made a face she once considered to be very nineteenth-century. It was a pose she'd associated with the boy poet A. Rimbaud, and one she saw again presently, standing before a painting by the seventeenth-century painter Claude Vignon, of David with the groaning, severed head of Goliath . . ."

Book Three

WEEKS BEFORE THE ATTEMPTED ASSASSINATION of Mayor Pablo Henry Crick and the destruction of the Big Tex Fish Cannery, Bettina Argyle was abruptly discharged as a worker-mother. The morning it happened, she lay in her bunk, wide awake but with her eyes closed, before the alarm sounded for the early-bird shift, as had been her routine since she'd switched from the graveyard shift seven years ago. She concentrated on a red dot beckoning her like a distant star beyond the fuzzy darkness of her eyelids. The red dot became larger as she floated closer to it in her half-asleep brain. It inflated like a balloon in the Thanksgiving parades of her youth. When she stood before the red dot, Bettina saw that it was actually a crisp red rose, sprouting at eye level from a crevice in a gargantuan dark wall. As she reached out to pluck the rose, three successive belches sprayed from the ceiling speakers, and she got up, along with a few other worker-mothers, for the first shift of a new day.

Bettina hit the showers and snuck in a cigarette before breakfast, stared at a yard with orange groves and daisies growing wildly beyond the northwestern perimeter fence. Bettina knew this was the only time that day when she'd be able to smell the heather-scented dawn without breathing in the miasma of processed verdillo fish.

A young pylon she'd made friends with, who occasionally

granted her certain liberties, signaled her with his bayonet rifle to hurry up.

Bettina stubbed out the cigarette, put the butt in her little plastic pouch, and walked to the mess hall. There she said good morning to her closest friends, worker-mothers like herself who had been there since Big Tex's founding over ten years ago: Katrinne, Sunset, Shamala, and Emilia, and when Bettina got in line to grab a tray, she remembered the recent death of Norway, the first worker-mother she'd become close with inside the fish cannery.

She ignored the armed pylons, as usual, and when it was her turn she chose the apple oatmeal option over the slimy eggs that came with cardboard corn tortillas and something called *chorixo*.

Bettina breakfasted alone, and everyone had learned to leave her be, since privacy and personal silence were coveted things at Big Tex. Sitting on one of the plastic yellow chairs in the pink cafeteria, Bettina stretched as far as she could the eleven minutes they gave all worker-mothers for breakfast, thinking of the book she'd recently finished reading, *Ghosts in the Zapotec Sphericals*.

Shortly before starting it, she'd realized what it was about the title that had initially piqued her curiosity: the word "sphericals" was also the word Norway had used to describe her hallucinations as she lay dying of pneumonia. Bettina remembered Norway reaching her hands out in her delirium, trying to grab one of the sphericals revolving above her bed. In her memory, Bettina could see Norway's face glowing orange and red from the orbs. Bettina now imagined these orbs in front of herself, too, as she finished her oatmeal and reached out with her hand, wondering what an orb would feel like closed in her fist.

She got up, discarded her compostables, stacked her tray, and made her way through the wide hall that led to the fields of verdillo fish in the fish cannery. Sunset was popping gum as Bettina caught up to her.

"Did you hear what's happening outside, in Three Rivers?" Sunset asked Bettina in a whisper.

"I did not," said Bettina, not mindful of her own tone.

Pylons relaxed their watch on the most senior worker-mothers, since it was widely known they were the least likely demographic to rebel. One time, at a card game during a work break, it had surprised even Bettina when Sunset told her: "Why do they bother with these handsome pylons standing over us still? Can't they see we prefer it in here to out there? It's not perfect, but neither is living in the city. In here at least we have the comfort of knowing we are feeding our children, that they're eating right, while their dads are out paving streets, or fighting wars, or who knows where. Out there, it's a nightmare trying to score a ration card to work, to get a can of soup or bottled water. No, thank you. You never know if there's gonna be electricity or gas in the winter, either. At least here we are part of a system that's holding up the social order."

Bettina had nodded and agreed, mostly because she dreaded having any kind of conflict with Sunset—their most minor dis-agreements tended to drag on, and their entire free time could be taken up with clarifying and apologizing to each other. The more she thought about these words of Sunset's, during work and on her breaks, the more Bettina looked around and noticed that maybe it wasn't just Sunset who preferred to have order in her life in exchange for personal liberty.

Sunset and Bettina waited in line to scan their work cards, and as they neared the fields of verdillo fish pools, Sunset said, "The people outside are protesting and rioting. They're burning cars and buildings, and who knows what they'll burn next. It makes me a little nervous, gotta say."

Thankfully, Bettina thought, they worked in different sectors: Sunset near the entrance of the fish cannery in sector 08, Bettina in sector 47, so the two women parted ways after this exchange.

Since she'd turned fifty-five, it had been Bettina's job to haul a barrel of verdillo fish after it got filled by the other worker-mothers. She'd slip a dolly under each barrel and wheel it a hundred yards into a tunnel and dump the contents onto a conveyor belt that moved the verdillo fish toward the peeling stage of production before they got canned. By this point in her career, Bettina had held every position at the fish cannery, excluding in the label department and on the clerical side that sorted the worked hours and the worker-mothers' dependents, who were then granted rations in Three Rivers. She'd been the timekeeper of several pools of verdillo fish, with a chronometer always at hand; she'd pulled bushels of verdillo with ungloved hands and had calluses from the razor-sharp bones that often pierced through the fish as they slapped wildly. Bettina had worked in the kitchen, and tweaked the recipe for sloppy joes using a combination of salts and spices, but working so closely with the food gave her an eating disorder that, with intervention from fellow worker-mothers, she had eventually been able to overcome.

Wheeling the verdillo fish barrels, a job the majority of worker-mothers dreaded, since it required serious repetitive heavy lifting, was mind-numbing enough—with intervals of waiting while barrels got filled—that Bettina had moments of free thinking and imagination, so she considered this position adequate.

During what was destined to be her final shift as a worker-mother, Bettina obsessed over the climax of *Ghosts in the Zapotec Sphericals*. In the novel, the Zapotec people live on their own planet, which is also something like an organic spaceship. Floating sphericals, which are orbs of light that act as statues on this planet, maintain the equilibrium of all its living things. One day the orbs become haunted by an imbalance within time and space that veers the planet off its natural course. During a debate between the genderless leaders, the Zapotec people are introduced to an idea by the only one of the elders who'd remained quiet throughout. This elder's idea is to bring forward one person—one specific person, who lives a specific life in a specific time and place—and then present to this person the dilemma of the haunted sphericals. This person, the elder insists, will hold the solution. When the other leaders ask who this person could be, everyone is surprised to hear the name of an earthling. They are all further taken aback to hear that this earthling is blind and the director of the Biblioteca Nacional de Buenos Aires, located in a time scale in the middle of the twentieth century. Not the library's first blind director, nor its second blind director, but in fact the third man destined to lose his vision while leading that distinguished institution. In the novel, this third blind director is referred to as *The Man Whose Name We Shall Not Speak*. Immediately, the Zapotecs summon their most astute, trustworthy tracker to pierce the space-time continuum and bring this human to save their haunted sphericals and aggrieved planet.

After the reader receives an exhausting introduction to this troubled but dedicated tracker, and follows a savage journey through space and time, the blind library director is brought before the committee of Zapotec leaders and elders. Upon hearing the nature of their dilemma, the blind director asks that certain texts be brought to him, which the tracker then retrieves. The tracker is also chosen by the blind director to read aloud, sometimes repeatedly, specific passages of these texts. Moments after the readings, the blind library director asks the Zapotecs to join him in complete silence. As nature and reality within the Zapotec world begin to be stripped apart like an old car, with earthquakes, tornadoes, and lightning, hot tea and snacks are brought to the blind library director.

Finally, he requests two simple things: a tall mirror, and a red rose. The exhausted tracker pierces space and time once again, and retrieves said things from Planet Earth. Before being handed the rose, the blind director instructs the tracker to position the mirror before him so the director's body is reflected from head to toe. The Zapotec planet is a powder keg by then—the blind man holds the red rose by the stem using his index finger and thumb, as his entire body's reflection faces the leaders and elders. The rose in his hand rapidly ages as it looks back at itself in the mirror, then turns to dust, while all around, ghosts howl in tortured agony and are exorcised from the planet's sacred sphericals.

The Zapotec planet is, at the last moment, saved, thanks to the cosmic wisdom of the blind library director. He stays for a celebration at the great insistence of the Zapotec people, and the novel ends with the blind library director going back to his native Buenos Aires, as he remembers that he left the current mystery he'd checked out from the library behind on the Zapotec planet—but it's too late to retrieve it.

For Bettina, it wasn't as impressive that this blind man figured out how to save the Zapotec world during this apocalyptic situation, but more that with the power of a single organic rose, an entire planet and civilization could be saved. The book opened her eyes to the fact that she hadn't seen a real red rose for many years. Bettina recalled their thorns, and something that bothered her about the book was that it made no mention of them, but then she admitted to herself that this petty annoyance was probably due to her admiration of the attention to accuracy found in technical nonfiction.

In the fiction section of the fish cannery's tiny library—the last library left in Three Rivers—only pedantic translations of classical texts were available. The library carried predominantly books and monographs and periodicals regarding patriotism, along with outdated magazines about the natural world. There was a greenroom down the hall from the library, where worker-mothers could sign up for fifteen minutes of total privacy each day, and in her later years Bettina took advantage of this privilege for extra time to read the books Neftalí would occasionally bring her.

Bettina was one of the few worker-mothers who had never given birth. Thanks to Neftalí's surprise visits when she was old enough, Bettina was able to recognize her former lover Angélica's face, and was able to remember the hardships and battles she'd suffered since her death to fulfill her promise to Angélica and take care of Neftalí.

She was tagged for a break at a quarter past the third work hour of the day—a rarity, and perhaps an error amongst the pylons, but she didn't complain. Bettina grabbed her sack lunch from the mess hall, and the young armed pylons looked the other way when she ate it sitting on a cinder block outside. As she was halfway through her wet sandwich, her eyes wandered past the northwestern perimeter fence keeping back the orchards and daisies—there Bettina spotted the manifestation of her current haunt floating in the air, or maybe held by a long gray stem: a red rose. She looked toward a young pylon, trying to hide her amazement, then up at the watchtowers and cameras that perched above the worker-mothers all day and night. The pylons had turned over many times through the years, with rumors circulating that they got shipped to the military after getting broken in. Unlike other gossip she put up with on a daily basis, this made sense to Bettina; it made sense that the city would teach these young men to practice cruelty within their community before moving them on.

Bettina stashed her sandwich back in the brown bag and crumpled the opening. She left it on the ground as she stood and became enchanted by that distant red rose with the gray stem. The young pylon yelled, "Excuse me!"

Did Bettina realize she was walking toward the rose?

"Excuse me! Worker-mother three eighty-three, return here this moment."

Bettina didn't look back. She wasn't afraid of the extra hours she'd receive as punishment for approaching the perimeter fence. The young pylon, confused about what to do, and sweating under his helmet, took the bayonet rifle off his shoulder. As he was about to use it, he was approached by a superior pylon and instructed to stand down. The senior pylon and the perspiring young pylon watched as Bettina walked the length of the field toward the fence.

Bettina felt the pylons would close in on her at any moment.

The red rose was growing from a hole piercing one of the hollow gray pillars supporting the fence. She admired the rose's undulations. Its face. She saw the wrinkles showing the rose's age, how tired yet radiant it was after its long journey through the dark pillar. This struggle against great odds, she concluded, had made the rose beautiful.

Bettina took out the cigarette stub from earlier and smoked the rest of it as she walked back and grabbed her sack lunch, then went into the mess hall to dispose of it.

On her way to sector 47, Bettina was intercepted by two armed pylons.

"Three eighty-three," one of them said to her. "You're done for the day."

Bettina squeezed past them, suspecting this was a trick, as worker-mothers always went back to work after their lunch. When the pylons barricaded her way again, she said, "Excuse me. I'm trying to hold the line here." She pointed to her position and saw that a younger worker-mother had taken her place behind the dolly, waiting for a barrel of verdillo fish to fill up.

A worker-mother was allowed to leave early or skip work only when they were sick or in the direst circumstances; in all her days, Bettina had been allowed to leave early once, after she'd fainted while serving in the cafeteria line. The pylons gave her energy-boosting pills to function through her convalescence, but she had to work full-time shifts like all other worker-mothers who came down with any sickness.

Feeling unsettled, Bettina passed by the basketball half-court, where she ran into a young new worker-mother shooting hoops on her own. The worker-mother scored over and over from behind the three-point line—it was obscene. Bettina waved and rooted her on, pumped her fists in the air for hoop after hoop.

The tiny library was closed because it wasn't Friday or Saturday, and when she passed the clipboard to sign up for private time in the greenroom, Bettina found her name was the only one, at the top of the blank form. The worker-mother in charge looked at the clipboard from behind a glass partition and buzzed her in for the next fifteen minutes.

Bettina thanked her, walked into the greenroom, and shut the door.

The room's swampy atmosphere, despite being a few degrees cooler than the rest of the factory, gave Bettina the momentary sensation she was elsewhere. Bettina never quite trusted this supposed privacy, and she had the nagging sense there were hidden cameras all over.

On the far wall of the greenroom, next to a round table and a chair, hung a long mirror—the only mirror at the fish cannery that didn't cut you off at the waist, so the privilege of being able to look at your entire body was reserved for the solitary worker-mother in the privacy room. Bettina walked toward the mirror, determined to expose its hidden camera once and for all, removed it, set it down, and found only the feeble little head of a nail. She studied the nail like a short, solvable equation. Bettina admired the nail's resolution and strength in holding up the mirror all on its own.

"You just keep being you, little nail," Bettina said to it, and remounted the mirror.

She untucked the denim work shirt and undid her overalls. Bettina watched as the red rose she'd picked earlier was revealed, reflected in the mirror against her bare stomach. She pulled its long stem from her left pant leg, the thorns catching in her hairs. Bettina removed all her clothes and stood before the mirror with her back straight, holding the red rose. She breathed deeply. The rose's color deepened within the confines of the mirror. Bettina let her hair down, holding this sacred yet profane red rose. She briefly invoked her ancestors, then remembered to leave the ancestors alone. *They've suffered enough*, she said to herself. *I don't need to bring them into this again.*

As Bettina stood there, the rose neither aged nor withered nor turned to dust, as it had in *Ghosts in the Zapotec Sphericals*. She slipped her clothes back on, tied her hair back while telling herself she'd never read fiction again. Bettina waved at the worker-mother behind the glass partition as she exited the greenroom, and once again was surprised there was nobody waiting to go in.

Whoever it is that's next, Bettina thought, *they'll be surprised to discover an apple-crisp red rose waiting for them on the table in front of the mirror.*

The pylons along the halls seemed particularly restrained in their bullying and harassment. Bettina had another cigarette break in the designated area by the basketball half-court. Rola, a worker-mother in her twenties who stuck to custodial work, was about to shoot hoops in her free time. She sat on the bleachers close to Bettina and said, "Three eighty-three, let me ask you a question. Can you read a label?"

"A label?"

"Yeah. I'm thinking of taking advantage of the Upwards Exam. Have you ever taken it? See, I hear you have to be good at reading labels in order to beat it. Then you can have a cushy office job. My kids are practically still babies, so that means I'll be here cleaning toilets and sinks for a while, unless something changes. It's not a bad thing to do if you keep telling yourself it's only temporary. So I was wondering if you had any advice for someone like me, who dreams of a comfy job in the label department?"

Bettina had much respect and admiration for Rola, not only due to her being the sole woman with teardrop tattoos on her face at the fish cannery, but also because Bettina could see that Rola was panoramic in her long-term view. One had to always be moving toward another position in one's early years at the fish cannery in order to find a place to settle and look forward to retirement.

"My advice," Bettina said, "if it were to be anything, is this: The exams are more difficult than you'd imagine. Filled with mathematical riddles. Not like shooting hoops, which you can get good at with practice. Don't have false expectations in here, try to learn new skills, and drink water. Lots of it."

Rola invited Bettina to shoot hoops, but she felt slightly winded, and declined. Bettina offered her a rolled cigarette and Rola took it. Rola dribbled the ball away as Bettina continued past the mess hall and the community area. Confused as to what to do with the unexpected time off, Bettina walked quietly back to the barracks and her bed, but when she got there she found another worker-mother sound asleep. She was about to shake the worker-mother awake and point out her error, but told herself it didn't really matter. The sleeping worker-mother was probably worn out and needed some rest. Simple mistake. Bettina looked around for her bag with her books and personal belongings but didn't find anything either—was it possible she'd stumbled into the wrong barracks, a place she'd walked into and out of the entire time she'd been a worker-mother?

Bettina rushed outside, and she was intercepted once again by two armed pylons. "Three eighty-three. Bettina Argyle. Follow us."

Working at Big Tex had made Bettina numb to resistance, so she followed the two pylons without questions or protest. From the distant working fields, like a scene projected on a screen, she could see Sunset trying to get water out of her chronometer, and other weary worker-mothers eager to finish their shifts. It came to Bettina's mind that she ought to be out there with them, holding the line in her sector. Bettina watched the eyes of overhead security cameras as she followed the pylons through a door that required buzzing in, then through a maze of hallways with doors labeled using complex decimal systems. When they arrived at room X87.Y23, one of the pylons scanned an identification card, opened the door. Bettina paused, not knowing what to do when he held it open for her.

X87.Y23 was bright, with casement windows revealing the cavitied, jagged molar landscape of Three Rivers beyond, as if regurgitated from a giant bird's mouth. Behind a desk with ornate family photographs and paperwork, Bettina was surprised to find a woman with washed-out hair standing tall on high heels to greet her.

"Bettina Argyle? Please, have a seat. Can we get you anything?" she asked. "Bettina, do you know why you are here? You're being dismissed as a worker-mother. You are no longer registered as a provider for one . . . Neftalí . . . Barrientos? This person is now a property owner. So your services here at Big Tex are no longer required by state law. Sign here, here, and here, or initial everything if it's easier. That's good, dear, that's good."

Bettina was given a blue canvas discharge bag with her belongings, a bus pass, and a newscube. The tall woman reminded her how important it was in the outside world to keep abreast of current events, and there was no better source for news than the newscube. Later, after reflecting on her discharge, Bettina concluded that the pylons who'd let her walk to the perimeter fence must have known it would be her final day. Otherwise, she would have been reprimanded, at best. The way it'd been carefully arranged hadn't allowed Bettina an opportunity to say goodbye to her friends.

———

On the first oblong piece of paper Bettina managed to sieve to-gether, she wrote: "Been working at the food bank since leaving the cannery. It's my designated workstation. There four days a week, seven hours a day. I clock in, allocate worker-mother hours into rations. Pass by two liquor stores on my way there and back. Easy to say no. Living in Arroyo North. For now. Not bad. Making my own paper. See?"

Since her discharge, Bettina had been assigned a near-sighted, bearded man as a parole officer, who briskly stamped her documents and mumbled too rapidly through routine civic instructions. During her first free week in the hollowed-out tech city, Bettina stopped three fights between men from escalating—on public transportation, in the checkout line at Billbert's Supermarket, and a few steps from her government efficiency apartment. All over Three Rivers she'd been pleas-antly surprised to find the names of Soraya, Maricruz, Yenifer, and other escaped worker-mothers killed by the state graffitied in remembrance, with calls for justice and portraits. People were finally boiling up, it seemed. Something was happening that her generation had lacked back when Angélica was lead-ing the fight against the encroaching technology sector, which had ultimately led to the city's privatization and collapse.

Bettina's designated newscube had remained stashed away in a kitchen drawer since her move-in date at the efficiency. On a few evenings, when she was bitten by the spirit of free-dom, she pumped herself up to visit Neftalí, then quickly talked herself down, knowing she needed more alone time— something she'd scarcely ever had as a worker-mother—before reconnecting with her past. She enjoyed taking meandering walks, trying to visualize the landscape of New Freeway from her twenties, remembering that the abandoned Chicken Shack used to be the Washateria, or that the Hollywood Horse Clinic was once a quinceañera supplies store.

Following a particularly stressful shift at the food bank, where Bettina messed up the rations for a few recipients, she tried to ignore the people downtown continually shading their eyes from encroaching storm clouds. A young woman hastily elbowed Bettina out of the way near the incomplete Hastings Building and King Ranch Tower, as if she was getting ready to catch a downpour of dollar bills.

Bettina was about to express her displeasure when she traced the young woman's astounded, heavenward gaze. The sky was blackening from the southwest, as if an almighty hand had knocked over a cosmic inkwell, spilling it over the entirety of the atmosphere. The ether's natural blue, orange, and capillary reds were gently smothered by droves of smoke-filled darkness, and Bettina squeezed past gawkers clustered along the sidewalks on her way toward her home. She bathed, surrounded by candlelight, in her efficiency apartment. Afterward, enjoying her cold canned peas, she opened the drawer beneath the plastic silverware packets, reached elbow deep into the back for the newscube. Bettina replaced its batteries, and listened as she ate her dinner, hoping to hear news of the phenomenon, and this is how she came instead to learn that the Big Tex Fish Cannery had been occupied by a successful revolt among her beloved worker-mothers.

A NIGHT WATCHER was extinguishing gas lamps along the sidewalk on the edge of Arroyo North, though it was well past what must have been dawn. He carried a handheld, battery-powered light, along with a three-foot ladder he used to reach the valve on each lamp. The night watcher stood before the lamp on the corner of 35 Mile Line and Toussaint and flashed his light through total darkness at crooked houses to see if anyone would be bothered by extinguishing this particular one. He climbed the ladder, opened the door with his night watcher's key, and shut the valve. Before continuing, the night watcher drank some water and gazed at the depthless, coffee-colored clouds making a trench of the entire sky.

His pocket watch buzzed. It was 2:45 p.m., which meant he was running fifteen minutes behind on his route.

The night watcher, like everyone else in Three Rivers, was still adjusting to the crude, shapeless smoke and ash blocking the sun and moon and stars. In before times, he'd been used to sleeping days and working all night, but now that life was stuck in mild, permanent darkness, the city had hired more night watchers and increasingly limited the gas availability. Demand for natural gas was sky high, and his shift leader had switched him to the daytime shift out of necessity. He'd initially thought it wouldn't make much difference, since it was always dark out anyway, but the time adjustment hadn't been easy.

He had picked up his ladder and was walking along when he heard footsteps approaching.

This new daytime darkness was different from nighttime darkness. It gave the world a dark red infusion that sometimes shifted to brown, orange, yellow, or a hollow gray like oil-stained concrete, revealing a bottomless crack in the earth.

The night watcher didn't like shining his flashlight directly at people, but the brown darkness of day often left him no choice. The light landed on some crumpled fast-food bags, shattered forties, and dirty underwear blowing in the wind around the corner on Thirty-Sixth. Then he saw across the street, heading away from him, a large figure—or maybe the figure merely appeared large to the night watcher because the person was covered from head to foot, embracing with both arms a bulky paper bag filled beyond capacity.

The first few squad cars he'd seen in nearly an hour passed him with dim headlights, and they honked at the night watcher, who took it as a sign of camaraderie from the officers. His job had always been important, but now that rationing the city's gas usage was essential, people's lives depended on the extinguishing or sparking of a single valve.

The night watcher carried the tools of his trade into the amorphous darkness, toward the next gaslight on his route, as the large figure carrying the bulky bag disappeared in the opposite direction.

———

The large figure wore a thick sweater and a scarf that covered their face and hair. They maintained a steady pace as they turned on Figueroa, slipped down Workers' Alley, and with a key opened the side door of a three-story brick building that had fading laundry-detergent advertisements on its side.

The door led into a very small kitchen. The one little window it had, facing the street, had been wheat-pasted from the outside with a fading advertisement. The person set the bag down on a small table, and using matches lit three candles placed strategically to make the cramped space feel luminous.

The person the night watcher had seen walking was Bettina, returning to her efficiency apartment from the food pantry. She'd taken the long way back, and had stopped by the remains of the Big Tex Fish Cannery. Though the charred grounds were barricaded and were under ongoing construction, she could still occasionally make out the entrance, a few sectors, the basketball hoop like a lone soldier on a shaved hill. Many times Bettina had hypothesized how it could have gone down: she'd imagined the rebellion starting at the mess hall, for some reason, over something that at a glance seemed trivial, like the quality of the fake meat, rubbery vegetables, or watered-down yogurt. The new generation of pylons was poorly trained; with a few determined worker-mothers leading the charge, anything could have happened. She regretted not having been there to witness the events that had brought about the fish cannery's demise, and half-jokingly told herself it was just another thing the state had taken from her.

At the moment there was no electricity in her confined quarters. She grabbed the newscube and flicked it on, as was her routine while putting food rations away. The newscube was halfway through a prerecorded bulletin, which replayed interminably until the news was updated.

"The volcanic eruptions in Mexico and the Middle East are rare events that hadn't occurred in eight hundred years," said the robotic anchor through the newscube. "We remind Texans to brave these challenges. Newscube will carry more bulletins on the governor rescinding the emergency declaration momentarily. For now, it is sixty-one degrees on July seventeenth . . ."

A midi version of the Texas Rangers theme played, then the news looped again to the same anchor. "Good afternoon, fellow Texans . . ."

Bettina let it play, though it was the same bulletin she'd heard earlier, only they'd changed the greeting from "good morning" to "good afternoon." The weather had even stayed consistent to the degree, according to the newscube, and she wondered if that was possible at three in the afternoon.

Growing up, Bettina had maintained a scrapbook in which she'd collected newspaper clippings of meaningful events that came to pass. Some chronicles were horrendous, others induced curiosity or inspired outrage. She remembered having a sense of accomplishment while flipping through the scrapbook, surveying the disasters she'd lived to document. Bettina had never used a newscube until she was discharged from the fish cannery, and lamented that the print newspaper days in Three Rivers were long gone.

Her rations stashed, she fixed herself a peanut-butter-and-cream-cheese sandwich and then stared at the books lined up against the wall next to her mattress on the floor. The titles were: *Quadrangles in Contemporary Woodwork*, second edition, compiled by the New Virginia Woodcraft Academy; *Metallurgy and the Upper Body* by Për Vjalkünd; *Modern Gears: Watchmaking*, edited by Karl Pintolls and family; *Pacific Volcanoes: Essays on the Ring of Fire*, this last one without a cover or credited authors or editors. Though her collection was small and unimpressive by her own standards, Bettina was proud of her modest acquisitions.

She walked into her little cramped bathroom. Gray mulberry tree shavings, hemp pulp, flax seeds, and essential oils floated on the surface of the water in the bathtub like a coarse fabric. Bettina poked at it using tongs, and the gray matter parted as she fished out a wide oblong piece of paper dripping with water from a sieve. She retrieved four more pieces of equal proportions and hung them on a nylon string that stretched over the tub. From the same nylon string Bettina removed the dry sheets and took them into the kitchen, where she laid them out on the counter by the sink.

Bettina used a ruler to make marks on each sheet. She razor-trimmed each page to five by eight inches, held each one in front of a candle: they passed the palimpsest test. She was pleased with this batch, and confident the paper would outlast her initial experiments. Bettina grabbed a generous pile of similar paper from a cardboard box, counted the sheets, and confirmed she was eleven pages shy of being able to bind an eighty-page booklet. She'd pre-collated the pages, and on top of page 1 had written the word *HEADLINES*.

Though it was now impossible to clip out news articles to keep track of current events, every time the bulletin in the newscube changed, Bettina would jot it down in these pages, and she envisioned this record being her first successfully bound homemade book. Since the beginning of this ritual, Bettina had filled three pages' worth of bulletins. She wasn't obsessive about documenting every single one—only the bulletins that gave her pause in some way.

The first newscube bulletin she'd managed to write down was also the only one beginning with the greeting "Good evening, fellow Texans." Then her writing went on: "Third-term mayor of Three Rivers, and founder of Big Tex, Pablo Henry Crick, is finally in recovery after an attempted assassination." The next bulletin read: "A young woman was taken into custody after she managed to sneak past security at the mayor's mansion and attempted the unthinkable. To take Pablo Henry Crick's life."

Bettina skimmed a few more, and the next one she'd written was "An explosion inside the Big Tex facility was believed to be caused by rebel employees, and has resulted in the tragic deaths of three government officers, bringing an end to this long rebel siege. There is no known connection so far between this incident and the attempt on the life of the mayor, who is attending to his duties better than ever."

She turned the page, believing each of these events contained tiny fleas of consequences that jumped onto the heads of other catastrophes, which in the end could be her own head, and she scratched behind her ears while reading the final written entry: "Heavy volcanic ash made its way northward from Mexico City, and the governor has issued an emergency declaration urging Texans to stock up on supplies and plan to stay indoors for the duration of fourteen days."

A brief succession of knocks rapped on the door, startling Bettina. She threw a blanket over her little bookshelf, put the shoebox of paper back in the cupboard, then shut the bathroom door. The afternoon darkness rendered the peephole useless, but Bettina didn't care who it was, and opened the door.

"Bettina Argyle? Ration ID 8D8-H986RZ?" A gust of wind silhouetted the person with dust. Bettina surveyed them up and down, noticed their braids and open-toed shoes, which were obviously carved out of an old tire.

"That's right. Who is asking?"

The person wore a bandanna over their face, and from a bag produced a document and handed it to Bettina, who was surprised to see actual paperwork. She admired and lamented how thin and expertly crafted machine-made paper would always be compared with her own.

When Bettina looked up from the paperwork, the courier had gone away. Bettina shut the door and sat near the candlelight to read the form. It had the next month's schedule for rationed electricity and running water for her block. The city had temporarily hired couriers to deliver personal messages to those pensioned. As a discharged worker-mother, Bettina recognized what a difference being a pensioned person made: it granted her running water for eight hours total, spread over the course of a week, which was more than most unpensioned families in Three Rivers got.

She had folded the machine-made paper, and was setting it

aside to recycle into one of her sheets, when another set of rhythmic knocks rapped at the door. Bettina glanced at the machine-made paper once again, to make sure it contained her correct information, just in case the courier had returned due to a mistake.

A muffled voice called from outside. Bettina leaned closer to the door, in no hurry to answer this time. The door shook as it was repeatedly slapped using an open palm, followed by desperate cries. The cries were small—it was the voice of a dormouse or a child, and when Bettina opened the door, she found a person much shorter than herself with their nose, mouth, and ears covered by an ash-resistant face scarf.

"Leonella?" the young person on the stoop said. "Wait. That's not you. Do you by chance know which of these places is where Leonella lives? I'm supposed to find her, and every building in this part of town looks the same."

"I don't know who that is," Bettina said. "I'm sorry. I don't know who a lot of people are, if that means anything to you."

"Me neither. Wait, maybe you can take her place. Are you hungry? Do you like tamales? We need another person to help us carry tamales to where the train derailed and the plane crashed. A lot of bad-off people have been living there. It doesn't pay money. Maybe you'll get a couple teddys as tips, if you're lucky. But you can bring home two or three dozen tamales. For sure, you can count on that!"

Bettina requested to be given a minute, left the person on the stoop, and shut the door. She looked around her efficiency, as if asking her little bookshelf or hidden shoebox to make this decision for her, thinking of volcanoes and worker-mothers. Only recently had Three Rivers authorities shifted their pursuit of the Big Tex worker-mothers from broad sweeps—carding every woman walking the streets—to targeted raids. Bettina grabbed her first-aid kit and ration identification card; she never left home without either.

Moments later, as the two of them turned the corner in front of the apartment building, the young person said, "What do you think about the rumors that the sun is no longer actually up there? That the government exploded the sun, and that's what the clouds actually are, just pieces of dead sun floating over us? Do you believe that the moon got really, really jealous? Jealous, like out of that passionate kind of love, and the moon killed the sun for looking at the Earth a certain way? Because that's what I think happened. It's weird, because really, it's the moon who has her eye always here and always there. Only showing you some of her face, depending on how she feels. Always keeping us guessing."

"I'm not sure what you're getting at," Bettina said. "Or that I agree with this assessment of the moon. But I have some other questions for you, if you don't mind."

"Okay. If I don't mind what?"

"If you don't mind my asking you."

"Okay, ask me. But the sun. The stars and planets. Just so you know, that's what I'd always rather be talking about."

"I feel the same way, to be honest. But there's still things I need to know. You say we're going to where the train wrecked and plane crashed? I don't get it: Did a plane crash from the sky and derail a train? Both accidents couldn't have happened together."

Two police cruisers sped through the street with flashing lights, which made them both slow their pace and pause their conversation. Since Mayor Crick's attempted murder and the destruction of Big Tex, the authorities had expanded their daily raids past book shredding—it took almost nothing to invite their executive overreach, especially to pedestrians.

When the cruisers were at a safe distance the young girl said, "Together? I don't know. But maybe. Do you have a bus pass? It's okay if you don't, we'll go another way. Sorry I forgot to mention it, I keep forgetting you're not Leonella and you have never done this with us before. Well. My mom and my tías spend all day a few times a week making tamales not just for us, but to give to others who need tamales and can't make any."

"Were your mom and tías worker-mothers at Big Tex? Or does this count as their job for the state?"

"At Big Tex? Never, Leonella, never. Sorry, I know you're not Leonella."

"My name is Bettina."

"Well, I'm Gia. Like 'day' in Spanish, but with a G."

They boarded the rarely on-time Orange Dillo trolley and sat in the first vacant seats at the front, behind the N95-masked driver. The Orange Dillo had its low beams on, as a solitary car passed them by. Three-quarters of the traffic in Three Rivers had disappeared after the arrival of the volcanic smoke, because people were afraid to drive in conditions with ground-level muddy clouds and sporadic rains of ash. Citizens had initially been advised to stay home by the local and federal government. But as the orders were rescinded by municipalities everywhere, more and more motorists, despite the challenging conditions, were braving high gas prices and impaired vision on the road to make ends meet. The effects of inhaling this ash, and the ash's relation to oxygen levels in the atmosphere, were not currently known, but communities had taken it upon themselves to inform one another that N95 masks or face coverings helped protect from prolonged exposure.

Gia removed her face scarf inside the Dillo, revealing what Bettina had suspected since their initial exchange: the freckled face of a child. Her curls fell over dark eyes, and she brushed them aside to blow her nose with a handkerchief. Bettina wanted to ask more questions but could tell Gia felt uneasy talking within earshot of the driver. They waited through eleven more stops in silence, then Gia pulled the cable, got up, and signaled to Bettina, who followed.

They were dropped off far from the tall clustered buildings that Bettina encountered on a daily basis in Arroyo North. She bent backward, in awe of the dark ceiling of concrete sky—never had it appeared so close to the Earth, yet so cavernous and infinite in its shapeless whorls of ash, knotting the void. There were no gas lamps in sight along the curb, and Bettina was surprised to see Gia turn on a battery-powered halogen lamp that illuminated the dark, hollow way.

A metal trash can with a contained fire revealed a rusted, bent sign above it: ANGELICA STREET, without the accent over the *e* in "Angélica."

"That's funny," Bettina said, pointing at the sign. "It's my first time seeing this sign since the street was renamed. They didn't even bother to add the accent on the *e*. I have an idea where we are now, though. This is Old Freeway."

A squad of boys on fixed-gear tricycles glided by, and Gia projected amiable shadow gestures at them as they pedaled away. Bettina and Gia walked toward Live Oak, an old brownstone tenement that was one of the oldest buildings in the city. Bettina heard teenage boys arguing from an indistinct alleyway, and everything smelled like burning banana peels, dog feces, or ragweed pollen. A plaque by the tenement building's entrance had once told of its complicated history, but it had since been repeatedly defaced, exhausted of any discernible meaning.

Gia said, "A strange man around here has been following not only me, but also other people. I don't see him right now, but I always look around just in case. He is easy to see, even at night."

"Has he harmed anybody?"

"Not that I know of."

Gia punched a code on the security pad and the door buzzed open. She signaled Bettina to keep quiet as they walked down a long hall and climbed the stairs, careful to avoid stepping on toy cars and one-legged tin soldiers scattered by other kids in an imaginary battlefield on the ground.

"It's the floor at the very top," said Gia, and this excited Bettina—she couldn't remember the last time she'd had to climb so many stairs. The kid must have been used to it, because after five flights Gia was still jumping three to four steps for each of Bettina's, until they reached the twelfth and final floor.

Bettina leaned on the railing for the last couple of flights, sweating and out of breath. She wondered what she'd gotten into, mixing herself up in this Leonella person's business. For a moment, Gia was concerned by Bettina's red face. Gia asked if she was okay, and Bettina couldn't reply as she gasped for oxygen; then she wiped the sweat from her face with her shoulders and huffed, "I'm fine."

Gia removed her face scarf again, revealing a gummy smile, then opened the door to the twelfth-floor hallway. The doors to all the government apartments were open, and over the whirring of fans and ranchero music turned low, voices were heard from the far end of the hallway singing in unison: "El día en que tú naciste, nacieron todas las flores."

Gia turned to Bettina, did a little hop of excitement, and sang along with them: "En la pila del bautismo, cantaron los ruiseñores."

Bettina had grown up on the Mexican side of a big Midwestern city, and although she hadn't heard it in years and didn't quite understand the lyrics, she knew it to be a traditional birthday song. One apparently credited to a King David. A loud mechanical cluster of sounds crawled from an open door, briefly drowning out the singing; Bettina peeked in and saw an elaborate conveyor belt taking up the entirety of a wide apartment. Little balls of masa circled the room on the conveyor belt, passed through an open bulbous oven running full blast in the center, and came out as glistening, steamed tamales at its other end.

Gia hurried her along, leaving the oven machine to its workings. They arrived at room 12-J, and inside the cramped space were about fifteen festive faces getting through the birthday tune. A small boy sat on a kitchen chair playing along on an accordion. A single candle radiated valiantly atop a cake with no frosting at the kitchen table, and before it an elderly toothless man smiled, hat by his side.

The elderly man blew out the haloed candle as the women

and children surrounding him clapped. They cut the cake into little squares and passed them around on pieces of foil along with plastic sporks.

"Everyone," Gia yelled, as she handed a piece of cake to Bettina, "this is—" and she nodded, cueing Bettina to introduce herself.

The non-English names sieved right through Bettina, but she noticed that aside from the young boy and the elderly man and Gia's mother, everyone was a tía. Gia's entire family had managed to take over the topmost floor of the Live Oak tenement building, and with their joint effort they made around a hundred dozen tamales two or three days a week, which kept the poorest people in Three Rivers fed. Although three of the tías oversaw the distribution, a few outside volunteers were always needed. The tías had learned not to trust the neighborhood boys or even the men for this task, and since the fish cannery was no more, finding volunteer women who wouldn't mind taking tamales home afterward as recompense posed no problem.

A tía with two long braids tied with rubber bands at their ends showed Bettina the coolers, and advised her to set tamales aside for herself, then offered her a nip of corn liquor from a rubber-stoppered beaker, along with a glass of twice-filtered water. Bettina drank gently from one, and had her fill of the other, then before she knew it she was helping to lift the coolers and move them down the hallway, toward the staircase. One of the tías pressed a button that flashed a circular blue light from the wall by the stairs.

Shocked, Bettina looked down toward Gia, and exclaimed,

"You mean this building had a functioning elevator we could've taken this entire time?"

"Oh, sorry. I like the stairs. But I should've said."

The elevator doors slugged open, and one of the tías used a crowbar to keep them ajar, as Bettina and two other tías hauled the coolers in. A tía reminded them that only one person could ride in the elevator with all that added weight from the tamales. Everyone agreed that Bettina should ride down, given her surprise about the elevator.

The elevator buttons were faded, but Gia peeked in and pressed the lobby button for Bettina, then quickly stepped out as the doors closed. The elevator stuttered down at first, then hardly seemed to be moving at all, as the smell of tamales summoned the poltergeist of a long-dead silver-screen actor, who joined her for the ride.

Bettina had heard stories about the league of bakers in her hometown, who distributed their own marbled rye after it became scarce; the monks who made their own brew and toilet paper; the rural ice farmers who reigned in counties that still got exceedingly hot; autumn soda pop and candy-corn dealers; the community Gregorian calendar keepers and stringed-instrument acoustics-compliance elders; and she had once been informed in great detail by an old bunkmate worker-mother of the underground sisterhood that gave away seasonal preserves, spices, and general cooking wares that were difficult to obtain.

The degree of niche that existed in the underground market, which helped sustain the order of survival, seemed equal parts astounding and pathetically fragile to Bettina—all this came to her on that slow elevator ride with the tamales. She was feeling awkward, not knowing if the elevator was moving at all anymore, when a loud knock came from the doors, along with a muffled warning to stand back. A crowbar was wedged between the doors, wielded by one of the tías in the lobby, and after some pressure the elevator opened on its own.

Only three tías stood in the lobby, along with Gia. Bettina lamented not having said goodbye to everyone upstairs, then she remembered she would have to return for her tamales, and that would give her the opportunity to thank them for the birthday cake, too. The women hauled the coolers to the front of the building, and one of the tías announced she would get the burro.

A camouflaged, spray-painted van turned the corner outside the tenement building and honked. Its old Texas plates read BURRO and depicted a cowboy cosmonaut riding a horse near a launching rocket, with the planet Saturn in the background. Though Bettina had been mentally prepared to haul these coolers around the city, it was delightful to discover that this was the vehicle the tías normally rode around town. Gia helped load coolers into the back of the van, and as the tías were buckling up, she stood on the curb waving, wishing them well.

Bettina rode in the back seat, behind the driver. She hated to see Gia—the person who'd brought her into all this—staying behind. But it made sense. And as the tías filled her in on where they were going—the site of the train wreck and plane crash—it made even more sense why they wouldn't want to take a child along.

FLIGHT 809, DEPORTING PRISONERS from an overcrowded immigration camp in Tulsa, was the ninth plane in the span of two weeks to inexplicably nosedive into Three Rivers, before flights were finally and permanently banned from the town's airspace. What made flight 809 more harrowing than the accidents leading up to it was that moments before the crash, the railroad steel on the ground below had inexplicably bent toward the plane's nose, then snapped, just as an Amtrak bullet train heading to Tucumcari was speeding by. The train shot up and crashed head-on into flight 809, the pilot and conductor locking eyes in those final moments.

This catastrophe occurred seven miles outside Old Freeway, and there were no accessible roads to the wreckage. Only heavy debris and derailed boxcars from the train remained, destined eventually to be taken over by a revolving cast of runaways, the unhoused, or wandering immigrants seeking asylum. People slept packed together in the boxcars and in the portion of the plane's tail that survived the collision.

On the way there, the tías informed Bettina of the three men who'd survived the plane crash. These men had been held as untried prisoners for entering the country undocumented, and after the crash they had convalesced on their own before discovering one another's existence. They were also the only men the tías had any business interactions with anymore. The tías made it clear this was due to several important reasons, the first being that they trusted these men, who'd overcome great odds to make sure this camp ran smoothly for anyone who might need it. Bettina inquired how long ago the accident had occurred, and after some discussion the tías agreed on three years. It was hard to picture the clear blue skies of those days, much less the airplanes that once flew over Three Rivers.

Burro carried the women from I-35 to I-37, then hit the caliche road softly. Where the caliche ended and dropped off into a steep canal, the headlights on Burro were shut off and one of the tías sparked her lantern. Since there were only four of them, the tías showed Bettina the most efficient way to carry the coolers. They checked in on one another to make sure they were properly hydrated. The braided tía passed around the beaker with booze, then each grabbed at their designated cooler handles.

It was probably close to evening, and the sky produced fiery color spectrums and theatrics, as if the northern lights were appearing in the trenches of a sewer. Bettina had not ventured this far outside the city since before her worker-mother days. She admired the furry shapes of the darkness moving through, thick as if hand-carved out of an onyx obelisk, or the tooth of a dragon, only to give way to patches of light that galloped like wild horses, revealing abandoned clotheslines and dead mesquite trees within clearings that were once baseball diamonds.

Bettina was holding the far-right handle on the cooler line, using her left hand. The braided tía to her approximate left helped her, and said, "Here's a trick for the children . . . If any of them run up to you . . . just keep an unwrapped dozen around for them. Only give them one tamal at a time. They're hungry, and hunger makes them careless. If you give them the whole dozen at once, they'll unwrap them wrong, and most will fall to the ground. They'll eat them anyway if they fall, of course, but I hate to see that happen. So give them only one at a time, por favor."

Less than a hundred paces later, Bettina found that even this warning couldn't have prepared her for the way people on the margins in Three Rivers lived. The first thing she heard was the mechanical hummingbird palpitations of a generator; beyond a tall agave ahead, two signals from a flare gun lit up the sky blue, then red.

"Somos las tías," the tías yelled in unison.

There were two boys behind the agave, and at hearing this they ran as fast as they could toward the sound of the generator. Bettina and the tías walked through brambles, weeds, shrubs, and avoided the gathered piles of branches. One of the derailed boxcars appeared, inclined like a ship sinking into the ground. Dogs yelped; gas and halogen lanterns shone; children were heard cheering and calling for their elders and siblings. A piercing whistle that served as a greeting from one of the tías revealed even more sparking lamps.

Bettina and the tías were standing on ground zero of the wreckage. Boxcars crookedly lined up like trailers fallen from the sky surrounded them in a half-moon to their right; to their left could have been the remains of a whale or a hydrogen blimp, but was instead the tail of flight 809. It had been severed from the missing rest of the plane and closed with a tarp, but the tarp was thrown aside by its residents as they climbed down.

The adults and children living at the crash site owned only one or two sets of clothes, so they each wore something fancy but ragged, as if the wedding or festivity they'd attended had not only gone on for days or weeks, but would also carry over into the book of Revelation.

Cacophonous voices chanted, "Tías, tías, tías, tías, tías, tías, tías, tías!" Small hands reached out but kept their distance by forming a circle around the women, as if there was a procedure to respect and strict rules the tías enforced. Bettina and the tías had set their heavy loads down, and the braided tía opened a cooler, then peeled the aluminum foil off a dozen tamales. Bettina watched as the braided tía gave single tamales to the youngest and hungriest, then Bettina followed her cue with a dozen of her own.

The two tías on the far left concentrated on distributing the tamales to a line of older residents. On the tops of three different boxcars were men standing watch, and to Bettina they very much resembled the men who'd watched over her as pylons at the Big Tex Fish Cannery. When the tías waved at the men, they each shouted a formal greeting in Spanish and climbed down. One of the tías threw each of them a dozen tamales, which surprised the men, and they exclaimed in a theatrical manner for laughs as they caught them.

Bettina watched uneasily as children sat around eating, or ran off into the dark, only to come back with glowing, greasy faces to ask for another tamal. Days later, when she reflected on this experience, Bettina would recall the electric, ghostly look of the children, how the hunger in a child was different from the hunger in an adult. The children could be openly feral and had to be reminded of the strict rules; otherwise, they'd push and shove anybody to get a tamal; the adults knew they must be complacent, and couldn't act out to get their way, so they formed a line and followed the process.

A tía had been pulled aside and was talking to a young woman; though Bettina couldn't make out the woman's face, it was clear from the tía's expression that her words were troubling. The tía whispered to another tía, then the news got to Bettina when the braided tía, drinking from the beaker, said to her, "We may need to take someone to the Red Cross. Don't worry. This has happened before. Sometimes people get gangrene from a cut, or huff something they shouldn't be huffing for a high."

"What's going on?" Bettina asked. "Maybe I can help. I have my first-aid kit with me."

Ever since the time she was on a city bus and saw a man get on with a face wound, and watched as the bus driver opened the first-aid kit to discover it'd been ransacked, Bettina never left home without her own kit, which she'd assembled and kept in a rectangular tin case. She'd needed it only once, after witnessing a kid fall off their skateboard and scrape their knee. The child had allowed Bettina to apply the alcohol and a Band-Aid decorated with extinct grizzly bears.

Bettina walked over to the young woman and the concerned tía as the two other tías continued the orderly distribution of tamales.

The worried tía asked Bettina, "Can you exorcise unwelcome spirits? Or deliver a child?"

"Pardon?"

"Tell her what you told me," the tía instructed the young woman.

The young woman told Bettina in a Cajun dialect that earlier in the day a pregnant person around her age showed up at the camp, and since then this person had been hallucinating, warning about a giant monster approaching.

"How pregnant?" Bettina asked.

The young woman demonstrated with her hands, then shrugged and said she didn't know; she claimed she was the first pregnant woman she'd seen in a long time—since she was a girl, she said—and this went for other people in the camp the young woman had spoken to as well.

Bettina and the concerned tía followed the young woman past people in line for tamales, and the remains of the great wreckage—everything flashed like smudged photographs or a burning postcard in Bettina's mind. The sun really must have been setting, because a gleaming purple iris bled from the leaden clouds beyond the west. The young woman guide held a gas lantern and illuminated the way. Far off, away from the main wreckage, Bettina made out the dark outline of a small, broken-down bus. It emitted an ultraviolet light from its windows and cracks, and there were muffled voices leaking through as well.

The tía and the young woman threw open the back doors of the bus. It had no seats, and at the front, past several pallets, crushed cans, and old clothes, lay a figure bundled in a blanket. Empty bookshelves lined the inner walls of the bus.

"Hwaaahh," the figure on the ground groaned.

The tía must have been familiar with this spot, because when Bettina turned to consult her, she already had a small fire going outside and had pulled out her portable cauldron to boil water.

Their young woman guide was holding the hand of the person on the ground. Bettina approached them, leaving the back doors wide open. "Nooo," the pregnant woman was saying, "follow the smoke . . . the monster . . . the maze . . . grackle . . . the grackle calls . . . for the monster . . . grackle calls for me . . . no . . . please, I never wanted this . . . don't take me there . . . your monster is your baby, says the grackle . . . don't you know . . . it will need a job . . . learn alphabets . . . your monster is your mother, my grackle . . . I'm your mother now . . . I'm adopting you . . ."

The person trailed off, louder, only nobody could understand her words this time.

"She's been doing this kind of thing," the young woman guide said, as the tía inspected the condition of the pregnant woman. "Is she well? Do you think her body has been possessed?"

The tía said, "She has a fever. And her water broke. We are going to deliver this baby right now. My sister the midwife stayed home with the kids, so there's a decision we have to make here."

Bettina was crouched by the pregnant woman, and had taken one of her sweaty hands between her own. She'd been listening attentively to what was being said, trying to follow and pinpoint all the words like cities on a map.

"Is she speaking in tongues because of what the baby is doing in her stomach?" the young woman guide asked. She was scared, stepped aside to give the tía and Bettina space between the neglected bookshelves inside the short bus.

"She's not speaking in tongues," Bettina said. "She's speaking another language. I'm in no way an expert. And I could be wrong. But it sounds like she's saying things in Arabic. Do you know her name?"

"No. Nobody does."

"Does she have her ration card?"

"I didn't check. What's Arabic? Like another tongue? Like Spanish or German?"

"Something like that."

As they stood there listening to the young woman's string of words, the tía nudged Bettina, who then rolled up her flannel sleeves. Bettina felt a bundle of something thick and heavy under the pregnant woman's head. When she replaced it with a rolled sweater, Bettina saw that the bundle consisted of one-sided, uncollated xeroxed paper. Wanting to admire not only the printed words but also the quality of the paper, Bettina set the bundle aside to concentrate on the task at hand. She grabbed the first-aid kit from her bag and handed the tía instruments to be disinfected when the water came to a boil in the cauldron a few feet away from the open rear doors.

Bettina washed her hands with the clean water they'd been drinking and used the disinfecting solution from her kit. Her hands came to a lather. She scrubbed all the way to her elbows and said, "I'm not an expert here, either. And I haven't done this in many years. But I've delivered babies before." Bettina had hoped the tía or the young woman guide would object, and counter with a better solution. But her statement was met with silence and faint nods. She didn't have time to analyze or second-guess.

"We need her awake," the tía said. "Otherwise, we'll have to cut it out of her."

Like a wraith springing from the abyss, a brown dog jumped in through the rear doors of the bus and snuggled by the pregnant woman's head of short hair. The brown dog smelled of jasmine, as if it had been rolling in a field of it before entering. This smell of nature and the affectionate dog brought the pregnant woman back to—she opened her eyes and looked around in great alarm.

The short bus was cleaned up by the tía and their young woman guide. Fresh blankets were obtained and rolled out. The jasmine-scented dog found its safe spot and stood watch near the driver's seat. Adults and children from the crash-site camp had quietly gathered around the dilapidated vehicle— they were eating tamales and keeping vigil as another dog rushed through the rear door. Soon after, all the people moved inside. One by one the entire destitute community crowded into the bus—silent witnesses to a child brought into this ash-covered world.

At night, if one stared into the sky long enough, the brightest stars often sparkled through the ashen clouds for a brittle moment, then soon turned to rust, falling dead once again in the night's eternal battlefield.

On the ride back to the Live Oak tenement building, Bettina considered acquiring a compass for her first-aid kit. *How would the ancestors know where they were going if they didn't have the stars?* she wondered. The braided tía had passed out in the back seat next to Bettina, clutching her empty alcohol beaker, while the two tías in front remained silent the entire ride. The tamale-free coolers in the back swayed in their lightness at every turn of Burro. Bettina was taciturn, yet shaken by what she'd been part of.

She helped haul the coolers up to the twelfth floor of the Live Oak tenement building, and assisted the inebriated braided tía, too. There were six dozen tamales, along with left-over cake with Bettina's misspelled name on a note waiting for her on the kitchen table of apartment 12-J. Despite repeated protestations, Bettina gave in, and let the tía who'd been her partner in delivering the baby take her all the way back to her government efficiency near Arroyo North. As she stepped off Burro, the tía, with a tired smile, told Bettina that if she ever wanted tamales, she knew exactly where to find some.

At her small kitchen table, by candlelight, Bettina tried recollecting that tía's exact wording regarding the tamales, and she was jotting it down when the power in her block punched through. She stood up, startled, looked with bleary, unfocused eyes at the candle's feeble flame under the ceiling's halogen beams, then confirmed that the water in her kitchen sink was running, too.

Bettina checked the pamphlet that had been delivered by the courier earlier in the day. This surge of utilities hadn't been scheduled in the "Power & Water Supply Itinerary." She quickly scooped out the pulp and paper coagulating in the bathtub, then took the longest, hottest shower to drain away the soot and dirt and grease and blood from her body, hair, and nails.

The medium flow from the showerhead calmed Bettina like the sea itself, while cleansing her life force and those of the living people around her: her old worker-mother friends, the tías, Gia, the young woman whose baby she'd delivered, Neftalí, wherever she was. Bettina insisted on replaying the most panic-inducing details of the earlier procedure in her mind: the young woman pushing, pushing, and, when she'd least expected it to happen, the baby's head thankfully in her arms.

She shut off the shower and, thinking in an abstract way of the city's less fortunate, felt the guilt of having used up so much water.

Though she would have answered anyone's questions truthfully, none of the tías had asked Bettina about her qualifications for assisting in a childbirth. In a way, Bettina hoped somebody would, was convinced that at any moment a more qualified person would interrupt, step in, and take over. When no such thing had happened, Bettina was forced to follow through, which evoked her days as a registered nurse and volunteer midwife in her twenties. It was how she'd met her late partner, Angélica. After delivering Angélica's only daughter, they had become great friends, and later had a small unofficial wedding ceremony with only the toddler as a witness. When Angélica was murdered during the second military occupation of Three Rivers, Bettina became the girl's legal guardian, and after the founding of the Big Tex Fish Cannery, it was Bettina who'd had to provide for Neftalí—but not before Bettina's problems with alcohol gradually deteriorated certain levels of trust between the two of them.

The past had a malleable meaning that Bettina was always

deconstructing. Once toweled off, she fished out the bundle of xeroxed paper from her bag and held its weight in her hands. She'd taken the unbound pages upon the suggestion of the young woman guide at the crash site, when Bettina had openly admired the paper after the newborn stopped crying and while the young mother rested.

Bettina sat at her kitchen table organizing the photocopied pages by their numbers, wishing life could be sorted out in a similar way. Only a couple of pages in the middle of the narrative were missing, and Bettina placed the title page at the top of the pile and stared at its title: *Brother Brontë*.

EARLY THE FOLLOWING MORNING in Old Freeway, inside a cramped closet space that had been partly converted to a bedroom in apartment 12-J, below hanging, handed-down clothes and her mother's old family dresses, Gia was rudely awakened by her little brother Jairo.

"The twins are looking for you," he told her, pulling at her staticky hair.

She slapped his hand, turned over, and waited until he shut the door to get up.

Gia brushed her teeth with no toothpaste and ate her cereal dry, grabbed the four dozen tamales she'd stashed, and shuffled down the staircase. The one-legged tin toy soldiers and cars that had been there the previous evening were gone. Outside, waiting by the defaced plaque at the building's entrance, were the triplets Huicho, Luismi, and Cua, all wearing clothes too big for them, which had perhaps belonged to the same person at one point. Gia flashed the tamales in her canvas bag, and the triplets signaled to her to walk.

They all lifted bandannas from their necks to their faces, for the low-flying morning clouds carried atmospheric soot that choked, and was also rumored to contain traces of tetanus. Cases of lockjaw had broken out, but the kids were all up-to-date on their vaccinations. The triplets moved in single file through the blown-glass darkness that the volcanic clouds had cauldroned up, and Gia had no recourse but to follow. Huicho, Luismi, and Cua stretched their arms out and made noises imitating aircraft.

Rolling power outages had rendered the use and value of ration cards fickle. Various underground markets, and innovative ways to barter, had sprung up, especially among the young. Gia felt nervous, but had been looking forward to this moment since stories of the tiger in their neighborhood began circulating. She'd heard the tiger had appeared in the city after a politician's ranch burned down, and every exotic animal he'd illegally acquired had tragically died or had had the serendipity to escape.

Huicho, Luismi, and Cua were some of the few neighborhood boys who didn't get around on souped-up tricycles, and therefore walked everywhere. Since Gia walked everywhere, too, she'd had various exchanges with them that had built something like trust.

Gia carried her savings of five teddys in case they proved handy. She knew tamales were not intended to be used as currency or for bartering, and if her family found out what she was doing, they'd be extremely disappointed. Even if she didn't get to see the tiger, Gia had promised herself she'd let the triplets have the tamales anyway, so she didn't feel entirely ashamed.

A series of reward posters for the remaining worker-mothers who had taken part in the destruction of Big Tex had been reposted in this part of the neighborhood. Some warned against sheltering worker-mothers and advised those who were newly pregnant to register with the state. As they passed by them, Gia tore one down, crumpled it up, threw it into the bleak bushes, while making a note to get the rest on the way back.

Huicho, Luismi, and Cua were humming and lightly singing the latest neighborhood children's rhyme: "The ground spit ash / when the mountains crashed, / so let's now bury our bones!" Those were, at least, the words Gia made out, but she was unsure, because everyone sang it differently. She'd heard the last lines sung as "So let's sit around indoors," and "But what should I do with this noise?" Though her mother had warned her against singing the dirty neighborhood rhymes, no matter how catchy, Gia found herself humming along with the triplets as they walked.

"Are you excited to meet her?"

"You're gonna like her."

"She's our friend," the triplets said.

"So she's a girl tiger?" Gia asked.

"Yeah."

"But you can't tell, because the tail's missing."

"She came to us that way."

They walked past Fourth Street on Angélica until they reached a dilapidated house with a drooping—almost falling, really—covered porch behind a chipped white picket fence. The faded, graffitied words CHUPACABRAS BRRRN were scarcely noticeable by its unhinged front door.

Thick, rusted fog parted behind them. Gia spotted a tall, dark figure trailing them about half a block back. The nerves at the back of her neck did a choral number and her shoulders tensed as she tried to contain her flippers of fear. The fog condensed and swallowed the block up. Though she didn't get a clear look at the dark figure, Gia was positive this was the man who'd been following people from her tenement building. The triplets sensed Gia's concern despite her face scarf, then as the ash-ridden fog parted again, with a longer gap of visibility, they saw the man as well.

He was bearded and sported a dark blue raincoat. From his pocket, the man removed something like a rectangular timepiece and brought it to his right eye. There was no fog in sight that could cloak Gia and the triplets, so the bearded man took this opportunity to snap a photograph using a tiny Edixa 16 camera.

The triplets stood idly in the middle of the street and watched as Gia fearlessly walked right up to him. She held out a dozen tamales to the man and said, "Sir, are you hungry? Is that why you're following us?"

The bearded man framed his shot past Gia and the triplets, once again took a photograph, advanced the film, and did it again. Gia turned toward the man's fixation. On the front porch of that dilapidated, vandalized house sat a Bengal tiger erect on her haunches, as if she was a statue come to life, standing guard over a pillaged ancient library.

The great animal pierced all of them with marbled glass eyes, their demeanors etched forever in tiny script on her turquoise irises as if by needles—even the Edixa 16 camera, from that distance, had a scent for the tiger to file away.

"That's not a thing to be living in the city," the bearded man warned. He took another picture.

After digesting the man's words, Huicho responded: "But it already lives here."

The bearded man put his photographic instrument away,

and took a moment to survey the small faces before him. He flicked a stick of spearmint gum into his mouth like it was a coin, and walked away in the direction he'd appeared from, but not before declining the tamales with a scowl.

Gia handed the promised tamales to the triplets, who commenced eating a few and asked Gia not to approach the tiger until they were finished.

A whirlwind of gnats had been making their way toward the tiger. They gravitated from the dead mother hive on the abandoned property next door. The tiger languorously moved down the steps of the porch, and Gia confirmed she really was missing her tail. When the tiger approached the edge of the white picket fence, she crouched, jumped over it, and stuck the landing on the sidewalk.

Luismi and Cua waved at their buddy the tiger, as Huicho rushed to chew his last bite of tamal. With great indifference, the tiger turned in the opposite direction and walked with slow, confident strides. A dusty cloud traveled close to the ground like the hem of a giant monk's robe, and it veiled the tiger as she gently made her way into the damp alley and vanished before Gia's and the triplets' eyes.

The tiger stopped in front of a pile of old telephones, looked up at some broken windows by the entrance to a trailer home. A vigilant cat sat by a cinder block below the trailer's broken wooden doorsteps. Bacon grease floated vaguely in the air— the tiger knew just where it was being fried, and how to break in to acquire some, so she ignored the cat. The tiger followed her soft paw prints embedded in the earth, and all the disheveled street creatures scurried away, hiding behind junked cars; haunted, abandoned homes; and squatters' palaces.

Streaks and orbs of orange and yellow leaked from the ash above as the sun was rising behind the brown, languid sky. Silver and gold bristles on the tiger's body glistened. The tiger was aware of the red-eyed grackles staring from the impotent power lines, but seemed uninterested in their order of existence. A blacksmith was shaping a flat piece of metal on an anvil, and stopped his hammering to admire the tiger. This near-daily sighting was the only thing in his life he considered majestic, and he had told nobody about it. The blacksmith wiped his brow with a rag, took a hit of bootleg alcohol as he watched the tiger leap over a fallen Southwestern Bell post and continue on her trek.

The tiger walked past broken tractors and fallen, outdated satellites onto Colonel Huerta's property. Her nose perked, taking in the dimensions of the land, and she walked around the perimeter of the house, past the musty stable, the well. The unkempt orchards seemed to part, making way for this creature, whose smell had become their smell, the same way the tiger now carried a faint musk of grapefruits and oranges everywhere she went. She walked through bulbous and decrepit scarecrow trees toward the irrigation canal, then toward the reservoir, which was now dammed at the point where it connected to the Frio River.

In a breezy clearing near the embankment stood a figure draped in a flapping shawl. Wormy ashes fell gently from the sky like unfestive ticker tape. This person's shoulders heaved, as their sobs were heard above the monthly air-raid siren test coming from the old high school football stadium. The tiger stepped closer, and when she was about ten feet away from this figure she sat at attention, licked her own nose. A gnat hassled the tiger, pricking her whiskers and ears, as the tiger fixed her turquoise eyes on a grieving Neftalí Barrientos. Neftalí mouthed words that arrived with no sound as she tried to contain her grief, to trap it like a firefly in a jar. Dark moats around her eyes told of insomnia, inner pleas directed to the buried heavens, repeating the words "This can't be happening, this can't be happening" like a mantra.

A pile of stones and knickknacks marked the spot in front of Neftalí as the site of a grave. The grave was marked with only one word, written carefully in white cursive on a wooden plank: PROSERPINA. Neftalí had made visiting her grave a daily ritual since they'd found her body at that spot and buried her. The wind shifted, and Neftalí turned when she got the feeling someone was spying on her.

"Hi, Mama," she said to the tiger, wiping tears on her shawl. "How long have you been there, baby? You can't sneak up like this. I know you think it's no big deal, but you can really scare the shit out of people, you know."

The tiger—Mama—walked toward Neftalí, who then petted her on the neck and ears, like she'd learned Mama liked.

Mama sat back on her haunches as Neftalí set a couple more precious stones on the grave, next to an array of others. She broke down in tears again, though it was something she avoided doing in front of Mama—Neftalí sensed that grief disturbed the tiger, who couldn't relate to this intensely human feeling.

"I'm sorry, baby," Neftalí said to her, but Mama couldn't

understand apologies either. Mama nudged Neftalí a few times with her face, then slightly nipped at her shoulder and hair. "Sure, all right," Neftalí said. "I know. It's time for you to eat, you brat."

Neftalí carried an extinguished oil lamp away from Proserpina's grave. The orchard's trees appeared to her like a procession of people frozen in time on their way to a harvest, or to fish. It was remarkable to Neftalí how most of their leaves were still green, since she was sure nobody watered or maintained them. With the sunlight so scarce, even plants fought for every bit of it, like seagulls fiending for scraps in a wet market.

Colonel Huerta had a steady flow of electricity rigged only in certain spots around his property, and this was how Neftalí kept the quartered chickens stored in a freezer. She made Mama sit on the porch as she prepared thawed quartered chickens in a bucket, and added a pouch of blood and gizzards for good measure. Mama struggled to stay still in anticipation, but she knew if she moved even an inch closer, her access to the food would be delayed, per Neftalí's strict rules. Mama salivated, licked her jowls and nose, stared with those darted turquoise eyes at the delicious pinks and reds swirling in the bucket.

"Okay, good girl," Neftalí said, and the tailless tiger sprang forth and ate, careful not to tip over the bucket, holding it still with her front paws. Neftalí never lost her sense of wonder and horror at watching Mama devour that nasty raw concoction. The tiger finished, then prowled over to an oak tree, where Mama liked to lie after a meal and observe the goings-on of the property.

The atmosphere had a lavender, orange tint that diffused

bright colors onto the ground and projected shadows so dark they approached iridescence. Neftalí reignited the oil lamp resting on the uneven back-porch worktable, reached for her worn hardcover copy of *Brother Brontë*, lying face down on her usual cushioned wooden chair, thumbed through it until she found the bookmarked page. She carried the book and the lamp toward the oak tree, careful not to trip on its popping roots, leaned against the cool trunk facing Mama.

Though she'd lost count of how many times they'd read this book together—the only book she owned, and quite possibly the last intact novel in Three Rivers—Neftalí dreaded getting to this flashback in the narrative. Pride, one of the central characters attending Our Brother Branwell Academy for Girls, has fallen in love with a shepherd boy, who almost daily passes by with his small flock near the fence. In their clandestine exchange of amorous letters, the shepherd finds a way to sneak Pride a tattered paperback book: *Jane Eyre*. Credited not to *Branwell* Brontë, like the multiple editions held at the academy's library, but to a *Charlotte* Brontë—an author she's never heard of. Pride presents this book to her older (by two minutes) twin sister, Prejudice, and the news travels quickly among the other girls. This disturbing revelation tangentially leads to a more dreadful one: that all graduating girls at the academy go on to become wives for ranking military officers.

Neftalí found her spot on the page and looked up as the triplets were walking from the alley toward the three-gabled Gothic house. Mama could feel their steps reverberating through the cool ground, but remained in her comfort spot, ready for the story.

"'Pride had always been an A student, so this was her first

time in the Director's cold office,'" Neftalí read to Mama, pretending not to see the triplets. "'"But it is not my wish to marry a man thirty years my senior, Madame Director," Pride said. The Director circled Pride while the girl sat on the guest chair below the candles of the office lustre. She leaned down close enough that Pride could count at least six legs on the spider growing inside the mole on the Director's face. "It is your duty," the Director said, and even the flames above shivered.'"

Huicho waved an aluminum-foil packet of a dozen tamales obnoxiously enough that Neftalí couldn't continue ignoring them. She marked her page, shut the book in a huff, and petted Mama, who was used to the smell of these boys.

"They're warm," said Cua.

"And super-duper good," claimed Luismi.

Neftalí set the book aside, reluctantly asked them to toss her the foil bundle. It was Proserpina who'd been close to and had had regular dealings with these boys. Now Neftalí humored their presence, especially since they'd helped her move her stuff out of Angélica Street and into Colonel Huerta's. Neftalí had claimed the property at city hall, and officials then carried out Huerta's body to the city's central morgue. The triplets also helped drag old furniture and clothes out of the house for Neftalí to burn on the dry patch of blackened dirt near the barn.

"What kind of tamales are they?" she asked.

"Corn. And green bean," the triplets said.

She felt bad for these neglected boys, but suspected they were presently well fed, and she could trust them.

"Did you see Alexei? Is he happy now, being a big shot for

the shot-up fucking mayor? I'm glad they maimed Crick's ass, and you should be, too," she said.

The triplets couldn't make eye contact with Neftalí when she was bad-mouthing Alexei, but they all nodded.

Cua approached Neftalí and handed her a leather medicine pouch threaded with plastic along its edge. The pouch was heavy, and she guessed its contents before pulling at the seal. Neftalí turned livid when she confirmed her suspicion, and held the individual teddys in her hand. The coins were heavier than she'd remembered, as if Professor Pantano had been using a different alloy than bottle-tops to mix newer batches. She smirked at the embossed profile of Theodore Roosevelt, but contained her laughter—the kind of maniacal laughter that comes after an extraordinary trespass or offense, and which leaves you closer to the edge of madness. The pristine anger from the girls who attended Our Brother Branwell in the novel came to mind, but Neftalí wasn't ready to be seen this way by the triplets.

Huicho, Luismi, and Cua had had a cautious fear of Neftalí ever since the discovery of Mama—a feeling that had only deepened after Proserpina went missing. They'd been witnesses to Neftalí's pendulum of emotions swinging fast and wide, crying about Proserpina one moment, then cursing Alexei or Mayor Pablo Henry Crick, only to be found reading her one book in peace moments later, not wanting to be disturbed. Neftalí kept connected to the triplets only because she used them as messengers, and they brought her news of the neighborhood since she didn't own a newscube anymore. The triplets were the first people who'd more or less told her the ash in the atmosphere that was blocking the sun and moon was caused by a volcano.

"How are you all doing on your vitamin D?" she asked the triplets. The triplets waited on the porch as Neftalí brought them a glass of water from inside to share, and placed a clear, cylindrical pill in each of their scrawny hands. Neftalí had turned her frustration and disappointment about Alexei into this thoughtful gesture, felt her anger abating as she watched all three swallow the vitamin D pills. She kept the teddys, but sent the triplets away without a message to relay back to Alexei, and was proud of herself for successfully practicing temperance.

Neftalí had decided henceforth to ignore Alexei, her former bass player turned lackey for the city, and live out her days alone at the house with Mama. This was how she decided to honor Proserpina's memory as well, and to honor their former band, Missus Batches, rather than talk and perpetuate endless, unnecessary shit.

Doña Julieta had passed away, but her daughter, Agave, who was once in the fish cannery, now ran the *depósito*, and Neftalí learned to survive from the scarce products on her shelves. She witnessed the days growing colder, the state's power grid pushed to its brink, ash tossing in the atmosphere like the putrid, shredded heart of an old crow. The cold season brought a stringy resinous rain that quickly coagulated into sludge. On one of those trips back from the *depósito*, Neftalí spotted a whirlwind of screeching grackles fighting for pieces of Styrofoam piled on the sidewalk. She ran through the darting birds, holding tightly to her bag of groceries, shooing them away, and stopped short when she saw the gray, lifeless body of a woman among the Styrofoam. Her cotton turtleneck sweater revealed multiple lacerations; the bloody fabric had crusted to the dead woman's skin and Styrofoam pieces. Rumor had it that Mayor Crick's attempted killer had been a blond woman, and as she walked home, Neftalí noted that this was the color of hair on the dead woman's body, too. Neftalí was haunted by her utter lack of options, since the last thing she wanted was to involve the police. Three Rivers authorities had moved on from book-shredding raids to random searches for Mayor Crick's attempted assassin, so the woman's killers could well have been the city itself. When she went by the following day, ridden with guilt, the decomposing body was gone.

Neftalí's remaining LPs grew moldy at Colonel Huerta's, and she often missed the sounds of distorted guitars and screaming in front of a microphone. She reminisced about her short-lived rock-and-roll dreams, and playing music with Alexei and Proserpina—and she thought how if she were to start a band or have anything to do with music again, she would never find a drummer like Proserpina or a wild animal like Alexei to let loose with four strings on a stage. Anyone can be a singer-songwriter wielding a guitar, she reminded herself, but exceptional bass players and percussionists are nearly impossible to find in any economy.

Neftalí swatted these thoughts away when she found herself tangled in their web. She admitted that her present reality could never allow a woman to be a traveling, working musician—at least not like before, so it was no use getting worked up.

Winters were hard on Neftalí. Reading *Brother Brontë*

aloud to Mama softened the passing of the days, and she never went more than five days after finishing it to start it anew. The long, unpaved driveway at the front of the house kept her separated from the nearest road, and she could understand how the deceased Huerta had gone mad, being so secluded from the community, in his own little world. She tested the water from the well every other day to confirm it was safe to drink, and went from feeding Mama eight chickens per meal to six—a change Mama definitely noticed. As neighborhood chickens and family pets went missing in Old Freeway, the rumors about the roaming tiger thrived.

One day, a sweet older woman showed up at Neftalí's door and bashfully pointed to a disemboweled lamb she'd dragged from her nearby property. Neftalí felt terrible and gave the woman four frozen chickens and a stick of duck fat in turn, then reprimanded Mama while holding her nose at the lamb carcass.

Another time, while doing food inventory math in her head, Neftalí found a hidden trapdoor on the kitchen floor, pulled it open, and discovered steps leading to a basement. Inside the basement were shelves of unexpired canned fish, bags of rice, flour, and—most important—a small bookshelf with hardbound, dusty books. Neftalí knelt before the shelf, filled with piety, unable to touch even one of the spines.

Mama peeked into the basement and followed her down the steps, hyperaware of the spiders curling their tiny legs around their webs and a scuttling pregnant rat somewhere behind a wall. She watched Neftalí pull a couple of the books from the shelf. Neftalí squeezed between Mama and the wall and went back up the stairs and into the kitchen.

Candles were scarce, but she lit a new one at the long dining room table, sat on the chair where Colonel Huerta had died, and read the book titles. One was Mary Shelley's *Frankenstein*; the other was *The Scarlet Letter* by Nathaniel Hawthorne—neither were books Neftalí had ever read, but she had seen cinematic adaptations of the former when she was a girl. She and Mama had just finished another reading of *Brother Brontë* the previous day, so the fortuitous timing of this discovery was not lost on Neftalí.

She got the idea to portion some of the rice and flour into jars, to possibly negotiate future chickens and more candlesticks at the Pulga. During these successful ventures, she locked Mama in the barn where they'd originally discovered her. Strangers, who were mostly men, had been passing through the property as a shortcut between neighborhoods. Neftalí always sensed customers and merchants at the Pulga whispering behind her back, and she knew from the triplets that people had been saying she'd murdered Huerta as revenge for his having gotten away with killing his wife and daughters, and that she also had forged the necessary papers to inherit his assets.

Neftalí laughed when the triplets first informed her of this, and loved that there was a bit of controversy about her in Three Rivers, so long as it didn't involve Mama.

Neftalí grew troubled when she was skimming fat from a broth one afternoon and dropped the wooden spoon onto the floor—*visita*, her mother would have said, for dropping a spoon was a clear sign you'd have an unexpected guest that day. Hours later, while reading the Mary Shelley book aloud on the back porch by torchlight, she noticed Mama's head abruptly turn as she picked up on a distant whirring. Neftalí followed Mama through knee-high dry grass to the front of the house. It took more than eleven seconds to make out the shape gliding across the driveway, before she could ensure that the blob of dust and light was not a government vehicle or a type of fallen spacecraft. A Chevy van with a strobing light arrangement was winding in from the road.

The driver's sales tactics must have clicked in as he approached the rotunda, because a loudspeaker within the Chevy shot a ragtime piano melody to life. Neftalí snapped her fingers to discourage Mama from making sudden movements, kept an eye on her as the van came to a halt about fifty feet from the old house. Mama's posture was erect, her bristles defensive yet unalarmed, whiskers poised, which reassured Neftalí to keep calm.

The sound of a door sliding open was heard from the van's other side, and then shut hard in two attempts. The lights on the van's roof fixture gyrated like fairies around a fig, silhouetting a person standing next to two suitcases on the rotunda, as the automobile drove away, blaring its grainy ragtime. Neftalí feared one of the scenarios she'd dreaded had come to pass: that a distant relative of Colonel Huerta's was here to claim the land and declare that the notarized will in her possession was moot.

The person had their head and body cloaked. Using one hand, they removed their hood to reveal a silhouette with shoulder-length hair.

A baroque cemetery, her mother, funerals, chipped stone

cemetery statues, decay, and the dead: these were feelings attached to the flashes of imagery that passed through Neftalí's mind. Thin patches of orange ash floated in the air, and white light in its most despairing forms shone through a mountainous range of red clouds. Uncharted colors leaked from the sky, and their prism briefly chanted in unison, before brown ash took over and the colors were flushed out once again.

Neftalí backed away from the person as they got closer, wheeling their suitcases behind them. Neftalí's voice cracked as she said, "We are not at your grave. There haven't been seven pink moons yet that we can tell. How is this apparition possible?"

"What the fuck are you talking about?"

Mama curled up and seemed to flirt, exposing her belly. The person crouched, petted Mama's torso vigorously using both hands and all their fingernails.

"Ask me something only I would know," the person said. "From way back. My memory is sharp now. Do it."

"Okay. Um. When we found all those caskets of whiskey after they stole our band equipment the first time, what album did we get loaded to as we drove around looking for our shit in JD's uncle's truck?"

"Come on. You're seriously asking me that? Too easy. What if I was a spy and already knew every single thing about you?"

"Why would I think you're a spy? At the very least, I'd think maybe a ghost, but you were riding in that van, which is weird. Like, why would a ghost be in a van—" Neftalí stopped talking mid-thought—this absurd banter proved more than any DNA test that the person who stood before her, covered almost head to foot in ash-resistant garments, was Proserpina.

Light pierced a thinning cloud of ashes, confirming that this indeed was her 'mana and former drummer, Proserpina Khalifa. Proserpina's brown hair was graying, her deep eyes filled with protective alligators and piranhas.

Neftalí took her hand and rolled back the hooded robe's sleeve, revealing scores of dark scars on Proserpina's wrist leading to her elbow, from slashing herself at shows and bleeding all over her drum set. She ran her other hand through Proserpina's bushy, unwashed hair—a stark contrast to the last time she'd seen her, with a buzzed head. Neftalí brought her nose close to smell the roots of her hair—the faint chrysanthemums took her back.

"We buried you. After the vultures had eaten your ass up."

"That's awesome. But how?"

"You disappeared. After I came out with Mama from the barn where you found her. The triplets said you'd gone wandering. And then we never saw you again. Where did you go?"

"Wait, your mama?"

Neftalí pointed to Mama by her side; the bristles that made up her stripes were as attentive to the atmosphere as her turquoise eyes. "Remember her? This is Mama right here—that's her name."

Proserpina undid her robe to reveal a bundle growing in her armpit that slightly kicked when a fresh gust of air swung by: a rebozo, holding a sleeping child. Neftalí had not been around a baby in her adult years. She tried to reach toward it like she did when she petted Mama, but she hesitated and watched as Proserpina uncovered the sleeping infant's face.

"I'm a mama now, too. But in a different way than this tiger. I knew you'd freak out. I can't believe it myself sometimes." Wormy ash rained for a few seconds, and Proserpina covered her baby back up. As soon as she did, the rain stopped. "Can you show us where I was buried?"

They walked through tall grass into the orchards and toward the edge of the ravine, which led to a little brushy trail by the reservoir and then to the clearing where they'd conducted the funeral. Neftalí stopped when they reached a pile of precious stones arranged around a wooden plank with a singular word in cursive: *Proserpina.*

A gust unraveled Neftalí's scarf and whipped it in the air.

"Tell me what happened, please," Proserpina said, cradling her child while staring at her own grave.

"I don't know what to say, 'mana. You found Old Man Huerta dead on the day the triplets discovered Mama in the barn and I got evicted, pretty much, from my childhood home. We think now that Mama escaped from a ranch somewhere during the wildfires. You disappeared. We couldn't find you. Even Po came out to help. Then after a few weeks he came across a woman's body out here by this ravine. She had no hair. All of us agreed it could've been you. We didn't know what to do. Po volunteered for a few shifts with the grave keeper so he could help us bury you. The grave keeper wouldn't move the body, because he was sick, so this is where it had to happen. Poor Po. He wasn't the same after he found you. A few weeks later he died of lockjaw from industrial pollutants in the fog, and that time it was me who volunteered with the grave keeper to bury him. Me and Mama moved into the house after I claimed the property, became a legit property owner, and even managed Bettina's release from the fish cannery before it burned to the ground. If you can believe all that."

They'd walked back to the house with three gables, and Proserpina gloomily watched as Neftalí unpacked and prepared four chickens in the bucket outside for Mama's meal.

Neftalí showed off Huerta's impressive survivalist fort: the hot spots with electricity; the heavy-duty walk-in freezer, where she'd discovered the colonel's stash of chickens; the cutting table where they were thawed; the well, water purifier, and untapped bottles of booze; the secret basement filled with dried goods, grains, and books.

Evening's shallow reds and violets streaked through the sea of chrome and the onyx ash sky. Neftalí flicked on the porch's incandescent lights and took a good look at Proserpina and her baby. Mama's neck fur stood taut like toothpicks as she got up and gazed suspiciously beyond the property. Neftalí grew concerned that Mama sensed a disturbance. She turned the porch light off and suggested they move inside.

Neftalí placed a candelabra with two beeswax candles atop the long table in the dining room. Proserpina had learned to appreciate moments with artificial light and admired the playful projections around her cast by the flickering flames.

"Weird how shadows don't exist outside anymore," Proserpina said, uncovering her baby completely, their singular shadow as mother and child bouncing around the room. "Not like they used to. Have you noticed? It's only when there is light indoors . . . or we have a flashlight . . . or something casts fake light . . . that our personal shadows return . . . I haven't named my daughter yet. Do you think she has any of my features? Or Po's?"

The distinctive *chik-chika-boom, chik-chika-boom* knock from the triplets beat on the porch door in the back. Neftalí rolled her eyes as water boiled on the stove. She grabbed the candelabra, carried it toward the back door, and set it down on the table below the key holder, looked through the peephole. Nothing: just the convex shape of the backyard. She opened the door to find the triplets, too short for the peephole's eye. Mama was behind the open door, shielded from jumping out.

"What's happening," Neftalí blurted.

The triplets wore stark white, long-sleeved shirts and fancy hats slightly too big for their heads, as if they'd returned from a black-tie funeral procession for Queen Mary. They had glum avian-flu faces. Huicho had a block of wood in his hands, and he extended it to Neftalí. In the candlelight, Neftalí could clearly see it was a newscube.

"What the hell do I want one of these bullshit propaganda things for? Did Alexei tell you to bring me this to fuck with me in a new way or something?"

She sensed the triplets were emotionally vulnerable. Their outlook on life had changed since the fish cannery burned down and their mother never returned to them.

"We don't run into Alexei much anymore," Luismi said.

"Instead, we help give tamales to other kids."

"We have a room at Live Oak, too."

"That's incredible news," Neftalí admitted, genuinely astounded. "Does that mean you brought tamales for your good ol' friend Neftalí, who's done nothing but look out for you little brats since day one?"

Cua pulled out two dozen tamales from his coat and handed them over.

"We saved you some of the *carne de res* ones."

"Nomás pa' que no digas," Huicho said, and all of them laughed, since this was a Three Rivers–ism much lampooned by its Spanish-speaking residents, used when anyone shared anything, whether information, food, drugs, or even a place to hide.

"All right," Neftalí said. "Calm down. All is forgiven, you little freaks. Are we cool? I'm upgrading you from brats to freaks, so you better feel lucky."

Neftalí waved the newscube in front of the triplets like a maggoty bone, saying, "I can't stand these things. What am I supposed to even do with it? The people they choose to read the so-called news always have the worst plastic voices, *guácala*."

Huicho said, "Did you hear who it was who tried to kill the mayor?"

"Pa'lo 'Enry Crick?" said Cua.

"Ha. No," Neftalí said. "Serves that criminal Crick right. Are you finally laughing about it with me? Whoever it was who tried to kill him should be made mayor automatically, to take his place. That's how it should work. Please, tell me who this person of twists and turns is, so I can light a candle in their honor and pour libations."

The triplets lacked the vocabulary to explain and left her with the newscube, since they always had extras. There were tamales lined up for them to distribute. Neftalí said thanks and shut the door, feeling karmically lighter knowing there were no longer bad vibes between her and the triplets.

She inspected the newscube next to the candelabra by the door. Mama watched her with curious eyes. Neftalí could remember a time in her girlhood when the news had aired on actual television, and even back to the regular circulation of city newspapers. She vividly recalled when the rolling blackouts began in Texas and the star-spangled government boxes had issued newscubes to the population—she'd been fascinated in those days, along with the other neighborhood kids, by what seemed like a sophisticated new toy.

Now, after she'd witnessed print phased out and libraries burned, Neftalí could connect the dots between those incidents and the creation of this perfect tool for streamlined misinformation. She reserved nothing but contempt and repulsion not only for the newscube, but for anyone who abided by what it claimed as the truth, which regrettably included most people in Three Rivers.

Proserpina emerged from the tarantula darkness at the west end of the house carrying her wide-eyed child. "I changed her," she said, "and left the dirty diaper in one of your chamber pots. You don't have to worry about it, of course, I'll take care of it in a bit."

Neftalí and Proserpina ate tamales at the long table, spoke little, and stared at the newscube placed right by a tall orange candle. The baby crawled on a blanket set down by the legs of

Proserpina's chair, a few feet from a sprawled Mama, who hardly paid any mind to the kid.

"Something I've been wondering about," Neftalí said, "that's kind of messed up, is that if we didn't bury you, then who is it that is buried in that grave? Because we buried a body for damn sure. We cried and sang your favorite songs."

"You did that for me?"

"Hell yeah. It was hard. Don't make me do it again. But about the body. It reminds me of an old story where a fisherman finds a suitcase in the river. And inside the suitcase is a mutilated woman. When the chupacabras, or whatever they called the police back then, announce the hunt for the killer, all these men appear at the station to confess to the crime. They're all sobbing their eyes out, shivering, ridden with guilt, so it's difficult to believe they're collectively making up their criminal pain. However, it's also hard for the chupacabras to believe that this many men killed only one woman. I mean, what kind of superwoman was she? In the end, it turns out that so many crimes against women went unreported that these men were *all* clearly guilty of killing a woman in the exact way the mutilated body was found. When they heard of the suitcase and the hunt for the killer, they each assumed it was their own particular crime and couldn't stand living with that terror, so they confessed."

"And who went to jail?"

"I forgot. Nobody, probably."

When they finished eating, Neftalí watched Proserpina neatly fold the tamal husks and flatten them, as if making paper airplanes, then reached over them, retracted the metallic antennae from the newscube, and pressed its singular button.

". . . In his first act since his attack, Mayor Pablo Henry Crick signed today the New Mothers Deal. This law promises to alleviate the sharp rise in hunger in Three Rivers by allowing unemployed mothers to participate in the reconstruction of the Big Tex Fish Cannery. The state government will also be seeking the death penalty for Moira Eeiyn, the disgruntled woman charged with the mayor's attempted assassination. Chorizo is twenty-three dollars and ninety-nine cents a pound. Tortillas are five dollars a kilo. Those thick clouds rolling in above the ash with the cold weather this weekend from the hill country—"

Neftalí clicked the newscube off and stared at her finger on the rectangular button. Proserpina was concentrating on the sunrise flame at the end of the tall candle on the table, as if she could see wild horses running over its buttery high plains and their old friend Moira appearing amidst the tumult. Neither of them spoke. The baby crawled out of the dining room, and Proserpina picked her up before she made it across the threshold. Neftalí collected the husks and slipped them into the husk bag, threw their forks into the dirty dish basin, then finally confronted the dishes, taking a good look at the built-up grime and filth.

She placed the dirty dishes on the ground, grabbed a jar of baking soda, and covered both sides of the sink with a thick layer, rolled a cigarette, smoked it, then sprayed hydrogen peroxide on the baking soda and scrubbed the hell out of everything using a sponge she'd been saving for the occasion.

As she did all this, Neftalí connected what the newscube said to the triplets' sheepish behavior—the fact that they'd bothered to bring it over for her to listen to in the first place.

She tried remembering how Moira had entered their lives. Moira was younger than Neftalí and her old crew, had never lived near their part of Old Freeway. Nothing came to mind. Still, the only person worthy of blame, as the chemicals in the sink created a viscous foam like the rabid saliva of a dog, was Alexei. She scrubbed her kitchen clean, imagining it was the incessant sickness and death pervading Three Rivers she was doing away with.

The teddy coins felt heavier as she pictured a person like Moira running from Three Rivers police; their engravings, though they were gibberish symbols alongside Theodore Roosevelt's embossed profile, maintained the semblance of actual worth in the street market.

As ration cards grew continually unreliable through the rolling power outages, and no more barracked worker-mothers at Big Tex provided resources, teddys had gradually become accepted as currency in neighborhood *depósitos* and *pulgas*, to Neftalí's surprise. She'd been witness to the gradual change in Alexei from being her bass player in Missus Batches, to the death of a salesman raving about starting his own business; it'd all finally become a madcap dystopia made in his own image, one that Alexei forced upon every neighborhood boy who'd idolized him from his musical days.

Neftalí was sickened to see what innocent dreams of being an artist can become when you live in a time and place that doesn't let you realize these dreams—a place that is nothing but a constant fight to merely stay afloat, and where nobody becomes anything but a decaying character in a perpetual, sludging, post-punk medieval drama.

She used boiling water from a kettle to finally wash away

the mold and mushroom growths that had accumulated in and around the kitchen, not only in her time living there, but in Huerta's time as well. By the completion of her task, the sink radiated, seemed to smile hugely, and she had made the kitchen brighter. Healthier. The kitchen even groaned like a giant who'd found relief after a tooth infection.

Neftalí stepped into the living room filled with mounting rage. The candle was snuffed out and both chairs were pushed in. Proserpina and the baby were gone. She found Mama by the door, ready to be let out, and Neftalí went outside to try to breathe cleaner air that could restore her. She followed Mama to a clearing behind the barn, and watched her gently, full of vulnerability, find a place to pee.

Neftalí closed her eyes, clenched her face, turned, and re-leased the most beastly, cathartic wail she could toward the rubble sky and the hidden sun, toward Alexei and the city of Three Rivers; she anticipated neighbors firing gunshots into the air, throwing Molotov cocktails, burning down satellites in solidarity with her primitive cry for justice.

A sound snuck up from behind her and rattled her bones and thundered in her chest and split the ground below—it was Mama's roar. The birds in Old Freeway sat like motionless droplets of rainwater on a still leaf. Neftalí felt proud, as if maybe by screaming she'd encouraged Mama to flaunt her creaturely side as well.

The Bengal tiger's eyes, however, were keenly focused on something moving at the edge of the property. For a moment, Neftalí thought it could be Proserpina, but it was too off the beaten path, coming from the Northface neighborhood, which also now had made its own currency using antique aluminum cans. Northface had been the setting of various neighborhood children's rhymes, and, with their revolving cast of petty thieves, was never portrayed flatteringly. In short, it was a neighborhood that Neftalí, and most people, tended to stay away from. The people there were rude to outsiders, and unwelcoming, but when the food or clothing drives happened each month, they were always the first ones camping in line before sunrise.

The terrain descended before Neftalí and Mama, and it was early enough that silver clusters of natural fog trotted in like migrating ghost horses. About thirty yards ahead of them, next to a downed telephone pole and tall grasses, stood a bearded man wearing a dark blue raincoat. He held a small rectangular instrument with both hands and brought it close to his face.

Mama moved toward the bearded man in a prowl, and right when Neftalí was going to give her word to stand down, the man pressed a button on his instrument. The instrument clicked, and a flash shot out. Mama roared again, and as the tiny stars in Neftalí's peripheral vision ran amok, she yelled, "No!" but it was too late. Mama had pounced on the bearded man, who panicked and squirmed between the five-hundred-pound tiger and the green mud. He broke free of the dark blue raincoat the moment Mama had shredded the hood to pieces, and he slipped on the ashy dew several times before regaining his balance.

The bearded man felt through his pockets, and along his torso and his limbs, perhaps expecting to have been torn to ribbons. Neftalí caught up to Mama and held her back, terror-stricken at the thought of what her child could be capable of, while the tiger stared menacingly at the man.

He found his Edixa 16 camera on the ground directly in front of him, pointed it again toward Neftalí and Mama, this time like a gun, as he walked away from them. "You won't get away with this," he yelled.

Neftalí frowned as she petted Mama, and exclaimed, "Sir. It was by your own free will that you trespassed onto our property. You are at fault here."

He was much farther away when he shouted, "It doesn't matter! That animal should not be anywhere within city limits. Period." The bearded man disappeared as the fog cleared, and the grackle-winged sky carried in darker clouds of ash.

Neftalí was struck dumb. Everything had happened so quickly; it was only after she was alone with Mama that she pieced together what the man had actually said—who even was he? Neftalí envisioned horror: battalions of chupacabras rushing the farm with their bayonet rifles, volleys sounding off at a roaring Mama on her hind legs, ready to lunge at them, only to die tragically trying to protect her.

She cried silent tears of anguish and confusion, as if she'd actually witnessed the killing of Mama before her eyes, and Neftalí petted Mama more aggressively, tugged at her rolls of fur, as she caught shedding orange hair on her sweaty palms. Neftalí hugged Mama, but Mama pushed away and moved toward the trough of water by the porch. Water splashed onto the floorboards and the ground as she noisily lapped up a good portion of it.

Mama set her eyes on another figure walking toward them from the orchard, and Neftalí felt weary. She was wrapping her arms around Mama to prevent her from moving closer when she realized the figure was Proserpina, carrying her baby in the rebozo and a heavy pail in her hands. She set the pail down, and Mama stuck her head in to get a closer sniff of the misshapen stones it contained.

"These stones were set on the grave out there by you and others, in mourning, thinking it was me who died," she said. "It's left me wondering about this person. The one who's really buried there. Thought about the people who miss them, who are hoping this dead person is still alive. I need to boil the stones. It should only be me who does it, since all their energy was directed toward me, to guide me in my afterlife. But I don't need that afterlife energy right now. The person who is buried in my grave does. Since we can't set the rocks out in the sun, or under a full moon, we can boil that old energy out of them to help guide this person."

Neftalí reluctantly carried Proserpina's baby girl while Proserpina filled a thirty-quart pot with cold water in the kitchen, set it to boil, and scrubbed each stone gently over the sink, as if they were potatoes, before tossing them in. Proserpina turned up the heat when there were no stones left; the two of them walked into the living room toward the newscube resting by an unlit candle. Proserpina relit the candle as they both took a seat. Neftalí pressed the rectangular button on the newscube. When nothing happened, she pulled out its antennae, and an anchor's voice fizzled to life, saying, ". . . and parts of Iowa and Minnesota received their first sustained sunshine in thirteen months. In his first act since his attack, Mayor Pablo Henry Crick signed today the New Mothers Deal. This law promises to alleviate the sharp rise in hunger in Three Rivers by allowing unemployed mothers to participate in the reconstruction of the Big Tex Fish Cannery. The state government will also be seeking the death penalty for Moira Eeiyn, the disgruntled woman charged with the mayor's attempted assassination . . ."

Proserpina pressed the newscube off. She walked with her baby toward the stove in the kitchen to adjust the temperature again, and put the lid over the pot of stones.

"Do you think Alexei convinced Moira to kill Crick for his own gain?" Neftalí asked her. "Him and Moira were close."

"Tolstoyevsky? Our old bass player? No way. That guy's a lot of things, but he's not a cold-blooded killer. Honestly, who has lived in Three Rivers and not daydreamed of murdering that asshole Crick? I know I have. You for sure, too. We literally wrote songs about it. He's been mayor here, like, most our lives. Maybe Moira, if she really did do it, did it on her own."

Neftalí pounded on the table, attracting Mama's protective attention from the other room and upsetting the baby.

She stood up, fixing her eyes on various objects around the room. "Before we saw you carrying these stones," she said, "there was a man on the property. A flash went off from his camera, and Mama attacked him. He ended up running away, saying awful things about Mama, how she shouldn't be here, and about the law, and things like that. I'm afraid he's going to get us in trouble, and they will take Mama from us."

Neftalí took Proserpina to the spot, and they found the torn dark blue raincoat with its arms spread on the ground, playing the martyr. Proserpina picked it up with a stick, and together with Neftalí she set it to burn in the property's blackened clearing. They kept Mama indoors, and she timidly watched the flames from one of the living room windows. A thin, gelatinous rain started drizzling. The fire steamed out, and the raincoat's remains curdled to an unctuous sludge.

Proserpina and Neftalí moved to the porch, watching the stringy rain of resin become a nuisance in their corner of Three Rivers.

"Alexei's taken over the roofed part of the city, 'mana. Where Professor Pantano's laboratory stood. I know we've always been sensitive about not vilifying him, because of our culture and history and everything, but he's the person we know who's closest to all this. The rising street value of those teddys has gone straight to his head. Only a matter of time before he gets burned. It's the triplets who've been trying to get me to talk some sense into him, and now I guess it's worked."

The pot with stones in the kitchen was boiling and spilling over. Proserpina turned the temperature down, used a wooden spoon to move around the stones, and seemed pleased. Neftalí strapped on her walking shoes along with a black, hooded garment that withstood the rain and kept her warm, too. She carried a knapsack and her favorite dark crystal—for safe travels and luck.

Proserpina and her baby followed Neftalí out the door. Affected goodbyes tended to disgruntle Mama, so Neftalí simply waved and left the tiger standing next to Proserpina and the baby on the back porch. They watched Neftalí make a trail through the rain sludge on the grass toward the alley, then vanish into the fickle darkness. Proserpina swayed with her hiccuping baby in the rebozo, petted Mama's head behind her ears. Mama lay on her side, licked her own nose a few times, then together they walked back into the house, as the winged red ants that emerged with the rain buzzed and conquered.

A CRYSTAL-BLUE HAZE was emitted by the streets of Three Rivers, brought on by the slimy rain and stray beams of light attempting to brew rainbows from sludge puddles under an uncooperative dome of volcanic ash. Squad cars patrolled the streets, sometimes shooting their long flashlight beams at huddled boys or older men, ringing their sirens in spurts before dispersing. Police had instructions to scan the ration cards of every woman they saw, to determine whether they'd given birth and to enforce the New Mothers Deal. Few women were seen walking the streets at any given hour as a result. Children were treated differently by the police, however, for often they acted as informants, and were rewarded handsomely with confiscated teddys.

No gas lamps were burning in any sector of the city, and the stoplights perpetually blinked yellow or red. Shreds of torn reward posters for escaped worker-mothers were still wheat-pasted on walls of empty buildings. Crosswalk signs had been vandalized or broken off, hanging by their wires.

Neftalí never had trouble or felt danger walking through Three Rivers, even during the shadiest of hours, so she was surprised when she reached Sinaloa Avenue and a squad car flashed a blue inspection ray in her face. She presented the police with her official ration card. In the city's database Neftalí was registered as a tax-paying landowner, so the officers let her go after a few routine questions.

A city bus approached as the police drove away, and she flagged it down. The bus had no number indicating its route. Its doors swung open, and the driver yelled, "Where you headed?"

"To the roofed part of the city."

"I'm not going anywhere near there. They cut off all the routes taking you there, as a matter of fact. You're gonna have to wait and see if you can catch a ride with the scrap dealer when he passes. But it's late in the day, he's probably far gone by now. I can take you as far up as Allandale, but you'll have to get off there."

Neftalí scanned the bus pass they gave to all property owners, and sat in the middle of the bus. Near the back there was one other passenger, wearing a fedora and chewing bubble gum loudly while humming a tune. He yanked on the cable and the bus stopped at the next corner. The man stumbled toward the front exit.

The driver said to the man, "Now, remember, pilgrim, just because you're sauced up and going back to your family, and you're not feeling as bad as you were earlier, it does not mean you don't owe anyone an apology. Remember what we talked about earlier. You need to listen to people. And you need to own up and say 'I'm sorry' when you mess up. All right? See you tomorrow."

The man stepped off and the bus continued. Neftalí moved to a seat closer to the driver. Since it was just the two of them, and there was a mysterious quality to the driver that Neftalí found intriguing, she asked, "What's wrong with that person? I know it's not any of my business, but . . ."

The driver kept their eyes on the road and said, "Nothing's wrong with him. He has the ability to act right. But he's not doing it. Comes on here every day and tells me his problems. What can I do? I got to lay it to him straight, so he quits bothering me. He's messing his life up, and only he can fix it. I'm not here to feel sorry for anybody. Here's your stop coming up. You be safe out there, too."

Neftalí stepped off, and immediately remembered to ask for more details about the scrap dealer. The bus doors shut behind her and it continued on its limited route. Neftalí was left with a face full of smog and one finger in the air, her question left hanging. She waited almost fifteen minutes at that stop, until she got impatient and decided to walk the remainder of the way. Neftalí was near the I-37 expressway, which funneled the ghostly moans of traffic jams past. She found a dark spot between two abandoned Lincolns turned abandoned homes, and peed.

A faint clop of hooves became increasingly loud from beyond a gated junkyard for discontinued water tower domes that used up most of the city block. Neftalí had her head covered by her hood, and waited until a rider appeared aboard a rickety wagon being pulled by a mature, strong burro. She waved for the rider's attention.

"Is there room for one more? To the roofed part of the city?" she yelled.

The man on the wagon made guttural sounds; the burro responded by huffing and coming to a halt.

"You got a fare?" the rider's gruff voice responded. His beard was thick and the few hairs left on his greasy head hung past his shoulders.

Neftalí pulled out a jar from her sack and said, "Please accept as a fare this jar of semolina grains that you can use in your food. They're good for digestion."

The man scrunched his brow and squinted at the burro, who seemed equally unimpressed.

"We'd perhaps consider it," he said.

Neftalí interpreted this as a yes and climbed aboard the left side. She was happy to see a thin wooden divider between her and the stern man. A basket of green and red apples also sat between them. Neftalí's eyes widened. She hadn't tasted an apple in so long that even the word itself seemed more like an incantation than a reference to a physical object. On the back of the wagon, rattling with every bump or turn, was the day's haul of old machine parts: broken space heaters, mangled book shredders, kitchen appliances, keyboards, mice, shattered projector screens, burned-out AC window units.

"I don't have teeth like I used to. Help yourself to one of them. Don't make the same mistake I made."

Neftalí saw he meant the apples. She reached into the basket and grabbed the reddest one that caught her eye. "Use that water there to wash it if you must. It's clean," he advised.

The man stopped the wagon at the sight of a pile of rubbish on the curb. He got off, rummaged through it like a bear tearing through a small car, now and again tossing a salvageable scrap onto the back of the wagon. A pile of large canvas paintings sat amongst the trash, and the scrap dealer held one up, looked at it critically, then threw it aside. He kicked through several imploded book shredders—now that most books in Three Rivers had been destroyed, the machines had been misused, as people tossed un-shreddable objects into their mouths, destroying the tiny blades and rendering them useless.

The scrap dealer climbed back on. Neftalí finished eating the apple and held the fresh core between two fingers. "Thank you for the apple," she said glumly. "It has been a while since I've had access to one."

"No need to mention it. It's what one does with apples. Scatter them, and pass them around."

"If you don't mind my asking, what did you mean when you told me not to make the same mistake you made?"

"Aye," he said. "It's the way it goes with apples. There's ancient imagination in them. If a stranger offers you one, you must take it. Or bear a misfortune. When I was young, I was a land baron. Had a swell education, and was engaged to the most beautiful woman these eyes ever saw. Mere days before we were to wed, the most abominable creature came my way. A ragged woman who'd stationed herself, begging for alms, right outside my business. I ignored this woman, see. Mere days before my wedding, this ragged woman held a red apple out to me as I was passing her by, heading home. I was confused, thinking she was selling apples. But there was only one apple in her possession, and she told me it was a wedding gift. From her to me. You could imagine my predicament. Who would want to take this hideous woman's solitary apple? I didn't know there was something inviolably ancient about this gesture from the woman. So I refused it. And I got home to discover my fiancée had changed her mind and left me. Following day, I was disinherited and pushed out of the company

I'd founded. Lost all my friends. Never saw this ragged woman again. All this, just for refusing the gift of an apple. Today I keep my own modest orchard. Set up lights for photosynthesis. Carry this basket and offer most strangers I encounter an apple, now that it's me who is the hideous old man."

"Thank you, sir," Neftalí said, somehow wanting to cry, and she held up the soft apple core. "Where can I dispose of this?"

"It decomposes into the earth. Chuck it out."

Neftalí did as instructed. A kitten crawled from the rear of the wagon and jumped onto the man's back. "There's my buddy," he said, and fed the kitten dry fish treats he kept in his pocket. The kitten crouched, full of wonder, on his left shoulder, as it eyed Neftalí up and down, meowing its questions.

"Can I pet it?" she asked.

"Probably not a good idea. Can get too friendly and scratch you bad. Looks like your stop is coming up," he said. "I am going to insist you take another apple. As many as you'd like. Even if you are not hungry, you can always use an apple for the road. They're useful also as weapons. For when you see a giant cockroach, perhaps. Simply aim it at their back, and throw hard. If you come to encounter a giant cockroach, that is."

Neftalí grabbed two apples, again thanked the scrap dealer, and stepped off the rickety wagon. As the lively burro clopped away, Neftalí regretted not having asked if she could pet the burro goodbye. The scrap dealer turned back—to her surprise—and waved.

As she lifted her arm to return the gesture, he and the wagon and the burro got swallowed up by a pale brown cloud sweeping across the width of the street. Neftalí took cover inside her long, hooded garment, turned her back to the cloud, and waited for it to pass.

The roofed part of the city sat at a higher elevation than the rest of Three Rivers, and it was originally designed to be the largest parking edifice in the world. The structure was fifty stories high, eight floors underground, connected to several abandoned, but once promising, buildings. Many areas were now difficult to access, even by the most experienced dweller. The main entrances and exits had been sealed off years ago. Unless there was an aggressive manhunt for a particular person, Three Rivers police mostly left this area alone, since it was well known that nobody could survive long in the roofed part of the city.

Neftalí turned on her halogen lamp, found shrubs and pesky little plants that slapped her ankles, stabbing their thorns through her socks. She stamped and fought off the plants as she walked along the edge of an expansive graffitied wall. A short whistle startled her, as she continued trampling the pesky vegetation. She shone her lamp at a spot on the cinder block fence where one of the triplets sat, deflecting the light with his arm.

"Which one are you?" she asked. "Don't lie."

"Cuauhtémoc."

"Where are your brothers?"

Cua looked at his shoes as he swung them bashfully.

"Take me to where they are," she told him.

Neftalí turned her lamp off, and in the darkness made eye

contact with Cua, before he jumped off the wall and signaled for her to follow.

"Did you hear the new-cube?" he asked.

Neftalí knew that Cua had trouble pronouncing his *s*'s, so was confident it was really him. "I did," she said. "That's why I'm here. To talk to Alexei about it."

"Do you think Moira really killed the mayor?"

"Well. The mayor never really died. He's not technically dead, so she never really killed anyone."

"What?"

"No, I don't think she did. Does Alexei think that?" She swung in front of Cua to watch his expression as she asked this. The darkness in the roofed part of the city proved itself near impenetrable, so she'd turned the light on again to illuminate the way; it revealed piled, dusty bricks, scattered clothes, debris, cigarette butts, used tampons, shattered glass, broken condoms, excrement. Mercifully, the stench of urine was faint.

"I don't know," said Cua.

There was a distant rumble, like an eternal shattering of windows coming from the far curvature of the maze Cua was guiding her through. No birds or rats were heard cooing. Neftalí and Cua gasped at the immense shadow of a spider in its web when the light flashed directly at it. They watched the spider crawl away, then they kept going to where the narrow passage curved into a brick tunnel, toward the perpetual shattering noise and an orange glow cast on a distant wall. The tedious passage reminded Neftalí of loading band equipment through the alleys of shady clubs back in the day.

Having Cua, her secret favorite of the triplets, as her guide was reassuring. She'd had second thoughts about coming out here, wondering what she'd even thought she could accomplish. When they got to the wall with the orange glow and turned right, a tall steel door with a brass latch was narrowly open and the sound of distorted guitars jammed through, along with crackling flames and cacophonous yelling.

Cua squeezed into the cracked door without touching it, and Neftalí did the same.

Two Marshall stacks were blaring incomprehensible music from the far end of the large dismantled laboratory. The absence of the teddy machine, Badebec, was only accentuated by dried grease and oil spots in the middle of the room where it had once stood. Leaks dripped in various rhythms from the tall mosaic ceiling. Buckets and trays were strategically scattered on the concrete floor to catch their sludge.

Huicho and Luismi were huddled in front of the Marshall stacks, among a few other boys Neftalí didn't recognize. All of them, with the exception of the triplets, were drinking forties and engaged in a card game on the ground, betting using broken tabs of aluminum cans as currency.

Cua silently, loyally joined them, leaving Neftalí standing by the sentinel steel door. Three metal trash cans were spread around the room, casting their raging light from hypnotic fires, except along the spot where the Marshall stacks and the boys were, which was illuminated by a lantern.

Alexei reclined on an old cushioned office chair propped up on a stage, away from the boys. The chair had a high back, and a purple curtain served as the stage's backdrop. The shadow Alexei cast on the curtain towered, stretched, and shrank continuously. Using both hands, he held a rectangular device with a tiny screen that illuminated his face with shifting color schemes. A crown with an array of antique bottle caps, winking teddys, and American coins welded or glued together was ensconced on his head.

Neftalí remembered an axolotl—a lonesome salamander in a lonesome aquarium—because as the smoke from the trash cans got sucked out of the air vents mounted on the dripping ceiling, and the boys hollered over the cacophonous music while playing their card game, this was what Alexei looked like. An axolotl. In the light of the fire he was also like a forlorn count bribing local villagers to be his friend before sucking their blood.

It was colder inside the large dismantled laboratory than outside, and she saw her breath in front of her—in that breath was a book, and Neftalí opened its pages. The book instructed her to presently look upon her own body, and Neftalí did just that. She found she was naked. Her lower half contorted until her legs twisted into the legs of a large bird, her body sprouted deep-rooted feathers, and her ass shot out a long, thick reptilian tail, which slithered along the concrete. Silver wings pierced the flesh of her back and spread wide open. In Neftalí's left hand she held a bugle; in her right hand, a harp; and she flew with great sorrow over a sea of drowning people on the streets of Three Rivers, before sounding the instruments that would put an end to their misery.

Neftalí snapped out of her fantasy and yelled, "Who put this shit on," pointing toward the Marshall stacks.

Alexei pressed the glowing screen against his chest and straightened himself in the chair; the boys drinking their forties and playing their game turned toward her voice.

Neftalí removed the long garment's hood from her head

and walked closer to a flaming trash can. She felt its biting concert heat. Alexei laughed and slowly clapped, as if Neftalí had won a long, epic round of *lotería*.

"Nef," Alexei yelled over the music. "Welcome." He shifted his coin crown, turned to one of the boys, and said, "Can we lower it down a little?"

A boy decked out in polyester and shades said, "Okay, but only a bit." He pulled a tablet out from behind the Marshall stacks, pressed a button. A pale glow revealed his thin, boyish face as he turned the sound level down a few notches.

"Get this," Alexei continued. "We are playing music from the wide-open air. But it's limited. The air only has music up to a certain era. All the bands that we grew up with aren't there."

Cua and Luismi and Huicho nodded slowly, as if it hurt their necks.

"Who gets to choose the music," Neftalí wondered.

The boy in polyester shrugged. "Mostly chooses itself. Do you know any names of songs?" he asked Neftalí. The boy was about a foot shorter than her, and his sneakers emanated a green phosphorescence, like fungi.

"Luna here," Alexei exclaimed, gesturing toward the boy in polyester, "is our gadgets man. He hooked everything together and made it work."

Neftalí's irreplaceable music had been broken by police, stolen, or turned moldy, so it felt like she'd walked across a long desert without hearing distorted guitars or Adderall drumbeats. She took a good look at each boy's physical features while the industrial music played. Other than the triplets and Luna, there were four other boys she didn't recognize, who all sat on a long wooden plank with their forties by their knees. They slapped one another and joked quietly in hushed voices, so the others could never quite hear.

Screeches and bat wings circled from above. One of the four boys she didn't know opened a big bag of pork cracklings, and the three others dug their hands in. Pork cracklings flew out of the boys' hands and mouths and the plastic bag as Neftalí watched.

"I can't eat more cracklings, I'm stuffed," Alexei told her. "But, please, help yourself. Take as many bags as you desire." He pointed to the hallway at the far end of the wide room, where Neftalí had spotted a stray dog with Proserpina on her previous visit. Shiny plastic bags were piled, almost blocking the doorway. She walked up to them and saw tiny fires reflected in each of the bags' crinkles and folds. Neftalí squinted, tried to make out their faded words and numbers.

"These expired eleven years ago!" she yelled. "They will make you all sick."

She turned around, saw that nobody had heard her warning.

Alexei had tilted back to his little screen, and as Neftalí approached the stage he shut it off and dropped it onto an aluminum folding table by his chair. An electronic piece nobody recognized started playing at a reasonable volume from the tablet attached to the Marshall stacks.

The boys continued their game of cards as if Neftalí had never entered, chugging their forties and slapping their knees. Only the triplets bothered looking in her direction every now and then. The menacing smoke unfurling from the trash cans, her metamorphosis fantasy, and the flapping bat wings gave her the courage to press her eyebrows together and ask Alexei:

"You heard that it's your old teddys partner, Moira, who's accused of an assassination attempt on the mayor, right?"

"Hell yeah," he replied. "Crazy Moira. Who saw *that* coming? She bailed on helping out in the teddys market in the end. All of us were left wondering what happened to her, and then come to find this out."

"So you're saying you had nothing to do with what happened to Crick?"

"*Do* with this? Like, you're asking me if I'm partners with Moira in her crime?"

"You two were partners when the professor was first making teddys—"

"Hey," Luna called out to them. "Gimme the name of a song, for God's sake. Any song." He'd cranked down the music, so the embers from the fires took advantage of the temporary quiet to really pop and fizz. The bats had stopped circling. Everyone waited on Neftalí for a response. Pressed to think of an old song, Neftalí drew a blank. Then from deep in her subconscious a ballad emerged like a lily through a prison wall—one Bettina had sung at Angélica's funeral, and that Neftalí associated with great longing and pain.

"'Black,'" she said, "'Is the Color of My True Love's Hair.'"

Luna repeated the words into the tablet.

Silence. The keys of a piano, ascending like a spiral staircase within the bare bones of a blood-filled mountain. Then a voice. A voice to turn bags of pork cracklings into fig trees.

"This is too slow," Luna protested.

With the added strength the opening bars granted her, Neftalí yelled back, "Let it play!"

Luna set the tablet down. The dynamics in the room

shifted with the song rocking the waters. Neftalí hadn't heard this studio version since her girlhood, during the last days of widespread internet, television, and radio.

"Nef," Alexei went on, "where do you think the professor and Badebec are right now? Pablo Crick arranged for them to be taken to a bigger facility after the professor saved his life, which essentially made teddys the official currency here. Why do you think me and the boys have full reign over this place? We own the roofed part of the city. It was in the contract with Professor Pantano that we could have it, and they transferred Badebec to the fifth floor of one of those electrified buildings by the capitol. So, unfortunately, it doesn't make sense that any of us would be partners with Moira. Especially not me."

Alexei paced onstage as he delivered all this, the coin crown poised at an angle, as if it was doing all his heavy thinking. Neftalí could see he enjoyed his height advantage over the kids. It reminded her of his time as a hooligan bass player. She'd dreaded facing Alexei, because she'd concluded that the only thing worse than losing a loved one to death was watching their spirit turn irrevocably worse, fighting for the wrong team.

But was Alexei really a loved one? Neftalí could not say. Now that there was no turning back to the old world, Neftalí had taken a good look at Alexei, and wondered if having played backup for two women made him posture a certain way with the boys now. When she'd seen what the teddys were doing to Alexei's self-image, to his sense of greed, their drifting apart had naturally accelerated. The feeling that there was something unresolved in their relationship and musical journey pricked at her.

"I wish I believed you, Alexei."

"Why would I lie about something this important? You can trust me to always tell the truth to you, Nef. And to prove it, I'll let you in on a little secret," he said, pacing the stage. "Something not a lot of people know about. You know how they say that the reason the sky got lower . . . the reason the sun and stars and moon went away . . . is because of some volcano in Mexico? Where your family is from? And all the smoke and lava the volcano shot out? Well, me and the boys know the actual truth. What people are saying is wrong. Because there was this big attack on the country nobody knows about. And they exploded a bunch of bombs. The bombs are still exploding, and until they stop the sun won't come out. That's why it's important to have leaders like Pablo Crick and his administration guiding us."

The boys had gathered around the stage to listen more closely. This was a topic that deeply interested all of them, and one they'd witnessed Alexei expounding upon many times. The boys had first heard this news of an attack directly from him, and continually struggled with context or to find the words to use to press him for greater detail. This was another advantage Neftalí could see Alexei wielded over these boys—he was older, and, like her, had at least a primary school education.

"Maybe," she said. "Maybe you're right, Alexei. It's not like we could do what our parents once did when they were our age and turn on the television, or read the local paper to figure out the truth. But why can't we hear the constant gunfire, if there's an invasion going down? Where are the sounds of these bombs going off? Are they really, really polite bombs that explode very quietly?"

"Okay. I get it, Nef. Say what you will. Is that what you came here for, to accuse me of being part of a political murder?"

"I don't know why I came here. Something pushed me. But now that I'm taking stock of things, I can see the bigger picture. And it's not pretty."

The four boys and Luna had wandered to the far end of the room, by a pile of gallon jugs and empty oil cans. Music from the Marshall stacks had been shuffled to a New Orleans ragtime number.

"Just tell me what you know about Moira, if you know anything to tell, and I'll get out of here."

"I'm telling you what I know, and I have nothing to do with any of it. I know this one thing for sure, though. She shot Crick with one of those forty-fives that burn your hand when you shoot. From up close, like five or six times, *BOOM, BOOM, BOOM*," Alexei yelled, winning back the boys' drifting attention. The triplets were each sitting in a different corner of the stage, listening closely, too. "*BOOM, BOOM*. She crushed one of his lungs. But the professor saved his life using an old invention. What he called an *iron lung*. He built it from a little submarine tank with chemicals used for putting out fires. The doctors took Crick's shot-up lung and replaced it with the iron one. They also sewed his ear back on, and glued his cheek together with lead. But one of his hands is partly gone forever, and that's the way it's going to have to be, everyone says, because there's no iron lung for the hand that's been invented yet. The professor also finally perfected the teddy machine. Look here, making us rich."

Neftalí noticed that the purple curtain behind Alexei was not so much a curtain but a cloak, and he threw it back to reveal a tall, rectangular red box, with large illuminated white words in front: COKE.

"Who's winning the game over there?" Alexei asked the boys.

"Our little man Huicho is," Luna said, pointing with both his index fingers.

"Let's cash those winnings in, Huicho," Alexei shouted, banging on the table.

Huicho gathered all the aluminum tabs he'd won with the help of his brothers, and together they fed them into the opening slot at the top of the Coke machine.

"I get it," Neftalí said, unimpressed. "Is this the big new baby now?"

"Sh-shhhhh," Alexei said, and gestured for everyone to step back. He pressed the large, unlabeled button at the machine's center, tilted his crown to the back of his head.

They'd all climbed onstage by now, and stood along its edge, giving the Coke machine plenty of room. Steam shot out of its rear vents as the machine sputtered. It did a little sideways hop like a man in a rabbit suit, then stood absolutely still. The COKE logo blinked, then one letter at a time. The bottom slot of the machine sucked in wind like a thirsty beast, then released the most squalid, mechanical howl Neftalí had ever heard.

The triplets were the only ones present to cover their ears

as the sound twisted into a wail, then a shriek that went on and on. Alexei stood there grinning, self-assured, with his arms crossed, the crown of bottle-tops, apocryphal teddys, and coins slicking his hair back. The Coke machine sputtered once again, the howl wheezed out, and an Arctic steam emerged from the machine's pores, forming a cloud that floated on the stage. When the cloud dissipated, the COKE logo was no longer visible through a thick layer of icy frost on the machine. Alexei, Neftalí, and the other boys approached it cautiously, like the machine was a sleeping giant they were trying not to awaken.

Six hollow clanks were heard from the front bottom slot. Alexei grabbed each cold, frosty coin using a pair of tongs and set them on the aluminum foldout table. Though she knew they were coming, the sight of the coins was deeply disheartening to Neftalí. She took two steps back. Neftalí pulled a medicine pouch from her bag, untied the strings, and opened it. Six mossy teddys fell into her hand, and she held them up for Alexei to see, like this was another score to settle.

Alexei took the teddys and was appalled at how filthy they were.

"Geez," he said, "where are you keeping these, by a swamp?"

"I'm returning them to you. It's funny, I'm actually charmed that you are able to have music in here. But you know what? Whatever the professor, or Pablo Crick, has you doing in this hellhole, paying you with teddys, it's not worth it."

"Hellhole? Neftalí, where do you think we are? Have the bomb fumes gone to your head and made you forget? We live in Three fucking Rivers, Texas. Where our parents had record stores or movie houses, what do we even have, other than the hope to find primitive tablets and speakers to play this kind of music from? Who can even score a record or a little TV here, when there's other, richer cities up north you can smuggle them to and actually make money? To live in Three Rivers and not be able to even get some sun, or see the moon . . . I can't imagine a greater hellhole than that, and that's where we are living. So, yes, thank you for that generous reminder. We do indeed live in a hellhole."

"You really know how to deliver a line on a stage, Alexei. I can see how these boys fall for your charm. Hell, I can see how *I* once fell for it. You were dynamic, playing music with us in Missus Batches. Everyone always said that you moved like an actual star in the making up there. But you also knew to do it for the show. You're even well aware of the show when you go on these little speeches."

"What show? What are you talking about? You're a show. I'm a show. Every day it's a show here in Three Rivers . . . Isn't there a saying like that? And we are all just performers in the show? You're the one who reads books, Neftalí, you ought to know."

"All right, Alexei. I'm going to say something, then. In this show. And on this"—Neftalí stomped down hard on the planks below her—"stage. Whatever you all have going on with these evil fucking men. The same evil men we grew up detesting, Alexei. To the point of even making music, so we could sing against them. Whatever these evil fucking men have you doing, it's not worth it. Remember that in the back of your mind. I know you're trying to, I don't know, ridicule me by pointing out that I read books. But one of the things books taught me is that there is a past, present, and future for our actions. What you did yesterday affects today. What you do today affects tomorrow, and so forth, forever."

"That's the thing," said Alexei, "that's the part you don't know about. The future. Teddys was the beginning. Remember my taco trucks? They're finally taking off. And soon there will be a whole fleet of them. The mayor's giving me a chance to go out there with my taco trucks and feed the people of Three Rivers. But one can only purchase an order of food using teddys. See? Pablo Crick and Professor Pantano are my primary investors. I don't think you're giving me enough credit here, Nef. My plan really is genius, if you think about it. We are creating the coins that will be used to feed people our tacos. In a way, we are heroes."

"Where are people gonna get these teddys? If you wanted to be a real hero, you'd give away the tacos for nothing."

"But where's the fun in that?" Alexei snapped, repulsed by her suggestion.

Meanwhile, Neftalí's song choice had permanently disrupted the algorithm on the tablet. A primitive guitar song now played, unleashing truth and consequences that awakened the bats above and got them circling again.

"Halfway here, I questioned why I was even coming," Neftalí said. "And to tell you the truth, I didn't have a good answer. Now that I see with my own eyes that you've lost your fucking mind, I know that's the reason I'm here. To bear witness. And be able to tell of the things I've seen. If you really gave a shit about feeding people, and the future, and all these things you claim to care about, then you'd care about what is happening to Moira, too. Your friend. My friend, too . . . I guess. But that doesn't matter. With how close you are to the professor, and to Pablo Crick, if I were you, I'd be helping Moira find a way out of this."

"A way out how? Like bust her out of jail?" Alexei laughed. "Hire her the best hotshot attorney teddys and tacos can buy?"

"Or finish the job for her. That's fucking right, I said it. Pablo Crick and the professor are not your friends. Whatever Moira is going through in jail . . . or wherever they are keeping her is tied to what all of you are doing right here in the roofed part of the city. And don't any of you fucking forget that. I ought to take away your tablet. It's bad luck to take away people's music, but I ought to take it anyway."

She hurried to the tablet and the others followed. Nobody would have stopped Neftalí if she'd unplugged the tablet and packed it up in her bag, but the moment she moved toward it, the song changed, and the opening notes made her stop in her tracks.

The grimy laboratory walls, mucky concrete, and metal-head trash can fires opened like a corpse flower—just as it had happened in her old living room the morning after the police raided her place for books. A golden cauliflower sun, sand along a beach, and crashing ocean spray projected around her. Alexei, the boys, the Coke machine all disappeared, and although the rays of thirsty daylight fell everywhere, Neftalí felt like the projection was herself, and she was unaffected by the elements while walking along the shore of this beach.

She watched a thin man with the legs of his trousers rolled up carrying a bucket to collect seashells. He hummed along to the song playing from the Marshall stacks—a song from the other end of space-time, like a lost relative dialing collect long distance. Neftalí watched this man inspecting shells, sometimes holding the concave parts to his ears, conducting an orchestra in his mind. She wanted to say something to him, but knew that in this illusion she could only observe and listen, not interact.

The song that stunned her was "Sobre las olas," and the man walking the expansive beach was a welcome vision of Juventino Rosas. Neftalí hadn't experienced one of his visits since before the volcanic ash had covered the atmosphere, since before they'd found the body by the reservoir that they'd buried thinking it was Proserpina.

A boy Neftalí didn't know was calling out from the corridor beyond the pile of pork cracklings and trash can fires. She heard his voice as a distant palpitation moving closer to her like a butterfly. The beach, along with Juventino Rosas picking up shells, melted into the ground, then disappeared, while the song "Sobre las olas" continued playing—a big-band version with extravagant flourishes that Neftalí had never heard before.

A volley of bewildered shouts and boyish shock rang from the corridor. Neftalí followed the triplets, powered on her halogen lamp, since the fire from the trash cans couldn't reach that narrow space. Beyond the mound of pork cracklings was a litter of pink baby possums suckling on a large silver mama possum as she lay on her back. The halogen lamp upset the mama possum; she exposed her fangs and scowled at Neftalí, which further astonished the boys. Neftalí flicked the lamp off and turned away from the scene. Juventino's song was still playing when she commanded, "Leave those loving animals alone."

Alexei threw a log into one of the trash cans. He was silhouetted, wearing his crown of real and invented coins, against the rising fire. Neftalí could see that that worthless crown really did grant him a certain esteem, even power. The triplets were the only ones among the boys who were eavesdropping when she said to Alexei, "I'm going to hold you accountable, Alexei. Not only for Moira, but if anything happens to any of these boys—"

"But, Neftalí—"

"I don't care," she interrupted, and threw the hood of her long garment over her head. Neftalí walked past a flaming trash can toward the tall steel door. She was gone before the tablet attached to the Marshall stacks shuffled randomly to the next track in the algorithm.

~

With the absence of regular sunshine, and the general scarcity of city lights, the color spectrum tended to carry the limited range of a rare monochromatic rose. One had to shine a lamp a few feet away from a subject to make out elusive greens, or oranges, fuchsia, or even stark white. Automobile headlights from drivers braving the haze often revealed patches of layered street graffiti and the fact that Three Rivers' street signs had originally been navy blue.

Neftalí decided to walk the entire way home, rather than wait for the scrap dealer's morning return or a bus that might never come. Despite her weariness, rage proved to be a much-needed fuel, and she replayed the encounter with Alexei in her head repeatedly, reenacting her own words as she maneuvered along potholed streets filled with pulpy resin from tetanus clouds. She found herself guffawing and scoffing over and over, as she pictured Alexei's reaction when she'd brought up Moira. The fact that "Sobre las olas" had played out of thin air lingered with her as a sign that she wasn't alone.

Neftalí climbed the pedestrian bridge and tried to ignore the piles of burning tires barricading sections of the freeway below, the bleak tent communities that had sprouted in place of traffic. There was always somebody heard coughing somewhere. As she crossed over, Neftalí squinted through the fumes, searching for the statue of Brown Apollo by the destroyed elementary school. She pointed her lamp in his direction, but the halogen couldn't pierce the low-flying ash and smog clusters between them, so she continued on her way.

Closer to Old Freeway, Neftalí witnessed copper smog swinging like the tall door back at the laboratory to reveal the Santa Genoveva de Madrigal cathedral. She flashed her light over the sidewalk, but couldn't find the outlines of the murdered worker-mothers and didn't see any stationed squad cars, either. The cathedral doors were shut, and she sat on its steps to rest. Neftalí fished one of the scrap dealer's apples from her bag and took a big bite without bothering to wash it. She crunched merrily on the green apple, tongued a sore inside her right cheek that was taking its time to heal, removed her shoes, and wiggled her unwashed feet, since it wasn't too cold out.

Neftalí considered all the wolves who are important players in fairy tales, but could not think of a single story featuring a tiger. Her mother had once given her a book by the Brothers Grimm, and the chupacabras pulverizing it was one of her greatest regrets, especially since Neftalí had forgotten her mother's exact wording in the inscription she'd written. These wolves reminded her there was no reason to take Alexei at his word. Neftalí imagined a future reality when she'd bust Moira out of her cell with the help of Mama and the other loose tigers sure to be roaming mid-twenty-first-century Texas. Neftalí remembered how her mother would organize with other women and protest on the steps of the capitol, steps not unlike the ones she presently sat on, before the capitol grounds were barricaded permanently from the public.

Gunshots rang out from a hollow distance; the wind carried a low psychotropic vibration, like the ghost of a whale attempting to communicate foreboding. There was yelling, rapid footsteps around the block, and something that echoed like a cry for help.

A police van with dim headlights zoomed toward the cathedral from the curving avenue. When the driver came close to jumping the curb and hitting Neftalí, the police van made a sharp left, then the noise of the vehicle was gone as it turned onto a darker, foggier street.

Neftalí heard a repeated banging, like the sound of bricks slamming against bricks, and men yelling procedural commands. She walked barefoot, with her shoes in her hand, crossed the cobblestone pavement, looked up at the name of the street she was peeking down as she turned its corner: Yesenia Avenue.

A dozen armed police officers were visible through the languorous passing fog, surrounding an unmarked door across the street from where she stood. The police officers wore helmets, visors, and each carried a bayonet rifle. The four officers nearest the building's unmarked door rammed against it repeatedly using a concrete burro.

"Three Rivers Police," a high, distorted voice called out through a bullhorn. "Come out with your hands up!"

Silhouettes of concerned neighbors peeked at the racket through the windows of surrounding buildings. A door to the immediate right of Neftalí cracked open as far as its security chain allowed. Neftalí noticed a pair of dark eyes below the chain; they were eyes full of bourbon and worry, eyes that she felt in that moment she could trust.

"What's happening? Do you know?" Neftalí asked.

The dark eyes retreated into shadows.

The concrete burro had two more officers helping to ram it against the stubborn, sturdy door, and a spotlight was cast on the scene from the hood of a police van.

"Worker-mothers from Big Tex have been living in that bunker," the dark eyes whispered, as the inevitable happened: the bunker door fell flat to the ground. Three Rivers Police boots stomped all over the door as they pushed their way inside the building, with their bayonet rifles and flashlights leading the way.

Neftalí heard agonizing screams echo from the bunker, followed by sparse, then rapid, gunfire. The coarse shouting of men and deathly screaming would ring in her ears until her dying days. A woman ran over the door across the threshold, and was seized by two police officers when she reached the sidewalk. The woman was naked from the waist up. She kicked, punched, struggled, cursing the officers as they subdued her.

Two sweaty officers walked back out over the rammed door, and using the sharp ends of the bayonet rifles they stabbed the woman all over her torso, until she stopped resisting, then moving entirely, and was left bleeding on the ground.

A scream to curdle the worst things Neftalí had ever heard came from a fully clothed woman running out of the bunker toward the other woman's dying body. She was seized as well; two officers cut off her top, and two others stabbed her torso over and over with the knife ends of their bayonet rifles.

An apartment door about fifteen paces ahead of Neftalí swung open, and a diminutive person walked up to the police squad car in charge of shining the spotlight. Neftalí could make out only their silhouette as this person raised their arm and in four calculated shots took down four Three Rivers police officers. The spotlight automatically moved toward them. A sniper's shot cracked from a window or a roof— Neftalí made direct eye contact with the armed, diminutive person, and recognized their dark eyes from the other door right next to her, which was now shut. But it was too late. Their head hit the ground hard. Neftalí saw the dark eyes bleed to death on the cobblestone street.

The police angrily sorted out the commotion and dealt with the downed officers, all while proceeding with their violent raid. Neftalí was nauseated and dizzy as she removed herself from the scene. It wasn't until she was blocks away that she puked up the apples and tamales from earlier. She'd been walking barefoot, and realized her shoes were missing. Neftalí mumbled incoherently, walked past hissing natural gas pipes and people sleeping in the crevices of buildings, or in tents below malfunctioning streetlamps. She came across many kids living with their elders inside those tents, and hud-dles of shadowed people sharing pipes with glowing bowls that barely revealed their emaciated faces.

Neftalí clutched at her own torso, and with a hint of jaun-dice in her eyes relived the horrific images she'd been witness to, feeling the sharp, cold bayonet rifles puncturing her own flesh and organs with scalding red pain. Though bayonet rifles had been ubiquitous among Three Rivers police for years, Neftalí had never actually seen them put to use until today.

The squid-ink darkness in the sky informed her it was still nighttime. Neftalí mumbled a passage from one of Jazzmin Monelle Rivas's books. The passage evoked a scene in which the protagonist of *I Was a Teenage Brain Parasite*, who lives in a petri dish, looks at their own feet, and in an act of foreshadow-ing has a vision of boiling blood between their toes. As she walked the trenched streets toward her neighborhood, Neftalí could feel blood boiling between her own toes, the character's monologues rolling off her tongue, all while in her hypersen-sitive imagination, the bayonet rifles continued piercing her torso, and she clutched her sides the remainder of the way.

A GOLDEN WINK OF SUNSHINE pierced the sky like a bullet through cardboard, revealing a hint of something like dawn climbing her throne over Three Rivers. Hunched over, fatigued, and depressed, Neftalí approached Angélica Street. She walked as if carrying the immense weight of every abandoned building in Three Rivers on her back. She could not articulate this weariness beyond the words "shadow," street," "car," "cat," as she encountered them, and when accumulated mucus throbbed in her nasal cavities, she blew her nose inside the long sleeves of her garment. Still, she found the strength to stand on a cinder block, and used a rat tail file from her bag to scratch in the accent on both sides of the street sign, so they now read ANGÉLICA—the way her mother spelled it.

Scores of people were gathered in front of the historic Live Oak tenement building half a block ahead, gazing helplessly at a bright fire in the sky. Neftalí realized the golden wink of light wasn't emanating from any sun, but from a raging fire in the northeastern corner of the topmost two floors of the tenement building. No fire truck stood by, and she approached a cluster of worried strangers on the sidewalk.

Masked neighborhood men were running in and out of the building, carrying hoses and buckets of water up the stairs.

One of the bystanders signaled to Neftalí and said, "Psst."

She couldn't quite see, but the person was her height, and

a group of women stood silently a few feet away from him, staring at the fire with profound sadness. Children wailed near the useless fire hydrant, where they were huddled.

The bystander calling her was Rayman, the retiree who grilled his onions and wurst to sell in the neighborhood at any given hour. He was famously an insomniac, and really got a thrill out of nighttime grilling. He was a sight for sore eyes on many a night when Neftalí had stumbled home wasted and starving.

"You're the girl," Rayman said, "who always used to carry a book, yes? And a guitar? We haven't seen you around in a while, welcome back. What a devastation this is, eh? I'm surprised we're not all crying, like the children are, for this building. This building is so old. Has a lot of lost history you can't dig up anymore . . ."

The women down by the curb were talking intensely among themselves; Neftalí heard their cries and protestations. Rayman made sure Neftalí was looking at him when he pointed with his eyes toward the women, and said, "The whole Trujillo family here is displaced now. The four sisters' entire family took up the whole twelfth floor. They made those red-hot tamales up there, and did an honorable, unsung service to the community. Those sisters can cook up tamales out of any old thing. Much like the elders distilled their whiskey, come to think of it."

Rayman pulled a chrome flask from his coat pocket. The flask reflected the towering inferno as he took a swig.

"Is that some of that famous whiskey the elders brewed?" Neftalí asked.

Rayman shook his head and extended the flask toward

Neftalí. "No. Unfortunately. But it's the next best thing around. This is Rayman's special quality shine. You can't find it in any *depósitos* or *pulgas*."

Neftalí took a power hit from the flask. When she handed it back, Rayman winked and said, "One morning, before the volcano happened, I was in my garden. A big shadow fell over me. When I looked up, I saw a mighty tiger on my neighbor's trash mound. Scared the wind out of me. But I have to say, it was also a holy sight. To be here in Texas and have the shadow of a tiger on me. *That* is holy. I have great respect for royalty like a tiger. So I am sympathetic. I know he belongs to you. A lot of the neighbors around here aren't so sympathetic. Do you understand what I'm getting at? Especially since a few of them have lost their chickens. Or goats. And Doña Ramirez's even lost one of her baby cows, believe it or not. I'm the one who found it half-eaten, alive still, in front of her yard."

"How terrible," Neftalí uttered.

"I put it out of its misery, helped clean and salvage some, and bury the rest. You know Doña Ramirez has only one arm. And the poor woman has a bad lung infection from the smoke, with nobody to care for her."

"I'm sorry you had to do that, Rayman."

"Don't lose sleep over it. Like I said, I am the sympathetic one. It's why I'm passing this knowledge on to you. People have been talking."

Tenants from the lower floors of the Live Oak building were spilling into the street toward the gathered crowd, looking surprised, then aghast at the burning floors above. Rayman's face changed to shades of orange and darkness as it reflected an aquarium of flames. Neftalí took another big hit from the flask—throwback style—when he passed it over.

"Somebody here," one of the Trujillo sisters screamed, as she made sure to make eye contact with everyone present to communicate her rage, "informed on us, and helped plant a bomb in my sister's apartment. Our father is in there! Our father is burning in there, dead! Do you hear me? What harm did we ever do? Who did our father ever hurt, to suffer a death like this? What business is it of yours if we feed people, if we care for our neighbors, instead of denouncing them? I am going to find out who did this, and you will pay!"

The screaming woman was hyperventilating, hovering above the ground with anger, as the raging fire behind her seemed to gain fuel with her words. A smoldering wall from the topmost floor collapsed inward, with cascading cinders. The spectators below gasped at the rumble of the bricks and crackling of precious heirlooms.

Neftalí felt tipsy and nauseated. She reached into her bag, pulled out the bright red apple she'd taken from the scrap dealer, extended it toward Rayman like it was a flask of better booze.

Rayman gave the apple side-eye, as if its contents were more toxic than any home brew. Neftalí simply held the apple there for Rayman to decide. The three other Trujillo sisters had come to the aid of their more vocal, desperate sister. They huddled together on the pavement by the curb, and sobbed loudly for their dead father, with occasional pious expressions of great farewell. Rayman took the apple from Neftalí's hand. He admired it, though in that lighting the apple's color, and therefore its essence, was ambiguous to Rayman.

Using a low voice, Rayman said, "I don't take an apple from just anybody. Just so you know. Because then I'd be owing them a favor. But I'll take this apple from you, young miss. Because I know you're a good person. So I don't mind owing you a favor."

He rubbed the apple on his forearm, admired his reflection in the skin. Then he took a bite.

"It's good," he said.

Neftalí nodded, then did a sort of drunk curtsy and walked away.

"Don't forget what I told you," Rayman yelled, and Neftalí saw him take another bite of the apple, then toss it.

She walked down the street toward her home. Her feet were in knots. Had Neftalí been more aware of her own body's needs, she would have remembered that her trusty spare *chanclas* were in her bag somewhere; that she carried a water bottle, half-full; and that she had a stashed day-old tamal that her rumbling stomach yearned for as it soaked in the alcohol.

Neftalí's spirit roamed beyond the clouds and the ash, and her organism was left on this earth to fend for itself as her spirit moved past abandoned cars on cinder blocks and downed power lines that children used as jump ropes, with not a bone in the sky above. If her old place wasn't so dilapidated, with a caved-in porch and doorway, Neftalí might have gone inside. Instead, she stood on the curb in front of it, by the faded, chipped picket fence. The low-flying tetanus clouds carried through a burnt-tire smell the moment Neftalí caught a light flickering from inside the abandoned house.

Her eyes watered and her nostrils flared. It made sense to her that somebody was already squatting there—the place wasn't a bad find in the broader context of Three Rivers. When she moved to walk away, there was a flicker from a cigarette lighter once again, accompanied by a loud whisper saying, "Nef."

Neftalí felt she really was tipsy now, needed to get some serious sleep, and her mind was playing tricks on her. She entered the picket fence gate, stood before the decayed crater of the house, switched her halogen lamp on. Inside the remains of her childhood home, standing next to the fireplace and broken bookshelves, was a person dressed in black, shading their face from the sudden intensity of light.

Neftalí dimmed the lamp, pointed it away, and the person put their hands down. Neftalí's chest inflated with the damp air circulating, and her head cracked almost in half. The person in front of her was Moira, with a buzzed head, like Proserpina's hair once was—but otherwise bundled head to toe in dark camouflage apparel. The two of them made sure nobody was around, then walked down the alley cloaked by a patch of natural fog, all the way to Colonel Huerta's place. The last thing Neftalí saw before passing out was her own bare feet covered in blood as Mama licked them clean with her warm, sticky tongue. *Must have been something I stepped in*, she thought.

MOIRA EEIYN HAD BEEN THRILLED to be in the company of Proserpina and Neftalí the day they visited the Big Tex Fish Cannery as a group. She was younger, and had met the two of them through Alexei long after Missus Batches stopped being a band. When the three parted ways inside Big Tex, after checking in—Proserpina downstairs to the label department, Neftalí to find Bettina on her smoke break—Moira made her way past busy worker-mothers and pools of verdillo fish to sector 88, where her own mother was stationed.

As she neared the sector, a worker-mother with an orange bandanna holding her red hair back, and with dozens of silver, shiny, slithering fish in her hands, hollered, "My glorious daughter!" The worker-mother dropped them into sector 88's barrel, wiped her hands on her overalls, then gave Moira a big, motherly hug. One of the shift supervisors shot her a nod from the watchtower's ground-floor entrance. The redheaded worker-mother sparked a cigarette, offered one to Moira, who declined, then upon her insistence took a puff. Moira's mother found three buckets and moved to the sidelines, out of anyone's way. She handed Moira a bucket, and both sat on the buckets' upturned ends, using the third bucket between them as a table. Moira's mother took out a complete deck of playing cards and handed them to her daughter, who knew what to do.

Moira shuffled and dealt the cards, while her mother said,

"Are you still working that business you're working out there? I'm in here doing what I can to help you out. You know that. Not just with the ration cards. We don't have a lot of time, so I'll tell it to you straight. Your sister came to see me."

Moira raised her eyebrows, looked over her shoulders, and dealt the cards.

"Yes," her mother continued, "your sister-sister. Out of the blue. I hadn't seen her in so long. Since the last time you saw her, too. And the last time we saw your father. When he took our Phoebe and split up the family. Abandoned you and me. It's my great regret, dear, that you didn't grow up together with your twin sister. You'll be happy to hear she's not doing too bad. Do you know what an anarchist punk is? They pierce their skin and color their hair. Scream this way and that about injustice. Well, that's what your sister is. She's an anarchist punk. But she doesn't have piercings . . . at least that I could see. And her hair color looked much faded. She has some things to say about injustice, for sure. I got the gist of it. I'm glad you came to see me, Moira. Because there's some details I have here that'll reconnect you with her . . ."

Later, on her way to the cooperative where she lived, Moira carried a bag filled with Proserpina's hair. As she passed by piles of trash stacked along the curbsides, Moira replayed the day's events: collecting bottle-tops, visiting her mother and Professor Pantano's laboratory, delousing Proserpina. City workers were trimming dense foliage obstructing power lines in her neighborhood, and Moira could smell the screaming trees in the sawdust blowing in the wind. Memories of living in a trailer by the southern border with her mother, father, and sister flashed through her like an out-of-body experience, then the fateful day when everything changed lingered in her mind. Moira had a hard time pinpointing on a timeline when this severance began, even when it came to recalling the number of years her mother had been working at the fish cannery.

As Moira approached the cooperative one of her new roommates, Jeff, who worked in construction, sat smoking a spliff on their front porch and said, "Hey," waving a Zippo lighter between his fingers. Since Jeff was at least twenty years older, Moira had been meaning to ask him for a recollection of how things used to be.

"Do you remember pasta?" she asked him, and immediately wished to take it back. Moira thought to rush inside the house, expecting a curt reaction from this hardworking, hard-partying man. Jeff let the spliff burn, as if it helped him think.

"Pasta? Like noodles boiled and stirred around?" Jeff paused a bit more to reflect, then chuckled and took a big hit from the spliff. He held in the smoke for five Mississippis, released it gently through his nose, and continued: "I remember pasta. You'd serve it on a plate, or a bowl. Usually topped with a fine sauce. They used to say the sauce made the pasta back then. Look at us today. That is clearly not true. A sauce can be created out of a shoe, or almost anything. But if you don't have starch, you don't get the dish. You got me being all nostalgic here now. They don't manufacture pasta in Texas, and we can't get anything imported, so it's hard to access. I bet you can still track down pasta, though. Not at any fancy restaurant or government kitchen or anything like that. But somebody, somewhere in this city, and in every town, is secretly making some fine pasta. Possibly even now. At this very moment."

Moira graciously declined the spliff and nodded, at a loss for a proper response to Jeff's impressive answer. She walked into her room at the cooperative, found Sonora sitting on the chair by the dresser, done up like she was ready for a cocktail-hour mixer.

"What's up!" Sonora exclaimed. "I let myself in. You're just getting here? We have to leave in a few minutes. What do you got in the bag? Hair? For what?"

"I'm gonna try to make little bouncy balls out of it. A friend of mine was lousy, and we had to cut it off. Don't worry, I made sure none of the lice was in this hair."

"Damn. I don't even know with you sometimes. But please hurry it up."

Sonora gave Moira her personal space in her room, found a spot to sit by an open window in the living room, and stared out into the street. She heard Jeff and a couple of people's muffled voices making dinner in the kitchen. A crew of kids zoomed by loudly on their souped-up tricycles—Sonora whistled shrilly and threw them the finger. Moments later, as if summoned by her whistle, a blue stretch limo pulled up.

Sonora stood on her high heels, filled with anxiety, mumbling epithets about Moira being careless and never on time.

"All right, I'm ready," Moira said, as she came out of her room and locked the door. "You got all your stuff, right?"

Sonora nodded vigorously and pulled her by the arm to walk faster. It was the first time a limousine had been sent for them, and both Sonora and Moira couldn't help but notice how incongruous the blue limo looked in their slapdash neighborhood. Both were thrilled at the sight, and wondered if their neighbors were, too.

The limo's back door was held open by a chauffeur who didn't make eye contact with either of them. Inside, they were both surprised to find only Ms. Cantú, dressed in a flashy burgundy suit and already holding a mixed drink.

"Good evening, girls," she said. "So generous of you not to keep us waiting."

Sonora and Moira smiled at each other and agreed, of course, that they could never be late for this extraordinary opportunity.

The limo started moving and Ms. Cantú handed each of them a set of stapled documents.

"No need for concern," she assured them. "This is standard industry practice. But feel free to skim through before applying your signature. I'm introducing you to a very important and well-respected clientele. I guarantee both of you this is the opportunity of your lives. Here is part of the money, in cash form. But I'll remind you that clients may also offer you gifts. Or bonuses. If the time you spend together proves exceptional."

Sonora signed her forms straightaway. As Moira scrutinized the small print, Sonora gestured with her eyebrows in a way that told her to sign them already. They handed their completed contracts back to Ms. Cantú, who filed them in a steel briefcase handcuffed to the limousine.

"It's probably too early for you to drink," Ms. Cantú told them. "Otherwise, I'd fix y'all one myself. Don't want to make a red-faced first impression. Pretty day outside, isn't it?"

The limousine entered the automatic gates of a wooded property, and cruised uphill along a winding driveway, past pines and pecan trees shedding their dry leaves. It came to a stop by a loud orange crystal fountain, near the faded steps of the largest mansion Sonora and Moira had ever encountered. The chauffeur opened the limousine door, and Ms. Cantú instructed her new employees to walk up the steps and press the red button to the right of the twenty-foot reinforced-steel door.

Ms. Cantú said goodbye and blew them a kiss, for she had other business to attend to. Moira and Sonora walked up the steps and pressed the red button as the blue limo disappeared down the leaf-carpeted hill.

There were things Moira did to make money in Three Rivers that she didn't tell anyone about: collecting bottle-tops with Alexei; tracking edible chickens for the butcher; shoplifting blocks of cheese and portioning them to sell individually. The work she did for Ms. Cantú in the passing weeks was just another one of those things.

Early one morning, after showering and wondering what there was for breakfast, Moira pulled out the bottle-top her mother had snuck to her at Big Tex during her visit. The address of a neighboring city was scratched into its underside. Having saved good money from her work with Ms. Cantú, Moira allowed herself the luxury of calling a cab, and less than a half an hour later she was on her way to George West.

Moira took the cabdriver's word when he said that a house down an unpaved road was the address. "I got old tires," the driver said. "And my axle and suspension need a ton of work. I have to be careful. Looks like the place you're looking for is that white place up the road."

She stepped out of the cab and looked down the dusty, bumpy way.

"Will you wait here for me?" she asked, standing beside the cab.

"And do what? Hopefully they got a landline in there. Judging by those cables running up there, they do. Just call up the cab number and I'll pick you up at this spot."

"What if I can't call?"

The driver chewed tobacco and stopped to think. He had been hoping to be gone by now. "I'll tell you what. So you can see I'm not a bad guy, I'll circle back over in a few hours. And if I don't see you, I'll go on and wish you well. How about that?"

"Thank you."

She walked down the middle of the road, between barbed-wire fences holding back overgrown grass and thick patches of dragonflies making fists in the air. A rust-colored pickup truck was jacked up with the hood open in front of the large white house the driver had pointed at. Moira panicked when she saw two legs poking out from underneath the truck. She heard writhing and groaning, and ribbons of weak light shot out from the open hood, as if the person below was having trouble tightening a bolt and keeping the light steady.

The person must have sensed movement, and slithered out from under the truck. He was a remarkably clean young man, free of dust and even of greasy hands. He held a small flash-light between his teeth, which he grabbed and flicked off.

There were a few seconds of suspicion and curiosity in his closely shaven face, before his expression turned to one of wonder.

"Hello," he said. "I'm Rolo. Taking a wild guess here . . . but you are Phoebe's sister?"

Rolo unjacked the truck, shut the hood, and invited Moira to hop in. They drove around the house, along a narrow road lined with oak trees that created a shady field and that tunneled cool, breezy air. Moira smelled something earthy, rough, and awkward that gave her a primitive comfort when she recognized it as manure. Cows were chewing grass by a tiny barn up ahead. Rolo stopped the truck and pointed a few feet off the road on Moira's side.

He honked the truck's horn, and a young woman with one long, faded violet braid spiked the shovel she was carrying into the ground, waved at the truck. When Moira made eye contact with her, the young woman stopped waving, dropped her smile, and leaned on the shovel.

～

George West, though only ten miles south of Three Rivers city limits, was a completely different reality, Moira quickly discerned. Phoebe, her long-lost twin, ran a garden there with other members of her farm community, who were up north for the season, which piled on extra work every day: tending the plants, feeding the animals, with little or no time for personal projects.

Rolo left the two of them alone and continued with the manure work Phoebe had started. Moira accepted a cup of coffee and agreed to a stroll among the older oak trees. The roots of Phoebe's hair were identical to those of Moira's, and they discovered other physical similarities while piecing together anecdotes about their separation and lives since. Moira was disturbed to learn that not every city had worker-mothers. In George West, the people were against the privatization of their city, and had done away with their mayor, commissioners, and police in an orderly upheaval. A rotating committee of diverse citizens voted annually to distribute resources and land throughout the community, and any disputes were settled democratically.

"The state governor," Phoebe informed her, "hates what we do here, but what's he gonna do? Send in his people to break down this tiny town? With the fucking wars going on? Maybe. Why do you think a law to implement fish canneries was even *passed* in your city? They've started so many wars and need new ways to keep their books balanced."

Phoebe guided Moira through waist-high grass and the shrill vibration of cicadas. They crossed a trampled clearing and came upon a mound of stones, where Phoebe unzipped a waterproof canvas bag that was sitting there.

"Check this out," Phoebe said, and pulled out a weapon the likes of which Moira had never seen. "See that target way out there? Shining in the sun? It's a glass bottle."

Phoebe loaded the revolver, cocked it, pointed, pulled the trigger—the glass bottle resting on a brick across the clearing not only shattered, but ripped a mean fire like it was giving birth to a great phoenix.

"I filled that bottle with a special powder mix of mine. Do you ever shoot? I can't get enough of shooting," Phoebe continued. "If it wasn't for shooting, I'd be dead. If only other people before us could've shot back, the world'd be different. I want to invite you to live here with us, Sister. I could show you how to shoot. Can you leave your life in Three Rivers behind?"

Moira told her of the cooperative where she lived, her friend Sonora, and how she'd learned to hustle a few dollars here and there to make ends meet. She watched Phoebe fire off a few more rounds at a distant painted target covered in bullet holes. When Phoebe offered Moira the gun after reloading, Moira remembered the nice cabdriver, and mentioned having to meet him.

"You want to head back already? But you just got here! Do you have business in Three Rivers today? Stay the night, then. I insist. Me and Rolo will drive you back in the morning. We have a landline. You can call the cab company if you're so worried."

Moira was reluctant to accept. She'd enjoyed being in that yellow cab, coasting along I-35, feeling the breeze biting into her cheeks under the blue Texas skies. Now that she was here, face-to-face with Phoebe—the near identical image of herself— she saw how it could easily have been the other way around, had her father chosen to run off with her instead.

Phoebe added: "Rolo was going to make a special dinner tonight of pasta carbonara. I know he would be delighted if you'd stay and join us. I would be, too."

Moira took this as a sign. She accepted. That night, during dinner, Moira even drank some cabernet sauvignon, which she'd never tried. She learned that her father had remarried and died of a heart attack years ago. Phoebe had been raised by an activist stepmother from Galveston, who published underground manifestos detailing the steps for safe, herbally induced abortions. Phoebe had learned about doo-wop, surrealism, guerrilla tactics, and sticking it to the man from her stepmother, and also things like gardening, and had even developed a taste for reading plays in her early teenage years.

Moira had to admit she'd never read a play, and struggled to sit with the fact that politics in Three Rivers would never allow for the lives Phoebe and Rolo presently lived in George West.

Phoebe got the gist of what Moira felt, however, and tried to untangle it further by saying, "Maybe what needs to happen is for George West and Three Rivers to become one singular city. We're only ten miles apart, with nothing but a desert of coyotes in between. But, yeah, they couldn't be more different, as cities. All the supposedly smart tech people, pushing Three Rivers to be the next tech capital, only for the idea to fall through. After buildings'd been erected, amusement parks built. Honestly, I'm not sure Dad would have even left, if the tech people hadn't destroyed everything. And that mayor that's been there since, Pablo Crick, has only made things worse."

Moira took the last sip of her wine, and surprised even herself when she said, "I know that man."

Rolo and Phoebe asked how she knew him. Moira told them she had done some freelance work for one of his assistants, and had met him several times at his mansion.

The evening's tone shifted, and Moira wondered if she'd

done the right thing—if by sharing that she'd been in proximity to someone so evil, it made her evil by association in Phoebe's eyes. Moira nervously asked where the trash was, to discard her plate and utensils after eating, and Phoebe told her they didn't throw anything away, and the plates were washed.

Five portable buildings with chimneys and several hammocks tied to papaya trees sat at the center of the property, along with lounge chairs and tables. Phoebe showed Moira the portable where she'd be sleeping. When she was left alone in the room, the silence made Moira feel something like safe. The portable had a skylight, and she gazed at the stars that shone through that four-by-four-foot window as she fell asleep.

Hours later: scratching, footsteps, a flicker of light.

"Hey," Phoebe whispered, waking Moira up.

The stars had made way for the moon, and Moira could see Phoebe in its pale light, standing by the door. Moira sat up. Phoebe pulled out a folding chair from a crevice on the wall.

"I know you must be tired, so sorry to wake you. I don't want to take more of your sleep time, but had to come talk with you. Me and Rolo have been discussing this. Because I feel it's too important, and all this must've happened for a reason. What if I take your place in the work you do? The work you do for Pablo Crick and his assistant?"

Moira had had a sense that something like this would happen after her reveal during dinner, but she wasn't prepared with an answer. "I don't think that's possible."

"Why not? You even said he probably didn't take a good

look at you. Right? How could he tell the difference? I mean, look at us."

Phoebe stood up and pulled Moira before the mirror that made up the top half of the wall opposite the bed.

"The kind of work that I do, he could tell," Moira said.

"How do you mean?"

"Well, I have to take all my clothes off to meet him and wait in a cold little room. When he gets there, he takes all his clothes off, and I have to give him a massage. Touch his body with oils, and wear stiletto shoes."

"And that's it?"

"Yeah. He's never said he's Pablo Crick, but I recognized him. We were in the mayor's mansion. It's obvious."

Phoebe sat on the bed, and Moira on the folding chair. The beam of moonlight floated between them like a thin placenta.

As if Moira had been insisting, Phoebe said: "I'll do it."

"Do what?"

"Go to the mansion as you. You tell me what I need to know about this Sonora and Ms. Cantú and all that. And you can stay here. Do these people know you are only nineteen?"

"I have a fake ration card," Moira said. "They actually think I'm seventeen. But I don't understand—do what? Why would you want to take my place instead of staying here in your paradise?"

Phoebe couldn't think of a way to phrase it. She looked around the room and noted that the water jug and chamber pot were there. "Forget about it," she said. "Never mind. I'm thinking crazy fantasies out loud. I pictured, you know, us making a pact, and me getting the chance to come face-to-face with Pablo Crick. Taking out my eight-shot revolver. Getting him where it counts. Right in the heart. Sorry I woke you up for this. You have to admit, it's a beautiful revenge fantasy."

Moira forced a smile. Both of them said good night a second time.

Streaks of orange and yellow from the skylight, and the braying of a donkey, awoke Moira at dawn. The words "You have to admit, it's a beautiful revenge fantasy" resonated in her head as she strapped on her shoes.

Moira stopped before the door to the room, turned the knob, and pushed, already expecting it to be locked from the outside. There'd been a hint of something in Phoebe's shaky voice and wild eyes that now alarmed her, so when the door opened effortlessly to reveal the South Texas hill country, she felt relief, and found the outhouse to do her business.

Moira wandered the property afterward, and spotted Phoebe walking toward her from the chicken coop, holding a woven basket. "Feel these eggs," she said to Moira, handing her a large brown one. Phoebe was wearing a wool hat that covered most of her hair. The egg was firm and cold to the touch—Moira couldn't close her fist around it.

Phoebe showed Moira the woodstove where they burned the property's lumber to cook their food, and pointed to a prepared breakfast. Rolo made aggressive sounds at the cows in the distance, shooing them away from a bad patch of grass.

As Phoebe and Moira ate their eggs and toast and potatoes, Phoebe noticed a restlessness in Moira.

"Are you anxious to head back to your cooperative?"

"No. It's not that. I didn't know what to expect coming out here. I've never seen how people outside Three Rivers live, like you and your community here."

"I get it. Which is part of the big reason I'm so angry. Where do people get books or videos where there's no bookstores or libraries? How does anyone even learn anything anymore? How do people communicate with each other? I mean, I'm sorry. I know living here, and not in Three Rivers with a fish cannery breathing down my neck, is a huge privilege. I'm lucky . . . that I've been able to learn, thanks to the library on the property."

They finished their meals and Moira asked to see this library. Phoebe led her through the courtyard to a trailer on the other side of a wooden fence—one Moira hadn't paid much attention to. Inside was a large room with floor-to-ceiling bookshelves on every wall.

"Kitty," said Phoebe, "who lives on the other side of that fence, made this place fireproof. It's always the same temperature in here, too. There's geothermal cooling from the ground below here. Do you think reading is something you'd like to do more of?"

Moira was thumbing through a book and said, "I don't know. I've never been around books much. But I have friends who like to read. Some who would actually freak if they saw a room like this."

The book she held had engravings throughout of pirates

on a beach, aboard a ship, and on seafaring adventures. As she read the opening sentences of chapter 4, Moira heard the shutting of a door and three clicks. Phoebe was nowhere around. Moira hurried to the window by the door and yelled, "Phoebe, stop!"

"I'm sorry, Sister," Phoebe said from the other side of the metallic window screen. "Ever since I decided to find our mother, I've been thinking a lot about destiny. And actions that shape our world. Which is why I'm so grateful that you came all the way out here. To reconnect with me."

Phoebe removed the wool hat she'd been wearing all morning, and let down her hair to reveal that it had been cut and dyed overnight to match Moira's.

"Did I do a bad job? Did it myself."

Moira shook her head and looked like a ghost haunting the little library behind that screen.

"Looks good," she said to Phoebe. "But they'll scan your ration card at some point. You're gonna need mine."

Phoebe held up Moira's ration card.

"I'm pretty good at pickpocketing. And I took the opportunity when I came into the room last night. Sorry, Sister. There's a little pantry in there. And a chamber pot in the closet if you really need to go. I recommend opening a tin of sardines, there's some crackers there that feel good to eat while you're reading. Try to enjoy the quiet."

"But what now? I'm a fucking Three Rivers girl, I can't be living in anyone's farm, turning pages in a book I can't read. I don't even know how to crack an egg!"

Cicadas played their early-morning violins, and a mockingbird recited the alphabet backward from the roof of the trailer. "You're cracking an egg *now*," Phoebe said, unlatching the wooden fence. Then she was gone.

~

Hours later in Three Rivers, at the cooperative, Phoebe was lying on the planks of Moira's room, dressed and made up for a fancy night out. She had her eyes closed, focused on the faraway, frosty mountain that always appeared when she meditated, and Phoebe floated toward it as if riding a slow canoe. The icy peak gradually approached her, more like a pristine blue flame than a mountain. Arctic birds had carved nests within the frozen rock and glided by her, admitting her into a kingdom few humans had seen.

Footsteps from the co-op's foundation rippled through her body like the underground strikes of a hammer, summoning her eyes to open. The door to Moira's room flung wide, and Sonora walked in on platform heels.

"What are you doing down there on the filthy ground? You look like you're ready to go, but are you? Clothes getting all messed up, being on the floor like that. When was the last time this floor was even swept? Here, let me help you."

Phoebe got up, and Sonora slapped her wardrobe free of dust. She pulled out a lint roller from her bag, and as she rolled it along Phoebe's back, Sonora thought she saw a tan line. Sonora tugged at Phoebe's top, compared the tone to that of her unexposed skin.

"Didn't you read the contract we signed? We're supposed to stay out of the sun, Moira. How'd your skin get that tanned so fast? Did you go swimming or something? You're almost as dark as me now. It's all right. Look, play it cool and nobody will say anything. I'm counting on making this money tonight, so I hope you're not messing this up."

Moira hadn't mentioned anything about a contract to Phoebe, and when the long blue limousine pulled up in front of the cooperative, she tried to keep her cool. The chauffeur opened the back door and both of them got in. Though she suspected this was a trick, Phoebe was relieved there was nobody inside the limo. Judging from Sonora's expression, she hadn't been expecting this either.

As the limousine rolled away, Sonora found the correct button and lowered the window dividing them from the chauffeur. "Excuse me," Sonora asked him. "But no Ms. Cantú today?"

"She's out with the flu," the driver said. "Stayed home. It's good for her to play it safe."

Sonora thanked him and raised the window, then sighed a gust of relief. "Thank God," she said to Phoebe. "We can chill for a bit. I wish we could mix ourselves a drink in here. The driver can't hear us through the glass, you think? One day we'll have a limo like this all to ourselves. And we can drink whatever we want. Do a bit of blow. You hear what's going on with the volcano down in Mexico? They're not saying it in the newscubes yet, but supposedly this huge volcano has been releasing gas over there for days. There's one in the Middle East doing the same thing, too, but everyone thought the volcano there was already dead. Gases are mixing with the oxygen, all scientific-like, and turning into this thick smoke. Smoke's covering the sky little by little, all over Europe and Japan. If it continues, they say the gas will cover the planet."

Phoebe felt bold and asked, "Are we heading to the same place as usual, you think?"

Sonora took a long look at the passing landmarks and street signs, and said, "Looks like it. What's up with your voice? Are you faking a bayou accent or something?"

The blue limo entered the perimeter gates and moved up the winding wooded driveway, past pecan and pine trees. The leaves from before had all been raked, bagged, and hauled away. It came to a stop by the mayor's mansion, near the noisy, orange crystal fountain.

Splashing and gurgling greeted them like a shaggy dog while the chauffeur held the limo door open. He nodded, mouthed farewell, and drove the limousine down the hill. Phoebe stood blankly by the stairs, in awe of the mansion's immense width and stature. She felt herself lifted by a whirlwind to scope out the layout of the grounds from above, saw the air-conditioning units and rats on the main roof, the rim of the driveway's foliage separating the property from the stark reality of the people in Three Rivers.

"C'mon," Sonora called out, after ascending the stairs.

Phoebe came down from her illusion. The tall reinforced-steel doors opened from the inside, and she was shoulder to shoulder with Sonora on the threshold when they were greeted by an elderly woman, who scanned their ration cards, guided them in, and looked at their left cheeks rather than their eyes when she spoke. Phoebe had never walked through so many dizzying hallways lined with framed portraits in oil on canvas. The portraits memorialized various founders and previous mayors of Three Rivers, as well as the women who'd played a crucial role in the city's privatization and autonomy from the state.

Sonora walked parallel to the elderly woman, both three paces ahead of Phoebe, who trailed to absorb as much of the art as she could, since visual art was a rare commodity anywhere. The woman opened a red door by a Roman vase encased in a vitrine. The door led to a small blue-tiled room. Sonora walked inside. Phoebe tried to follow, but the elderly woman stopped her, as if reading her mind, before she could.

Phoebe witnessed Sonora starting to remove her clothes, as the woman shut the red door, locked it, and guided Phoebe farther down the decorous hallway. A bust of Pallas Athena stopped her cold, and she admired the chips and slight cracks in the marble. The elderly woman pushed open a green door to the left of the bust, gestured with her hand for Phoebe to enter. The woman stood there watching as Phoebe walked around the single massage table in the small room. It was tiled from floor to ceiling in an abstract mosaic style, with a few inches of corkboard wrapping around the walls at her knee level.

Phoebe made eye contact with the woman, who seemed to be waiting for something, then remembered to disrobe. The elderly woman watched Phoebe do so entirely, but Phoebe kept her stiletto heels on. She shut the door and locked it from the outside. Phoebe felt each passing second like a goose bump on her skin in that cold mosaic room—so many chaotic possibilities rolled through her mind that their immensities were canceled out; every moment she'd calculated felt at risk, but she breathed deeply, knew who she was deep down and what she was there to do.

When the doorknob turned and the door pushed open, it did so quietly. A bulky, towering man with broad shoulders walked in, and behind him was a shorter man, as tall as Phoebe, wearing a bathrobe and nothing else. The bulky man walked around inspecting Phoebe as a precaution, lazily pushed at her dress and undergarments on the floor with the toe of his right boot. He walked back around the massage table, and before closing the door Phoebe noticed him winking at the robed man, who did his best to suppress a grin.

The door was shut. Phoebe heard the outside lock click. As the robed man circled Phoebe, admiring her nakedness, he extended his hands around her waist, while stopping shy of actual touch, as if measuring something. He got onto his knees in front of her, gently caressed Phoebe's stomach with his knuckles, grazed his mustache hairs in the area below her belly button. The man leaned back, looked into her belly button like it was the face of a person, whispered sweet nothings that Phoebe couldn't hear, and stuck his nose right into its center. He landed soft little kisses all around her belly button, near tears the entire time. Then he got up and stepped away.

When looking back on this event, Phoebe was incredulous about how she'd decided things—why had she not grabbed the Webley-Fosbery from the dress on the ground first, after she'd gotten lucky with the bulky bodyguard not noticing? Moira hadn't mentioned anything about security on entering the room with Crick.

While the mayor disrobed, Phoebe detached an ice pick from her right stiletto heel and threw it, aiming square for Pablo Crick's neck. Out of sheer boyhood reflexes, Crick tried catching the knife like a ball, and did so by the blade, slicing his left thumb open. In that second or two, Phoebe flew at him holding a stiletto with a heel for a blade, forced her underwear into Crick's mouth, and stabbed him three times in his hairy chest.

Phoebe never did reconcile why her actions unfolded in the order they did, but after she stabbed Crick, he grabbed her throat with both hands, trying to choke the life out of his assailant, biting down hard on the soft underwear in his mouth. Phoebe dropped the stiletto blade, and in a flailing attempt successfully grabbed the knife she'd first thrown, used it to slice open Crick's right cheek into a half smile, and he dropped to the ground, spit out thick, bloody saliva and Phoebe's stained underwear.

She stabbed his left earlobe to the lining of corkboard on the wall, and crawled toward the revolver hidden in her little pile of clothes. Crick removed the stiletto heel from the corkboard and his earlobe as his torso and face bled profusely, the blood pouring from the river or the moon, anywhere but his own body. He remembered the white button under the table to be used for emergencies. Blood gushed from his flapping sliced cheek down his bare chest, coagulating in his body hair, and it sprayed onto the mosaic tiles when something like a scream crawled out of his throat, his eyes almost touching out of sheer rage.

Phoebe was covered in Crick's blood, too. She was holding the Webley-Fosbery in her hand the moment Crick reached over to press the white emergency button. It summoned the green door to immediately open, and Phoebe got the bulky bodyguard and his companion in two clean shots. The bullets hit them like pickaxes through their torsos, leaving the men writhing against the tiles. Pablo Crick tackled Phoebe and wrestled her to the ground until a booming shot rang out, followed by five more.

The artisan-tiled room was postmodern with splatters and pools of blood. Pallas Athena's bust was outside this entire time, waiting by the green door. Her impervious, cracked marble eyes watched as Phoebe cautiously walked out holding a smoking, empty-chambered revolver. Pushed by adrenaline—as if in that moment the goddess of strategy and wisdom had placed her own prized helmet on Phoebe's head—Phoebe ran down the mansion's hallway toward an exit, naked and smeared in blood that was not her own.

NEFTALÍ DISCOVERED DEAD LAMB REMAINS about twenty feet from the back door upon waking, so she was surprised when she encountered a disemboweled rooster off the edge of the porch, too. Filled with grief, she recognized the dead rooster as Miss Gernandez's prized companion—a despised-by-some early riser in the neighborhood. She used old paper bags and the garden hose to clean up while Mama was kept locked inside the house. Neftalí felt clueless about how to properly discipline the Bengal tiger. Mama watched from behind the casement window, licking her whiskers, piercing Neftalí's every move with her needlepoint eyes.

Neftalí walked to where she burned trash on the property, set the carcass bags down, sprayed starter fluid, and lit them on fire.

"I'm sorry, little animals," she whispered to the flames.

Mama shadowed her as soon as she stepped back inside the house with three gables, thinking that Neftalí was, in fact, preparing her food out there. She shooed Mama, walked into the living room, didn't see anybody, went toward the kitchen. On the long dining room table, Neftalí found a fully decomposed human skeleton—still wearing burial garments, sprawling the length of the table. It was the body they'd mistakenly buried as Proserpina.

The stones Proserpina had boiled were all placed in strategic disorder around the dusty skeleton's bones, creating the effect of a dining room as a burial altar. Neftalí lit three long-stemmed candles in the middle of the table. The worm-picked bones were illuminated and seemed to dance with the stones to the flicker of the flames. She searched the house for Proserpina, even went upstairs into all the rooms, to no avail.

Mama was right behind her as Neftalí descended the stairs. The tiger had been glued to her all along, then Neftalí remembered she was probably hungry and fed her four chickens already thawed and quartered. She watched Mama slurp everything up in the feeding bucket outside on the porch, near the spot where she'd found the mangled rooster.

Though Neftalí uncovered plenty of undeniable evidence on her own, it was difficult to imagine such a majestic creature as Mama hurting another living thing. Cutting it open with her jaws and talons. Chomping, getting her soft bristles greasy with blood. A memory of discovering the jungle on a television program as a girl flashed before Neftalí—if it hadn't been for those broadcast images, accessible now only through memory, how would she know what creatures living in nature even were? How would the existence of a bear, great ape, or white tiger come to be known, if not for once-accessible media? she asked herself.

She grappled with these thoughts while carrying a gas lantern outside, looking for Proserpina in the diffuse brown daylight, moving past the orchards toward the canal. Proserpina was walking directly to Neftalí along the same narrow path, smiling and looking well rested, talking softly to her baby in the rebozo.

～

Moira sat at the head of the dining room table with one hand resting over the skeleton's bony left hand. The three long-stemmed candles projected tall, murky shadows against the walls as Proserpina and Neftalí entered, the latter's stomach grumbling. She grabbed the last dozen tamales, warmed them up, and smashed coffee beans in the *molcajete*. The baby made like she was going to cry, then Proserpina sat on a chair to breastfeed her.

Moira described the commune in George West as this happened, then tried to get as quickly as possible to the part about Pablo Henry Crick being dead. "There's no way," Moira insisted, "any human being could've survived what happened, the way Phoebe told it. Unloaded almost the whole pistol on the guy. Can't imagine five or six bullets, all inside your chest and body, and surviving that. A person like Crick is just like you and me, not some monster. I know what everyone is hearing on the newscubes. They've announced they've caught me . . . or my sister . . . and Crick's ghost is out creating laws somewhere, I guess. All these things are obviously . . . I mean, bullshit. Here I am. What more proof do you need? I liked it out there, in George West. At first, at least. It was a good place to be when the volcano erupted. Life slowed down a lot for the first time. I didn't have to do any chores, and I got better at reading. Like, actual books that you'd love, Neftalí. But I mostly felt bad out there. I was happy with my sister, seeing her life, and learning how incredibly different we are. But Phoebe and her friends argue pretty much all the time, it drove me crazy. Some of them think what Phoebe did was stupid and selfish. Which I can't understand—I mean, how can someone be selfish if what they did is liberate people from the clutches of this awful man? But some got pissed, saying it only made everything worse in Three Rivers—"

Five loud knocks came from the front door, the door that usually went unused. Neftalí noticed that Mama was feeling uneasy, with her sharp eyes and erect ears focused on something beyond the walls, but surmised she'd been tracking a bird. A standoff between the knocking and Moira's story hung in the air like a clothesline. Neftalí walked to the front door only when a fist knocked five times yet again.

She made sure Mama was out of sight, then cracked open the door. Eight neighborhood faces stood at the outer edge of the small front porch, all of them older than Neftalí except the young boy in overalls clutching the side of a woman in a bonnet. None of them appeared pleased or happy to see Neftalí step out of the house to meet them. There was an older man holding a pitchfork—an accessory Neftalí found a little much.

A tall, thin, clean-shaven man stepped forward holding a piece of thick matte paper in front of Neftalí. She took it and saw it was a gruesome photographic print of a dead calf. The thin man handed her another, this time of a gutted rottweiler. Another: a glossy photograph of Mama on the verge of pouncing. In the background of that print, off focus, Neftalí made out her own image, and that of this house.

When she handed the photographs back to the thin man,

she recognized him as the person whom Mama had torn the coat from, only he'd shaved his scraggly fisherman's beard.

"You can't have a wild animal like that here, untaxed, within city limits," the thin man said, with great authority in his enunciation.

"Excuse me," the woman in the bonnet—Miss Gernandez—interrupted, "are we the state damn comptrollers or something? We don't care about any damn taxes. Young lady, what I care about is just minding my own business, and looking out for my family and property's well-being. Your animal has killed our three good milking goats, and eight of our egg-producing chickens. I've had it up to here. We haven't heard our beloved rooster for days, too, and I'm prepared to find it dead any moment. How are we supposed to know when the sun's supposed to be risen now without our rooster?"

"I'm sorry. I don't know what else to say."

"You don't have to say anything," the man with the pitchfork throatily proclaimed. "All you have to do is hand the big cat over. Or stand aside and let us handle it. Whichever you prefer."

"I don't have to do either of those things, and you know it. But what I can do is tell all of you, nicely, to please leave my property. And don't come back to threaten me and my family ever again, unless you're prepared to go all the way."

The posse scoffed at Neftalí's firm words. One of the women said, "The only reason you are even living in this house is because you were Mr. Huerta's no-good floozy. May he rest in peace. You think we are ignorant idiots? We've known all this time you more than likely poisoned him. Even after everything that poor man was falsely accused of, and all he suffered, just to have some floozy like you take what's left of his good name."

This string of words came as a surprise to Neftalí. She opened her mouth but couldn't come up with any retort. What she really wanted to do was laugh. Maybe throw up a little. But she stood there before the angry posse, mouth agape, when the young boy in overalls pointed at the window by the door behind Neftalí and yelled, "Look!"

Mama was sternly gazing at the crowd from inside, framed by the casement window—the red drapes acted as a background, which gave her a heightened, royal look, like she was sitting for an official portrait. The posse's collective eyes widened. Everyone, except for the man with the pitchfork and the thin man, retreated a few steps.

The man with the pitchfork turned to Neftalí and said, "All right, then, ma'am. We will do as you suggest, for the time being. But we'll return. And perhaps then we shan't be so understanding."

"Or courteous," Miss Gernandez said, shielding her young boy. The posse retreated, but the thin man stayed behind, looking at Neftalí with great contempt. Just then, the unmistakable cry of a baby came from the house. The thin man grinned. "You are aware of the new jurisdiction, signed recently by our brave mayor, I'm assuming? They've restarted the worker-mother initiative. Three Rivers is ready to get back to normal. As a property owner, you can lose your rights if you are caught harboring an unemployed woman who qualifies as a worker-mother. Just a reminder."

"Sir," Neftalí said, "look around. What does 'unemployed' even mean? All of us are unemployed. All of you who have no real skills, especially. And you love taking it out on people like me. There's women out there being killed by this jurisdiction. I saw a woman last night being *killed*. And you all are hungry for even more blood? You came over to my house, and for what? What were you planning to do? To murder this rarest of creatures, because you lost a few fucking ducks? Get out of here. Get real. I am not your fucking enemy, and neither is Mama. That's right, she has a name, and that name is Mama. Think about that name long and hard while you are thinking also of your murderous fucking illusions of murdering exotic beasts."

By the time she finished her diatribe, the posse and the thin man had walked past the property, but it felt good to yell all her feelings out. She went to Mama's side in the house, desperate to put her arms around her and keep her safe. Mama sniffed Neftalí's hair with that pumice of a nose, then moved closer to the door and pawed the knob, asking to be let out.

Neftalí locked the door, walked into the living room, where Proserpina and Moira were busy eating tamales. The baby looked like the calmest creature as she slept in a blanketed cardboard box propped on a chair.

"The neighbors are upset with Mama," she said to them. "I've been trying. Trying hard to learn about her diet, to feed her right. But obviously I have very limited resources to learn anything about raising a Bengal tiger. I don't even know how old she is. But I suspect she's young. She can still be taught things, right? We can teach her to not do bad things like kill other people's pet animals, right?"

Mama sat by Neftalí, who continued petting her, but nobody had any answers—she pulled her hand away, tried to wipe off the staticky silver and orange hairs stuck between her sweaty fingers. The old house creaked with the powerful rolling cyclones passing through, and somewhere deep in the walls a mother rodent scuttled with her litter toward the dining room's corner.

Mama tracked the walled critters using her crosshair sense of smell. The dancing candlestick flames reflected in her turquoise eyes and multiplied as she zeroed in. The tiger crept toward the northeastern corner of the dining room, below a moldy, framed oil still-life of green and red grapes, and kept her pumice tiger nose against the wall's chipped trim. Mama caught something in her mouth, and everyone heard the cutting shreds of tiny screaming. A furry, fat rat with an orange belly was struggling within Mama's clamped jaws, as countless baby rats protested in their high-pitched rat language. A miniature symphony of screeches spilled from a widening crack in the wall: pink and brown balls of fur wielding toothpicks as weapons in their tiny hands.

Mama looked at Neftalí with proud, gleaming marble eyes that said: "Look, Mother, look what I can do, look how strong and capable I am. This is my offering to you."

"No. Drop it," Neftalí yelled, which was a command Mama had learned.

The baby rats were swarming around Moira, Proserpina, and Neftalí, trying to bite their feet and ankles, climbing their legs in retaliation. Proserpina lifted the cardboard box with her baby over her head. Mama simply moved her jaw once in a clockwise motion; two loud crunches came from the rat mother, and it stopped struggling. Since Mama was eager to go outside at any given moment, Neftalí tried to move the action away from the house, and opened the front door. Mama took big lunges out, celebrating her kill by spinning in the yard several times, the baby rats chasing her angrily.

Moira had taken refuge on a chair; Proserpina was kicking at the rats as they came toward her, still holding up the baby, who slept soundly; Neftalí backed away, trying not to hurt any of the smaller rats, trying not to cry, while making sure all the critters ran outside. She approached her beloved tiger under the decayed brown sunlight of the day. Mama brought the dead rat to Neftalí's feet proudly, as a tribute. When baby rats tried to bite Mama, she playfully pawed them to the side, or pushed them down, suffocating them against the colorless grass.

Neftalí spread her arms wide, trying to spook Mama away from her prey and its bereaved litter, but it did not work. Although she hated doing this—and practiced it only when there was no recourse—Neftalí took out her lighter and a stick of cherrywood and lit one end on fire. Mama cowered at the sight of the flame, hurried toward the shed with her ears back and head down.

Neftalí knew fire brought terrible, invasive memories for Mama—she felt awful.

The stick of cherrywood was burning quickly. Neftalí brought it closer to the masticated rat mother, since she didn't have a lamp handy. The rat babies screeched and cried around their mother's shredded body. Mama's razor-sharp teeth had sliced the rat mother's stomach right open. Neftalí could see by the tiny balls of pink, bloody flesh peeking out that she'd been significantly pregnant.

She stepped back, waved the cherrywood stick until the flame fizzled out.

Mama peered from behind the stable, watching Neftalí walk toward the back porch, where Moira and Proserpina stood watching. The cardboard box cradling the infant was on the porch's worktable.

Baby rats continually scuttled from the house out of their damn minds.

"I'm mad at you," Neftalí yelled at the indifferent tiger, as she stepped closer.

Proserpina pulled out a paper halceamadon from her secret pocket, unfolded it like the tiny puzzle it was, hung an oil lamp on the hook above the porch table away from her baby's eyes, and set the parchment paper down like a battle map. A title was revealed in the upper-right-hand corner with the aid of a magnifying lens: *The Southerns: The Worker-Mother Tales*. She scanned the tiny script to find the relevant passage: "Here it is. Read it yourself, if you want. In this story, a woman from New York befriends a woman from the Panhandle, here in Texas. The woman from the Panhandle gifts the woman from New York a baby Bengal tiger during a visit to the Northeast. But when the tiger grows up, it starts killing and eating the neighbors' cats and dogs. Even their talking parrots . . ."

Neftalí had taken the magnifying lens but had a difficult time reading the tiny penmanship. Her mind had trouble adjusting to reading it backward, from right to left, as it was written.

"She writes to the woman in the Panhandle and tells her something needs to be done about her old gift, the tiger, because she's come to the painful conclusion that tigers shouldn't be living in the city. The woman in the Panhandle ends up getting her unemployed son and a buddy of his to secretly take the tiger out of the apartment building in Staten Island and bring it to the Panhandle. Then that's it, if I'm remembering it well. The story doesn't really end there, it just moves on to the next story, the way they all do in *The Worker-Mother Tales*."

She handed Neftalí and Moira each a halceamadon. They both intricately unfolded them to find exact copies of the parchment paper with *The Southerns: The Worker-Mother Tales*.

"I made all these copies. And I'm still making them, by hand. Each one takes me like three weeks. My mother gave it to me the last time I saw her, and it's the least I could do for her and the women at the fish cannery. Even if most of the mothers never made it out of the fire, at least these stories they put together can survive."

The noxious baby-rat chorus reached a crescendo. Neftalí made sure Mama was secure inside the house. Moira pointed the hanging halogen lamp at the commotion. The baby rats were moving on from where the dead rat mother lay. Nothing was left but her rat bones and a pool of blood seeping into the thirsty soil. The baby rats had taken everything they could from the mother, even their unborn siblings, and were frantically scurrying away from the house over patches of dead grass and gravel.

"Something like this also happens," Proserpina said, "in the stories. An unemployed woman's children drown in a lagoon by accident. The community ends up blaming the grieving mother. Calling her a witch and a slut and all that. The community burns her house down while she's sleeping, and they kill her. But the rats that were living in the house run away and give birth to baby rats, who then give birth to more rats. All the rats end up infesting the houses of everyone in the community who killed this woman. Some of the people's babies are even eaten by the rats, everyone gets the plague, and they also die . . ."

Mama watched from the casement window inside the house, backed by the red velvet curtain once again, as the orphaned baby rats fled in search of anything they could chew through and digest in the neighbors' houses.

WALKING HOME ONE DAY, to will the smoke and volcanic ash in the atmosphere magically away, Gia imagined future times with clear blue skies. Dried tears were caked with soot on her face. She pictured the clouds above cracking open like an inflating pig bladder, giving birth to the giant moth that would spray its mouth juices onto Three Rivers. It was colder than most days. Gia feared what her mother and the tías had been discussing, about this coming winter being perhaps the coldest ever.

Everyone in the community rallied to raise the little donations they could in the aftermath of the Live Oak tenement fire, and the tías were able to pitch a tent in the vacant lot behind the remains of the building. At first, they shared the space with a circle of wandering, gambling teenage boys; when the boys had a falling out amongst themselves, Gia helped her tías set up a stove, and they switched from making tamales to small batches of gorditas, but only enough to feed the family. Still, Gia often used gorditas for secretly bartering with the neighborhood kids.

She found her mother and three tías huddled together when she arrived at their temporary tent home. The makeshift oven was unattended, with an aluminum foil pouch keeping the gorditas warm. Gia grabbed a gordita, bit into it, tumbled it around in her mouth because the veggies inside were hot. Her mother waved, invited her daughter to join their huddle, which made Gia feel this adult conversation could be important.

"Mi'ja. I'm glad you are here. We have to make a decision, and we need you. That young woman just paid us a visit, the one who lives with the tiger. Are you friends with her? Well, she's in big trouble. And she's sympathetic to our situation after the tragedy . . . and your abuelito. She made an offer for us to come live in that big house where she lives. But we have to help her. We don't mind helping her. But you're the only one among us who is still growing up. Me and your tías are already grown-ups. If we do this, you'll be living in that house with us, as well. The tiger won't be there, so don't be nervous about that. The young woman just left here to make arrangements with Mr. Rayman. Says Mr. Rayman owes her a favor. Your tías and I were discussing what to do if Mr. Rayman refuses this favor. We'd be having to help her figure out how to move the tiger ten miles south to George West."

The three tías, Gia, and her mother, along with her cousins, decided not to dismantle the hovel under the tarp, and left the stoves and sleeping pallets behind. They didn't have many belongings to carry, and took a shortcut through the uneven alley to reach Colonel Huerta's house. Moira, Neftalí, and Proserpina were waiting for them on the back porch. The baby was alert in Proserpina's arms, eager to absorb the surroundings with her eyes. After introductions went around, the talk of the neighborhood was brought out.

The tailless Bengal tiger had eaten, and approached them

with the same curiosity, pomp, and gaiety she used on any stranger who was standing still. Gia's knees trembled, and her heart beat faster as Mama sniffed her crotch and her legs. The tías and Gia's mother tried to look fearless, and each delivered adulatory whispers. Ten dark brown hands ran through Mama's thick, striped fur, petting her, saying hello. They avoided her exposed, singed flesh, which had never quite healed. A soft purr came from deep inside Mama, like the spinning gears of a clock reminding them of the danger and power she held, which could indiscriminately turn on anyone at any moment.

Gia stuck around to hear Neftalí explain the unfortunate but real situation she found herself in with Mama. She had eavesdropped on a woman talking with the bus driver earlier in the day regarding something going down by the *depósito*. Gia wanted to stake it out in case it involved the police, so when nobody was looking she told her mother she had to go on an errand.

She ran down the alley all the way to the beginning of Angélica Street. When she got to the corner, Gia saw Mr. Rivera the mechanic carrying a big jug of gutrot wine in one hand, a pitchfork in the other, then he passed the jug to Eusebio, the bread maker, who walked by his side. Gia had not only heard rumors of Mr. Rivera using that pitchfork to kill stray dogs and cats; she'd perpetuated and exaggerated some of those accounts herself.

The mechanic and the bread maker crossed toward the *depósito*, sloshing that gutrot jug back and forth. Three adult loiterers she didn't recognize stood around the corner of the little store. One of them, a short man wearing a scarf, lit a pipe, while a tall, thin man refused the jug from the bread maker upon his offer. As she continued watching from a safe, veiled distance, Gia realized this thin man was the same one following people in the neighborhood. The last time she'd seen him was on the evening of the Live Oak tenement fire. He had been in the stairwell, which had frightened her because she had never actually seen him inside the building. He was the same man who had snapped a photograph of Mama and the triplets on Angélica Street.

Gia grew concerned, thinking these things over. The woman she'd overheard on the bus joined the group by the depósito. They conspired loudly among themselves, and Gia clearly made out the words "animal" and "kill" several times, without context. Her mind raced to fill in the gaps of those statements using the most innocuous phrases—nothing appeased her rush of fear and dread. She turned and quietly hurried back the way she'd come.

It was the third day Proserpina had the gowned skeleton airing out on the living room table, along with the decorative boiled stones. The tías and Gia's mother had gotten acquainted with the remains, and were now helping prepare them for a real burial.

Gia grew emotional watching them do this, thinking about her grandfather's recent passing, and the small ceremony they'd had after they gathered his remains. She found it difficult to communicate to anyone what she'd seen at the depósito, and stayed out of everyone's way. The tías, Gia's mother, Moira, Neftalí, and Proserpina all walked through the orchards with the remains, while Gia stayed inside the house with Mama. Gia admired the way Mama sprawled confidently on the rug by the open window, where she kept an eye on the orchard, awaiting everyone's return.

Mama's stripes glowed like black lightning. Gia sat on the first step of the stairs, admiring Mama's breathing, her tiger torso inflating and deflating. The house grew darker, and Gia jumped abruptly to her feet, immediately followed by Mama. Gia climbed back a few steps to give Mama walking space on the ground floor. She was trying not to fear the tiger, but found the instinct difficult to suppress. The candles on the bureau near the entrance had been snuffed out, their smoke ribbons elongating into a light fog. Gia had run out of matches the day before, but set her halogen lamp to the lowest setting, and walked toward the bureau behind Mama. Three hardcover books were piled on a nice cushioned chair by the bureau. Gia glanced into the kitchen, annoyed by a drafty open window letting in strings of exterior ash. Mama's nostrils fluttered, and Gia thought she could hear voices. She looked over her shoulder toward the orchard-facing window, but didn't see anyone emerging quite yet. Gia grabbed the topmost book, recognized only one of the title's words on the worn, white cover, "Brother," and admired the two dots above the *e* in the second word. She opened it to the first page.

When she turned again toward the kitchen window, a pair of scowling eyes belonging to a bald head were framed by the trim. They startled Gia, making her gasp and shut the book. Mama snarled at the man, who was too short for the window, and who climbed down in a hurry at the sight of the beast.

"There's the lion," Gia heard from outside. "With the curly-haired tenement girl!"

Gia placed the book on the chair, and forgetting her fear of Mama, embraced the tiger with both arms.

"Let's go over here, c'mon," she whispered.

As they stepped away, a ball of fire flew into the room through the open kitchen window. Mama jumped back with a fright, pounced toward the living room. Gia approached the flaming intrusion—it was an old boot afire. Gia emptied the metal kitchen trash can and flipped it upside down to cover the boot, putting her body weight on top, diminishing the oxygen flow. After a moment, she lifted the trash can to find the size-eleven boot steaming and black.

"Mama!" Gia yelled, remembering both the tiger and her mother.

Another flaming shoe flew inside, and when she turned, several more were kicking through the air, until they hit the curtains or a wall, gradually catching them on fire. One landed on the cushioned chair with the three books. Gia found Mama hiding behind the living room couch, half her body almost comically sticking out.

"Let's go, Mama," Gia insisted. "We have to leave here." She tried pulling at Mama, when suddenly Mama's head shot out and snapped at Gia, tearing one of her sleeves. Gia fell backward on her ass, as Mama escaped up the stairs. The teenager sat catatonically as the chorus of flames throughout the house raised their pitch. Mama's bowl of water was a few feet away from Gia. She grabbed it and dumped its contents on the rapidly burning curtains, then tried running into the kitchen, but its doorway was on fire.

Frightened for herself, for the house, for Mama, Gia panicked and had trouble working the doorknob to the back door. A clear path appeared for a moment through the flames, toward the stairs. Gia didn't give herself time to think, and when she saw the flames rapidly incinerate the book she'd just been holding a few feet away, she went down the path, toward the stairs, not knowing if the fire or Mama was the bigger threat.

"Mama!" Gia cried out.

Smoke rose from the floorboards of the second story as she looked from room to room.

The tías walked ahead of their eldest sister, and Neftalí, Moira, and Proserpina with her child, so they were the first to spot the fire's smoke after the burial ceremony. They ran toward the house with three gables and worked as a team, ignoring the posse armed with shovels, picks, and rifles surrounding the calamity. One of the tías pumped water, as another guided the slack of the hose and the third sprayed down the flames.

A stout man among the posse swung an axe in the air and stepped toward the water hose. As the blade was about to strike, Gia's mother kicked the man's wrists, making him miss the hose entirely. The axe stuck itself to the ground, the man tumbled over, and the posse's numbers seemed to multiply.

"There's a little girl in there," Gia's mother yelled, desperately keeping from clawing her own face out of fear.

The tías were deep inside the house, working to put out the fire while ignoring the posse's curses and admonitions.

"Anything that happens here," a red-faced woman yelled

angrily, "will be due to the negligence of this floozy." And she pointed at Neftalí.

"It's against the law to have a tiger within city limits," the tall, thin man said, with greater determination and judgment than ever.

The fiending flames had spread in a frenzy to the eastern and southern gables of the house. Gray light distilled through the dark rusty whorl of clouds, delivering more jokes for the fire's continuous laughter.

"Worst of all," the angry woman continued, "you besmirched poor Mr. Huerta's name. The man lost the entirety of his family. And he was a veteran of foreign wars. To have you living in his home furthers his besmirching."

Neftalí saw Rayman's truck rolling up the driveway. As he got closer, she squinted toward the angry woman's dress at something she half recognized darkening her wardrobe: a shadow cast by the sun.

The posse's primal anger was swept aside by a blanket of clean daylight unrolling from the junkyard sky. Everyone fell silent as this chariot descended. Some shielded their eyes, having grown unused to the spectacle of the sun.

A young boy within the squinting posse pointed toward the one gable without a fire directly above them. "Over there," he said.

Mama stood on the awning extending from the open second-story window and roared a low elegy as the fire easily overtook the house around her. Gia climbed out the window behind Mama. Fearing that Mama was losing her balance and about to fall, Gia clutched at the tiger's thick fur the moment before Mama leaped into the air.

The man in the posse who was carrying a rifle put it quickly to his shoulder, pointed at Mama's chest.

Moira had hoped she wouldn't have to use the weapon when she'd packed it, but she pulled out the Webley-Fosbery her sister, Phoebe, had given her on their most recent birthday. It wasn't the piece that had killed Pablo Henry Crick, but nearly identical. She pointed it at the rifleman's trigger hand.

As Mama's and Gia's shadows descended upon the astonished crowd, growing larger and larger like the giant moth Gia had dreamed of, only one gunshot rang out under the long-awaited daylight and terrible, pitiless flames.

~

A deep crimson darkness; bursts of light shooting within a whirlwind, as if inside a glass filled with muddy liquid; Mama's fur, and Gia clutching it, refusing to be separated from Mama. Other than these rudimentary sensations, Gia had difficulty recalling the details of that day, or of her family's exodus to George West. It was her mother who decided at the last minute to put her with Mama in the bed of Mr. Rayman's truck, after they'd sedated the tiger for the move.

Even when her tías and mother came to George West weeks later, Gia had a hard time adjusting to farm life. There was no public transportation, but even if there had been, where would she go? she often wondered. There were no sirens and no distant screaming or ominous coughing in George West; no half-dressed bus riders to avoid; and, strangest of all, she'd stopped worrying what her family would be eating every day. It was unfair to her how two cities like Three Rivers and

George West could be so close together, in the same state, yet be so unalike.

Gia's mother and tías adjusted to farm and communal life readily, since it reminded them of their rural childhood in Puebla. Neftalí was given the old schoolhouse past the locust grove as her living quarters. It was separated from the main property by a few hundred yards and had its own sturdy perimeter fence to keep Mama in. Rural life was a drag at first, but Neftalí took it upon herself to read to the younger children, and Gia often listened in, sitting as close to Mama as she could. The library on the property was a place of wonder not only for Gia, but for all the children. She quickly realized that the grown-ups hardly had time to read. There was no order to the library as a result. Though Gia was barely literate, she enjoyed thumbing through books when she finished her daily chores.

One day she walked past the locust grove toward the schoolhouse, and found Neftalí like she was most days: drunk, listening to her records, staring off into the mesquites and arid land, with Mama soaking in the sun nearby. Neftalí knew Gia had developed an attachment to Mama due to their shared experience in Three Rivers.

She welcomed Gia and, unprompted, said: "There will come a time, kid, when you're my age. And you'll be very surprised nobody remembers those dark days. When we couldn't see the sun. Never forget those days, kid. Never forget when you lived in a city named Three Rivers, and nobody could decide if it was a volcano that erupted, bombs exploding, or some giant reptile's nasty breath . . . but one of these things covered up the stars at night . . . and our big blue sky. I am glad you are here, Gia, because I have decided it's you who will have to read to the future children. It's you who will set the record straight for the generation after us. Long after I am gone, and Mama here is gone, someone is going to have to keep all these stories going. So I am—with your mother's permission, of course, and if you really want me to—going to teach you properly how to read. You'll no longer be a kid to me, but my 'mana. It's short for hermana, but you probably already know that. What do you say?"

SOMETHING LIKE ACTUAL SEASONS PASSED. There came an evening when Neftalí called out to Mama for her supper, and it took the tiger longer than usual to return. The cicadas were shrill in their lament for another bygone day. Neftalí feared Mama was out hunting cattle again, and walked along the perimeter fence to the far end of the property to see if there were any breaks she could have escaped through. She found Mama by the cluster of old oak trees, three buzzards looking down on her as she struggled to breathe.

Mama didn't make it through the night, and was buried at dawn the following day, with everyone living and working on the farm present at the ceremony.

Neftalí was devastated. She concluded that Mama's current weariness and trouble with her weakening hind legs had been more markers of old age than permanent damage from the leap she'd taken out of the burning house in Three Rivers. Neftalí grew even more reclusive, and it was only when they carried her weekly provisions to the schoolhouse that anyone besides Gia interacted with her.

A farmer's market had inadvertently started in George West's old town center. Parents and workers on Phoebe's farm debated whether they should go, and everyone decided they could do so only as a small armed group. Gia sat in the bed of a truck with her tía Lupe, her mother, and a boy named Robbie, while an armed Phoebe and Rolo rode in the front. The market was under a large gazebo. The local vendors were amiable toward Gia, though she was shy about talking to anyone or even smiling back. Gia hadn't seen so many strangers so close together who weren't collectively suffering or protesting some injustice. She saw portioned pumpkin seeds, sunflower seeds, nuts, radishes, grapefruits, lemons, all for sale, and fresh lemonade, which she had a free glowing cup of.

Across the street from the gazebo, under the shade of a great sycamore tree, sat a large van with its doors open, and on the sidewalk in front of it was a sandwich board with the word BOOKS written on it. Gia told her tía where she'd be, and was instructed not to be out of sight, and to stay vigilant and safe. Gia sipped her lemonade as she crossed the street. She saw that the van was more of a short bus, with bookshelves set up and room to walk around inside.

Gia stood by the entrance and looked toward the finely dressed proprietor sitting behind the steering wheel. Part of her wanted to run away, but the books made it difficult.

"Welcome to my little bookshop on wheels. Please, feel free to wander in. I try to carry a little bit for all tastes, so if you are looking for rare technical manuals, I got some real handy ones. Like look at this one. *Whittle a Spoon Out of Anything* by Hobart Messier. The title tells you everything. Don't you love a book like that, where the title is enough to tell you what it's all about? Or how about this. You look like a youngster who is interested in learning the laws of thermodynamics. Here is *Western Thermodynamics*, the rare, corrected third edition, issued to students your age a long time ago. But I can see that's not your type either. Tell me, are you a person who enjoys reading books?"

Gia nodded while thumbing through *Western Thermodynamics*, eyeing the shelves, and making sure her tía could see her—all at once.

"Great to hear. May I ask, what is it that interests you to read about most?"

"I love anything about animals, unless it dies or something. Or when stories involve outer space, with black holes and asteroid stuff."

"Fabulous," the bookseller said. "Feel like we already know each other. I got one here that may be just the ticket for you. Let me see. Here it is. *Relativity from Here to There*, a scholarly study financed by Princeton Press, during their golden editorial era. I can attest firsthand that this book is a gem of its genre."

From across the street, Tía Lupe waved her arm at Gia, calling her over. Gia grew nervous, her arms full of these heavy, tedious books, and said, "Sorry. When I say 'outer space,' I mean more the kind of outer space about saving the world. About the galaxy having problems, stuff like that."

"I got you. Say no more. I've only been doing this a short while, so perhaps I tend to push my own subjective tastes on customers. Here's one. It's kind of special to me. Even though it's not the regular kind of thing I read."

The cover of the book the bookseller put in Gia's hands was missing, and a piece of cardboard had been cleverly sewed on as a replacement. Gia opened it and read the title page aloud, like she would to Neftalí in their reading lessons: *Ghosts in the Zap . . . otec Spher . . . icals.* By Jazzmin. Monelle. Rivas."

"Very good," the bookseller said, and since Gia appeared anxious and in a hurry, told her the price.

"I don't have any money," Gia said.

"Nothing to trade, either?"

Gia shook her head.

"Well then. What is to be done? I can't be giving away my inventory. Most of these books are not easy to come by. Especially this one, by this niche author. I treasure the books I sell. But I can't eat these books to stay alive. I need to at least make something so I can chow down. And get corn fuel for the bookmobile here. Do you live in George West?"

Gia nodded.

"All right. Well. I'm posted here another month. You are lucky I have a soft spot for energetic youngsters like yourself, who are curious about this troubled world. I can loan you the book if you promise to return it. If you keep your promise and bring it back, then maybe I can trust you enough to loan you more."

Gia got through the loaned book, occasionally stopping to ask an adult what certain words meant, and as it got closer to the weekend she hinted to her mother and tías about her desire to return to the farmer's market, but was disappointed when it didn't pan out. The only person besides Neftalí who enjoyed reading was Rolo, and he had figured out on his own why Gia walked around carrying such unrelatable anguish. Rolo reminded Phoebe about the dried mushrooms she'd harvested, and they invited Gia and her tías to the farmer's market the following weekend, since the tías had been making their own tamal husks to trade or sell.

Gia walked as fast as she could toward the bookmobile. The bookseller clapped once as she approached.

"I knew I'd see you again. And I'm glad it was today. Hello there, you, too, sir," the bookseller said to Rolo, then proceeded to give him the rundown of the shop as Gia greedily browsed the shelves. She returned the paperback with the cardboard cover to the bookseller, while feeling the intense rush of the novel's final pages all over again.

"This rough-looking book is a difficult one," the bookseller said, "for me to part with, believe it or not. You are a person of your word. Thank you for returning it. It was given to me by someone special. It's funny. You actually remind me of her. I will keep my end of the bargain as well and loan you another. Let me show you something truly unique by this same author."

The bookseller pulled out a large bundle of pages crudely bound with clear plastic thread. Gia tried her best not to wince at the heavy, smelly manuscript when the bookseller put it into her hands, and she flipped the dusty pages open.

"This was the first book I found here. In this vehicle. It came with the shelves already built in. The book is not about outer space, however. But the main characters are girls around your age, at an all-girls conservatory, who discover a dark, painful truth about their lives. The binding is nothing to brag about, but I did it myself with the limited resources I had at the time. I would let you take this one, only thing is that this version is missing three pages. But this one—"

The bookseller pulled out a white hardcover book. When Gia looked closely at the clothbound texture, she read aloud the embossed words: *Brother Brontë*. She pronounced the second word "Brontt." The two dots at the end of the last *e* were familiar flourishes that made Gia wonder if she'd encountered this title before.

She traced the words with one finger and stopped listening to the bookseller and Rolo, who were having a hushed exchange. Rolo was telling the bookseller about their farm and invited them to stop by. Proper introductions went around as Gia turned the pages of the book, and she learned the bookseller's name was Bettina—a familiar name. She pretended to read when the bookseller told Rolo about the trouble the authorities outside George West had been giving them for selling books without a license.

As pedestrians approached the shop, the bookseller turned to Gia. "For you, take the complete, official version of the book. I found that unexpurgated first printing at the annual banquet of the rogue booksellers' guild in Corpus Christi. Met a bookseller from Odessa with three copies, so I, of course, had to barter for one, if only to know what happens in those three missing pages. It turns out one of those pages—I'd even argue all three—are integral to the plot."

The bookseller grabbed a short stool and stood on it to retrieve a wooden box from the top shelf, then sat on the stool to open the box. Rolo and Gia took the carefully folded piece of parchment paper the bookseller handed them.

"One more thing for you. These papers folded into a funny, complex shape are called *The Southerns: The Worker-Mother Tales*. I give one for free to all paying customers. It's the stories, so they say, that the worker-mothers at the Big Tex Fish Cannery in Three Rivers spent their time collecting and recording. You need a magnifying glass to read all of them. And they're written backward. I bartered a bunch off the same bookseller from Odessa. You'll have to find your own magnifying lens, unfortunately. I don't have an extra."

The unabridged first edition of *Brother Brontë* by Jazzmin Monelle Rivas was 312 pages. One chapter in, Gia made herself stop when she overheard her mother and tías talking about their options of staying on the farm or moving farther north, possibly to live with their distant cousins in Chicago. They were tired of being the only Mexican women, other than Neftalí, on the farm and needed a change.

Gia walked to the barn where they kept the bales of hay, sat on a stack, and read there until she ran out of daylight. When she finished the book at first light the following morning, Gia remembered the time Phoebe had described her girlhood experience with a tornado out in the plains, her use of the words "vortex" and "suction," because this had been the only way to describe how she was feeling. The novel was complex, beyond her reading level, but Gia didn't let this stop her, and pressed on until the end. There were plot points that confused her, words she didn't know, and she questioned if certain details were real-life things or not. She wanted to talk about it with somebody, and knew if there was one person on the farm who not only tolerated but welcomed Gia talking about books, it was Neftalí.

The noon sun pushed everyone's shadow straight down like a nail being driven into the coffin earth. Gia held the hardcover novel with both hands and could see Neftalí standing on the schoolhouse porch next to a rocking chair, pouring a dark brown liquid into a steaming, fragrant cup of coffee. Neftalí gulped at the coffee, poured in some more of the dark liquid, mixed it with her finger, and gulped again.

"Ey, little 'mana," she said. "I thought that was you. Just got up. Everything is still fuzzy."

She focused on the book in Gia's hands, took it from her. "Hell yeah. You're into the hard shit already. Look at you. You got it made. There was a long time when all I had was this book. Would read it every day to Mama. I know it probably by memory, feels like I practically wrote it. I lost my copy back when they burned down Huerta's house. Of course, you remember that horrible fucking day. You'll probably never forget it. One day, you'll be on your deathbed, and the last thing that will come into your mind is riding Mama down to safety from a burning house—"

"I have questions about this book. Were the Brontë sisters real people who actually wrote those real books that are in the story?" Gia still pronounced the surname as if it ended with a t: "Brontt."

"As real as the sun shining right now. They existed in England . . . across the Atlantic Ocean . . . a long time ago."

"But in this book, those other real books are not credited to the Brontës? They're credited to their brother? Branwell? And they even name the girls' academy after their brother: Our Brother Branwell Academy for Girls?"

"Yeah, but then Pride and Prejudice, the twin sisters, figure it out."

"Twins. Like Phoebe and Moira?"

"Exactly. And like Phoebe and Moira are very different people, so are Pride and Prejudice. See how hardworking and dedicated Phoebe is to be living here on the farm? The woman is a machine. Give her a medal. And Moira, she couldn't stand it here another minute. Went back to Three Rivers as soon as she could. Prefers to be wanted there. Said she belonged in a chaotic city, not out here in the country. To be honest, I get it. With mosquitoes biting here already this early in the day, who would want to be here?"

Gia asked Neftalí about the two dots above the *e* in "Brontë," but the only thing they meant, according to Neftalí, was an instruction for how the *e* was pronounced.

Neftalí cut short their almost literary conversation by pointing into the swaying thicket ahead and saying, "I am going to let you in on a little secret, Gia. But you can't tell anyone." She grabbed a long, thick rope and signaled with one arm for Gia to follow her. They walked about thirty yards out, to a spot near the locust grove. Neftalí had trouble with her balance, but it might just have been the strong wind.

"Mama has come back to me, Gia. You see her? She's right over there. Looking at us."

Neftalí pointed at a glistening metallic wreath about twenty steps ahead near a patch of fruiting cacti, then the warning rattle of its tail punctured the hum of day. "Don't you recognize the classic beauty? Same spirit. Same aura. And look." Neftalí stepped aside, whipped the long rope into action. She twirled a perfect circle about ten feet out, despite the pestering gusts.

"Me and Mama have a trick to show off. I taught her while also teaching myself to lasso. That way we teach each other."

Gia clutched the hardcover book and stepped aside.

The rattlesnake sprang like a coil from the ground, jumped through the open noose of the lasso in the air.

"Waah-hoo! You see that? She learned that trick fast, too.

New Mama's got it, just like old Mama. New Mama's got it good. You're a careful reader, Gia. I've been impressed by you. You pick up things in stories that others easily brush off. Do you remember the last words of *Brother Brontë*? After all these years, as many times as I've read it, that's what comes back to me the most, those last words in the story. I say them out loud to myself, in times of trouble or distress. While the Branwell school is burning down and our protagonist Prejudice roams the halls, waving an axe around . . ."

Gia opened the book to the final page. Neftalí shifted the direction of the lasso, made it dance in the dusty gale, then presented the loop to the rattlesnake like the opening eye of a portal. In her imagination, as she looked up from the typeset sentences, Gia saw an axe instead of a rope in Neftalí's hands, an evil boarding school director instead of a reptile in the snake, a burning hallway instead of George West, Texas.

"Ophelia," Neftalí yelled, quoting the book from memory in her best embodiment of Prejudice, pumping the perfectly taut lasso like a kite against the sky. "Opheliaaa . . ."

A crowd cheered from the snake's rattle as it leaped through the noose in the air.

". . . I am picking out your birthday present."

Gia followed along on the page.

ACKNOWLEDGMENTS

Drafted spring 2015 to fall 2021 on an Olivetti Underwood Lettera 32. Couldn't have been finished without cosmic help from: Nina Simone's 1969 Rome concert version of "Suzanne"; Josephine Foster's *Hazel Eyes, I Will Lead You* and *Graphic as a Star*; the music of Brother Theotis Taylor; the works of Clara Schumann as played by Hélène Boschi; the secret art of Henry Darger; the photography of Vivian Maier; Jimmy Scott's version of "Nothing Compares 2 U"; Emahoy Tsegué-Maryam Guèbrou's sublime piano compositions; the music and liner notes of Cairo Records comps; Mississippi Records (thank you, Cyrus Moussavi and María Barrios) and Little Axe mixtapes; Ted Barron's photography and radio show; Maria Monti's *Il Bestiario*; Neko Case singing Roky Erickson's "Be and Bring Me Home" as if from the tallest mountain in Dante's *Inferno*; Tom Jarmusch's photography; my man Juventino Rosas; pretty much everything LuLu Gamma Ray and Roxy Monoxide have recorded, especially *Excerpts from the Holy Scumbrella*, *Slink to Intensity*, and the song "L'Atalante," respectfully.

Thank you, Soumeya Bendimerad Roberts, for believing in my work always, since day one. Thank you, Jackson Howard, for your guidance and wisdom and friendship. Thank you so much, Na Kim! To Ella Wang. To Caitlin Van Dusen. To everyone at MCD/FSG, past and present in my tenure, especially Sean McDonald, Mitzi Angel, Jenna Johnson, Abby Kagan, Brianna Fairman, Carrie Hsieh, Claire Tobin, Flora Esterly, Devon Mazzone, Sam Glatt, Julia Judge, and Chloe Texier-Rose.

To all my bookselling coworkers at Malvern Books and Alienated Majesty Books, especially Julie Poole, Celia Bell, Stephen Krause, Becky Garcia, Stephanie Goehring, Annar Veröld, Claire Bowman, Schandra Madha, C. Rees, Matthew Hodges, Taylor Pate, Kelsey Williams, Michelle Zhang, José Skinner, and Melynda Nuss. Thank you to Joe W. Bratcher III, and to Ian Bratcher. To the Kitaiskaia family: Zhenya, Sasha, and Roma. To Steven Ray Martinez for the photographs. To my hermanos: Angel and Elias Serda. My RGV people: Carl and Sofia Vestweber, Derek Beltran, Amanda Elise Salas, Kirsten Alyssa Salas. Thank you to Elva Baca, Ramona, and James Graham; to Billy Baca; to Christopher Hutchins and Azaleia; to Stephanie Hannay and Leslie Scott; to Travis McGuire; to Phil Lovegren; to Corey Miller. To my sisters, Anna y Alba; to my father, Fernando Flores Moreno; and always to my mother, Olga Elena Robles de Flores. To Andrea, Roman, and Anna. To my own tías: Alma, Pati, Mappy, Sol, and my tías who are no longer with us: Delia and Anna. Thank you to all my primas y primos también. All my tíos, too, for good measure. To my film world people: Jim Mendiola, Cruz Angeles, and Raúl Castillo. Wore my Superheater shirt through writing Book Three—thank you to Max Bray and the gang. To Night Viking. Special thanks to fellow booksellers, authors, and book world friends: Josiah Luis Alderete, Madeline ffitch,

Tatiana Luboviski-Acosta, mónica teresa ortiz, Nina Mac-Laughlin, Raquel Gutiérrez, Christopher Brown, Daley Farr, Mandy Medley, Paul Yamazaki, Riley Rennhack, Mark Haber, Jen Fisher, Mesha Maren, J. David Gonzalez, Charley Rejsek, Camilo A. Sánchez, Lucy Sante, Ben Roylance, Edward Carey, Elizabeth McCracken, Laura van den Berg, Ursula Villarreal-Moura, Annie Tate, Tomás Q. Morín, Matt Bell, Christina Vargas, John Phillip Santos, Caitlin Murray, Tim Johnson, Mathew P. Zuniga, Dobby Gibson, Eileen Myles, Joshua Edwards, Kali Fajardo-Anstine, Donald Quist, Connie May Fowler, Ed Park, Stephen Sparks, Robert Sindelar, Deb Olin Unferth, Will Evans, and Uriel Perez.

Thank you to Little Max, to our Adira, and, of course, to Taisia Kitaiskaia forever.

A Note About the Author

Fernando A. Flores was born in Reynosa, Tamaulipas, Mexico, and grew up in South Texas. He is the author of the short-story collections *Valleyesque* and *Death to the Bullshit Artists of South Texas* and the novel *Tears of the Trufflepig*, which was long-listed for the Center for Fiction First Novel Prize and was named a Best Book of 2019 by *Tor.com*. His fiction has appeared in the *Los Angeles Review of Books Quarterly, American Short Fiction, Ploughshares, frieze, Porter House Review,* and other publications. He lives in Austin, Texas.